Germania

Germania

A Novel of Nazi Berlin

Harald Gilbers

Translated by
Alexandra Roesch

THOMAS DUNNE BOOKS
NEW YORK

First published in the United States by Thomas Dunne Books,
an imprint of St. Martin's Publishing Group

GERMANIA. Copyright © 2013 by Harald Gilbers.
Translation copyright © 2020 by Alexandra Roesch. All rights reserved.
Printed in the United States of America. For information,
address St. Martin's Publishing Group, 120 Broadway, New York, NY 10271.

www.thomasdunnebooks.com

Design by Meryl Sussman Levavi

The Library of Congress Cataloging-in-Publication Data is available upon request.

ISBN 978-1-250-24693-6 (hardcover)
ISBN 978-1-250-24694-3 (ebook)

Our books may be purchased in bulk for promotional, educational, or business use. Please contact your local bookseller or the Macmillan Corporate and Premium Sales Department at 1-800-221-7945, extension 5442, or by email at MacmillanSpecialMarkets@macmillan.com.

Originally published in Germany by Droemer Knaur

First U.S. Edition: 2020

1   3   5   7   9   10   8   6   4   2

Germania

Prologue

———+———

The light was positioned to simulate ten in the morning. The urban canyons of the capital of the German Empire shimmered blindingly white. But nothing moved, everything seemed suspended, frozen solid in an eternal winter.

It would be a while until the daily chaos of Berlin reached those corners. At this moment, the streets still radiated symmetry and order in their abandonment. There were no vehicles parked on the curb, nobody strolling along the tree-lined streets. The only disruption of this orderly impression was the remnants of dried glue that, despite the architect's diligence, had welled out onto the street from under the building blocks.

The wide road axis ran straight as a die toward a mighty dome that would be visible on the horizon from several kilometers at some point in the distant future. What now dominated the horizon in white splendor was one day to outshine the entire city in its green gown of copper patina. The Große Volkshalle, a hall providing seats for 180,000 people, was a site for unprecedented victory celebrations.

A whisper sounded high above the roofs: "Magnificent, Speer."

The voice was not the distant rasp with the rolling *R* that every member of the German nation knew from the radio or the newsreel, nor was it the hoarse bark the dictator called forth from his repertoire when he needed to whip up the crowds. In front of the thirty-meter-long model of what would soon be the street of glory, the voice, utterly private in its natural baritone, seemed lost in thought, almost gentle. His backside poking out, a pose he usually avoided, the dictator bent forward to assume a near-ground perspective.

It could not be denied that in Albert Speer he had found an architect who occasionally managed to surpass even his principal's bold ideas in size and scale. Paradestraße, a road running at a length of more than five kilometers; the triumphal arch with its shady colonnades, which would be almost fifty times as large as the Arc de Triomphe in Paris; the vast Große Volkshalle, planned as the world's largest building, whose dome arched to a height of more than 220 meters on the inside. The entire city planned to compete with other metropolises, a display set in stone of deeply hurt national pride that now wanted to show its superiority with all its might.

The center of the Reich's capital would be transformed into a huge stage for military deployments and parades. The question of whether anyone could actually live in this city only rarely occurred to the dictator. The surrounding housing blocks were little more than uniform quadrangles that could easily be divided up yet again if traffic planning required this.

There was no room in this monumental vision for the old Berlin with its contradictions, for the brash, sometimes deeply provincial metropolis. For some time now, the dictator had been thinking about making this quite clear from the start. *Berlin* sounded too disdainful in his ears. A new name was required, one worthy of a capital of world renown. A name like *Germania,* perhaps.

Time and again, the dictator's gaze was drawn to the dome of the Große Volkshalle. Eventually, he cast a critical gaze across the structure on its spire, where the imperial eagle was enthroned on the swastika. Then, gripped by a sudden realization, he shook his head. "We have to change that, Speer. It's better if the eagle doesn't preside over the swastika anymore. The crowning glory of this building must be the eagle atop the globe."

When Hitler had left, Chief Architect Speer turned back in the doorway once more. Only the arrangement of lamps, which enabled him to give a realistic simulation of daylight atmosphere, lit up the academy's exhibition room. The model of the city rested in the otherwise dark room, a bright mark in the black infinity, a promise for the future. A lot remained to be done until then. Speer switched off the light.

Night descended upon Germania.

1

Oppenheimer had drowsily placed his arm around his wife when suddenly he felt Lisa's body grow tense. But everything was quiet outside. Because of the blackout, not the slightest glimmer of light came in. No siren wailed through the night, no bomber droned in the air, no antiaircraft fire drummed in the distance. So it couldn't be a bomb alarm that had frightened Lisa. At first, Oppenheimer had turned toward her, but then he, too, perceived the stranger standing very close by.

They've come to fetch me, Oppenheimer thought. Instinctively, he pulled the covers around himself.

The shadowy figure kept still, his breathing calm and regular. A spark danced in the darkness, moved upward, and transformed itself into a flaming point when the intruder inhaled. The smell of tobacco was blown toward Oppenheimer.

The stranger had to be a Gestapo man. Through Oppenheimer's knowledge of Berlin's criminal community, he knew that no normal burglar would stray into a designated "Jewish House" only to then nonchalantly smoke a cigarette and wait for his victims to wake up and notice him. *Oppenheimer knows his crowd,* had been the much-quoted quip among his colleagues during his years with the police force. No burglar would risk getting on to the Gestapo's radar for a few lousy coins, and the Gestapo men considered it their very own privilege to seek out and rob the Jewish residents of these houses. Even though there hadn't been any more raids in the last few months, Oppenheimer could recall them all perfectly. On these occasions, the Gestapo arrived in bulk. It was considered normal for them to beat the residents around the head, spit at them, and call out obscenities. But this man had come alone, covertly. This was a particularly bad sign. When the Gestapo people rabbled, you knew where you stood. However, if they were silent, anything could happen.

Oppenheimer and Lisa remained in their positions for a seemingly endless moment, him motionless in his bed, her next to him, and the stranger leaning against the doorway. Then the man's voice rang out. "I know you're awake, Oppenheimer. Sicherheitsdienst. Don't you want to get dressed and come along?"

This was posed as a question, but the tone was unmistakable. The speaker would not tolerate a refusal.

Oppenheimer did not dare switch on the bedside lamp. Shaking inside, he got up and fished his clothes from the back of the chair. He didn't have time to ask himself what a man from the National Socialists' so-called Security Protection Service, the Sicherheitsdienst, or SD, was doing here. Mechanically, he walked through the kitchen they shared with the other residents of the Jewish House. It always surprised Oppenheimer how readily he obeyed when he was scared, when he knew that his fate lay in someone else's hands. He briefly thought of Lisa, whom he had to leave behind without protection. But as an attested Aryan, she would be better off anyway if they killed him. Afterward, she would be free and no longer excluded from the community of the German people because she had married a Jew. Although he acutely feared for his own life, this thought gave him a certain comfort.

The light was on in the hallway, and Oppenheimer saw the stranger for the first time. It was a sobering sight. The man wore glasses and was quite small. But the hand in the baggy coat pocket betrayed the fact that he was carrying a firearm. Oppenheimer was surprised that none of the other residents were up and about. Not even the Schlesingers were creeping down the corridor, curious to see what was going on. It seemed that he was the only target tonight.

The SD man looked at the suitcase his prisoner was carrying and frowned. It had been a reflex. Oppenheimer had picked up his air raid suitcase on his way out. All his important belongings were stowed inside so he always had them with him when he had to go down into the cellar during an air raid. There were a lot of such suitcases in Berlin.

"You won't be needing that," the SD man said and waved him back. Oppenheimer turned and placed the suitcase in the dark kitchen.

Two SS men were waiting outside the building with guns in their hands. As soon as the SD man had pushed Oppenheimer out onto the pavement, they got moving. Clouds obscured the night sky. The moon behind them was nothing more than a diffused light that refracted dully off the SS men's steel helmets. Anxious, Oppenheimer stared at the gray backs, moving in unison, and heard the metallic clatter of their carbines. What could he do? Was there any way to escape? Oppenheimer instantly discarded the thought. As long as the SD man's gun was pointed at the back of his neck, there was nothing he could do.

They reached a car discreetly parked in a nearby side street. The back door opened, and Oppenheimer was engulfed by darkness.

■

It had been uncommonly quiet in Berlin during the last few days, and there wasn't an air raid alarm tonight either. But everyone knew the silence was deceptive. The airplanes would return at some point. Myriads of bombs had destroyed buildings and laid waste to the capital of the Reich. New gaps in the rows of houses testified to the latest attacks. The inhabitants had long gotten used to the constant change. Life in Berlin had always been hectic, but even by these standards, after Hitler seized power, the construction mania was remarkable. The scars could be seen everywhere. The National Socialist rulers had the most beautiful squares in the city center flattened into parade grounds, while fountains and statues were moved. They had even relocated the Victory Column from the Reichstag, the parliament building, to the star-shaped central square known as Großer Stern right in the middle of the municipal park called *Tiergarten*.

As they drove along, Oppenheimer looked out of the window and started with fright. For a brief moment, he thought he saw a scared face staring at him. But when he looked more closely, it turned out that the moonlight had played a trick on him. The sunken cheeks and deep-set eyes were Oppenheimer's own. The realization that he had been frightened of his own reflection made him feel stupid.

Outside, the plinth of the Victory Column, in itself high as a house, slid past them. The SS man at the wheel turned left, heading straight for the city center on the east-west axis. After a while, they drove through the Brandenburg Gate. Despite the darkness, Oppenheimer had no trouble finding his bearings. He knew every corner here and didn't need to look up to know that wings of stone swooped past them above their heads, reaching far into the night.

The street they were driving along was called *Unter den Linden,* but Hitler's architects had made a mockery of this description many years ago. For lack of anything better to do, they had chopped down all the old linden trees that gave this street its name to make space for countless marble pillars, which now served as thrones for a formation of imperial eagles and dwarfed the newly planted replacement trees.

When areas controlled by the League of Nations were returned to the Reich, jubilant cheering filled the street. Even-greater euphoria roared when the first successes from the front line were announced and the German Wehrmacht rushed through all of Europe from victory to victory.

But when the bombs fell, the resounding approval began to wane. Then came Stalingrad.

The military debacle in the remote Russian steppe had marred the taste of success and had undermined the trust in Germany's well-oiled war machinery.

During the day, Hitler's blindingly white marble pillars continued to outshine the city center, but night transformed them into a sinister forest of shadows in the midst of a gravel desert, through which the car now laboriously carved its way.

The driver swerved around a barely repaired crater in the road. Startled by the headlights, gray shadows with gleaming red eyes hastened to find cover. Rats. Myriads of them housed in the ruins. Despite all the destruction, they regained their terrain, inch by inch, mile by mile.

■

The SD man opened the door for Oppenheimer as he became vaguely aware of another car parked nearby. Men holding flashlights stood farther back in the darkness.

"Get out," the SD man said. Oppenheimer hesitantly clambered out of the seat. The drive had taken unexpectedly long. At some point, he had finally lost his sense of direction in the darkness. The panic that had initially seized him had increasingly turned into astonishment. When they crossed the Spree River and he recognized the mighty AEG factory buildings, Oppenheimer knew that they were in the suburbs of Oberschöneweide. Every inhabitant of Berlin knew the imposing industrial buildings that lined the northern banks of the Spree, but he couldn't fathom what had induced the SD to drive him here in the middle of the night.

Oppenheimer's escort pointed in the direction of the dancing light. He pulled his gun from his coat pocket and directed it toward Oppenheimer, who reluctantly started moving.

Security led Oppenheimer to a green area with a block of stone, three to four meters high, with granite steps leading up to it. The stone did not seem to fulfill any recognizable purpose in its crudeness. It was probably the meager remains of a memorial. There were countless numbers of these in Berlin. Most of them were quite recent, reminders of the horrors of the last war. Now that the world wars had been numbered, it had become known as the First World War, but in common parlance, it was simply known as Anno Scheiße. Given that any sort of metal was scarce in these heroic times, these sizable reservoirs of metal pieces were being melted down as soon as the new, even bigger war had started. Where a sculpture once had towered, there was now nothing but a gaping void.

But on this morning, something else disrupted the site of a memorial.

Someone had laid a large square of cloth over something directly behind the stump. Oppenheimer immediately recognized its outline: a human body.

In the dim glow of the flashlight, Oppenheimer also better recognized the faces of the two men. Both wore the gray battle dress of the SS. A large building that had to be a church loomed up behind them.

Snippets of conversation drifted through the cold morning air.

"Right bloody mess, this is," one of them whispered to the other and stared grumpily at the covered body at his feet.

"Do you really think it's a good idea to consult a *Jew*, of all people?"

"I've got my reasons, Graeter," the second man said and lit a cigarette.

"Say what you like, Vogler. I think it's a mistake." When the speaker realized that Oppenheimer was approaching with his escorts, he fell into an embarrassed silence.

The other man turned to the new arrival. "There you are, Oppenheimer."

The SS man called Vogler pointed his flashlight toward them both. The beam of light rested briefly on Oppenheimer's yellow Star of David. An expression of uncertainty flitted across Vogler's face, but it quickly disappeared behind the forced self-confidence that was so typical of Hitler's elite.

"I'm Hauptsturmführer Vogler. This body was discovered two hours ago."

Vogler went over to the body. Although the expression of the other man in uniform—Graeter—was deliberately blank, he sighed meaningfully before the cloth was folded back.

When Oppenheimer saw the dead woman, he felt the familiar stab in the pit of his stomach. He had dealt with numerous deaths during the run of his police career, but he was not so jaded that the sight of a murder victim left him completely cold. At the same time, he also felt the reflex of a homicide detective kick in. He felt his brain get into gear in the old familiar way and told his reluctant eyes to take a closer look.

"Tell us what you see," Hauptsturmführer Vogler commanded.

There was no doubt that this woman's body had been destroyed. When Oppenheimer noticed the steel marker posts that had been rammed into the ground alongside the body, he realized that the forensics team had arrived with the special vehicle they used in murder investigations to carry out the examination. Oppenheimer instinctively wanted to look for additional evidence that the specialists might have missed, but he paused.

The question of what he was actually doing here occurred to him. He had been suspended for a long time now. Following Hitler's rise to power, Oppenheimer had been removed from public service, like all Jews. Officially, he was not allowed to set foot in the crime squad offices, and yet here he was, standing before a new victim.

He looked at those around him, panic creeping up inside him. Did they want to frame him for the murder? He wouldn't have considered the SD to be that imaginative. A simple open grave and a bullet to his head would have sufficed to get rid of him. Why go to all this trouble?

"Are you not able to give us any indications?" Vogler asked. "You disappoint me. I had placed a certain degree of hope in you." He handed Oppenheimer his flashlight.

Hesitating, he took it. So they wanted pointers from him. He had no choice but to go along with it.

Thoughtfully, he turned to the corpse, beginning to speak, his voice raw.

"I'd put her at around twenty-five. There are strangulation marks on her neck. That is probably the cause of death."

Was that what the men wanted to hear from him? Their gloomy expressions showed indifference. Only Hauptsturmführer Vogler tried to follow his deliberations. Oppenheimer wanted to touch the body, but he stopped and turned to the Hauptsturmführer.

"Can I touch her?"

"Do whatever you consider necessary," Vogler answered.

Oppenheimer carefully manipulated the jaw. It barely moved. However, the muscles of the hands were relatively loose.

"Rigor mortis is not very pronounced. It has only set in partially in the lower half of the body. The murder is therefore probably quite recent; I am guessing around six hours ago. But I could be wrong, as the cold slows down the rigor. The doctors will be able to determine this more precisely. Her wrists are chafed, so she was probably tied up."

Oppenheimer stood and looked at the body in its entirety. The young woman's lower body was precisely aligned with the stone stump of the monument, her legs spread as if in the act of love. The position of the body appeared to have been specifically selected. The perpetrator had spent a lot of time arranging the dead body in this obscene way in front of the monument.

Oppenheimer suddenly noticed a small, crusted smudge of blood on the inside of one of her legs. He bent down next to the body to see where the blood had come from. The SD man who had brought him here turned away with a shudder. Did he not want to watch a Jew looking up a murder victim's skirt? Oppenheimer knew that the dead were not sensitive, and he lifted the hem.

The sight he was faced with instinctively made him jerk back. He instantly understood the SD man's reaction.

"Is something wrong?"

Oppenheimer tried not to vomit. He drew a sharp breath and then reacted as he had used to in similar situations. He pushed his revulsion aside and concentrated on approaching the matter methodically.

The woman was not wearing any underwear. Her pelvic area was a single massive wound.

"There is a large injury here. Her genitals have been mutilated, maybe even removed."

When Oppenheimer felt he had seen enough, he got up, aware of his surroundings again. Leaves rustled somewhere over his head. While he could just see the outline of the surrounding houses, the body was still enveloped by darkness. Oppenheimer's mind sorted the facts, while life slowly began to awaken around him.

Although he couldn't see any of this through the darkened windows, Oppenheimer sensed some of the residents getting up at this early hour as usual, although they didn't need to go to work today, shuffling to the bathroom or getting breakfast ready. Others, unaware that something terrible had happened nearby, were still in a blissful slumber, which for once had not been disturbed by an air raid. It was like any other Sunday. The first vehicle clattered past nearby, but the noise faded between the houses' façades. Not much longer and the churchgoers would arrive for morning prayers. To get to church, they would be heading straight for this square.

"And what is your conclusion?"

Vogler's voice tore Oppenheimer from his thoughts. Two more men had appeared with a stretcher to remove the body. The others shuffled their feet restlessly. Only Vogler stood quite still, staring at Oppenheimer, who cleared his throat in embarrassment. His years of experience helped him to not make a complete fool of himself and to outline his observations in a few brief words.

"At first glance, I would say that she wasn't killed here. There is hardly any blood. There are a few little spots underneath her skirt, and some close to the wound, but that's it. No blood on the ground, no traces of blood in the surrounding area; no, she was killed somewhere else and then brought here. I have never seen a body presented this way. I consider it unlikely that this is a coincidence. This is a public square. The danger of being caught is high. No, gentlemen, the man responsible for this planned it in advance. And he carried out that plan to the letter. Successfully so—otherwise, someone would have noticed him. The only conclusion that can be drawn from this is that we are dealing with an incredibly cold-blooded person here. Only someone with a bestial disposition can mutilate a body as brutally as that and then go on to present it. I don't hold out much hope of catching the perpetrator. It won't be easy."

∎

The siren sounded its protracted howl. That meant full alarm. Oppen-heimer automatically started moving, but he was not really bothered by the enemy bombers flying toward the city.

After he had given his evaluation of the murder case in Oberschöne-weide, he was driven back to the city center. Nobody had made the slight-est effort to explain the situation he had suddenly found himself in. As soon as the pre-alarm had gone off, the SD man had dropped him off at the Hansa Bridge and had raced off in the car. That didn't matter, as the Jewish House was just a few hundred meters away.

Oppenheimer should have been tired after this long night, but his mind was in overdrive. The impressions wouldn't leave his head.

As he approached his current dwelling place, he tried to assess the men who had been waiting for him at the site where the body was found. The SS men had worn identical uniforms, so it could be assumed that they were both Hauptsturmführer. But Oppenheimer was unable to say what SS men had to do with a murder case like this.

In contrast to the two Hauptsturmführer, his SD escorts had more of a reason to be present at a murder site. Officers from the Sicherheitsdienst were quick to arrive at the scene in the case of a serious legal offense, even though this particular organization initially had nothing to do with the criminal police. Early on, the Sicherheitsdienst of the Reich Leader SS were nothing more than the NSDAP party-internal intelligence agency, but when Hitler came to power, the borders between the German state and the National Socialist party apparatus had gotten increasingly blurred. The various NSDAP organizations received ever more responsibilities, so it was just a question of time until the security services, Gestapo, and crime squad were integrated into the newly founded Reichssicherheit-shauptamt, the Reich Security Main Office. Regular crime officers no lon-ger had any say. They were lackeys, permitted to act independently only in the case of minor offenses. Serious crimes had to be handled by party members. It was unclear what decided whether a case ended up with the SD or with the Gestapo, due to the general wrangling for responsibilities between the individual party organizations.

Oppenheimer was so lost in thought that he didn't even notice the

ghostly silence that had settled heavily on his surroundings. He had un-
dergone a decisive change this morning; for the first time in ages, he had
felt in control again. For a brief moment, he had once again been Inspector Oppenheimer and not the former civil servant, dismissed from public service because of his Jewish lineage. Suddenly, he wasn't a victim of
Hitler's despotism but a hunter. And so he didn't slink through the streets
with his head and gaze lowered but instead entered the Jewish House as if
it were the most normal thing in the world that he lived here.

As an air raid sounded, Oppenheimer went downstairs. The residents
had converted the cellar into a makeshift bunker. There had been no alternative, as Jews were not allowed into the big high-rise shelters with their
meter-thick concrete walls. On account of the head-high wooden beams
that had subsequently been wedged into the cellar rooms, Oppenheimer
thought it looked like a mining tunnel. Despite all the precautions that
had been taken, the measly wooden ceiling would hardly have offered any
resistance to an actual bomb hit. Strictly speaking, it would have made
more sense to seek shelter out in the open, as there was less danger of being buried by rubble there. As potential public enemies, the Jews had not
been allocated any gas masks, nor were they permitted to have a radio in
the cellar, not even a wireless one, to monitor what was going on outside.

When Oppenheimer entered the cellar bunker, the other residents of
the Jewish House were already seated: the Bergmanns, the Schlesingers,
and Dr. Klein, who was guarding the medicine chest as usual and had his
medical bag within reach for emergencies. Old Mr. Schlesinger squinted
at Oppenheimer from beneath his steel helmet, a souvenir from the First
World War.

"Is your wife in the factory today?" the old man inquired. "She didn't
come down with us."

Oppenheimer was surprised. "That's news to me. She didn't mention
anything."

"I told you to check, Schlesinger," Dr. Klein grumbled from his corner.
Clumsily, he pushed his massive body up.

"Don't worry, Doctor," Oppenheimer said. "I'll take care of it."

Oppenheimer was just taking the last few steps up to his flat when he
froze. Gas!

Something was not right. He ran up the remaining steps and flung open the kitchen door.

He was hit by the stench of gas. Stunned, he took a step back. Inexplicably, the kitchen window was closed. Normally, Lisa made sure it was wide open during air raids so the glass didn't break from the blast of a detonation.

Oppenheimer took a deep breath and dived across the room. His efforts to open the window were futile. He was too agitated. Without hesitation, he picked up a bucket of sand from the floor and used it to smash the window.

Oppenheimer gasped for air at the opening. He had just managed to refill his lungs with oxygen when he saw that the gas was lit on the stove. The kettle was on one of the burners, but someone must have forgotten to turn the gas off underneath.

In two strides, he reached the stove and switched off the gas. He had barely opened the door to his bedroom when he spotted Lisa. She was lying on the bed, unconscious, fully dressed. Oppenheimer rushed over to the window and wrenched it open.

Cool air wafted across his face. At the same moment, he heard heavy engines roaring over their house and the shrill whistle of falling bombs.

It was as if they were caught beneath a freight train. Outside, a deafening inferno was raging. Detonation after detonation. Oppenheimer could clearly see the contours of airplanes pushing themselves in front of the gray clouds. When they were flying this low, not even the antiaircraft guns had any effect. But he had no time to worry about such things. He grabbed Lisa underneath her arms and dragged her to the window. Panicked, he slapped her cheeks.

Suddenly, she opened her eyes and took a deep breath. Oppenheimer held her tightly, felt her body spasm as she coughed the gas out.

2

———

The Jewish House had emptied over the last few months. This increased the probability of the remaining tenants having to move to new, even more cramped dwellings in the near future. The former residents had disappeared one after the other: window dresser Schwartz, who had constantly sketched drawings and like Oppenheimer was married to an Aryan; the Lewinsky family with their four children; an orthodox Chassidic couple called Jacobi, who had annoyed him terribly with their constant praying; and the distinguished lawyer Dr. Kornblum, who called himself a liberal and showed no sympathy for Reform Judaism or orthodoxy and had to live next to the Jacobis. The mildly proletarian glassblower Franck, who had always had strong reservations about eastern European Jews, had also disappeared. They all left empty spaces in the building following their evacuation by the Gestapo, locked rooms one was not allowed to enter.

Of course, the word *evacuation,* the official term used by the authorities for the removal, was just window dressing. This had nothing to do with protecting the Lewinskys or Jacobis from the bombs that pelted down on Berlin. On the contrary. They had been shipped farther east to concentration camps. Oppenheimer's neighbors had heard the rumors and knew that they were as good as dead. But they refused to give up hope, down to the last minute; even when the Gestapo came to bundle them off into the railway carriages, they wanted to believe that the whispered horrors were exaggerated, that they would somehow manage to survive. The Gestapo would probably be coming to pick up Dr. Klein soon. As his Aryan wife had passed away a week ago, he was no longer under the protection of a mixed marriage. Dr. Klein hoped that, due to his age, he would be taken to Theresienstadt, which was generally considered less terrible. Soon his room would be empty too.

And now Lisa, too, had almost left a gaping hole in the house under tragic circumstances.

"I must have forgotten to light the gas under the kettle," she mumbled dazedly. "All the excitement with Richard . . . wanted to make some ersatz coffee."

"It was a good thing the gas was turned off because of the air raid, Mrs. Oppenheimer; otherwise, things might have ended badly," said Dr. Klein. He replaced his utensils in his battered medical bag. Oppenheimer looked thoughtfully at the two red Gestapo time cards fixed to the door opposite. "Unfortunately, the Lewinsky family isn't here anymore. They would have noticed the smell of gas."

Dr. Klein scrutinized Lisa, who was sitting at the table. The kettle began to whistle. Oppenheimer had boiled some water on the doctor's instruction.

"Right, I think you really need some ersatz now. Or, wait a moment . . ." Furtively, Dr. Klein fumbled in his medical bag and conjured up some coffee beans. "Here, to get your circulation going again. Better than that old coffee substitute," he remarked.

The effect was similar to him having dropped a lump of gold on the table. For a few seconds, Lisa's accident was forgotten; they were much too busy staring in shock at the coffee beans. Provisions such as meat, eggs, or milk were rationed and were primarily only given to *purebloods*. Scarce goods like tomatoes or cauliflower were forbidden for Jews. Lisa was the only one in the Jewish House to occasionally receive a few grams of Aryan coffee. It was mainly handed out as special rations after particularly heavy air raids, which was why it soon came to be known as *bomb coffee*. Despite their stimulating effect, the black beans were clearly an effective means of keeping the population calm.

While Oppenheimer ground the coffee beans, he considered where the doctor might keep his secret stash. Given his considerable corpulence, there was every reason to assume that he hoarded provisions somewhere, but neither the vigilance of his fellow residents nor the Gestapo's lootings had unearthed even a single crumb of his supplies.

"We've had numerous departures since I've lived here," Dr. Klein remarked. "This is particularly painful to me as a doctor. You understand, the Hippocratic oath and all that. On the other hand, I can understand someone in our situation taking death into their own hands. But it shouldn't happen by accident."

He winked meaningfully at Lisa. Was he trying to imply that she had turned the gas on intentionally to kill herself? Oppenheimer was not sure.

Lisa ignored the doctor's insinuations and sipped from the steaming cup that Oppenheimer had placed in front of her.

"I'm much better," she mumbled. "We need new sand for the firebombs; Richard poured it out. And Schlesinger has to do something about the broken windowpane."

When she made a move to get up, Klein placed his hand on her shoulder. "You must rest now, Mrs. Oppenheimer. I'll inform Old Schlesinger. You'd best stay here, Mr. Oppenheimer."

A telltale glimmer appeared in his eyes. Oppenheimer understood. "Do you need to"—he searched for the right words—"report the incident?"

"If our caretaker doesn't ask, then I won't have to lie. But don't be surprised by your next gas bill. If I were you, I wouldn't question it."

After the doctor had taken his leave, Oppenheimer awkwardly placed his arm around Lisa. He felt guilty toward her; it was only because of him that she was in this situation. But Oppenheimer was not only plagued by guilt. Fear had crept into their love over the last few years. Oppenheimer knew that this situation wasn't new to Lisa; she had always worried about him. After all, during his time with the police, he had often dealt with dubious characters. But ever since the first bombings began and put Lisa's life in constant danger, too, Oppenheimer could appreciate what she had gone through all those years. When they weren't together, there was always the fear that something might have happened to the other one.

"Where were you?" she asked.

"It was nothing. A murder investigation, routine stuff," Oppenheimer reassured her.

"But you're not with the crime squad anymore."

"I don't really know what they want. Me, of all people. It's completely mad, but it seems like the SS needs me as an advisor."

The mention of the SS made Lisa shudder. Panic flared up in her eyes.

"It could have been worse." Oppenheimer tried to allay her fears. "They let me go again after all."

"You've got to go to ground," Lisa urged him, "immediately. You can't stay here tonight; otherwise, they'll catch you."

"They won't come again."

"You can't be sure of that. Go to Hilde. I have to go and see the Hinrichs later anyway. I promised Eva I would come by."

"You heard what Dr. Klein said," Oppenheimer reasoned. "You shouldn't go to the Hinrichs'; you need to rest. I can't leave you alone now. After all, I don't need to visit Hilde *every* Sunday."

Lisa shook her head. "You don't understand. She's helped us before. She should do something for you. You said she has connections. She knows people underground. It's too dangerous if the SS is already turning up. You have to disappear!"

At first, Oppenheimer was reluctant, but he had to admit that Lisa was right. Hilde was his only hope. "All right, maybe it is possible to organize something. But it's not necessary."

"Richard, promise me you'll disappear?"

Oppenheimer mumbled something incomprehensible. He hated when Lisa made him promise something. It was her way of giving orders.

It felt good to escape the Jewish House at the weekend. Although Oppenheimer and Lisa had a harmonious marriage, being confined to their accommodations was a test of their resilience. This was the reason why over time they had each gotten into the habit of doing their own thing on Sunday afternoons. Lisa rarely accompanied Oppenheimer when he visited Hilde. He knew that a different wife would probably not have allowed him to meet, unobserved, with another woman every Sunday. Even though Lisa had never been the jealous type, it was striking how relaxed she was about it all. Oppenheimer could only speculate about the reasons. Maybe it was because Hilde was a good ten years older than he, and Lisa didn't see her as a rival. Maybe the fact that she could be certain he was safe also played a role. Hilde had repeatedly proved that she could be counted on.

Oppenheimer, on the other hand, had encouraged Lisa to cultivate her own circle of friends in the last few years, as he did not want her to rely on him too much. He could not rule out that he would be fetched by the Gestapo at some point. Too many Jews in mixed marriages had been killed for anyone to rely on being protected by their Aryan partner.

When Oppenheimer finally picked up his coat and hat, ready to leave, he hesitated. Eventually, he took the small vial out of the inside pocket of his coat.

"Here, take it," Oppenheimer said and pressed one of his Pervitin pills into Lisa's hand.

Lisa hesitated. "But you need them . . ."

"I've got enough for a while," Oppenheimer lied and embraced her. He was unwilling to let her go again, but he had to leave.

■

Before Oppenheimer dared to go through the front door of the building, he, too, took a Pervitin pill. As he didn't have any water, he chewed it and swallowed. When he wasn't worrying about Lisa, he barely felt anything else. Too much had happened in the last few months. Death was part of everyday life. One could barely even influence his own fate. But he knew that in just under half an hour, the effect of the methamphetamine drug would set in, and then nothing could affect him anymore. One pill gave him the necessary energy to make it through the day. Given that after several months of regular consumption the effect slowly began to weaken, Oppenheimer should have increased the dosage, but because of his supply shortage, he only permitted himself one pill per day.

Thus strengthened, he stepped out into the street. The smell of burning assailed his nose. The light was hazy, the sky overcast in sulfur yellow. Although it was only two in the afternoon, night seemed to have fallen prematurely in the east as black smoke clouds enshrouded the city center. Oppenheimer briefly considered whether it made sense to take the tram or the subway to get to Hilde. But then he rejected the thought. The departure times would probably be all muddled after today's attacks. He needed just under two hours to get to Hilde's house on foot, so he strolled across the Hansa Bridge toward the Victory Column as if he were taking a Sunday morning walk.

As a rule, passersby were rarely unfriendly when they caught a glimpse of his Star of David. Sometimes they even nodded understandingly. But you had to be on your guard when faced with children or overzealous

Nazis. The Gestapo had been strangely quiet in the last few months, seemingly ignoring the Jews who'd remained in the city. Although that was probably due to the fact that the Gestapo had more important problems to deal with ever since the Allied air raids, Oppenheimer found it impossible to trust the calm.

Previously, the Gestapo had clamped down with an iron hand. Oppenheimer had not been spared either. Nearly two years ago, one of the Gestapo's so-called Dogcatchers had stopped him in the subway and taken him in to check his papers. At the time, Oppenheimer had resolved not to play along anymore, an act of defiance. Like many others, he could have traipsed to the Reich Office of Genealogy, laden with old photographs, family documents, and other papers, to somehow show that the family resemblance was not particularly strong. If you were a so-called cuckoo child—or even better yet, adopted—you could hope to be classified as half or quarter Jew. Oppenheimer, however, had not even considered this, but instead sought a way to surreptitiously get rid of his Star of David.

As he was now drawing nearer to the Victory Column, the time had come for him to enact his very personal Aryanization process.

He turned left at Großer Stern. Albert Speer, in his function as the inspector general of buildings for construction, had had the Bismarck memorial moved here together with its enormous column. Poured in bronze, the first German Reich chancellor stood on his podium of red granite, set back from the roundabout, flanked by the statues of his highest-ranking military officers Roon and Moltke. Each of these generals had been given his own alcove, separated from the surrounding park by a low stone wall. Today, Oppenheimer selected the memorial of Count Albrecht von Roon.

After having made sure that no one was watching, he began walking slowly around the podium, looking up toward the count, whose rigid visage with the demonic eyebrows and the pointed beard would have been reminiscent of a second-rate actor in the role of Mephistopheles had he not been wearing a splendid uniform, with his helmet held casually at his hip. The back of the podium was wide enough to hide behind. With a resolute tug, Oppenheimer removed the Star of David, which was sewn on only perfunctorily, and put it in his inside pocket. In Berlin, many wearers of the star did this because they knew they were protected by the anonymity of the big city.

As he stepped out from behind the memorial, no one would have paid any attention to the middle-aged man. Oppenheimer was perfectly disguised without the star. No one would have suspected that he had an identification card with a capital *J* for *Jew* on it and that for several years now he had been forced to use the additional first name *Israel*. Any passerby would have sworn that Richard *Israel* Oppenheimer could be nothing other than a true Aryan.

Oppenheimer's relationship to the Jewish faith had been ambivalent since his early youth. Although his parents had not attached great importance to religion, he celebrated his bar mitzvah when he was thirteen as a matter of course. Oppenheimer enjoyed the ceremony in the synagogue, during which Jewish boys take on the religious "obligations of being a man" and become full members of the community, and he enjoyed the fact that he was allowed to read from the Torah in front of the entire community even more. But when, in the months leading up to this, he had to learn the mitzvoth, God's 613 "positive and negative commandments," he rebelled. Maybe he couldn't see the purpose of some of these commandments, maybe adherence to the mitzvoth was just too inconvenient—Oppenheimer couldn't really explain it afterward. In any case, his doubts became skepticism, which later turned into an aversion against all types of religion. Oppenheimer was a born skeptic who had seen too much to still believe in the existence of a God.

When he reached Potsdamer Platz, he saw where today's bombing had caused the most damage. An impenetrable smoke cloud had formed parallel to Saarlandstraße, and he deduced that Wilhelmstraße was probably the worst hit.

Women were heading toward the fires from the high-rise bunker at the Anhalter Bahnhof train station. Wearing head scarves and with spades on their shoulders, they marched in pairs in a long row. Oppenheimer was able to make out blue labels with the word *East* stitched in white on their clothes—they were forced laborers from the East.

About three weeks ago, around the date of Hitler's birthday, which was celebrated with great pomp and circumstance in Germany as usual, the fear of Berlin's citizens had reached its zenith. As instructed by the propaganda ministry, countless red swastika flags hung from the windows. Some jokers had even decorated the piles of rubble in the street with paper flags. But no one saw them rustling in the wind, as the streets were long empty. Those able to afford it had squeezed into the overcrowded trains to escape the much-feared air raids. However, it turned out that the strategists in the Royal Air Force headquarters didn't give much thought to trifles as the führer's birthday. A birthday gift in the form of several tons of explosives failed to materialize, and so, against all expectations, the day had passed calmly.

The big hit had happened last Saturday.

As Oppenheimer crossed the hall of the Anhalter Bahnhof, he saw the significant progress that the clearing operations had achieved since then. You could hardly tell that during the air raid a driverless express train with burning carriages had borne down on the terminal at full speed. The train had hurtled into the station like a flaming missile, rammed through the buffer stop, and plowed up the platform alongside the tracks. But the remains of the train had already been removed and the gaping hole in the paving covered with new stones.

Oppenheimer had to force his way through a cluster of people at the exit to Möckernstraße. Beneath the stone arches, surrounded by the few possessions they had been able to save from their destroyed homes during the last air raid, stood those who had been bombed out. Children mute with shock, countless suitcases and bags, in between an old man in a rocking chair—a panoply of private catastrophes.

"Retaliation had to come." The old man's voice was full of apocalyptic ardor. "It was obvious that the English wouldn't stand for Coventry."

"Just leave it, Father," his daughter silenced him and looked around surreptitiously for denunciators. Just to be sure, she added, "Everyone knows that the English started the bombing."

A passerby wearing a gray felt hat tried to enter the station. "Please, everyone! People still have to get through! Thank you."

"Just wait until our robot planes begin their attacks," a twelve-year-old said, the circular insignia of the Hitler Youth proudly displayed on his chest. "They'll get their dues when we hit back."

"I hope our wonder weapon is ready soon," said another boy with the same insignia. "It's about time we showed those bastards."

"Stop talking rubbish," the old man sputtered. "You saw what happened. These terror bombers are flying in broad daylight. *In daylight!* How are we meant to oppose them?"

"Our fighters couldn't get up there because of the clouds," one of the squirts explained expertly.

Once again, the old man wanted to say something when his daughter pushed him firmly back down onto his rocking chair. "Be quiet now!" She looked toward the boys as if she wanted to excuse the old man's utterances. But he wasn't having any of it.

"They can't harm me anymore. Everything's gone! Everything!"

That was the last Oppenheimer heard of the discussion. There were enough people who harbored a grudge against Hitler. Hilde had told him that there was increasing bewilderment overseas about the fact that the bombings had not roused any resistance in the German people. They complained, but that was it.

■

Hildegard von Strachwitz owned a large house on the edge of Berlin-Schöneberg. Her uncle, an officer of the Imperial German Navy, had had it built at the turn of the century. With no children of her own, Hildegard became his sole heiress, as she had cared for him with great devotion during his last few years and was his only remaining relative not scared off by the old man's increasing eccentricity. The fact that she was a doctor and had a good deal of experience with difficult characters had probably come in useful. Of times prior to that, Oppenheimer only knew that Hilde had been married. But the marriage had not gone well and had been annulled after a few years, after which she had taken on her maiden name again.

Next to the impressive mansion, there were two smaller buildings on Hilde's property, subsequently built by her uncle: a garage and a separate house for the chauffeur. Since Hilde needed neither a chauffeur nor a car, she had turned that house into her doctor's surgery. But as the National Socialists thought she had more than enough space at her disposal, over the last few months, families had been billeted to live in the main house after their houses had been bombed out. Without further ado, she had packed her belongings and had moved into the doctor's surgery.

Oppenheimer was relieved to see that Hilde's property had survived today's attack unscathed. As usual, he turned into the small side street, where he could enter via the small back gate. He had often wondered where Hilde found the courage to meet him alone. After all, they risked being tried for *racial defilement* if it came to light that Oppenheimer was a Jew. But Hilde rarely paid any heed to the National Socialist rulers' regulations.

As Oppenheimer headed to Hilde's surgery, a woman staggered toward him, probably in her early thirties. She had just about reached him when she stumbled and clung onto his arm.

"Oops!" she cried cheerfully. "Those steps weren't here earlier."

As far as Oppenheimer could tell, there weren't any steps now either.

"Sweet Jesus! Don't say you got it from me, but that stuff the doctor lady has is much better than any liquor."

Following this statement, she swayed toward the pavement. Oppenheimer was too surprised to consider helping her. Instead, he pressed the doorbell.

The door opened immediately, and Hilde stood before him. She didn't normally go out at this time, but as usual, she wore subtle makeup and her hair was immaculately styled into waves. Her figure was growing increasingly plump with age, but she was able to hide this to some extent with her choice of smart clothes, and her graceful appearance continued to be untouched by the passage of time. Every inch of Hilde showed the observer that this was a woman of the world. Although she had experienced a great deal in her life, her eyes widened at the sight of Oppenheimer.

"Bloody hell, you look like something the cat spat out!" she exclaimed.

3

To say that Hilde swore like a trooper would be an understatement. In fact, her verbal diatribes were similar to those of a burly sailor. Oppenheimer grew nervous. The seriousness of his situation had suddenly caught up with him. "I might not be able to come by in the near future."

Hilde paused briefly, then she pulled him inside. "Come, take off your coat first."

Feeling despondent, Oppenheimer entered the small treatment room. He hung his coat and jacket on the stand and followed Hilde through another door into her cave-like dwelling. Almost every free inch of surface in the private section of the chauffeur's flat was used to store countless books, which made it feel smaller. Even the windowsills were overflowing with papers.

It was by no means just specialized medical literature that piled up here. Any National Socialist with even a partial knowledge of literature would probably have a heart attack in Hilde's flat, given that the majority of her collection consisted of books that for some years had been considered *un-German*. Kurt Tucholsky's works could be found next to Erich Maria Remarque's novels, Karl Marx's tractates stood alongside Albert Einstein's scientific works, Kafka met Hemingway, Kästner stood in intimate companionship next to Maxim Gorky—all books that National Socialist students had thrown into the flames of the pyre on the Opernplatz just a few years ago.

Incensed by the audacity of the book burning, Hilde had immediately begun to collect so-called corrosive literature. And she didn't do things by halves. Hilde wanted to set an example, wanted to store the outlawed literature for future generations and preserve the thoughts that had flowed in printer's ink so that in the future, the authors would once again be able to speak to the reader from the pages of these books. Oppenheimer almost felt as if the many books along the walls formed some sort of ideological palisade that shielded Hilde's soul against the madness raging out there. In any case, the works of these ostracized authors had found their place of refuge in this small flat, and Hilde was their patron saint.

"Oh, I almost forgot," Hilde said and reached for a magazine lying on a chair. "I'm tidying up."

"Because of your visitor earlier?"

"You met the brainless creature? Gosh, I didn't let that old Nazi cow in here."

Hilde placed the magazine on a pile and went into the kitchen. Oppenheimer sat somewhat lost in the oversized armchair. The silence that entered as soon as Hilde left the room felt oppressive to him. So he half-heartedly tried to make conversation.

"Not very nice to call someone that," he said.

"Oh, come on, that blunderbuss was from the National Socialist Women's League," she replied. "Now tell me, what do you think of a woman who calls her children Adolf, Joseph, and Hermann? In precisely that order."

"Good German names."

Hilde appeared in the doorway. Although the chances of being overheard by her neighbors were infinitely small, she whispered, "Yes, they're the names of good German assholes. Brainlessness really is the nicest thing one can ascribe to her."

Oppenheimer knew that Hilde sometimes liked to make things easy for herself. "I know a Jew called Adolf," he tried to draw her out. "He was in the army for years. No idea what became of him. Maybe he had to change his first name."

"That doesn't happen to be a certain corporal who now occupies the Reich Chancellery?"

Oppenheimer waved her off. It was pointless. He didn't know how she did it, but Hilde always seemed to be two steps ahead of him.

"What did she want from you?"

Hilde came back with a glass and a pack of cigarettes. "That was the best bit. She had been instructed to scour the neighborhood and convince all women without a job to take on voluntary labor in community service. As if I didn't have anything better to do. A lot has to happen before I break my back for the Nazis. Instead of discussing that with her, I got the silly cow drunk in the treatment room. The way she was putting them away, she's unlikely to remember anything by morning."

Oppenheimer scrutinized the half-empty bottle that Hilde had brought with her. "What a waste of schnapps," Oppenheimer said without much enthusiasm.

"Well, I think you need it more than she did." She filled the glass and pushed it toward him. Oppenheimer stared at the liquid as if wondering whether it was well disposed toward him.

"I distilled it myself. You won't find any better," Hilde persuaded him. "Come on, one for Mummy . . ."

Oppenheimer finally overcame his revulsion and swallowed the contents of the glass in one gulp. His eyes involuntarily narrowed to watery slits as Hilde's schnapps etched down his throat.

She heaved an exaggerated sigh. "Why do you always have to make such a fuss? Well, at least the boozer from earlier appreciated my stuff." She handed Oppenheimer two cigarettes. "I'd better give these to you straightaway. Here."

He took them gratefully. She usually gave him a couple every Sunday as a parting gift. Oppenheimer dug around in his jacket for his cigarette holder. While he inserted the cigarette and lit it, Hilde scrutinized him.

"There's nothing like going out in style, right? You can't be doing that badly. What actually happened?"

When Oppenheimer told her about his nighttime excursion with the SD, her face lit up with excitement. Psychology was Hilde's pet issue, in particular research into the criminal mind. Oppenheimer had already guessed that she would be interested in the case. But right now, she focused on a different issue.

"Well, I'll be damned. Why on earth is the SS working on this murder case?"

"It can only mean that this matter is very important to the party. But I have no idea what's behind it. They didn't tell me anything."

"What does a dead woman have to do with state security?"

They sat thinking in silence for the next few minutes. When Oppenheimer inhaled the smoke of the second cigarette through the meerschaum mouthpiece, he noticed how greedily Hilde sucked in the blue haze.

"Don't you want to treat yourself to one?" he asked.

"No, I'm all right. Too precious. Do you have any idea what sort of things you can arrange for a cigarette on the black market? It's better than any cash. I prefer to abstain."

"You're making me feel guilty."

"Oh, don't you worry, I have enough reserves. But, Richard, I'm not sure if that's clever."

"What do you mean?"

"This idea of you disappearing. I can of course understand Lisa, but it seems to me that the SS has already become aware of you. If you disappear now, they'll notice straightaway. I'm sure they've already found out where you work."

The führer or the community of the German people or whatever other entity had decided that even a Jew like Richard Oppenheimer had to support the war effort. Which was why for the last few months he had been slaving away, polishing machines in a small factory.

"Maybe they won't come by anymore and will leave me alone," Oppenheimer objected.

"In that case, there would be no need for you to disappear."

"We're going around in circles." He groaned. "I'm guessing you still have your contacts?"

"I'll find somewhere for you if necessary. There are options. It's not easy, but maybe we should give you a whole new identity. Because of all the bombings, a large number of new identity cards had to be made. The ministry hasn't been able to check all the details for a while now. First of all, we have to get an attestation of a bombing from one of the district authorities. If you're lucky, you might even get a substitute Aryan ration card for a month. If we manage to smuggle you in somewhere for registration, there's even the possibility of you getting a fully valid citizenship under a fictitious name. As long as you don't get caught with your pants down, they won't notice anything."

"And if it doesn't work?"

"Then all you can do is hide out privately somewhere and keep your mouth shut. And you'll have to keep changing your lodgings. You'll be on the run the whole time. I hope you realize this."

"I fear I have no choice," Oppenheimer replied despondently.

Hilde thought for a moment. "All right. This is what we're going to do; you think about it while I get things moving. We can always call it off. In the meantime, you need to get ready."

"I've already packed the few things that I own."

"What about work?"

"I can miss two days without a doctor's note. Any longer and I need one from an independent medical examiner."

Hilde considered the options. "Hmm. Which colleague do you have a good relationship with?"

"Well, there's Arnold. I told you about him once, the Jew who polishes machines with me and who looks like the knight Sigurd in the flesh. And then there's Ludovic. He always comes and chats with us, although he's not really allowed to."

"A Frenchman?"

"Yes. Unfortunately, his German is just as bad as my French. He's a young chap from Avignon, that much I've discovered. He was drafted from there for a voluntary labor stint."

"Ah, so they dragged him to Berlin. Ridiculous." Hilde briefly shook her head. "Right. Then start playing them some symptoms tomorrow. Dizzy spells would be best, breathlessness, something like that. Come up with something, but don't exaggerate. I know what a bad actor you are. Come and see me tomorrow. I should have managed to sort most of the other things by then."

"All right. I have quite a lot to do, then."

"And one more thing—if someone asks Lisa about your whereabouts, she should say that you've disappeared because you were having marital problems. Then she should be off the hook."

"I hope so," Oppenheimer said gloomily.

Hilde leaned forward. As usual, she was able to read his mind. "I will keep an eye on Lisa. It's going to be over soon anyway. This is the last gasp of Hitler's mob."

"I've been hearing that for the past eighteen months, and still nothing has happened."

"No, really. It's all over town that there's going to be an invasion soon. The British radio has been calling on their resistance fighters in the west not to strike until the order is given. Our Nazis will soon be fighting a war on two fronts. Then things will come to an end quickly."

"I'm not convinced."

Hilde nodded toward the record player. "Time for Johann Sebastian?"

"Definitely. How is my gramophone?"

"It hasn't complained yet. But you know that I don't have any use for it."

When Oppenheimer, like all Jews, was ordered to turn in all his valuables, he had hidden the apparatus at Hilde's. It would have been pointless to try to pretend that Oppenheimer's gramophone and record collection belonged to Lisa. There was no other alternative, and Hilde's Ark for forbidden literature seemed the suitable place for his gramophone. With the countless Brahms, Bach, and Beethoven records, she would have been well equipped for the time after the brown deluge, if only she had any understanding of music. He had tried to educate her on this several times, always without success. And so it sometimes happened that on his Sunday visits he did nothing but listen to music for hours on end, while Hilde was busy with other things.

While Oppenheimer let his gaze roam over his records in order to choose one, Hilde said, "It's a bit chilly out, isn't it? You'd hardly believe it's already May. Wait, I managed to get hold of a nice specimen this week."

She returned to the kitchen with a book. "Here," she said, proudly handing over the volume.

Oppenheimer flipped through the pages. "A wedding gift?" he asked.

"Of course. But look, leather cover, with a personal dedication from the führer."

He gazed at Hitler's scrawl, but the name of the recipient meant nothing to him. He must be a bigwig. Despite himself, Oppenheimer began to smile. Although almost everything was rationed nowadays, there was no lack of copies of *Mein Kampf.* If you really wanted to, you could probably get hold of dozens of copies of Hitler's tractate. And Hilde was an expert in this area.

"To celebrate the occasion," said Hilde and picked the book up again.

Then she opened the door of the black stove in the corner of the room, stood in front of it, and proclaimed, "For Stefan Zweig." Then she threw the luxury edition of Hitler's *Mein Kampf* onto the coals and lit it with a match.

"Joy, bright spark of divinity!" the choir belted from the gramophone as the book went up in flames. Hilde turned in surprise.

"Not very original," she commented on Oppenheimer's choice of music.

"But appropriate," he retaliated.

"Ah, that's better." Hilde stretched her hands out toward the warmth that began spreading throughout the room. When she saw that Oppenheimer was sitting in front of the gramophone, his eyes half-shut, listening to the music, making no move to speak, she said, "Will you excuse me? I have a few things to do."

Slowly, Oppenheimer grew tired. There was nothing more for him to do. Everything had been discussed and arranged. He could only ponder how much of a difference one day could make.

Hilde was working noisily in the treatment room. Oppenheimer was aware of this without paying any heed. He was just happy that she made it possible for him not to have to pretend or be careful. She demanded nothing in return for her friendship. It almost seemed as if his presence was reward enough for her.

After a while, Hilde returned and sat down next to him. "Here," she said and gave him a cardigan. "I noticed that you're running around in darned clothes again."

Hesitantly, Oppenheimer took the gift. He was a bit embarrassed by Hilde giving him such generous presents all the time. But a warm cardigan would come in very useful in these times of strict rationing.

"And you really don't need it?"

Hilde shook her head. "It's not my size, and beige doesn't suit me. Better I give it to you than let the Nazis get their hands on it next time they collect material for spinning."

"Thanks." Oppenheimer had to chuckle. "I wonder how the SS came to choose me of all people. There are enough inspectors trained in murder investigations out there. Surely they could have found a line-toeing crime officer. So why get me out of bed in the middle of the night and whip me over to where the body was found?"

"I think it's obvious what happened. They dug around in the files and discovered that you were involved in the investigation into Karl Großmann."

Oppenheimer flinched when he heard the name of that monster, after all these years. For a doctor like Hilde, who was interested in the psyche of a pathological murderer, Großmann was just what she'd been waiting for. And although many years had passed since then, the residents of Berlin still shuddered when they remembered this man's inconceivable deeds. Oppenheimer had spoken to Hilde about murder cases on more than one occasion, but now he almost regretted having gone into so much detail. Recently, he thought of Großmann less and less often, but the memories of that man's deeds slumbered in the recesses of his mind and were just waiting to be awakened. It had been the first case he'd been involved in as a young officer, and it had turned out to be the worst case he would work on in his entire career.

"But that happened ages ago," he protested. "And anyway, I was just an assistant. I was just a runner and wrote the occasional protocol of his interviews. That was all."

"Großmann is considered the classic sex killer. Maybe the SS think that they're dealing with a similar type here."

"I can't see a correlation," Oppenheimer replied stubbornly. In actual fact, he'd had this thought a while ago, but part of his mind rebelled against the notion that he might once again be dealing with such a beast in human form.

■

When Oppenheimer left, Hilde remained standing in the doorway, watching him disappear. "God be with you," she said in a toneless voice. Of course, he couldn't hear her, but as nowadays every parting could be the last, she got sentimental quite easily.

She went up the stairs into her bedroom and closed the door to the wardrobe from where she had taken the cardigan.

Erich's cardigan.

Back in the deepest recesses of her cupboard, there were still a few items of her husband's clothing. Hilde had met him during her medical training. She had admired his intellect, which was accompanied by a marked ruthlessness. For a few years, Hilde had really believed that she'd met her soul mate.

Initially, the marriage had been quite harmonious. Hilde had accepted her fate of playing the housewife that Erich wanted, although she had always seen it as her destiny to run her own doctor's surgery. But when her husband started to take a growing interest in genetics and eugenics, he had slipped away from her.

Hilde had fought for her marriage, but when Erich finally joined the SS, where, as Hauptscharführer Hauser, he trained to become a military doctor, Hilde took the appropriate action and ended things.

Since then, Erich had risen up in the Nazi hierarchy. Despite everything that had happened, Hilde still felt some sort of affection for him, a feeling she resented herself for. However, he protected her. Erich would do anything to prevent his reputation with the senior party members from being compromised. He had laid himself open to blackmail. And Hilde knew it. She could afford to take certain risks, knowing that if things went wrong, Erich would sort them.

She longed to forget him. For this reason, she had started giving away Erich's clothes. Hilde had set herself the goal of driving him from her mind completely as soon as all the clothes were gone. So now she was giving away her memories. Piece by piece. One more harsh winter and Hilde would have forgotten Erich. At least that was what she hoped.

As Hilde closed the cupboard again, wondering if Oppenheimer also expected his wife to run the household, there was a knock on the surgery door. It was only now that she remembered she was expecting someone. The excitement about Richard had distracted her.

Hilde opened the door.

"Am I in the right place . . . ?" The young woman with the freckled face broke off anxiously and looked at the piece of paper in her hand. Then she handed it to Hilde.

A brief glance sufficed. "Yes, you're in the right place. You'd better come in."

The young woman had taken off her coat and stood in the treatment room, clearly uncertain.

"Don't worry," Hilde tried to calm her, "I am a doctor. Nothing is going to happen to you. How old are you?"

"I am . . . I'll be seventeen next month."

Hilde guessed that she was at least two years younger. She sighed at the thought.

"I've got everything ready. If you don't want to do it, then we don't need to go ahead. One word from you and I'll call it all off."

The young woman followed Hilde's instructions, lay down on the treatment couch, and spread her legs.

4

———————

The night had passed without interruption. They had even been spared by the so-called Mosquitos, isolated planes that dropped their bombs at random. It was early morning when Oppenheimer trotted listlessly down the stairs and made his way to work.

As soon as he stepped out onto the pavement, he spotted a man at the next street corner. This chap had to be Gestapo or SD. After just a few steps, he heard a voice close behind him.

"Mr. Oppenheimer?"

He turned around and stared into the stranger's face.

"Yes?" Oppenheimer asked.

"Sicherheitsdienst. Please come with me."

"I have to get to work . . ."

"Don't worry about that," was the laconic answer.

■

A metallic clinking reached Oppenheimer's ear. Followed by shouts and further clinking. A few seconds later, the two white figures stood facing each other, motionless, appraising each other.

"Sit down," the SD officer commanded. Oppenheimer had no choice but to obey and watch the two fencers in the gigantic hall. At the end of the fight, the winner took off his mask. It was Vogler. This was the first time Oppenheimer saw him in daylight. He estimated him to be in his midtwenties. Ash-blond hair fell across his forehead. Oppenheimer's sister-in-law, who worked as a hairdresser in Leipzig, liked to call this indefinable color *dishwater blond*. Vogler came toward them with a spring in his step and pulled off his gloves. Oppenheimer noticed the jet-black SS insignia on the white metal vest and frowned.

"Come along, Oppenheimer," the Hauptsturmführer said by way of a greeting. Oppenheimer got up and trotted along behind him. Once they'd reached the changing rooms, Vogler mustered him with interest. Then he began to get undressed. Oppenheimer felt a bit queasy, as he didn't know what sort of game was being played here. The situation was similar to the fencing match just now. Both were waiting for the other to make the first move. Vogler took a towel and strutted around naked in front of Oppenheimer. This was probably his not unsubtle way of showing those around him that he had nothing to be ashamed of.

Finally, Oppenheimer asked, "Why am I here?"

In passing, Vogler said, "I'll keep it short. We need your help in solving this murder case."

Silently, Oppenheimer followed him to the shower. Of course, he was tempted by the case, but he had no idea what he would get himself into if he worked for the SS. And there were other things to consider. After all, Oppenheimer had a job to report to every day. If he didn't, he would get into serious trouble. He considered whether the other man might interpret these deliberations as refusal. Finally, he said, "I work as a machine polisher."

Vogler stood under the water jet and waved the objection aside. "Your employer has been informed. You will be on leave until the case is cleared up."

Oppenheimer didn't know what to say. It seemed to be a done deal. "Why did you choose me, of all people?"

"I think you're just the sort of man we need. You are said to be one of the best crime investigators there are."

"I'm not in the service anymore. And anyway, there are enough colleagues who are just as good."

"Not for this case."

Vogler was interrupted by a sudden clatter. The SD man came rushing into the changing room. "Heavy, five!" he called.

"Damn, it was forecast that they'd change course!" Vogler said angrily. "Quick, into the bunker. No time to lose." Hastily, he dried himself and grabbed his clothes.

Outside, the sirens were already howling as Oppenheimer and the others ran down the steps to the shelter. When the heavy iron door closed behind them with a dull thud, Oppenheimer realized that there was no one else there. He, Vogler, and the SD man were the only ones sharing the cellar vault.

"As we're likely to be spending quite a bit of time down here, we might as well have a look at your dossier," Vogler said. He sat down on one of the wooden benches and had the SD man hand him a slim folder. As he looked through the pages, Vogler's brow furrowed. Something had awakened his interest. "You were in Verdun?"

"Yes."

Although it was a long time ago, Oppenheimer could still remember clearly storming out of the trenches into no-man's-land, where every single step could be a deadly mistake. He'd been a soldier then, much too young to be confronted with the carnage of what war meant. The mixture of uncertainty and fear he felt today was not dissimilar to the feeling he'd had under enemy fire back then.

The corners of Vogler's mouth twitched disdainfully. Oppenheimer had no trouble discerning what was going through his mind. He did not correspond to the image that Hitler had painted in countless speeches. Oppenheimer was living proof that the stab-in-the-back myth, according to which communist Jews intended to weaken and demoralize the brave German army, was a lie. Nothing had been further from Oppenheimer's mind. In his youthful idealism, he had simply considered it his patriotic duty to fight for his fatherland and the emperor. He had even received the Iron Cross for bravery, albeit second class, but nonetheless. Given what had become of Germany since then, it might be childish, but Oppenheimer was still proud of this award. However, the cross was no longer in his possession, as it had been stolen by the Gestapo during their last ransacking of the Jewish House.

"I see you have a daughter. Why is this mentioned here?"

"It seems someone has done their research," Oppenheimer replied curtly.

Vogler rustled through the papers. "Hmm . . . admission to the Prussian police force, initially foot patrol, then detective sergeant, finally promotion to detective superintendent. And then . . . yes."

Expulsion from service, Oppenheimer mentally completed his own biography.

"Who was this Großmann chap?" Vogler suddenly wanted to know.

Oppenheimer flinched inwardly. "You've never heard of Karl Großmann?"

"I had hoped you'd be able to enlighten me. What was he? An antisocial element?"

"That's probably what he'd be called nowadays. He slipped into obscurity over time. People only remember Friedrich Haarmann or Peter Kürten."

Vogler looked across at Oppenheimer with interest. "I have heard of the Haarmann case."

"Haarmann? Yes, well, Haarmann was a pederast. He lived in Hannover. He would bite into his boy toy's throat or carotid artery during the sexual act. Then he would dismember the body."

"And Kürten? What about him?"

"He was known as the Vampire of Düsseldorf. He was convicted in 1930. Another mass murderer. He stabbed his victims to death and drank the blood from their wounds to seek sexual gratification. But that was nothing in comparison to Großmann."

"And what did Großmann do?"

"He would kill women during the sexual act. Prostitutes, often homeless women whom he'd promised a place to stay. Some of them even worked for him as housekeepers. If they weren't willing, he would rape them. Sometimes he would mutilate their sexual organs and their anuses with kitchen equipment. He didn't shy away from children either. He would dismember the bodies. They repeatedly found body parts near his flat. What's more, he sold meat products. It is possible that he processed some of the bodies into sausages or tinned meat. There were rumors that he ate parts of his victims himself. It was . . . well, yes, there is probably no point talking about it."

"What did you want to say?"

"We were only able to pin three murders on him and were still busy with the investigations. Of course, we wanted to know exactly how many victims there had been, but then the case was taken away from us. It seemed there was a hurry to get him in front of a judge. Großmann was only accused of three murders. He hanged himself during the trial. We shall never know how many people he killed. There was a whole string of unexplained sex murders that we were able to link to him. There must have been dozens. At least. I have never met anyone like him since."

Oppenheimer had portrayed Großmann's deeds very drastically. He wanted to see if it was possible to draw Vogler out of his reserve. But the other man didn't bat an eyelid during the recital of the gruesome acts.

"If you look at the police photographs, you can clearly see that he was subhuman. An Untermensch. The structure of his skull, the nose, a typical example."

Vogler held the photograph out to Oppenheimer. It had been in the files all this time. After all these years, Oppenheimer was staring into the visage of the monster once again. When he saw the face above the collarless white shirt, the hairs on the back of his neck stood up. Großmann's narrowed eyes, two dark slits, stared at Oppenheimer with hostility. For a few seconds, he couldn't help but gaze at the photograph as if hypnotized.

Großmann's face triggered other connotations too. The mattress, stained with blood and feces, the indentation of the rope cut deeply into the victim's skin, the poor woman's bruises, the lacerated flesh between her legs, the kitchen utensils on the floor in a foul-smelling, dark liquid— all this combined to form an image that was deeply etched into Oppenheimer's memory.

Finally, he cleared his throat. Thought. Then he slowly began to shake his head. "I'm sorry to disagree, but in my experience, a person's face does not tell you what is going on inside them. There may be certain theories on the matter, but I can only speak from practical experience."

When Vogler gave him a skeptical look, Oppenheimer realized that he'd probably gone too far. He had to be careful. He sometimes grew careless under the influence of Pervitin. He hastily added, "Maybe I am wrong. Times have changed. Why not also the criminals?"

Vogler chuckled but said nothing.

Suddenly, the steel door was yanked open by an SS man. "All clear!" he shouted into the cellar vault.

"Already?" Vogler asked in surprise. Oppenheimer hadn't expected the all clear yet either. Normally, you had to spend three to four hours in the bunker during a raid.

The distant all clear could be heard through the open door. Vogler stood up and looked over toward Oppenheimer. "Nothing is going according to plan today," he said. "*Almost* nothing. Mr. Oppenheimer, I will make you this offer only once. There is a murderer whom I want to arrest at all costs. You are being given the opportunity to help the investigations in an advisory function. It will not be to your disadvantage. You need to decide here and now. If you don't take up this offer, there won't be another opportunity."

Oppenheimer considered the wording *it will not be to your disadvantage.* But then a more obvious question arose. "What happens if I don't accept the offer?"

"Then you'll have to reconcile that with your conscience. I don't have much time; there's a murderer running about out there. You can stop him. So what do you say?"

This is all madness, Oppenheimer's logic protested. At the same time, the notion of ridding himself of the stupid machine-polishing job he wasted his days on was decidedly attractive. Vogler's gaze rested on Oppenheimer while he tried to weigh up the consequences. He had to make a decision, but did he even have a choice? Oppenheimer hesitated. He begrudged Vogler the triumph of a straightforward acceptance. Instead, he asked, "When do we start?"

■

The metal sign with the skull and crossbones vibrated in the wind. Beneath it in big letters, the inscription: UNEXPLODED BOMBS!! MORTAL DANGER! Oppenheimer chuckled at the ruse. Whoever had been charged with keeping unwelcome visitors from the place the body was found had had a true inspiration. Although countless signs warning of unexploded bombs characterized the daily lives of the citizens of Berlin, they had lost nothing of their terrifying effect. Those not wanting to take any unnecessary risks gave them a wide berth. Two SS men were standing at the cordoned-off area in full uniform when Oppenheimer approached with Vogler. One of the guards saluted the Hauptsturmführer before he lifted the chain to let them both through.

"Has anything happened since I left?"

Vogler's brusque tone instinctively made the SS man freeze to attention.

His heels clicked together noisily. "No, nothing to report, Herr Haupt-sturmführer!" he replied.

Oppenheimer himself had received many orders, both from his superiors in the police force and during his time with the military, but the SS tone had a different quality. It had little in common with the self-important blustering he had grown accustomed to in the barracks from his sergeant major. The SS people made a particular effort to appear snappy, and they had the nasty habit of chopping all their words into syllables so that each one could be spat out with great fanfare. When a superior addressed a subordinate, it reminded Oppenheimer a little of the disdainful tone with which Gestapo men spoke to Jews when they were bullying them. He asked himself how the two might be connected.

"Come along," Vogler said to Oppenheimer in his other, civilized voice.

"Has an autopsy been carried out yet?" he asked.

"There is a slight communication problem, as the phone lines are down. But we'll soon have a radio set at our disposal. I hope to receive the autopsy report as soon as it's available. As I said, there is no reason to come here. Everything has already been photographed."

"Hmm. I wanted to see the site again in daylight. A camera cannot pick up all the details. Are there no other witnesses?"

"Only the air raid warden who found the body."

They stopped in front of the stone block, at exactly the same spot where the body had lain yesterday morning. Behind them, a narrow path separated them from the redbrick church that rose above a ledge of white stones. Oppenheimer looked up. The architect seemed to have been bent on interlocking as many building elements and battlements as possible. The result was unusual, but impressive.

The upper floors of the houses opposite were barely visible through the four linden trees. They offered the perfect visual cover for the perpetrator.

"I'm not surprised we don't have any witnesses," Oppenheimer said. "Were there any more traces of blood in the vicinity?"

"We didn't find any."

"Good. That means that the body was transported here somehow. I'm guessing that the vehicle was parked right here. Between the church and the memorial. It's only a few meters to the place where the body was found. Although this is a public square, no one would really be able to see what was going on behind this block of stone. Possibly the residents on the first and ground floor, but it was nighttime, and the windows were blacked out as of nine thirty. The risk of being interrupted was minimal."

"So it's not a coincidence that the body was found here?"

"That would really surprise me. Everything indicates that the perpetrator knows this place well and chose it specifically. I just don't understand what the whole thing is about."

Oppenheimer let his gaze wander thoughtfully. Then he pulled his cigarette holder from the inside pocket of his coat and put it in his mouth. With his gaze fixed on the ground, he walked around and chewed on the meerschaum mouthpiece. Vogler watched this spectacle for a while, then he asked, "Would you like a cigarette?"

Oppenheimer looked at him in surprise. "Cigarette?" he repeated, but when he realized what he had been doing, he felt a bit stupid. "Oh, thanks. No problem. The thing with the cigarette holder—it's an old habit of mine. Please excuse me, but it helps me to think."

Vogler raised his eyebrows. Whatever he might think about someone who needed a cigarette holder to think, he didn't comment. Instead, he asked, "So the perpetrator had some sort of vehicle?"

"At least he managed to transport the body without attracting attention. It wasn't necessarily a motorized vehicle. A wheelbarrow would have been enough. However, that would mean he lives in the immediate vicinity. Did any of the neighbors notice a vehicle during the night?"

"You must understand that this investigation is top secret. We cannot interview the neighbors without raising suspicion. This is why we have informed the block wardens in the surrounding properties. They will make inquiries with the residents and pass the information on to us."

"That of course presupposes that the neighbors tell the block wardens everything." Oppenheimer couldn't suppress a suggestive smile, but Vogler didn't seem to get the innuendo. The block wardens were doubtlessly all loyal to the party line and would keep mum, and they were predestined for this sort of discreet sleuthing, as it was their job to spy on the residents. This was also exactly the reason why, as a rule, they weren't particularly well liked.

Oppenheimer looked back toward the church. "The vicar?" he asked.

Vogler had anticipated Oppenheimer's thinking. "Has already been interrogated. He was giving a service on Saturday evening. He didn't notice anything afterward."

"And what about the sexton?"

"He locked all the doors at ten in the evening and didn't see anyone."

"Good. Next question: Why this place? The body was brought here. If I think about how we found her, then it's pretty obvious that she was placed here on purpose. Her legs were spread and pointed directly toward this structure. What is it, actually?"

Oppenheimer went around the stone block until he found an inscription.

"Ah, here it is." He read out loud. *"They died for the Fatherland in the 1914–1918 World War."*

Oppenheimer paused for a moment. Lost in thought, he tapped against the heavy stone. "So we can summarize: The body was found in a church square. It was placed before a monument for the fallen of the First World War. The way it was placed makes it look like an enactment. The perpetrator *wanted* her to be found in this state."

"Maybe he just wanted a location where she would be found immediately?" Vogler interjected.

"Possibly. We will have to take that into consideration. The fact that there was so little blood might be an indication that the victim's genitals were only mutilated after her death. So we cannot exclude the possibility that we might simply be dealing with a necrophiliac. The rope marks on the victim's hands and feet indicate otherwise, but there are plenty of corpses available these days. Maybe he found the young woman's body somewhere and then mutilated it. The likelihood is extremely low, but we won't know for sure until we have the coroner's report. Until then, we have to consider the possibility that maybe the perpetrator didn't kill her himself."

Questions upon questions. Oppenheimer was under no illusion. The clues were very poor. It was going to be an extremely difficult investigation.

Vogler seemed aware of this too. After some thought, he asked, "How should we proceed with the case, in your opinion?"

"The most important thing is to identify the body. That would advance matters a bit. Usually, there is some sort of connection to the perpetrator.

So we must find out as much as possible about the life of the victim. We might find some sort of clue as to the motive in her biography."

"Which measures are the quickest to yield a result?"

"If only it were that easy. I fear there are no hard-and-fast rules. We shall have to prepare for a lengthy investigation. Whether weeks or months—impossible to say. We don't even know if our measures will be successful. It's often just a silly coincidence that gets you on the right track. And that, you can't plan. In principle, there is only one thing we can do: be alert and beware of drawing hasty conclusions."

5

The rain falling on Oppenheimer from the gray clouds above had not managed to clear the air. Although there was no more smoke in the skies, a stubborn cloud of dust continued to hang over the ruins of the city.

After his discussion with Vogler, Oppenheimer had gone to see Hilde and tell her that for the time being he didn't need to disappear. When she then told him that bombs had fallen near the borough of Moabit, he had quickly set off for the Jewish House. While in the bunker with Vogler, he had ignored the thought that his tiny place might be damaged during the bombings. As usual, his first thought had been of Lisa, relieved to know that she had already gone back to work today and would have found a place in the bunker there.

As Oppenheimer stumbled through his neighborhood, across chunks of stone and glass, he saw that the streets really had been badly hit this time. Each step triggered a scraping noise. He didn't think the soles of his shoes would last much longer before they finally fell apart. Despite everything, however, there was still a certain order in the chaos of ruins, bodies and machines that presented themselves to Oppenheimer, because the worst was over. The bucket brigades for extinguishing the fires had already dispersed. Several people remained standing in corners of houses or entrances to cellars, blinded by the acrid dust and soot. A helper from the Red Cross with a flowing black cape and white hood, together with two young women from the League of German Girls, gathered the last of the blinded to bring them to the mobile military hospital, where their eyes could be washed.

The dust in the air made Oppenheimer's eyes water, too, although several hours had passed since the attack. Gas was pouring out of leaking pipes somewhere, polluting the air. This was a usual problem after a bombing. Oppenheimer hoped that no one would come up with the idea of smoking a cigarette.

When the first bombings had occurred, the citizens of Berlin had clustered round the ruins to gawk in shock. At the time, they marveled at the bombing as something new, something unheard of, but eventually, the novelty had worn off. As night attacks had long become normality, the newspapers only reported of daytime attacks, mostly in a couple of lines, laconically stating that *"the population had suffered losses."*

The air raids had become part of daily life, and with it came routine. The salvaged goods that those who had been bombed out had managed to save—furniture and odd bits and pieces—stood by the road outside the destroyed buildings, guarded by their owners. Some of them sat on their air raid cases, exhausted, while others had settled themselves on chairs covered in plush upholstery or other furniture they had managed to rescue from their burning homes with the last of their strength.

Just a few meters on, the dead who'd been pulled from the ruins by the emergency services had been laid out in a row in the middle of the pavement. While passing them, Oppenheimer could not stop himself from taking a hasty glance. He saw a man, dragged out from underneath tons of rubble, whose deformed skull looked like a soft-boiled egg without its shell.

A banner hung off the skeletal ruins of the houses behind the bodies. It read: THIS AREA HAS BEEN SEARCHED FOR CASUALTIES. Like all areas where the emergency services had given up the search, the detritus of the former building had been sprayed with chlorinated lime to disinfect the terrain.

Convicts in striped clothing were in the process of clearing the street from rubble. SS men were guarding them, hands always resting on their weapons. Oppenheimer passed women from the Fire Protection Police who were busy rolling up the water hoses again. In their dark uniforms, heavy shoes, and side caps, they were an unfamiliar, strangely masculine sight.

"Oppenheimer!" someone to his right called out. Dr. Klein approached from a side street. Despite his corpulence, he danced nimbly around the rub-ble piles. "How wonderful to see you! I thought you might have been hit!"

"Silence!" a man wearing headphones hissed from a nearby ruin. Klein flinched and stood still. The man paid no attention to his apologetic ges-ture but only pressed the headphones tighter onto his ears. Slowly, he squatted down next to the listening devices with which he filtered out knocking signs from within the rubble.

"Nothing's happened," Klein whispered. "All good. The house is still standing. We got lucky this time; the fire almost reached our neighbor's gas cellar. Luckily, it was extinguished in time. Old Schlesinger is suffering from smoke poisoning, but it's not too serious."

Another voice called out nearby. "Richard!" Lisa came toward them.

"Thank goodness," Klein said. "I was just about to ask after you. Won-derful. At least all the residents of our house managed to escape."

Lisa's face was red with excitement. When Oppenheimer hugged her, he noticed that she barely dared to breathe.

"Richard, why are you still here?" she finally managed to say.

"It's all right," Oppenheimer whispered into her ear. "They picked me up again this morning, but I'm not in danger. Do you understand? They need me."

"What do they want from you?"

"I'm to help them with the investigation."

"Richard! Are you mad?"

"They gave me no choice. If you think about it, it's probably the best thing that could happen to us. As long as the investigation goes on, we're safe. I'm practically under SS protection! And I don't need to polish any machines for the time being."

Oppenheimer looked into Lisa's eyes. He tried to seem positive, but Lisa was too clever for such maneuvers. He sensed an unspoken question in the air. Doubtlessly, Lisa was asking herself what would happen once the investigation was over.

Dr. Klein approached and pointed toward another smoking ruin. "Do you see that? It hit just one house. The ones alongside it are still standing. Seems to be some new sort of bomb." He went over to the edge of the crater and inspected it with curiosity. "I've never seen anything like it. The impact is much deeper than usual. The surrounding area is completely unharmed. Very strange."

Oppenheimer cast a distracted glance at the crater the bomb had made. His untrained eye only saw that the roof of the cellar had been bombed through. The limestone lay in the open cellar room like snow. He was not really interested in the technical finesse of warfare. Instead, Oppenheimer observed his fellow resident. Over the last few days, the doctor had been gripped by a peculiar frenzy of activity. Probably his way of dealing with the death of his wife. Oppenheimer thought about how Dr. Klein would react once he had calmed down and faced reality.

"They were able to retrieve only burned corpses from down there," Klein explained and pointed to the destroyed cellar. "No idea how many there were. The attack came so suddenly that they didn't have time to make it to the bunker at the station."

Oppenheimer heard a murmur go through the crowd. Klein looked over his shoulder. "Ah, word has spread that the ration post is open now. They promised coffee beans. Interesting to see how quickly people can run when there is something to be had."

Lisa and Oppenheimer looked at each other. The tempting prospect of coffee beans made them consider going as well. But for Oppenheimer, at least, it was pointless trying to ask for something—there was always someone from the neighborhood ready to sneak on him as being from the Jewish House. Only Klein remained standing firm as a rock. With his secret stash of provisions, it was easy for him to remain calm.

■

Oppenheimer woke with a start. Something was clinging to him. He hadn't imagined it. An arm. Although the air was pleasantly cool, his brow was covered in sweat. Remnants of his dream swirled through his head. He remembered swimming through a sea of severed limbs, heading for an island that had turned out to be a bone-crunching mouth. The thought made him sit bolt upright, afraid to look around.

In the dim shimmer of the light bulb, Oppenheimer recognized his surroundings. The pit in the cellar. So he was in the bunker, lying on the ground on his traditional spot. The arm resting on him was Lisa's. Old

Mrs. Schlesinger lay a bit farther back. He recognized her jacket that once might have been red. Her deep breathing told him she was asleep. The remaining residents of the Jewish House lay on the ground a little farther off. Now Oppenheimer vaguely remembered having heard a siren during the night. There must have been another bomb attack. But it was quiet outside. Deadly quiet.

Oppenheimer had probably never had as little sleep as in the last few months. And yet, despite the citizens' lack of sleep, the city functioned as usual. Everything ran its usual course: administrative offices were open, mail was delivered, and even electricity and water worked most of the time. Oppenheimer remembered that it would be full moon soon. The attacks usually relented then. For a few days, it would be possible to sleep through the night and not have to hasten down to the cellar half-dressed. Lisa squinted at him from a few inches away.

"Awake again?" she inquired.

Oppenheimer nodded. "Did I sleep for long?" he asked.

"Maybe half an hour. You were very restless."

"Hmm," he muttered. Then he leaned against the wall. It was strange, but he wasn't able to remember the dream that had been so present just moments ago. Finally, he cleared his throat. "I wonder if it's unpatriotic," he whispered.

Puzzled, Lisa looked at him, and he explained what had been going through his head. "I am horrified every time an air raid takes place, but on the other hand, I hope that they'll win. It's crazy, right? Maybe it's down to not being part of the German people."

Now Lisa sat up too. "If you start thinking like that, then you're playing into their hands. I know few people more German than you. There is no such thing as the Jewish race. There are lots of people at my workplace who also hope that the Nazis will lose. And they are Catholics and Protestants. And they ask themselves the same question. I don't think it's unpatriotic to wish for defeat. After all, the Nazis aren't Germany."

Later that night, as Oppenheimer was lying on the ground again, staring at the ceiling, this last sentence kept going through his mind, until Lisa finally turned on her side to cuddle up to him.

Unbidden memories welled up, the events of the last year, when the SS had arrived long before dawn in large lorries. They had driven

Oppenheimer and other men onto the loading platform at gunpoint because the German race was to be free of Jews within six weeks. That morning, they had rounded up all Jews in the city who were married to Aryans
and herded them into a temporary camp near Rosenstraße like cattle for
the slaughter. But while they waited there, a crowd gathered outside. It
was a vigil held by the wives, who did something no one in Germany
would dare: they refused to remain silent but instead voiced their protest
in public. Lisa, too, had stood outside the doors of the building and defied
the cold March nights to get Oppenheimer back safe and unharmed. The
crowd of women had grown ever larger, until the constant press of people
outside could no longer be ignored. As a result, the Nazi state had actually
caved in and without further comment let Oppenheimer and the other
prisoners go free.

And now Lisa was cuddling up close to Oppenheimer as if he were
able to protect her, when really, it was exactly the other way around. Oppenheimer wondered what he had done to deserve this love, for he knew
that his biggest flaw was his inability to protect Lisa from all this madness.
Right now, he felt like a fraud.

■

When Oppenheimer got out of the car in the early hours of the morning,
he couldn't make sense of his surroundings. The trees in this place could
definitely not be mistaken for their domesticated fellow species in the city
parks. Right now, Oppenheimer stood in a deep, impenetrable, typically
German forest.

Just as arranged with Vogler, the driver had shown up at seven o'clock
to pick him up. Oppenheimer assumed that his companion, who had only
introduced himself by his last name, Hoffmann, was also going to keep
him under surveillance. But what with the happy prospect of being able to
move throughout the city in far more comfort than before, he didn't really
care. Hoffmann had been instructed to bring Oppenheimer to their headquarters, from where Vogler coordinated his efforts to arrest the killer,
first thing every morning. But now, Oppenheimer stood in the midst of a
fairy tale instead.

He couldn't tell whether the noise in the air was the city traffic or the
rustling of the forest. His surroundings smelled of moss and pine needles,

and the light got lost in the tops of the high trees so that a pleasant twilight prevailed in the forest, only pierced by the occasional beam of light. Memories of his childhood were awakened, of his mother reading him the story of Hansel and Gretel and the witch's cottage. He spotted witches' cottages here, too, not just one like in the story by the Brothers Grimm but several, lined up one next to the other in solid bourgeois style. The houses were in no way luxurious or particularly large, the saddle roofs covered with tiles, the dormers clad in dark wood, the lattice windows flanked by large shutters.

Hoffmann had turned off directly behind the entrance to Argentinische Allee and parked the car in a cul-de-sac, Am Vierling. It seemed almost absurd to Oppenheimer that the narrow streets in this wild area of beauty should carry names at all.

He filled his lungs with the tangy air and gazed up into the branches. He could imagine that someone might not shy away from murder to own a house in this exclusive location. After all, they were in the southwest of Berlin, close to the Grunewald forest. At this moment, Oppenheimer could not possibly know how prophetic this thought was.

Hoffmann pointed to the nearest doorway and said, "There. Just ring the bell."

Before Oppenheimer reached the door, it was opened from within. Vogler waited for him on the doorstep in his uniform and waved him inside.

The building looked like a normal residence, just like it did on the outside. Although the rooms were not particularly big, they seemed enormous to Oppenheimer, compared to his current residence.

"Take off your coat. What can I offer you? Coffee? Cognac? Champagne?" Vogler mentioned these delicacies with a casualness that Oppenheimer had not heard for a long time when it came to food or even spirits. He took off his hat and only managed to utter, "Coffee."

"Take a seat," the Hauptsturmführer said and pointed toward the sitting room. The house was completely furnished, but at a closer look, it seemed to be a hollow shell. The glass cabinet and shelves in the sitting room were empty, and there were no personal items anywhere. Only the sonorous ticking of the wall clock structured the silence into seconds. Vogler reappeared, a cup of coffee in his hand.

"Who lives here?" Oppenheimer asked.

"We do," Vogler answered and lit a cigarette. "At least until the case is solved. This room is yours to use as an office. Telephone and radio set are in the cellar. A radio technician will be on constant standby when I'm not here."

Oppenheimer just nodded and sat down in the next-best chair. He suddenly felt that Vogler in his uniform and upright stance formed a strange contrast to the sitting room's flowery wallpaper. Oppenheimer sipped the dark brew to check whether it was proper coffee. Of course it was. His nose had not deceived him.

"Have you made any progress in identifying the body?"

"I'm afraid not. My people are still working on it. What do you think we should do?"

"As long as we don't know who the deceased is, there's not much to go on. At best, we can check whether the perpetrator was a necrophiliac. It would be preferable if you could contact the corpse identification command centers. They aren't likely to give me any information. Ask them for corpses that have disappeared or similar irregularities. I will check out the cemeteries."

Vogler looked at him in surprise. "Are you really planning on canvassing all of Berlin's cemeteries?"

"At least as long as we don't have any proper leads. I will work my way from Oberschöneweide toward the city center. Maybe we'll get lucky."

"Very good, then that's how we'll do it," Vogler said and put his hands on his hips. "We'll meet here every morning at eight to discuss the situation. Any other questions?"

"No," said Oppenheimer, although numerous questions were going through his mind.

■

Morosely, Oppenheimer trotted across the gravel path. The cemetery caretaker had to be around here somewhere, but in the office, they hadn't been able to be any more specific. The pale gray sky hurt his eyes; he felt as if his head was going to burst. Maybe he was coming down with a cold. Oppenheimer's hand instinctively slipped into his inside pocket. He wanted to take a Pervitin tablet to get through the day, but after long consideration decided against it, as there were only about a dozen left in the vial. These were his last ones, and he had no idea how to get his hands on more. It was not easy to procure Pervitin. It was impossible without a prescription, and he didn't want to bother Hilde with it. Maybe Dr. Klein had a solution.

Hoffmann stayed a few steps behind him, his motorbike goggles dangling rakishly from his cap. They had switched to a motorbike, the ideal way to get around the city, even if Oppenheimer did have to wedge himself awkwardly into the sidecar each time. The vehicle was versatile enough to navigate around the piles of rubble and bomb craters, which tended to appear out of nowhere. Despite all that, Oppenheimer would occasionally have preferred a car or at least a different driver. He was beginning to suspect that Hoffmann had misinterpreted his instructions of wanting to go to the cemetery, as he was driving along the road at such breakneck speed that more than once, Oppenheimer's heart almost stopped while he desperately held on to his hat with one hand and used his other to cling to the vehicle.

The cemetery on Baumschulenweg was adjacent to the woodlands of Königsheide and just a few kilometers away from where the body had been found. The vast area was quite confusing, as it was sectioned into two halves by the access road. Oppenheimer thought it quite possible for a body to disappear from here.

As he strode along the rows of graves, he spotted a man gesticulating wildly to two gravediggers not far from the crematorium.

"I don't care when you take your break," the man ranted. "These bodies have to be put in the ground today, and that's that!"

"Wouldn't it be easier if we dug one large pit?" one of the men armed with a spade asked. "The three of us can't dig a dozen graves in a few hours."

"No chance. Mass graves are forbidden. Instructions from the führer himself." At the mention of the führer, the gravedigger instinctively ducked his head.

"We've barely got any ice left. Are we just going to let the bodies rot? No, I don't want any trouble with the ministry. Even if it means shoveling around the clock. The foreign workers haven't arrived yet, but I can't help that!"

The other gravedigger bashfully tugged his cap. "Well, we just wanted to say, it's not fair," he demurred.

"Life is not fair, and neither is death. I'll try to find some new workers as quickly as possible. But until then, we have no choice. So get on with it!"

"We can't split ourselves into four," the first gravedigger grumbled querulously and jumped into the half-dug grave. His colleague also reached for his shovel and whispered, "There's just no justice in the world."

That seemed to put an end to the conversation, and Oppenheimer cleared his throat loudly to make the officials aware of him. "I presume that you're the cemetery administrator?"

"Yes, that's right," the man answered, already marching on. Oppenheimer had no choice but to trot alongside him. "Have you found a relative? Then please register with the caretaker. Together with the death certificate, you'll receive a coffin certificate. You'll have to bring this back here, and we'll take care of the rest. You'll have to inquire about a date for the burial. Bringing clothes for the dead person to be buried in is prohibited. Clothing material stipulation—you will have heard of it. The body will be buried in the clothes it was found in. I hope that explains everything?"

"I'm not here about a burial," Oppenheimer replied. "It's about a criminal case."

The administrator stopped in surprise and gave Oppenheimer a scrutinizing look. Then he noticed the Star of David.

"Wait a minute, what's going on here?" he asked skeptically. He turned to Hoffmann. "Has the Jew got any authority?"

Hoffmann pulled out his SD identification and discreetly took the administrator aside. While the men chatted quietly, Oppenheimer thought that it would be a difficult investigation if every person he talked to first had to question his status as an external advisor. The administrator turned back to Oppenheimer.

"I'm sorry, I had no idea. Name's Krüger." He wanted to shake Oppenheimer's hand, but after a sideways glance at Hoffmann, he changed his mind and rubbed his hands together, embarrassed. "What's up? Are you looking for a dead person?"

"On the contrary," Oppenheimer answered. "We wanted to inquire if you might be missing a corpse."

The administrator looked at him in surprise. "Goodness me, how am I supposed to know that? Have you any idea how many dead people we get delivered here every day?"

"Do you keep lists?"

"Lists?" he snorted in disdain. "There's a bit of a challenge with lists. Do you see over there?" He pointed toward a piece of lawn where sunlight reflected off countless brass plaques. "We bury people without knowing who they are. Then their gravestones remain empty. And each time the British lay their eggs, we get new ones. It's a complete shambles."

"Is there no one who can help us?" Oppenheimer asked helplessly.

"Go over to the morgue," the administrator said, shrugging. "Maybe one of the caretakers noticed something. If you ask me whether it's possible for corpses to go missing here, then I have to say yes, it's possible, and it's likely that no one would notice."

■

The dead lay in the cold-storage room. Figures dressed in black moved among them in a random procession. Worried glances searched for the brother whose flat had been bombed, for the wife whose place of work had been engulfed in a sea of flames, for the child who had not come home for lunch for days. In between the occasional happy face. Relatives whose hope was renewed, as their fears had not been confirmed, until they entered the next morgue to search for a loved one.

Oppenheimer watched a slight man step through the curtain. His face reflected neither hope nor fear. Instead, he was enjoying a bite of his chewing tobacco. He was unquestionably part of the furniture.

"Are you the caretaker?"

The man scrutinized the yellow star on Oppenheimer's coat with disdain, only to then pull the corners of his mouth up into a crooked grin.

"Well, will you take a look at this! There's still a few of you around," he said in a broad Berlin accent.

It seemed he didn't want to say any more. At this point, Hoffmann intervened. After he had explained the situation to the caretaker and asked him to cooperate, the man finally answered Oppenheimer's questions. But the hostile glimmer in his eyes remained.

Oppenheimer soon realized that he might have spared himself the trouble. In principle, the conversation was little more than a repetition of the information he'd received from the cemetery administrator. The mortuary was usually locked up at five in the afternoon. As was the latticed entry gate to the cemetery grounds. Occasionally, the place was opened up outside the usual operating hours during night air raids to let in lorries on which the emergency services delivered the victims of the bombings.

"Could someone smuggle themselves in during one of these night openings?" Oppenheimer wanted to know.

"Possible," the scrawny caretaker answered vaguely. "I don't know them people doing the driving." Oppenheimer realized that his hypothesis was probably a dead end. He could remember that there had been the occasional night alarm in the last few weeks, but bombs had only actually fallen during the daylight raids. And the concept of someone smuggling a dead body out of a cemetery in broad daylight seemed pretty unlikely.

The caretaker spat out his tobacco. As if by coincidence, the brown sludge landed just a couple of centimeters away from Oppenheimer's shoe. He looked straight at the caretaker, but the man seemed perfectly uninvolved.

"What's behind the curtain?" Oppenheimer wanted to know.

The caretaker turned briefly and then grinned. "That's our special department. Don't think you want to see that. That's where the body bits are kept. We have them in all shapes and sizes."

The man stared at Oppenheimer, challenging him. It was a childish game. Whatever was behind the curtain was irrelevant to the investigation, but at the same time, Oppenheimer begrudged the caretaker the triumph of getting him to back down. Furthermore, he couldn't stand it when someone tried to intimidate him. Without giving it much thought, he stepped through the curtain.

6

———

Over the next few days, Oppenheimer was busy checking out more cemeteries. The situation was similar in all of them. If they had a special morgue or a chapel where the dead were laid out, this was normally locked outside of visiting hours. Oppenheimer finally put together a list of companies that delivered to the cemeteries, addresses of coffin makers and florists. The employees of these companies were potential suspects. The next step was to clarify who owned a vehicle in which a body could easily be transported. But the list grew and grew, and by Friday, Oppenheimer had to concede that it was almost hopeless to try to find out anything this way.

For the time being, at least, the question of how he would get something to eat during the day had been sorted. Oppenheimer had feared he would have to find a pub near his new investigation headquarters that offered a standard dish without asking for a ration card. And then there was the small detail of the publican not officially being allowed to serve a Jew. But on the first day, once Oppenheimer had compiled a list of the cemeteries, Hoffmann appeared around lunchtime with a large food pack. And when they were out and about over the next few days, he always had an ample supply of sandwiches with him. Given that over the last few months, Oppenheimer's nourishment had consisted mainly of potatoes, this was a bonus he gratefully accepted.

Now it was already Friday, almost the weekend. Oppenheimer wondered whether he would be expected to work through it. They hadn't received the autopsy report yet. The criminal authorities were clearly more affected by the bombings than Vogler had envisioned. The administration had taken to having their documents delivered by children on bicycles in exchange for some pocket money, and so it was not surprising that the occasional document got lost. Meanwhile, Oppenheimer had gotten as far as Neukölln in his search of the cemeteries. Admittedly, the borough was several kilometers from where the body had been found, but he had decided to be thorough. During the day, he had worked his way along Hermannstraße. Oppenheimer knew his way around here. Within a small area, there were no fewer than eight cemeteries. They were crowded together on narrow plots of land south of the subway station Leinestraße. He had saved his last visit of the day for the cemetery attached to the Jerusalem Church. Oppenheimer expected this to take longer, because he wanted to visit someone there.

He found the caretaker without any problems and made the usual inquiries. Then he inspected the grounds. He encountered several workers on their way to an open grave with shovels on their shoulders. On closer inspection, Oppenheimer realized that it must be the crater of an explosion. The cemetery administration had told him that they often took a hit, as they were situated directly alongside the airport Tempelhof, which was a favored target.

Oppenheimer couldn't say whether this hit was a result of yesterday's daylight attack. The cleaning-up operation, at least, was still in progress. Scattered among the bushes were coffins waiting to be put back into the soil.

"Would you mind leaving me alone for a moment?" Oppenheimer asked.

Hoffmann stopped in front of the first available grave and mimed a mourner. He did this with the typical discretion that probably only SD men had in their repertoire, one of their most important jobs being to spy on the population.

It had been a long time since Oppenheimer had visited Sonja's grave. She had been a secretary in the crime department. Sonja used to arrive late almost every morning and then hurry to her office. But she always had a smile for him when they occasionally met in the corridor before starting work. Over time, Oppenheimer started to go out of his way to meet her in the corridor. And at some point, that evolved into something more.

The fact that Oppenheimer was now standing here was probably just further proof of his inadequacy. All this probably wouldn't have happened if his daughter had still been alive. Some couples were bound even closer by such a loss, but Oppenheimer and Lisa had grown apart in the months following Emilia's death. Oppenheimer's relationship with Sonja was an episode that he still regretted. He and Lisa finally managed to save their marriage, although it had taken quite a while. They had only really found their way back to each other when the Nazi terror was already raging on the streets.

Looking at Sonja's gravestone, he wasn't sure what he was doing here. Graves had always had this effect on him. They were nothing more than randomly chosen places. Oppenheimer told himself that people needed these places and rituals to have the illusion of being closer to the dead. He couldn't relate to that and had decided that it didn't work for him. And yet here he was, standing in front of Sonja's grave, not really knowing what had driven him here.

Through his confusion, he noticed heavy steps approaching. But it was Vogler, not Hoffmann, who appeared in his line of vision.

"A friend of yours?" he asked, examining the headstone.

"A colleague." Oppenheimer suddenly found Vogler terribly annoying. "Any news?"

"We know the dead woman's name. She was called Inge Friedrichsen."

Oppenheimer's heart began to beat faster. This could be the breakthrough.

"Her landlady, a certain Mrs. Korber, reported her missing," Vogler continued. "The description fits."

"Has she already been identified?"

"Mrs. Korber has been asked to come and identify the body."

So it wasn't confirmed yet. Vogler still had a lot to learn. An experienced crime officer would never have claimed with such confidence that a body had been identified if this hadn't been definitively established.

"Well, then let's take a look," Oppenheimer said and started walking.

"Where are you going?"

"To the morgue, where else? Then we can also inquire where the autopsy report is."

■

When they got there, Mrs. Korber had long since left. She had identified the body as her tenant Inge Friedrichsen in the morning.

They went into the cooling chamber with one of the assistants. His pupils swam like two fish in an aquarium behind his thick glasses. Of course, Vogler had to give a laborious explanation of what Oppenheimer was doing here. But the assistant still couldn't help himself from taking the occasional surreptitious glance at the Star of David as they were walking, almost as if Oppenheimer's presence were a test and he was uncertain whether he had passed it.

"Sixty-three years old, I thought she was going to faint right here," the assistant said of Mrs. Korber.

"And you allowed that?" Oppenheimer asked. "Was there no one else to identify Inge Friedrichsen?"

Vogler just shrugged. "There were no other tenants, and her sons are at the front. There was nothing else for it."

"Right, we're nearly there," the assistant said. Cold air confronted them when he led them into a room full of cold chambers. The assistant studied the list in his hand. "Inge Friedrichsen, that would be number 46,513." He was just about to look for the corpse when Oppenheimer held him back.

"One moment," he interjected. "I've already seen the body."

The assistant looked up. "So what is it that you want? The protocol of the clinical autopsy?"

"We've been waiting for that all week! This investigation has the highest priority. I hope I've made myself clear. Who carried out the autopsy?"

"Ahem, Dr. Gebert."

"Old Gebert?" Oppenheimer hesitated briefly. He'd had a few altercations with Gebert in the past. Their temperaments were simply too different. "Hmm, well, it can't be helped. Is he busy dealing with another body right now?"

"I don't think so."

"Thank you," Oppenheimer said curtly. He turned and left the assistant standing there.

"What are you doing?" the assistant called after him.

"I'm going to clarify the matter with Dr. Gebert."

"You can't just do that! Dr. Gebert is a very busy man!"

"So am I," said Oppenheimer and left the room.

It didn't take long for him to remember where Gebert's office was. When he reached the door, he paused for a moment and pumped some air into his lungs. Then he knocked and entered without waiting for a reply.

Gebert was sitting behind his desk, working on some papers. He looked up. "What's the matter? I told you . . ."

His annoyance dissipated when he saw Oppenheimer in the doorway. He leaned back in his chair in surprise.

"Well, well, well. That might just be our Inspector Oppenheimer. Who else would storm into an office as he pleases?" Then he nodded briefly. "Nice to see you," he lied.

"You carried out the autopsy on Inge Friedrichsen?"

"Friedrichsen? The name doesn't ring a bell. I'd have to look at the notes."

"Came in on Sunday, around twenty-five years old, blond, with massive mutilation to the pelvic area."

Dr. Gebert said, "Yes, I remember. But what's your interest in this case? As far as I know, you've left the police force. A wise decision, I feel."

Vogler entered the room. He must have heard the last few words through the open door. "Heil Hitler! Hauptsturmführer Vogler. I'm heading up the investigation."

Gebert gazed at him, raised one eyebrow, and then looked back at Oppenheimer. He understood. "Heil Hitler. Please take a seat, gentlemen. How can I help?"

Vogler sat down and pointed at Oppenheimer, who picked up the conversation again. "What was the cause of death?" he asked. "I'm assuming she was strangled?"

"Definitely."

"And the mutilation in the pelvic area took place *post-mortem*?"

"We can definitely assume that, yes. There was no bruising. Blood circulation must have stopped beforehand."

Oppenheimer thought what a blessing this would have been for the poor woman. "How were the cuts executed?"

"As far as I can make out, with quite some precision. They were made purposefully. The surrounding tissue was barely damaged. Whoever was responsible for this knew what he was doing."

"So someone who knows how to handle knives." Oppenheimer was thinking out loud. "What was the time of death?"

"We can assume it was Saturday afternoon."

Vogler chimed in. "Were there any other unusual findings?"

"Indeed there were. One moment." Gebert got up, opened a cupboard, and returned with a glass jar containing something metallic. "I've seen a lot in my time, but this . . . We found two items in her head."

Oppenheimer swallowed hard when Gebert showed him the jar. Inside were two six-centimeter-long metal nails.

"Where were they?" he asked tonelessly.

"I found them in her ear canals. They had been driven in so hard that they were lodged into her brain."

Oppenheimer's eyes narrowed when he tried to picture this. "Was there any bleeding?"

"Massive. She was definitely still alive when this happened."

For a moment, the men sat in silence. Each seemed to be dwelling on their own unpleasant thoughts. Oppenheimer turned the jar in his hands. The nails scraped against the inside of the glass.

"Thank you for the information," Vogler finally said. "We won't take up any more of your time." He got up. "I must point out that this investigation is top secret."

Dr. Gebert got up and made an acknowledging gesture. "Of course."

Vogler raised his arm. "Heil Hitler!"

"Heil Hitler," Dr. Gebert replied with the Nazi salute, which was not quite as snappy.

Oppenheimer instead raised his hat and turned to leave.

"Of course, you can take the evidence with you," Gebert added.

Oppenheimer stopped and realized that he still had the jar with the nails in his hand. He nodded wordlessly.

"And one more thing, Inspector," Dr. Gebert added. "I don't know who you're looking for or how long it's going to take, but I hope that you find the bastard."

■

Oppenheimer and Vogler left the building and stood on the pavement for a while. The Hauptsturmführer gazed into the bright blue sky, but his expression was gloomy. He fished around in his coat for a hip flask and took a sip. Oppenheimer stood next to him, indecisive.

"The hypothesis that he's a necrophiliac cannot be sustained," Oppenheimer finally summarized. "The victims were tortured when they were still alive."

"I think it's pointless continuing with the cemetery line of inquiry," Vogler said.

"Hmm, it probably won't lead to anything. According to the landlady's information, Miss Friedrichsen left the house alone on Friday evening. She was murdered at some point the following day, and her body was then discovered that night in Oberschöneweide."

"Why there?" Vogler asked. "Why at this specific statue? Her flat was north of there, in Pankow."

Oppenheimer chewed on his cigarette tip, ruminating. "Another important question would be whether it was a coincidence that the murderer chose her or whether he had had an eye on her for a while."

"Assume that this deed was planned in advance."

The assertiveness with which Vogler stressed this theory made Oppenheimer listen up. "What makes you say that?" he asked.

"I think . . . ," Vogler began. For a second, he seemed caught out. "I think it would be the most practical approach for our investigation."

Oppenheimer pretended not to have noticed Vogler's uncertainty. "Maybe you're right."

"We'll meet Monday morning and talk about the next steps." Vogler waved his car over, which had been parked at the side of the road. When he opened the back door, he looked at Oppenheimer once more.

"Listen, as long as you're involved in the investigation . . . I think it would be best if you didn't wear your Star of David." He uttered the last sentence quietly.

Oppenheimer frowned at the unexpected instruction. To be sure, he asked, "You're telling me to *remove* the star?"

"This is an investigation that requires extreme discretion. That thing makes you stick out like a sore thumb."

"Well, I don't know what to say. If someone asks me about it, can I refer them to you?"

"Don't you understand? This is an order!" With that, Vogler slammed the car door shut. The vehicle left, and Oppenheimer turned to Hoffmann, who was waiting a few meters away with the motorbike.

"An order is an order. You're my witness," Oppenheimer said, shrugged, and removed the Star of David from his coat. Hoffmann's expressionless face showed he didn't care in the slightest.

7

Anyone living in the busy center of the capital of the Reich would find the leisurely pace of life in the Berlin suburb of Marienfelde very strange. On this Sunday morning, the small town seemed particularly sleepy. In the dawn twilight, a lone figure strolled through the center of town. An unusual sight for the first churchgoers, especially as this was an SS Hauptsturmführer. But none of the inhabitants would have guessed that it was a murder case that brought the visitor here.

Vogler unbuttoned his coat. The sky was cloudless. The sun would soon warm the cold morning air. But this chill was nothing compared to the biting frost he had come to know at the eastern front. In his mind, Vogler went through the things Oppenheimer had said in Oberschöneweide, where the body had been found. He had observed the former inspector closely over the last few days in order to learn from him. Now Vogler tried to put the new insights into practice. First, he began to look for parallels between Oberschöneweide and Marienfelde. There was a memorial in both places, surrounded by several trees and a church.

And both in Oberschöneweide and Marienfelde, they had found a murdered woman near the memorial.

Vogler stood on the tapered green lawn where the road through the village forked. He mustered the surroundings carefully, then glanced at his watch. Half past seven. Several months before the Friedrichsen case, the body had been discovered here at almost the same time of day. More and more churchgoers approached the church. Oppenheimer had said that a camera could not capture everything. Vogler would have been happy to have any photos at all of Marienfelde. However, no one had informed the SS at the time, which probably explained why no one was really interested in solving this murder.

IN MEMORY OF OUR BELOVED KILLED IN ACTION AND LOST IN WAR, it said at the top of the stone monstrosity that loomed above Vogler, the surface engraved on all sides with countless names arranged by date. A three-meter-high row of bushes shielded the monument, but right behind it lay a pond, and just a few hundred meters farther on stood the simple church, which from a distance appeared particularly medieval with its rough brickwork. The only other building that stuck out between the squat row of houses was to Vogler's right, on the opposite side of the road. It was a three-story building and even had the extraordinary luxury of a stone balcony. Although the building seemed like a respectable residence dating from the turn of the century, a butcher's shop was installed in the ground floor. Although Vogler was originally from the Hunsrück region, he felt that Marienfelde looked quite similar to his hometown. He felt the same sort of special small-town atmosphere that had always made him feel depressed.

Vogler sighed in frustration when he realized that his thoughts had wandered off. He was forced to admit that although he was able to take in his surroundings, he didn't have the slightest idea what conclusions he was supposed to draw from them. It had been nothing more than a gut instinct that had driven him here. Although there were only a few concrete clues, Vogler was pretty certain the cases were linked. But his decision was final; he didn't want to disclose this information to Oppenheimer.

Vogler found it best not to divulge everything to those who were thought to command respect. However, as a Jew, Oppenheimer had undoubtedly not enjoyed any respect for a long time. Which was precisely the reason that Vogler had selected him among the other inspectors. The fact that he had Oppenheimer's life in his hands was also a guarantee that he would have him under control.

Vogler lit a cigarette. Although he couldn't really do much here, he found it hard to leave the place. Here of all places, he had finally found the quiet he had been missing over the last few years.

Vogler considered in what way Oppenheimer resembled his father, the grumpy old Latin teacher who had terrorized the entire family and had always considered himself terribly important. Many years ago, Vogler Sr. had kicked up a great fuss when his junior had joined the Hitler Youth. In his obstinacy, he had insisted that his son immediately withdraw. Instead, Vogler Jr. had turned the tables and denounced his father to the local SA roughnecks. They had arrived just a few days later to arrest the old man.

And it had worked.

When they released him the next morning, he had changed forever. The SA had forced him to drink castor oil, and he had crapped all over himself. Vogler's begetter, who had so admired his own mind, was forced to admit that he, too, had a body. Later, Vogler had realized that this had possibly been the biggest humiliation one could inflict upon one's father. After that, the patriarch was a shadow of his former self who no longer dared to discipline his son. The sonorous bass that had so often droned through the house had been silenced for good. Vogler had broken his father and for the first time felt the intoxicating sensation of having power over others.

And National Socialism had continued to offer him the opportunity to do so. Vogler internalized the ideals of the movement, later joining the SS. Although he occasionally rubbed his superiors the wrong way, it hadn't damaged his career. No one could dispute that Vogler was the born warrior, which was perhaps down to the fact that for most of his life, the party organization bred him to be so. Although he did not really make a name for himself as a daredevil at the front, he had always achieved the desired results, because he never shrank from radical brutality when chasing his goals. Vogler had destroyed lives, injured bodies. But he felt that his reckless practices were justified, given his good motives. He had distinguished himself through his cold-bloodedness several times; one promotion followed the next. However, Vogler had not envisioned he would perform so well that his superiors would decide to send him to Berlin to be deployed in the regimental headquarters.

But the current situation was too confusing for Vogler to feel honored by it. Away from the front, he was on unfamiliar terrain. When he arrived in the capital of the Reich, he had initially been pleased with the new challenges. But the first disappointment came shortly afterward. Just after his arrival, he'd been assigned this idiotic murder case instead of more important tasks. And so as to humiliate him even more, he was forced to work on the case with this unpleasant creature Graeter. During combat, Vogler had felt alive, but here on the home front, he felt increasingly useless. To make matters worse, he and Graeter had now wasted three months without delivering a result. The more time passed, the bigger the pressure exerted on them. Calling in Oppenheimer had been an act of desperation, the final straw he had clutched.

Gloomily, Vogler looked over toward the butcher's shop one last time. The stone faces that had been affixed as decoration above the windows on the first floor stared directly at the place where the body had been found. Vogler wondered what they might have seen during the night in question.

Almost all the villagers were now assembled in front of the church. The morning service would soon begin. Vogler became aware of the curious faces. Occasionally, one of the passersby raised an arm in the Nazi salute, but faced with this German normality, Vogler felt separated from them. He had already seen too much in his lifetime to delight in this village idyll. He had spent the last few years almost exclusively abroad. But the image he'd had of home while he was away did not correspond with reality. His fellow Germans were not nearly as heroic as he had imagined. In his eyes, they were obtuse figures that only cared for their small vanities, led petty lives. Had he actually fought for them? For these old men with hollow cheeks, for the women whose skirts were too long at the sides because their hips had narrowed so much?

When Vogler asked himself what distinguished the proud German race from the haggard figures he had seen in Poland and Russia, he was overcome by a strong feeling of anxiety. He had been presented with too strong a dose of reality in the last few months. He knew he wouldn't last much longer here.

■

This Sunday, Oppenheimer had chosen the route along Potsdamer Straße for his weekly visit to Hilde. He had grown cautious since his first meeting with Vogler. Now each time he met up with his good friend, he took a different route, allowing the occasional detour. It was an old trick to ensure that he wasn't being followed. The last time he'd been forced to deploy this tactical deceptive maneuver, it had been because of the terrible weather. But now that it had stopped raining and the cold no longer crept up his trouser legs, he enjoyed the walk. The air was pleasant. He couldn't imagine a stronger contrast to the stuffy intimacy of the Jewish House. He strolled happily past flowering red poppies adorning the fields with bright red dots and examined the lilac bushes, which had suddenly sprouted great white dabs as if by magic. So far, Oppenheimer had been relatively sure of not being followed. But this was about to change on this lovely spring day.

Oppenheimer turned into Kolonnenstraße when he noticed something behind him. Initially, he couldn't say exactly what it was, but when he stopped and pretended to tie his shoelaces, he perceived a figure out of the corner of his eye who also stopped, only to look demonstratively at his watch. At first glance, it was simply an inconspicuous man wearing a light summer hat. Finally, Oppenheimer took off his jacket and slowly wiped the sweat from his brow. Day-trippers were streaming all around him to get to the train station, entire families pushed past him, a small group of giggling League of German Girls in their obligatory dark blue skirts, with white blouses and black neckerchiefs, doubtlessly on their way home from a weekend of ideological indoctrination and still delighted to have escaped from their parents on this sunny day. But the man with the summer hat remained motionless. He was the only figure not participating in these busy goings-on.

Maybe Oppenheimer was mistaken. In any case, he decided to put it to the test. Instead of crossing the Kolonnen Bridge, he left the pavement and headed for the undergrowth. It was just a couple of meters to the subway tracks. Oppenheimer clambered down the bank between the unruly bushes and cursed his worn-out shoes. After checking that there was no train coming, he ran across the tracks and aimed straight for the opposite embankment. He noticed how out of practice he was. He started panting after just a few strides, and when he pulled himself up the opposite bank on a bush and looked back, he realized that his pursuer was no better off.

The man with the summer hat stumbled across the gravel on the tracks, swearing under his breath. So Oppenheimer hadn't been mistaken. But instead of savoring the triumph of having unmasked his pursuer so quickly, he gathered his strength and fought his way up the embankment, sweating all the while.

The round cement block that Oppenheimer was headed for rose up ahead of him. When he'd first spotted the structure, he had assumed it was a high bunker or a water reservoir. But Hilde had later explained to him that this ugly block had been set into the landscape by Albert Speer himself. As the gigantic triumphal arch was supposed to be built nearby, the static engineers had voiced concern as to whether the soil in Berlin could actually carry the weight of the monumental structures that were buzzing around in the führer's head. So they had cast this block in several cubic feet of cement, to test how far it would sink in.

Oppenheimer crossed General-Pape-Straße as quickly as he could and headed straight for the cement block. The surrounding wooden fence provided ideal coverage. He ran along it until he came to a spot where he could peer through the fence to observe the opposite side.

It didn't take long for the man in the summer hat to appear. He looked around. Panting, he removed his hat and wiped his sweaty brow. He was probably in his midthirties and slim, although his shirt was suspiciously tight around the stomach area. He was without a doubt ideally suited for the role of an inconspicuous observer. He looked up and down the street.

Oppenheimer drew back in alarm. Something seemed to have drawn the man's attention to the cement block. Oppenheimer tried to hold his breath and listened carefully. Hesitant steps drew nearer. Had the pursuer spotted him? Did he want to drive him out of his hiding place? Sweat appeared on Oppenheimer's brow. Slowly, he walked backward, paying attention not to make any noise. He looked around frantically, searching for a way out.

A sudden creak. Oppenheimer flinched.

Two of the slats were loose, just hanging by a single nail. Without hesitating, he pushed the boards aside and squeezed his way through the opening. The circumference of the base of the cement block had been kept small to raise the point load. The resulting niche beneath the block was just high enough to stand under and to look out from the shadows at the surroundings, almost without being noticed.

Oppenheimer dived into the niche, breathing a sigh of relief, but soon realized he wasn't safe. He had no idea whether there was another way in. If his pursuer thought of checking this particular niche, Oppenheimer was trapped.

He took a few careful steps backward until his back was up against the round cement block. Heavy breathing became audible, then got louder. It was the man in the summer hat. He slowly crept along the fence, trying in vain to quiet his breath. Finally, he stopped and stared through the fence. He cleared his throat in frustration and thrust his chin up in the air. He seemed to be contemplating whether it was possible to get onto the top of the cement block.

After taking a few more steps around the block, Oppenheimer's pursuer finally gave up. Hesitantly, he turned back to the path and returned to the main road.

The man walked away, and Oppenheimer relaxed. He knew that he had outsmarted his pursuer.

■

"Have you heard the latest about Mr. Conti?"

Oppenheimer had barely had time to put down his hat when Hilde waylaid him with this question.

"Conti?" Oppenheimer unsuccessfully routed through his memory. "I'm afraid the name doesn't mean anything to me."

"Yes, Conti, Leonardo Conti, the bastard. He is our minister of health. He has now demanded—you won't believe this—*Top Birth Output* from mothers so that their husbands can go to the front feeling reassured. Anyone would be happy to get killed knowing that offspring was guaranteed, right?"

"It's probably a question of priorities," Oppenheimer replied lamely.

As usual, Hilde then gave him a rundown of the latest news she had picked up from the BBC in the shelter of her home, being an incorrigible secret-broadcast listener. The Allies had begun their offensive in Italy. It didn't look much better for the National Socialist gang elsewhere either. Eighty percent of the Leuna works had been destroyed during an air raid. A petrol warehouse had also gone up in flames.

"They tried to get commodities from the eastern front," Hilde concluded her report. "Now that's not working, they are left with just the final reserves."

Oppenheimer was only half listening, as he was busy going through his record collection. He selected the first Mozart symphony he came across.

It was the right moment for a piece that just pattered along so that one could simply relax and listen. In heretic moments, he often thought that the music from the eighteenth century was primarily composed for just this purpose. It was only toward the end of that century that young hotheads like Beethoven had appeared, demanding greater attention from their audience.

In contrast to many music lovers, Oppenheimer had never had a particular preference for Mozart. He quite liked the operas but found it hard to differentiate one symphony from another. He owned the recordings of the *Prague* and *Jupiter* symphonies only to complete his collection. However, he was still reluctant to listen to the famous Serenade No. 13 in G Major, K. 525, which was more commonly known as *Eine kleine Nachtmusik,* as he found it terribly banal. Despite Mozart's popularity, Oppenheimer had wondered for a while now why no Nazi bigwig had thought of declaring his music degenerate. After all, as a Freemason, the composer had belonged to a population group that Hitler hated just as much as Jews and communists. With this in mind, Oppenheimer placed the needle on the ridge of the black disk.

"I'm guessing you had a close shave on Monday?" Hilde asked.

Initially, Oppenheimer didn't know what she meant, but then he remembered the daylight attack. There had been so many bomb attacks recently that he could barely tell them apart anymore.

"Luckily, Lisa was at work when it happened. They've got a good bunker there. Our building is still standing, although it doesn't really deserve to." Then he changed the subject. "You haven't asked me how the investigations are going."

"Are you trying to tell me that you've already had a result?"

"Well, at any rate, I am under surveillance."

Hilde looked at him in amazement. "How long have you known?"

"I found out a few minutes ago."

Oppenheimer told Hilde about his adventures and then recounted the latest developments in the murder case. When he described the colony where his new office was, Hilde choked on her schnapps. Gasping for breath, her face bright red, she uttered a few garbled words that Oppenheimer failed to understand.

"All right?" he asked when she finally got her breath back.

"Do you have any idea where you were?"

"We were somewhere in Zehlendorf."

"Damn right. Bloody hell! Well, it's not quite the lion's den, but not far off."

Oppenheimer looked at her uncomprehendingly.

"Nice area you described, with all the houses and so on." She snorted with contempt. "You'll also find some charming neighbors there. All line-toeing Teutons of racially pure blood. You naïve idiot! Have you never heard of the Kameradschaftssiedlung in Zehlendorf, the SS housing colony? Wherever you look, everyone is a member of the SS. That's where they live out their petit bourgeois ideals with their families. If you ask me, I wouldn't lift a finger for these people."

Oppenheimer sighed. "I know, I know, but what else am I to do?"

"It doesn't look like you can stall them much longer with your cemetery visits."

"Well, at least they're including me in their plans, for the time being," he reassured himself. "Otherwise, they wouldn't have summoned me for Monday morning."

"In any case—what's that arse-faced guy's name again? Vogler? He at least seems to have given you security clearance. No wonder you have an escort on your heels now. Did you find anything strange in the postmortem?"

"Yes, indeed. The number of injuries. I noticed that straightaway when we found the body. But I couldn't explain it."

"Let's take a look at the process, shall we? First, he drives nails into the victim's head. That looks a lot like sadism to me. But the question is, why does he mutilate the woman after he's killed her?"

"Yes, and then he even deposits her in a public location, a site where she *had* to be found." Hilde wanted to say something, but Oppenheimer waved her off. "I know. Of course he wanted her to be discovered. That's the only possible explanation. Hmm, when I think of it, the stone, the spread legs . . . it's almost as if he"—he searched for the right word—"as if he had *orchestrated* it all."

"What reason could we envisage for someone not making a dead body disappear but rather putting it on prominent display?"

Oppenheimer mulled this over for a moment. Then he laughed, a little embarrassed. Even before he spoke, he knew that his answer was wrong.

"The simplest solution would be that the murderer's superego is resisting the acts. The perpetrator wants to be caught so that someone can stop him from carrying out more murders."

"Oh, for goodness' sake, stop talking rubbish!"

"I expected that reaction," Oppenheimer replied with a broad grin. "But even if we don't go with that—just the fact that he arranged the body in a certain way suggests that he wants to communicate something."

"There's just one flaw in your theory," Hilde pointed out. "If someone wants to communicate something, then there must be someone specific to receive that communication. The fact that the air raid warden found the body was more or less a coincidence. It could just as well have been someone else. Who arrived after that?"

"SD, SS, the crime officers with their special vehicle, and finally me," Oppenheimer replied.

Hilde thought for a moment. "Could it be that he wanted to communicate with *you*? With the investigators?"

Oppenheimer knitted his brows. This thought was disturbing because it created a direct connection between him and the perpetrator. "Possibly," he admitted to Hilde. "If you think about it, it is possible."

"Do you know what I first thought of when you described the place the body was found? It wasn't Großmann. He mutilated his bodies so that one wouldn't be able to identify them and so they could be disposed of more easily. This doesn't apply to our case."

Oppenheimer nodded. "I know. Then there's still Kürten. That had also occurred to me, but the parallels only go so far."

"That may be. What differences are there to the Düsseldorf Vampire? Kürten choked some of his victims. Our woman, however, was strangled."

Oppenheimer nodded. "Kürten drank the blood and raped the victims," he mumbled. "Neither can definitively be proved in this case. Kürten didn't hide the victims but simply left them lying at the crime scene. He wanted to get away quickly and didn't care if they were found. That would be difference number one. But in our case, the scene of the crime and the place where the body was found were not identical."

"Are there indications yet where the crime was actually committed?" Hilde asked.

"As far as I can gather, they're still groping in the dark."

Hilde stared into her glass, lost in thought. "Another difference, of course, are the wounds. The injuries inflicted by Kürten were directly connected to the act of killing or the acting out of his sexual urges. Stab wounds, head traumas, vaginal tearing. But the way he wielded the knife was quite amateurish. In actual fact, that guy was nothing more than a boring little slasher."

"His victims wouldn't have thought that," Oppenheimer said reproachfully. "But you're right; the cuts are difference number two. Kürten tended to injure his victims with his stab wounds. When he cut someone's throat, the execution varied. In our case, the cuts are precise and clean. We can work with this information. Who apart from a doctor would be able to do that? Hmm. A butcher, of course. That would be the most obvious."

"Then we'd end up back with Haarmann and Großmann. Both were butchers. Most mass murderers have a past of carrying out violent acts on animals or were arsonists. Quite a few of them were both."

Oppenheimer paused. He had thought of something. "Have you ever noticed how many potential sex offenders there are?"

"Maybe that's the price we have to pay for having a steak on our plate."

"After I'd had to write the minutes of Großmann's interrogation, I wasn't able to eat any meat for ten months," Oppenheimer remembered. "And I still don't particularly like it."

"You're perfectly adapted to our war-torn society. No more meat until after the ultimate victory. Until then, turnips and potatoes will have to do." Hilde chuckled to herself, but quickly grew serious again.

Oppenheimer asked, "Have you had an idea?"

"No," Hilde replied slowly, "I'm just thinking of Kürten. Do you remember what happened when they found all those naked bodies of women and children around the Düsseldorf area? There was a mass panic. And when those underground murders occurred here in Lichtenberg a couple of years ago, it was a similar situation; things got to a critical point—and there weren't even any bombs falling at that time."

Oppenheimer nodded. "It's no wonder that the SS showed up so quickly this time. They don't know how people are going to react when they find out about a murder like this."

"Haven't you realized that we live in the land of smiles? No? Then you should listen to the propaganda. There must be no crime in an untainted

racial community. Maybe the press can be muzzled, but the party is powerless against rumors. Frightened people are capable of a lot. Maybe that
would be the final straw."

"Hang on a minute—there haven't been any indications yet that we're
dealing with a mass murderer; otherwise, we would have found more
bodies by now. But yes, it doesn't change the fact that I'm helping the system if I catch the murderer." Oppenheimer sighed dejectedly.

Hilde shrugged. "The way things look, you're not going to get out of
this situation. Your only option would be to leave Germany, but to achieve
that, you'd have to be Harry Piel or, better yet, Houdini. The borders have
been hermetically sealed off, and now that the invasion is imminent, even
more so."

"First, there's a murder to be solved," Oppenheimer argued.

Hilde had to smile. "That's typical of you, you workaholic."

Oppenheimer pondered for a while and then said, "No, I don't think the
comparison between Großmann and consorts is going to get us anywhere."

With that, he went over to the gramophone and raised the tone arm.
The *Prague* symphony stopped. Oppenheimer carefully inserted the record back in its sleeve and rearranged it in the collection. "I think I'll head
off. It's late."

When Hilde handed him the obligatory cigarettes, she asked, "What
shall we do now? Will you be able to come again even though you're being
followed?"

"Give me a couple of days. I'll think of something to lay a false trail so
they don't get suspicious. I'll be back with new information next Sunday.
You can count on it. You know, when I think about it, maybe we could
actually solve the case together."

Oppenheimer looked at the cigarettes in his hand. With a longing sigh,
he carefully put them in his cigarette case and let it snap shut. The time
had come to make sacrifices.

8

———

Inge Friedrichsen had occupied a small attic room. Mrs. Korber stood in the doorway while Oppenheimer inspected the room. He could sense the landlady watching his every move. As the resolute woman clearly had no intention of leaving his side, he thought he might as well question her in the process.

"Who lived in this room originally?"

"My nephew," Mrs. Korber answered. "Theo. He's at the front right now, and I thought he wouldn't mind if I rented out his room until the ultimate victory."

Oppenheimer noticed the matter-of-fact way in which Mrs. Korber used the phrase *ultimate victory*. There was no irony in the way she said it. She seemed to believe in it like a law of nature. Oppenheimer had anticipated something like this when he'd spotted a small altar in a corner of the living room, with an artfully bound copy of *Mein Kampf* lying in front of a replica painting showing Adolf Hitler in a shining suit of armor, of all things. Despite it all, Oppenheimer doubted that Mrs. Korber had ever actually read Hitler's book. Even among his most zealous followers, there were very few who voluntarily did that. Similar to a dusty family Bible, the work was more of a devotional object used to show your disposition than reading material that you perused to uplift yourself.

Oppenheimer let his gaze roam across Inge Friedrichsen's room, which was dominated by the pitch of the roof. Although there was a window in the dormer, the daylight was not enough to illuminate the room.

"May I?" Oppenheimer asked and switched on the light. A bare bulb drove away the shadows. The room contained nothing more than a bed, a huge wardrobe, a chair, and a bedside table. Almost nothing showed that a woman had lived here. Everything was utilitarian; the only decorative items were two framed photographs on the wall. One depicted a young man in uniform. The second showed the same young man among his friends, raising his glass to the camera.

"Your nephew?" Oppenheimer asked and pointed toward the pictures.

Mrs. Korber nodded. "The boy is going to the aeronautical college. He needed frontline experience to apply."

"Where did Ms. Friedrichsen keep her things?"

"I allowed her to use the right-hand side of the cupboard and the bedside table."

Oppenheimer opened the cupboard and looked at the contents. It was not much, only two pairs of shoes, three blouses, which Ms. Friedrichsen had evidently altered, and a heavy winter coat, which she had clearly bought before the spinning-material directive came into force.

"How long had she been living here?"

Mrs. Korber thought for a moment. "It must be about ten months now. She moved in last July, I think."

"Where did she come from? Did she have any friends or relatives in Berlin?"

"I don't think she had any relatives here. At least she never spoke of them. She came from somewhere near Hannover. She always went out in the evenings, although I kept telling her that it wasn't suitable behavior for an unmarried woman. Well, that's what happens."

"When did she leave the house on Friday?" Oppenheimer sat down on the bed and looked through the bedside table.

"Early in the morning. She didn't come back here again. She often did that at the weekends, said that she was with a girlfriend. A likely story . . ."

"So you didn't see Ms. Friedrichsen again after that?"

"Only when she was already dead."

Oppenheimer looked at Mrs. Korber sharply, but then he remembered the morgue assistant's report. "You mean when you identified your tenant?"

Mrs. Korber swallowed hard and nodded.

"Where did Ms. Friedrichsen work?"

"She worked for a liquor retailer, as far as I know. Ücker or something like that."

"Ücker? Never heard of them. Well, my colleagues will find that out."

Vogler's people had already searched Inge Friedrichsen's flat on Saturday. However, Oppenheimer wanted to check for himself to make sure that nothing had been overlooked. There was an empty water bowl on the bedside table, and next to it, an alarm clock. In the drawer, he found a playbill like the ones that had been available in cinemas everywhere until recently. He flicked listlessly through the pages. At the front was an ad for *Immensee,* featuring Carl Raddatz and Kristina Söderbaum, who was nicknamed "the Reich Floater" because she often embodied tragic heroines who all found a watery death in the end. Next in line was the ad for *I Entrust You with My Wife,* with the hugely popular actor Heinz Rühmann in the lead role, *Melody of a Great City* with Werner Hinz and Hilde Krahl, and then many more that Oppenheimer didn't bother looking at.

Although most of the films were just a few months old, the photographs looked like archaeological findings from a bygone era, which had been lively and happy and had nothing to do with reality. In between the images of beautiful, happy people, Oppenheimer came across a picture folder. When he opened it, he was looking at Inge Friedrichsen's face.

Sometimes it was a shock to see photos of people whom one had only seen as a corpse. Through the pictures, the anonymous dead changed into real people and could no longer be perceived as an abstract problem. It was only now that Oppenheimer was able to understand the complete extent of the tragedy of this case.

Inge Friedrichsen didn't pay attention to the camera but was smiling down at a baby that seemed to be just a few days old. Her gaze shone with pride and disbelief at the miracle she cradled in her arms. Oppenheimer had seen this gaze several times in his life. It was unmistakable. Lisa had had it during the first few days following the birth of their daughter. Inge Friedrichsen had to be the mother of this baby.

"Where is the child?" Oppenheimer asked.

Mrs. Korber didn't seem to understand. "What do you mean?" she stammered.

"Ms. Friedrichsen's child. Where is it?"

"I say!" she called out indignantly. "She was not married! She *can't* have a child. At least, I know nothing about it. If she had told me about such a thing, I would never have let her live here! This is a reputable house!"

Oppenheimer saw Inge Friedrichsen in a new light. From now on, she was a woman with a story—and a secret.

■

Hoffmann was already waiting for Oppenheimer when he emerged from Mrs. Korber's house. As soon as Hoffmann saw him, he swung himself onto his motorbike, ready for another nightmarish journey through the obstacle course that had once been the streets of Berlin. Oppenheimer mustered the sidecar without enthusiasm and thought for a moment. It was only lunchtime, but without the address of the ominous liquor retailer where Inge Friedrichsen had worked, he couldn't do much right now. He also had an urgent job to do that the SS shouldn't find out about.

"Thank you. I won't need you anymore today," he said to Hoffmann. Magnanimously, he added, "Enjoy the rest of your day. I'll see you in the morning."

Hoffmann stared at him through his motorbike goggles without saying a word, raised two fingers to his leather cap in a farewell gesture, and started his engine. *You weren't expecting that now, were you?* Oppenheimer thought when he saw his driver disappear. He was sure that Hoffmann or one of his colleagues would be back shortly to observe him. So time was of the essence. He had to get to Big Eddie and talk to him; otherwise, his plan was worthless.

Ten years ago, when he'd still been with the force, he would have known immediately where to find the little thug. Oppenheimer sincerely hoped the Berlin underworld had not changed since then.

Hurrying through Pankow in the direction of the borough Prenzlauer Berg, he realized to his relief that it wasn't hard to find his way, even though the streets looked different due to the gaping holes and the bombed houses.

The small corner pub he wanted to pay a visit to was still there. As usual, the lunchtime rush was on. Oppenheimer saw many new faces among the guests, but Corpulent Carl still staunchly manned the bar. And yet, time had not failed to leave its mark on him either. His impressive twirled whiskers had disappeared; instead, his face was now embellished by the narrow mustache that Reich Chancellor Hitler, in his sideline job as a fashion icon, had made popular throughout the entire German nation. The big paunch the landlord used to carry with him had also disappeared. Maybe the fact that he had halved his body weight was down to rationing, but the hollow cheeks made Oppenheimer think he might have some stomach-related issues. Carl was in the process of polishing a beer glass and looking around the room. When he saw Oppenheimer, he paused.

"What can I get you, Inspector?" he asked when Oppenheimer approached the bar. Carl had intentionally raised his voice. As if by command, several of his guests left the premises when they heard the word *inspector*.

"I need to talk to Eddie."

"Eddie? Never heard the name in my life."

It was the same old game. In the company Carl and Eddie kept, you only gave a policeman a direct answer if it could not be avoided. Oppenheimer didn't know why, but today, he took perfidious delight in this verbal grandstanding.

"Don't make out you're even dumber than you are," he snapped back. "I know he's a regular here. Tell me where he is, or I'll come back with a police battalion and take the place apart."

The threat didn't seem to bother Carl in the slightest. However, he had satisfied the etiquette of the underworld sufficiently by not obeying a policeman without putting up some resistance and now didn't bother messing around anymore. In his broad Berlin dialect, he said, "Ah, you mean *E-Edward*, Inspector? Yes, I think I have seen him here today. But I've no idea if he's still here." Suddenly, he shouted over Oppenheimer's shoulder across the room, "Hey, Paul, can you take a look and see if *E-Edward* is around?"

A pasty-faced beanpole with a flatcap got up and stared at him uncomprehendingly. "Which Edward?" he asked in surprise.

"Come on, get to it, you silly bugger!" Carl commanded.

Paul took a hearty sip from his glass and disappeared behind a heavy curtain.

"I'll take a look myself," Oppenheimer said. Having been announced in this way, he entered the smoke-filled room behind the curtain. Four men were sitting at a table, holding playing cards. The man called Paul stood next to them, looking lost.

"Eddie?" Oppenheimer called into the room. A bull-necked man raised his head and looked at him with expressionless eyes.

"What do you want from me?" the brawny man drawled. "If you've finally come to pay my rent, you can leave the dough at the bar."

"A couple were attacked and robbed in the Grunewald Park last night," Oppenheimer lied. "I want to talk to you about it."

"What's that got to do with me? Nah, it's not me you're looking for. I'm a reformed sinner, so to speak. I don't do no dodgy stuff anymore."

"I'd like to convince myself of that."

"Up yours!" Eddie answered grumpily and turned back to his card game.

But before he could pick up his cards again, Oppenheimer had grabbed him by the scruff of the neck and pulled him out of the chair with a routine movement. When he stumbled over toward the back entrance, Eddie protested loudly, "It ain't legal what you're doing, Inspector! Not legal!"

Within a few seconds, Oppenheimer was out in the backyard with his prisoner and pulled him down the first cellar steps they came across.

"Well, look who it is, old Oppenheimer," Eddie said in a familiar tone once he had rearranged his collar and sat down comfortably on the steps. "And I thought they'd strung you up a long time ago."

Oppenheimer remained standing so that he could keep an eye on the courtyard. "So far, I've been able to prevent that," he said curtly.

Eddie pulled out his handkerchief to wipe his gleaming forehead. Oppenheimer had occasionally deployed him as an informer in the past. They had always got on well, although this fact must not be made public. Eddie had never screwed him around. If it concerned a case that violated his particular type of hoodlum honor, he had no qualms about ratting on his colleagues. "If it's information you're wanting, I've got to tell you that I'm sort of in retirement."

"Well, you don't forget how to ride a bike either, do you?" Oppenheimer retorted. Eddie grinned. "I'm no longer with the police force," Oppenheimer added. "I'm here in a private capacity, so to speak."

Eddie looked at him with interest. "Go on, then."

"I need a hideout."

Eddie understood immediately. "Is someone chasing you?"

"It's probably best if I tell you straight—the SS is tailing me. I have to get them off my heels occasionally."

"Phew." Eddie frowned. "That won't be easy, boss. It's best not to tangle with the SS. You got a few pennies going spare?"

Oppenheimer pulled out his cigarette case and showed the cigarettes he'd gotten from Hilde. "Four a week. That's all I can do."

Lost in thought, Eddie looked up at the sky, which from this perspective was just a blue square above their heads.

"Hmm, that's fair, actually, but what with the SS, it's going to be hard to find something. Unless . . ." Eddie thought for a moment. "We do have a room over in Moabit. We sometimes use it to store things. It's empty the rest of the time."

"I'd come at short notice. No chance of telling you in advance."

"Understood. As soon as it's settled, you'll get the key and the address. I'm sure it will work, but I need to know where I can find you, Inspector."

Oppenheimer tore a page from his notebook and wrote down his address. "I owe you one," he said on leaving.

"I'll hold you to that," Eddie said.

Oppenheimer had no doubt that he would.

■

The warehouse of liquor retailer Höcker & Sons was filled with stacks of sealed crates. Inside these, carefully packaged in wood shavings, was highly coveted produce. Oppenheimer wondered how many liters of high-proof alcohol might be stored here. Surely it would be possible to knock out an entire army company for several days with this amount. But there were no hard-drinking soldiers in the warehouse; the only one stomping through the labeled rows of shelves was a storeroom manager named Häffgen.

He was a forced teetotaller ever since the doctors had ordered him to give up alcohol. Doubtlessly, this fact had facilitated the owner Gerd Höcker's decision to give Häffgen the responsible job of warehouse manager. Not a single drop was allowed to leave the warehouse without Häffgen's authorization. Judging by the suspicious way he mustered Vogler and Oppenheimer during their tour of the company, he guarded what was entrusted to him as if it were straight from the Nibelung treasure.

That morning, Vogler had informed Oppenheimer that Inge Friedrichsen had worked here. The company was small. Höcker employed eight people; besides Häffgen, there were four drivers, two apprentices who stacked the crates, and a secretary. According to Höcker, he had employed Inge Friedrichsen as an additional secretary last July. Ms. Friedrichsen was always punctual, carried out her duties conscientiously, and was also a member of the NSDAP, which in his eyes confirmed her trustworthiness. Before that, she had worked in Klosterheide, a tiny village about sixty kilometers north of Berlin. Oppenheimer wondered who might have needed a secretary in such a remote location.

After Höcker himself had given them a guided tour of the company and passed on the most important information, Vogler and Oppenheimer decided to talk to the staff, and Vogler withdrew to a separate room to do this.

When the SS man had left the room, Höcker looked uncertainly at Oppenheimer.

"Oppenheimer," he mumbled, "I used to know an Oppenheimer. We were in the same regiment, back in the war."

Oppenheimer suddenly remembered where he had seen Höcker's thickset figure before. He recalled the bad jokes Höcker had told to keep his comrades entertained. "It's a small world, Gerd," he replied.

"Goodness, Richard," Höcker said, clearly delighted, and squeezed Oppenheimer's hand with his large paw. When they had been in the military together, they had not been very close, although they had not avoided each other either. But Höcker did not seem inclined to let this small trifle impact the nostalgic memories of their mutual war service. Content with having found an old comrade, he gossiped about their drunken sergeant major and inquired after other comrades whose names Oppenheimer had never heard. Finally, Höcker asked quietly, "I didn't want to mention it while Vogler was here, but as far as I know, you're a Jew, aren't you? How come you're working for the SS now?"

"I converted." It was the first lie that popped into his head. He didn't feel like giving a long explanation of why he was involved with the case. Oppenheimer knew that a conversion to Christianity would not have fundamentally changed his delicate situation. The Bergmanns also had to live with Oppenheimer in the Jewish House, although they had both

converted and had been christened as Catholics. At least they hadn't evacuated the Bergmanns as so-called Jewish Christians yet. But Höcker was
satisfied by Oppenheimer's banal reply.

"Very sensible, Richard, very sensible. No point in messing up your life
by being a showcase Jew, right? Just so you don't misunderstand me, I've
nothing against Jews in general. But there is no doubt that a Jew cannot
be a German. And all these stories that are told about Jews, there *must* be
some truth in it, right? Although, just between us, I've a feeling that the
führer is exaggerating his Jew policies just a bit. After all, there are excep-
tions, like you. But no one wants to hear of it."

Oppenheimer was in serious doubt whether he should feel honored
or not.

Höcker took a cigar from a box on an imposing office desk. "Would
you like one?"

Oppenheimer nodded and pocketed two cigars. He would have taken
them from his archenemy. His heart bled as he watched Höcker bite off
the tip of the cigar with his teeth and then light it. "Do you need a light?"

"No, thanks," Oppenheimer said. "I'll keep it for later."

"Ah, right. Nice. Anything else you want? Gin, whiskey, maybe a glass
of wine?"

"Many thanks, but I think I'd best make a start on the interviews."

"Of course. Work can't wait. Right. I'll be off, then. Please feel free to
use my office. Can I call anyone for you?"

"Who worked with Ms. Friedrichsen?"

"Hmm, that would be Ms. Behringer." Full of pride, he added, "My
main secretary."

"Then I would like to speak to her."

"Right away," Höcker said and pranced out of the room. Given his
stocky figure, this was a ridiculous sight.

■

When Oppenheimer saw Ms. Behringer, he immediately realized why
Höcker had employed her. While secretaries like Ms. Friedrichsen needed
a knowledge of spelling and good references to get a job, Ms. Behringer
was one of those employees that bosses liked to adorn themselves with.
Despite that, Oppenheimer did not find her at all vulgar. She was dressed

simply but effectively. As if she had foreseen the tragic occasion, she was wearing a black trouser suit. The only colors on her were her chestnut-brown hair and the red lipstick, which shone into Oppenheimer's face like the rear light of a car.

Initially, he would have assumed a rivalry between the two women, but after just a few minutes, he had to revise his prejudice. Ms. Behringer had heard of Inge Friedrichsen's death that morning and was clearly devastated. During the interview, Oppenheimer concluded that she was an intelligent and vibrant young woman. Going by what she was saying, Inge Friedrichsen had shared these characteristics. The two of them had gotten on so well that they spent a lot of their free time together too.

"We went out together on Friday night, but then she suddenly disappeared."

"What time did you meet?"

"She came around to my place straight after work to freshen up. Then we went to Bahnhof Zoo. We met Günter there. He had a friend with him—Hans-Georg, I think his name was."

"Who is Günter?"

After Ms. Behringer had hemmed and hawed for a while, it turned out that she was secretly engaged to Günter. No one in the office except Inge Friedrichsen knew about it. Oppenheimer made a note of Günter's address.

"What were you planning to do that evening?"

"We went for a drink. There is not much else to do now since the dance prohibition. We wanted to go to the cabaret later on, the Berolina club near Alexanderplatz. But then we lost track of time, and the show at the Berolina had already started at five thirty. Inge wanted to go to the cinema. To the evening showing."

"Did she watch a lot of films?"

"Yes, all the time. But that weekend, every place was showing Heinrich George's most recent film. *The Defense Has the Last Word* or something like that. The only other film on was in the Titania Palast out in Steglitz. Something with Hans Moser. That's the one she wanted to see. But I couldn't be bothered to drive out to Steglitz, and I don't like Austrian films anyway. So Inge set off by herself."

"No one accompanied her?"

Ms. Behringer's lips quivered at this question. Finally, she took a deep breath and said, "I know, we should have. But Günter wanted to stay with me, and I fear Hans-Georg wasn't quite sober anymore. I'm guessing I could have prevented it all. Sometimes it seems as if one always makes the wrong decisions."

"What time did she head off?"

"Around five thirty. The film was due to start at seven thirty. Did she suffer a great deal?"

Oppenheimer decided it was pointless to burden Ms. Behringer with the truth. "No, she was dead immediately. She didn't feel a thing."

"Thank God. At least that."

Asked about the work atmosphere at Höcker & Sons, Ms. Behringer didn't hold back. "Just between us, she was happy not to have to deal with the old goat," she said, referring to her employer. "Luckily, I can cope with my bosses chasing after me and know how to defuse the situation. I don't know how Inge would have reacted to it." Once more, her eyes filled with tears.

"Was Mr. Höcker propositioning her?"

"No. I'm absolutely sure about that. She would have told me. And anyway, she wasn't *one of those,* if you get my meaning."

"Was she engaged?"

"I think she had a fiancé at the front. She never told me his name."

"And what about when she went out? Did she ever flirt with anyone?"

Ms. Behringer shook her head emphatically. "Never. At least not when I was present."

"So there was no one else in the city whom she had any sort of closer connection to?"

"She had no relatives here, and she never mentioned any friends."

He wasn't going to get anywhere by continuing with this line of questioning. Oppenheimer changed the subject. "Where did she work before?"

"I don't know exactly," Ms. Behringer faltered. Then she burst out, "In any case, Inge was a very good person."

Oppenheimer pricked up his ears. He wondered what this outburst had to do with his question. "Now, now, I did not question that at all, young lady," he appeased her. "I didn't mean to insinuate anything, but I must find out what happened. Any small detail could be relevant."

Oppenheimer sensed that Ms. Behringer was hiding something from him. He decided to go full attack.

"Where is the child?"

"What do you mean?" she asked, shocked.

In reply, he pulled out the photograph of Inge Friedrichsen with the infant.

At the sight, Ms. Behringer clapped her hands in front of her face and began to sob. "I—don't—don't—know," she gasped between her fingers. "She didn't want to tell me. She just said that he was being taken care of."

They had reached the critical moment. Oppenheimer sensed that Ms. Behringer would now tell him everything. "Let's start from the beginning, shall we?" he suggested in a calm voice.

Everyone had heard rumors of the Nazis' breeding program at one time or another. The organization that was responsible for it was called *Lebensborn;* it was a registered association, controlled by no one less than Heinrich Himmler, which implied that the project was prioritized within the party apparatus. The association owned a handful of buildings, which were scattered all over the country, away from the big cities. Nobody really knew what went on night after night behind the seclusion of the thick walls, dedicated to the *belief in the führer and in the will for Aryan blood to be everlasting.*

It was Lebensborn's declared aim to strengthen the Aryan race and to produce children with the purest blood possible. As there was very little public information on this project, there were massive rumors and speculations about the ways and means this was carried out. For a long time, there had been rumors of Himmler ordering the SS and the police to produce children *of good blood* with German women. If necessary, this should also take place without regard for convention or morals, as in his opinion, the end justified the means. Most people associated some sort of posh brothel with the term *Lebensborn,* where veritable sex orgies were celebrated with Hitler's blessing. According to the rumors, SS breeding studs were said to service very young girls with blond plaits to make the dream of the superiority of the Nordic race come true.

These were also the images Oppenheimer conjured up when Ms.

Behringer first mentioned Lebensborn. For a few seconds, he found it difficult to reconcile the photo of the beaming Inge Friedrichsen with his notion of unbridled Nazi orgies.

"You said Lebensborn?" Oppenheimer asked, to make sure he hadn't misheard.

"Yes, they have a home out in Klosterheide. Inge was a secretary there."

"And what was her . . . job?" Oppenheimer asked hesitantly.

"Not what *you're* thinking of." Ms. Behringer rolled her eyes. "She did the paperwork. Certificates, forms, things like that."

"And what's that got to do with the child?"

"Inge came to Lebensborn when she was pregnant with Horst."

"Her son is called Horst?"

"Yes, that's right. She was pregnant and not married. She didn't have much choice but to go to Lebensborn. There she could have her child without anyone finding out. First, she was in a place called *Haus Friesland,* somewhere near Bremen. She didn't have a job and didn't want to go back to her parents, because they weren't allowed to know about Horst. And so she made some inquiries with the Lebensborn association as to whether there might be a job for her."

"And then she was given a job as a secretary with Lebensborn?"

"Yes, she was sent straight to Klosterheide. There is a house with a day nursery attached to it. So she was able to be with her son. But after a while, the work became too repetitive, I'm not sure. Maybe she didn't want to work there anymore because Lebensborn had such a bad reputation. Maybe she just wanted to be in a city. In any case, she looked for something here in Berlin, and Horst was put in a Lebensborn home. That's how she ended up with us."

"Did she ever talk about the father of her child? Do you know his name?"

"I just know that he came from her hometown."

"The fiancé from the front that you mentioned?"

"Yes." Ms. Behringer suddenly looked at him guiltily. Abashed, she added, "Only the bit about her being engaged wasn't true. Sorry. He dumped her when she got pregnant. He was called up shortly afterward."

■

These were the only useful bits of information that Oppenheimer was able to glean that day. The other people he talked to were largely clueless. The workers in the warehouse had only rarely caught a glimpse of Ms. Friedrichsen. She had occasionally stepped out of the office to collect delivery bills from Mr. Häffgen or to hand him an urgent order. It was only through persistent questioning that Oppenheimer managed to discover a rumor that Inge Friedrichsen had something to do with Lebensborn. It seemed that subsequently, one of the warehousemen called Bertram Mertens had started making explicit proposals, according to Ms. Behringer, without success.

There was one unanswered question left. Oppenheimer was only able to ask it when Höcker knocked on the door and peered into the room. "Sorry, I don't want to rush you, but I need to get at some of my papers."

"Come in. I'm done here. I have one more question. Who else owns the company? I'm assuming your sons?"

"There are three owners. I actually have only one son, Karl. The place is called *Höcker & Sons* because it sounds better that way."

"And where was he when Ms. Friedrichsen disappeared?"

"I'm guessing he was in Italy."

"He is stationed there?"

Höcker sighed meaningfully. "Yes, indeed, Italy of all places. The Americans launched an offensive down there on Friday. Well, at least he'll get some field experience from it. Character-building stuff. We're perfect examples of that, aren't we?" He laughed, then growing serious again, he leaned over to Oppenheimer. "I'm not really sure about the boy. But you've probably come across it before too, Richard. At first, he didn't want to join the army—imagine that! But then I told him, Karl, you can't cop out when the Fatherland and your führer are calling. It's your duty as a good and proper German! Well, yes, and when I threatened to disinherit him, he finally signed up. Young people these days . . ." He shook his head in resignation.

"You mentioned three owners," Oppenheimer reminded him.

"Oh yes, of course. Yes, the third owner of our company is the SS."

Shocked, Oppenheimer asked, "How did that happen?"

"Didn't you know? We used to deal in mineral waters and lemonades.

A few years ago, they became a partner. Of course, the SS use a different name. They have a few of their own springs and later took over some others. Niederselters, Apollinaris—you wouldn't believe all the pies they've got their fingers in. They control three-quarters of the mineral water market now, can you imagine. Well, yes, ever since then, we're supplied almost directly by the party. However, I realized that the profit margin is higher with alcoholic beverages, which is why I founded a new company and changed our product range. It wasn't a problem, I just had to discuss a couple of things with my counterparts in the Economic Administration Department, and then we were off. It's just a bit difficult to get hold of a halfway decent beer. I can organize anything you like. Whiskey, scotch, sherry, even Bordeaux or champagne, large amounts, whatever you want. The SS can organize anything. There is a huge warehouse in the occupied territories. But beer? You'd think so—no chance! But honestly, what do French people know about beer? They still have to work on that." Höcker smiled broadly.

■

Later, Vogler and Oppenheimer sat down together in Zehlendorf to exchange information.

"Did you interview Bertram Mertens?" Oppenheimer asked.

"Mertens? Just a moment." Vogler checked his papers. "Yes, Bertram Mertens. Apparently, he asked Ms. Friedrichsen to go out with him a couple of months ago. She turned him down. He couldn't say much more. He claimed he was at the Wannsee at the time in question. Went for a walk around the lake. It's going to be hard to prove it."

"We haven't checked Ms. Friedrichsen's background properly yet."

"What are you thinking, specifically?"

"Well, firstly, it would be interesting to know who the father of her son is. An illegitimate child can certainly be a motive for murder."

Vogler looked at him in surprise. "She had a child?"

Oppenheimer handed him the photograph. "Here. Your colleagues must have overlooked it. She worked in a Lebensborn home called *Kurmark*. It is possible that our killer also came from there. It's not too far to Berlin. Doable by train. I think it makes sense to extend our investigation to Klosterheide. Her former colleagues' alibis also have to be checked."

"Hmm, she worked at Lebensborn." Vogler frowned. "Interesting, the things you managed to dig up, Oppenheimer. This means that the number of potential suspects has suddenly increased."

"I'm afraid so, yes. That's the way these things work. We can't afford to ignore anything. When shall we go and visit the home?" Oppenheimer gave Vogler a challenging look.

9

The house in the Kameradschaftssiedlung in Zehlendorf remained a mystery to Oppenheimer. He spent most of the next few days there, sorting the information. After the morning briefing, Vogler drove off and left him behind with the radio operator, who sat by himself in the cellar in front of his devices. As Oppenheimer felt relatively unobserved, he carefully checked out his surroundings when he was able to tear himself away from his papers. The ground floor consisted of a hallway, the living room where he worked, the kitchen, and a large cupboard. The kitchen was fully furnished, but there was a serious shortage of food. The initial impression that no one lived here seemed to be confirmed. Luckily, there was a large tin of coffee beans that Oppenheimer could grind to perk himself up from time to time. Added to this were the sandwiches that Hoffmann brought by. Oppenheimer didn't hesitate to make extensive use of these luxuries.

He didn't see much of the top floor. The doors of the rooms were closed so that the stairs led into darkness. Those were probably the bedrooms. However, Oppenheimer only dared to quietly go up two or three steps and peered through the bannisters. But he wasn't able to find out anything new.

It was a completely different matter with the employees at Höcker & Sons. He was bombarded by information. The first reports arrived on Wednesday morning, and the next day, the stack with painstakingly compiled lists of names and details grew further. Vogler primarily seemed to use SD people to do the groundwork for him, which made sense. At first glance, the information on Inge Friedrichsen's colleagues was anything but out of the ordinary, though that could not be blamed on Vogler's spies. At this pace, Oppenheimer was pretty certain they would soon have interviewed every single witness.

This was the start of a phase of the investigation that Oppenheimer always found tiring. Routine work. As usual, he noted down the names of suspects on small cards. The radio operator supplied him with drawing pins, and Oppenheimer pinned the cards to the wall. In doing so, he followed a system that only he understood properly. He had once tried to explain the system to an aspiring inspector, but after one frustrating week, he'd given up in exasperation. Although he himself thought it perfectly simple.

First, he stuck the card with Inge Friedrichsen's name in the middle of the wall. This was followed by the remaining cards to form a wide circle around the first one. The closer a suspect's name was to the murder victim in the center, the more likely he was to be the perpetrator. After brief reflection, Oppenheimer placed the name Bertram Mertens several centimeters closer to the center. He had been snubbed by Ms. Friedrichsen, which might have been a motive. Oppenheimer proceeded in the same manner with the other cards. The more evidence he gathered, the complexer his chart became.

By Thursday, Oppenheimer had come to the sobering conclusion that despite all his shifting around of cards, nothing much had changed. He also realized this would be the harmless part of his work. Once the information regarding the suspicious persons from Klosterheide was added, the wall would probably be completely covered with notes.

Nonetheless, Oppenheimer discovered an important difference to his previous work. In the past, when he'd been working on a case, he'd occasionally had to fight to keep track of things. He'd always had a problem remembering names and faces of all the people he encountered during an investigation. Sifting through stacks of files had often been too much for him. But now, as he worked through the files, he realized to his surprise that his brain took an almost perverse pleasure in dealing with the smallest of details. His mind almost seemed like a dry sponge that had been waiting all these years to soak up information, to evaluate, organize, and connect things once more.

Oppenheimer had arranged to visit the Kurmark home with Vogler on Friday. Honestly, he was quite looking forward to getting out of the city. He wasn't a true nature lover, but in view of the constant bomb attacks and surveillance aircraft, he enjoyed the trip to a calmer and more intact landscape.

Hoffmann had taken the opportunity to get behind the wheel of the black car to escort them to the countryside of Ruppin. If his mind hadn't told him otherwise, Oppenheimer would have thought that the landscape he saw just a few kilometers outside Berlin was a long-forgotten dream. On more than one occasion, he found himself staring out the car window with his mouth wide open. After an almost endlessly long time spent in the city, his gaze now lost itself in the wide-open landscape, and he was unexpectedly gripped by the feeling of being pleasantly foreign here.

Buildings became scarce. Alongside the redbrick structures that could be found all over Berlin, there were small houses covered in plaster whose sharp gables pointed toward the sky. Occasionally, they passed guest-houses where city residents had sought refuge from the bomb attacks. Locals walked the streets with rosy skin and honest gazes. But Oppenheimer knew this was wishful thinking. Of course, the people here were no better than those elsewhere. Hilde had told him that people in the country were particularly true to party principles and sniffed at city slickers' lack of values. But at this moment, Oppenheimer simply wanted to believe that despite everything, there was a positive alternative world, yes, that he was driving through a picture-postcard idyll. Nobody was running toward a bunker to escape an air raid. No alarm signals cut through the air. There was a peacefulness around him that he hadn't thought possible anymore. They drove past a church whose bell tower reminded him of the battlements of a medieval tower. In the next village, a different place of worship, built in timber frame, proudly presented its dark, stained wooden construction to the outside world. The few houses standing forlornly at the side of the road, the gently curving hills, the dark pine forests they were driving through—this reality had continued to exist the whole time, although it hadn't appeared in Oppenheimer's concept of the world for too long.

About forty-five minutes into the journey, Oppenheimer tried to concentrate on going through the facts once more. At the speed Hoffmann was driving, they would arrive soon, and he didn't want to get there unprepared.

"So the last time Inge Friedrichsen was seen was on Friday evening," he summarized. "The murder must have taken place at some point the next day, given that her body was discovered on Sunday morning. It would normally take one and a half hours to drive from Klosterheide to Berlin by car, the train journey around two and a half hours. There are five connections per day; the first train to Berlin is at 5:27 a.m., and the last one leaves at 8:10 p.m. It's basically the same in the opposite direction. So there are a lot of ways to get to Berlin, but we should assume that the murderer spent the entire Saturday in the city. We should focus our investigations on those that were there that day."

Vogler nodded in agreement. Then he looked at the empty cigarette holder that was hanging from the corner of Oppenheimer's mouth.

"Here, have this," he said and handed him a cigarette. "You don't need to smoke, but please put it in the holder. Otherwise, it irritates me."

Of course, Oppenheimer accepted. This way, he was able to add another cigarette to his collection.

The village where the Lebensborn home was situated was right on the southern edge of the Mecklenburg Lake District, which reached as far as Wismar. Three large lakes dominated the area around Klosterheide: the Große Strubensee, the Wutzsee, and finally the largest, the Gudelacksee, which was where the Kurmark home was located. Oppenheimer would not have been surprised if the Lebensborn home had towered over the nearby village on a steep cliff, a forbidden place with an unwelcoming façade like the castle of Count Dracula, radiating a dark aura across the few roofs of Klosterheide that were clustered together as a means of protection. But nothing could have been further from the truth. The village consisted of a handful of houses that had been built a good distance from one another. There was more than enough space here.

Just before they left the village, Hoffmann suddenly turned off the main road to the left. They came to a country lane leading directly into the woods. Oppenheimer almost believed that Hoffmann had gotten lost, but the man drove unerringly through the woods until he found a narrow lane between the dense, leafy wall of trees. Instead of the sky that Oppenheimer had expected to see through the treetops, an impressive yellow-brick chimney appeared. It stood there like a whim of nature, among all the other growths, a tree that was not true to type. When they got closer and stopped at a small square, he saw a building behind a closed gate. They had arrived.

■

A nurse led them to a large, completely empty hall. The light coming in through the windows, whose dusty curtains seemed to have been untouched by human hand for decades, refracted on the parquet floor. A good dozen swastika flags were draped on the opposite wall, with a monolithic black bust of the führer in front of it. Oppenheimer could not see any other objects in the room.

"If you'd just wait here for a moment," the nurse said, glancing at Vogler shyly. "I'm afraid we're just in the process of preparing for a name-giving ceremony." Then she disappeared in the twilight behind the doorway like a hallucination.

"Name-giving ceremony," Oppenheimer repeated. "Are they expecting us to contribute something?"

"I—I don't think so," said Vogler, who didn't know what he was supposed to do and therefore kept switching legs every few seconds.

Oppenheimer walked along the flags. In the middle hung a portrait of a woman. He examined it curiously. "Hmm, who do we have here? I'm guessing this is the founder of the home? Judging by the photograph, the lady is probably somewhat older."

Vogler sighed at Oppenheimer's lack of knowledge. "That is the führer's mother."

"Oh, oh yes," was the only thing that Oppenheimer could bring forth in his surprise. With a decent portion of feigned contriteness, he finally added, "Sorry, my mistake." Of course, he should have guessed that a picture of Hitler's mother would be hanging in every Lebensborn home. "Beautiful frame," he said, but Vogler's silence only seemed to grow icier.

Suddenly, two panting figures in gray smocks forced their way past, carrying chairs. When they noticed Vogler's uniform, they both immediately put down their load and called out, "Heil Hitler!" Before Vogler could even nod to indicate that they were permitted to continue with their work, they had picked up their chairs again and hastened into a corner of the room. As Oppenheimer looked around in irritation, a nurse appeared in a white gown. The white collar and bright white bonnet, fastened to her dark hair with clips, did not differentiate her from the other carers. But her self-assertive appearance and the reaction of the other staff suggested that despite her small stature, she held a certain authority.

"Good day. I presume you are Inspector Oppenheimer. I am Mrs. Berg, the senior nurse here at Kurmark." She shook Oppenheimer's hand firmly. "The doctor cannot receive you right now, as he is attending to a birth. You will have an opportunity to speak to him later."

A group of perspiring cleaning ladies carried bucketsful of soapsuds into the hall, reverently steering clear of Mrs. Berg.

"As you can see, we are in the middle of preparations for our name-giving ceremony. It's probably best if we find somewhere quieter. If you like, I can show you around."

Oppenheimer had no objections to being led around the premises, but he had to admit that he was disappointed. The plush parlors he had imagined were nowhere to be found. Nor were there any other amenities that might have induced one to joyfully procreate. As they walked along the boring corridors with their stuffy smells, the home reminded him less of a brothel and more of a maternity home. And this indeed did seem to be the sense and purpose of Lebensborn.

"Originally, this building complex was a convalescent home belonging to the Army High Command. We also have a crèche alongside the maternity ward."

"Who runs the home?" Oppenheimer asked Mrs. Berg.

"The position is currently vacant. The doctor and I share the responsibilities."

"Then I am sure you can help me. Ms. Friedrichsen worked here as a secretary. I can't picture what this would entail. What exactly were her responsibilities?"

"The secretary administered the funds and completed the paperwork."

"What would that involve?"

"There are official papers that she would make out—birth certificates, death certificates—and she managed the books and the registry. I think Miss Inge once even married a couple."

"Is there not a registrar here to perform such tasks?"

"You have to understand—our children are well-kept secrets. A large part of our work consists of admitting SS members' wives for delivery. But we also have other responsibilities. This includes enabling unmarried women to deliver their children without anyone finding out. We take care of the offspring, and should the mother decide to give her baby up for adoption, we try to place them with families that are true to party principles. We are committed to the highest possible discretion. Therefore, the usual registration requirements don't apply to the children that are born here."

"So Ms. Friedrichsen was entrusted with confidential information?"

"Well, you could say that. The secretary compiles all the information. She knows the mothers' real addresses, knows which of them were married, and in some cases, she even has information on the fathers. Like all other secretaries before her, Miss Inge was made aware that her position was subject to the strictest secrecy by the doctor."

The fact that a secretary like Inge Friedrichsen was entrusted with confidential information surprised Oppenheimer. This could be a possible motive for a crime.

Mrs. Berg left the main building with them. It was a four-story edifice whose portal was flanked by two impressive dormers. There were also several side buildings. No one who spotted the lane between the trees that served as a driveway to the home would have thought that such a vast property with its massive stone buildings was hidden here. Without a doubt, Mrs. Berg and *the doctor* were in charge of a significant operation. Oppenheimer tried to estimate how many potential suspects there were here. It had to be several dozen.

Despite its size, the terrain was shielded from all-too-curious glances by a row of trees. Oppenheimer could see something gleaming between the tree trunks. The Gudelacksee glimmered to his left; to his right lay a small pond, little more than a dark spot on the landscape.

"That over there is the small lake where our staff occasionally like to go," Mrs. Berg explained.

"Very interesting. How many people work here?"

"The doctor will be able to give you the precise numbers. It's probably around one hundred thirty people. Nurses, midwives, our nursery school staff, kitchen staff, of course, gardeners, chauffeur—all that amounts to quite a few."

Oppenheimer was not happy to hear these details.

"Is there anyone Ms. Friedrichsen had close contact with?"

"I'm afraid I don't know."

"How did she get this job? Didn't she need to have particular references to be entrusted with such confidential information?"

"Initially, Miss Inge was herself a guest in one of our homes. I cannot tell you which one. This information is confidential, and only the doctor has access to the central files."

"She was a guest?"

"Sorry, I should have explained. This is what we call the women who are admitted to our maternity ward. Each of them is only addressed by her first name, to protect her identity. We also don't call any of our ladies *Miss*, as in the mothers' interest, we don't want to give out any information regarding their marital status."

"So Ms. Friedrichsen came here through the home where she delivered her son?"

Mrs. Berg nodded. "Exactly. She had excellent references regarding her character and ideological suitability for the job. She had joined the party during her time on the maternity ward. Management had also confirmed that she had participated in all the courses with great interest."

"Which courses would that be?"

"Each home conducts courses for its guests. We try to inform the mothers about everything that is important for raising a child and for the general health of the German people. We offer a wide-ranging program. Sometimes we broadcast speeches given by the führer; occasionally, there is a communal singing evening. However, our responsibility goes even further. Apart from the children and the home, there is, of course, political schooling. After all, we want to educate our mothers to be good National Socialists so that they leave our home in an ideologically stable state."

"What about Ms. Friedrichsen's son? Is he still in Lebensborn?"

"Horst? Yes, he's here in our crèche. She visited him every second weekend. He's over there with the others." Mrs. Berg pointed to a field where several children were romping around. If one of them was Inge Friedrichsen's son, then he was playing as happily as the others, clueless that someone had robbed him of his mother.

A certain unease overcame Oppenheimer that he hadn't anticipated when he'd assumed he was dealing with a simple breeding station. Daily life in the home was much more normal, and perhaps that was why it was far more shocking. The fact that Inge Friedrichsen worked at Lebensborn did not mean that she was a nymphomaniac. She had seen a chance to earn some money, be independent, and at the same time keep her child. But she had to adhere to the rules, and she did that without question. Whether she had joined the NSDAP out of conviction or consideration could no longer be deduced beyond doubt. Oppenheimer considered the likelihood that the Lebensborn courses had played a role fairly low. The way Mrs. Berg described these events, they were different from the indoctrination that the German people had been exposed to for years, be it at school, at the workplace, through newspaper reports, or on the radio.

But after his conversation with Mrs. Berg, Oppenheimer had gotten an idea of how this was all connected. The party's motivation for helping mothers bring illegitimate children into the world—as long as they conformed to their requirements of raciology and were of *good blood*—was not human kindness. A war was being conducted at this seemingly idyllic place. Skirmishes were carried out every day, not concerning the current situation at the front in Russia but for battles that lay in the distant future. The National Socialists were getting ready, not with new, ingenious machines of destruction but with human material. The average German mother had to deliver as many children as possible and would at best be rewarded with a Cross of Honor of the German Mother for uncompromisingly sending her sons into future wars as cannon fodder.

The future pool of leaders, however, was to be born in Lebensborn. An elite according to Hitler's taste that was meant to establish itself as senior leadership with their perceived pure genetic makeup. That, at least, was the theory. Inge Friedrichsen was a small cog in the big wheel of this plan. Her assistance was not critical, and yet she, like many others, had made a contribution so that the system could function smoothly.

"I think the doctor ought to be available now," Mrs. Berg said and headed toward the main building. As Oppenheimer followed her, he heard noises that he could not classify. He wondered whether he had misheard or whether in this place, which was dedicated to purifying the German race, someone was speaking a foreign language. Oppenheimer looked around and saw a young boy, maybe three or four years old, holding on to a leather ball. His blond hair was almost bleached white by the sun. He looked up at the nursery school teacher stubbornly.

"*Pilka,*" the boy said and held on to the ball.

"No, say *ball,*" the teacher admonished him. "It's called a *ball.* You have a ball. I don't want you saying *pilka* again!"

The boy's face darkened. He shook his head fiercely. A girl in a dress, with plaits sticking out from the side of her head, watched the showdown before a nurse led her away. The teacher sighed audibly, looked at her recalcitrant charge, and placed her hands on her hips. "Do you not want to understand me? Either you say *ball* by this evening, or there will be no dinner."

Oppenheimer turned to Mrs. Berg. "What language was that?"

"A child from the East. Occasionally, we get some to see if they can be Germanized."

"Where do the children come from?"

"Mostly from Warthegau. There are homes in Brockau and Kalisch that we work with. Naturally, it is part of our remit to return children of good racial background to the Aryan ancestral home."

Oppenheimer didn't dare ask where these children's parents were. Had the children been taken from them? When he looked around again, he saw the purple-faced boy standing in the middle of the field. He didn't seem to know what he was doing here and what was being asked of him. Everything he had relied on in the past had lost its validity from one day to the next. When their gazes crossed, Oppenheimer briefly felt as if he were gazing into his own face.

■

"I need to lodge a complaint," the lady in the simple dress said. She had insisted on wearing an expensive, glittery necklace, although the management of the home asked their guests to keep an unpretentious appearance.

"One moment," Mrs. Berg said and led her visitors to the doctor's office. But the lady was not letting it drop and continued with her complaints.

"The meals are intolerable. No one can tolerate that much cabbage. I don't want my little one to get flatulent."

Mrs. Berg paused for a moment. "He's just been born. How is that supposed to happen?"

"It will be passed on through my breast milk, of course."

Mrs. Berg frowned ominously. She asked Oppenheimer and Vogler to enter, but they still heard some of the conversation through the closed door.

"I also demand to have a better room. Don't you know that I'm the wife of SS Officer Krug?"

"Mrs. Lore, I have told you several times, there is no preferential treatment here."

"Hauptsturmführer Vogler and Inspector Oppenheimer, I presume?" a voice came from behind the desk. When Oppenheimer turned to look at the man, he had already raised his arm in the Nazi salute. "Heil Hitler! Please take a seat."

The doctor did not bother to introduce himself. As every other person in the home only spoke of him as *Doctor,* Oppenheimer considered whether this might actually be his last name. During their conversation, he simply confirmed what Mrs. Berg had said. He was unable to say in which Lebensborn home Inge Friedrichsen had given birth to her son. Although Oppenheimer had already been given the name by Ms. Behringer, the doctor wanted to double-check.

"You have to understand that these matters are highly confidential," the doctor explained. "I can only give you data like this following confirmation from headquarters in Munich."

"You don't seem to understand. This information is important to our investigation," Oppenheimer insisted.

"As I said, I cannot give you a different answer."

"We will sort this," Vogler intervened. He turned to Oppenheimer and added, "The Lebensborn project is subordinated to the Central SS Office for Race and Settlement. I will contact someone there directly."

"That will probably be the quickest way," the doctor agreed.

Oppenheimer, sitting next to them, could see how they fed each other lines. Both Vogler and the doctor belonged to the same organization and understood its structure, whereas its manifold interconnections and the omnipresent wrangling for competency were inscrutable to Oppenheimer. This was why in this situation he felt less like an investigating inspector and more like a passive observer in a foreign world. The men stared at each other in silence. Vogler seemed to be waiting for Oppenheimer to ask another question, but the only thing that came to mind was whether he would be able to accomplish anything here at all.

Finally, the doctor broke the silence. "I presume Mrs. Berg has already shown you around the premises, Mr. Oppenheimer?"

"Yes, we've had the tour."

"And what do you think of our home?"

Oppenheimer answered truthfully, "It's very different from what I'd expected."

"Lebensborn has an important function. Most people forget this. It is a fact that since the beginning of the war, the willingness to procreate has diminished. In addition, fewer and fewer elite children are being born. We will reach a deficit in the near future that must be compensated for, and we have to include this in our planning. It is in the interest of the German nation to have a new generation of outstanding human beings. After all, someone will have to head up state and society when the führer is no longer among us. Many people simply don't want to understand this. Even many SS officers refuse to carry out their procreation duties toward the German Reich."

"I have to admit that I was expecting something completely different here."

"What do you mean?"

"The Lebensborn homes are commonly seen as a sort of brothel."

The doctor smiled patronizingly. "Ah, the matter of the procreation helpers. Unfortunately, this is always misunderstood. But perhaps it's quite a good thing that I have the opportunity to clear a few things up here. To put it quite bluntly, Lebensborn does not want to undermine the institution of marriage. Nothing could be further from the truth. But a marriage can only be seen as a foundation of the state if it produces many children. It is true that we are considering offering help to mothers who are willing to bear children and who cannot find a partner to realize their desire to get pregnant. We can assist by providing them with special procreation helpers. But this most certainly has nothing to do with prostitution. However, this plan has not yet been realized. Yes, there were trials, and I don't wish to deny that so far, they were not very successful, which is why the project has been deferred for the moment."

"What sort of problems were there?"

"Well, so far, the genetic makeup and disposition of most of the men who came forward as procreation helpers was below average. We here at Lebensborn are aware of our enormous responsibility, and for the time being, we have stopped actively looking for candidates. Our association does not consider it a priority to arrange partnerships. But I believe that after the ultimate victory, every woman will see it as her duty of honor to give the führer and the Fatherland a child. And at that point in time, we will again intensify our efforts in regard to the procreation helpers."

The doctor had gotten into his stride. While speaking of something that was his expertise, the doctor managed to do something rather unachievable: he strutted while being seated.

"Do you know, the Reich Leader SS advocates a fascinating theory. He has found proof that procreation helpers existed in Teuton and Dorian times. So it is an old tradition, which we are reintroducing and reinterpreting in the sense of genetic responsibility. If a woman of marrying age could not find a husband, then for a long time, it was tradition that her father would choose a man from among the villagers for her. The chosen man had to mate with her on the ancestral grave at night and remained anonymous during the sexual act. Imagine, in some areas this custom still exists." After these words, the doctor's gaze wandered into the distance.

Speechless, Oppenheimer looked at the man in the white coat. The conversation had unexpectedly taken a strange turn. Oppenheimer shifted around on his chair. He decided it was best to steer the conversation back to the investigation.

"Do you happen to know whom Ms. Friedrichsen was closer with?"

"I don't know. I assume she probably associated with the nurses. However, some of them have since been reassigned by the NSW."

Once again, one of these insufferable abbreviations. The Nazi organization was full of them. "NSW?" Oppenheimer asked.

"The National Socialist Welfare Service. They decide where personnel gets assigned."

"Would it be possible to receive a copy of all staff members who were employed here at the same time as Ms. Friedrichsen?"

The doctor looked at Oppenheimer and Vogler in surprise. "I don't understand the question. I gave you the list when you were here the day before yesterday, Hauptsturmführer!"

■

Oppenheimer was seriously upset. He sat in the car, sulking, his arms folded across his chest, trying to calm down. By the time they were several kilometers away from Klosterheide, he felt he had managed to rein in his anger. He now felt he was being figuratively taken for a ride by Vogler too.

"We can play games, of course," Oppenheimer began. "But I think the case is too serious for that. After all, we are trying to solve a murder. I don't know why you brought me in on the case in the first place. I can only work properly if I have all the information. We can carry on as before, but we'll waste a lot of energy and time. There is also no point in me following up leads that have already been explored. I have to have an overview of the current status of the investigation; otherwise, I can't help you. I'm sorry."

When they approached the nation's capital, it was already getting dark. But Oppenheimer immediately saw that black smoke was hanging in the air. There had probably been further air raids. After having spent the whole day in the rural idyll, far from the smell of death and depravity that pervaded almost every corner of Berlin, the sight was a shock that catapulted Oppenheimer back into the reality of the capital. It was a reality in which he still lived in the Jewish House, was still ostracized, in which his life was worth nothing. This thought made him realize what danger he had put himself into when he reproached Vogler, even setting him an ultimatum. The SS Hauptsturmführer held Oppenheimer's life in his hands, could have him killed on a whim at any moment. Impossible to say when this might be the case. It was probably enough for Vogler to feel offended or bored. Nobody would hold him accountable. The illusion of leading an investigation had made Oppenheimer careless. But it was too late to take back what had been said.

10

O ppenheimer, I fear that I underestimated your abilities," Vogler said by way of greeting. Hoffmann had driven Oppenheimer to Zehlendorf the next day at the usual time. He had even been a little faster than usual, as there was not much traffic on a Saturday morning. When Oppenheimer entered the living room, there were two piles of paper on the table. He had a sense of foreboding.

"It was stupid of me not to bring you in the loop earlier," Vogler continued. "But I had to make sure you met the high standards I hold this investigation to. I have seen that you were on the right track thanks to your intuition, even though you didn't have all the facts. You were right when, upon seeing the injuries, you presumed that the perpetrator knew exactly what he was doing. That he was practiced in what he did. It was not his first time. He's killed at least two other women in the same way."

Oppenheimer had to sit down. He didn't feel the soft padding that he sank into, didn't even realize that he was still wearing his hat and coat. The only thing that entered his mind was the bitter realization that he had not been wrong.

"And?" he uttered tonelessly.

"Julie Dufour and Christina Gerdeler." Vogler paused briefly to allow the names to sink in. "Those were his other two victims. You'll find the complete investigation reports with photographs, witness statements, and everything else on the table. You have complete insight."

Suddenly, Oppenheimer revived. He shifted to the edge of the chair and interrupted Vogler. "Hold on. Let's proceed chronologically. What time frame are we talking about?"

"Christina Gerdeler was murdered in August 1943. Julie Dufour in February this year."

"So this has been going on for nine months?"

"The SS were consulted only after Ms. Dufour was discovered. Her"— Vogler hesitated—"her employer, SS Gruppenführer Reithermann, called us in. We later found out about the Gerdeler case. It was more of a coincidence. We were following a lead in the Hotel Adlon when we were told about a similar case that took place several months prior. I fear that the investigating authorities didn't examine the case all that carefully. Both Ms. Gerdeler and Ms. Dufour frequented the Adlon on a regular basis. There are indications that the cases were connected. Since Ms. Friedrichsen's death, we have certainty."

It was happening again. Oppenheimer felt strangely weary. Once again, he was chasing a madman, a serial killer. As if his experience with Großmann hadn't been enough. Once again, a merciless creature was bringing terror to Berlin, and no one could foresee what nightmare this would lead to. From the window, Oppenheimer could see a few rays of sun shining through the pine trees, though for him, it was anything but a nice day. He thought of what Hilde would say in this situation.

"Bloody hell."

Vogler looked at him in surprise. Oppenheimer figured he must have not only thought the words but also spoken them out loud. But there was nothing to make light of. "Bloody hell," he said again, took off his coat, threw his hat into the opposite corner of the room, and got to work.

■

Whether the first victim, Christina Gerdeler, was simply crazy about men or whether she purposefully instigated relationships with wealthy middle-aged men was up for debate. Oppenheimer at least was quite convinced that her prime interest lay in the financial conveniences that such sexual relationships brought with them. Her savings account spoke volumes. There had been regular large cash payments. They had also found a tatty school booklet among her things, where she had meticulously noted down her expenses and earnings. Christina Gerdeler, in her late twenties, lived in a room in the city center that she shared with another tenant. She spent most of her money on elegant clothing, probably unavoidable expenses for an adventuress of her sort. She was a frequent guest at the Hotel Adlon, which served as an oasis for the members of the upper crust while the bomb war raged outside. Any self-respecting man made sure he passed by the Adlon at least once a day to eat in a cultured environment, to exchange important information, or to enter into an occasional adventure with willing and cultivated ladies such as Ms. Gerdeler, who were on the prowl for men in the noble hotel. And Ms. Gerdeler was cultivated, that much was proved by the small but exquisite collection of German literature that had been found alongside all the sophisticated clothing.

Oppenheimer examined the three photographs included in the file. Ms. Gerdeler clearly had them taken by a professional to promote herself among the gentlemen. The photographer had done a good job. The first photo showed her in half profile, wearing a tailcoat and top hat. She had regular features; her eyebrows had been shaved off and replaced with two dark painted lines. The picture emphasized the model's pretty appearance and its light-dark contrast made it highly appealing from an artistic perspective. If the photograph of a woman in men's clothing was quite daring, the second photograph—optically, at least—brought Christina Gerdeler a lot closer to party ideals. The picture showed her sitting on a tree trunk in traditional garb, her hair in two plaits, smiling at the camera. Oppenheimer had no idea what sort of costume she was wearing, but there was no doubt it most certainly emphasized Ms. Gerdeler's impressive cleavage, thereby probably serving its main purpose.

In contrast to this picture, he doubted whether the third photograph of Ms. Gerdeler was presented in public all that often. In it, she was depicted lying naked on a plush chaise longue. Her body, supported by her arm, rested on the extended seating area, and she had bent back her head so that her hair was displayed in its full glory. Reflecting light made her hair shine, and shadowy areas were combined with an optical brightener, which gave Ms. Gerdeler's body a radiantly enticing outline. This picture was most certainly designed to be passed on to special clients. An effective advertising method, Oppenheimer thought.

These were the only photographs in the file. It seemed that no pictures had been taken of the crime scene or the discovery of the corpse. In

Oppenheimer's opinion, the entire Gerdeler case had been handled in a shockingly unprofessional manner. Her body had been found on Sunday, August 8, 1943, near the Protestant village church in Alt-Marienfelde. An early churchgoer on his way to Sunday service had perceived something light on the grounds, which on closer inspection had turned out not to be rubbish but the dress that Ms. Gerdeler had been wearing. Her body lay in front of a memorial for the fallen of the First World War, but foul play had not really been taken into consideration. Similar to the Friedrichsen case, Ms. Gerdeler's exposed lower abdomen was facing the stone monument, and the genitalia had been removed. However, the police report said that it was likely stray dogs had a go at the corpse, a conclusion that ignored the strange circumstance that only the woman's genitalia had been mutilated.

The fact that the police hadn't looked deeper into the crime scene was probably because bodies were nothing unusual during wartime. And yet Oppenheimer could only shake his head. The investigators seemed to have been primarily concerned with removing the body as quickly as possible. No evidence had been collected. A hastily written report, no police photographs, no witness statements. Oppenheimer considered his colleagues' unbelievably sloppy work a total fiasco.

The second batch of documents contained the papers pertaining to the Dufour case. This was a completely different situation as far as the material was concerned. While Oppenheimer barely found any information regarding Julie Dufour in the notes, Vogler's men had done an excellent job of documenting the circumstances under which this body was found, as well as the investigation results. It had happened almost exactly six months after the first murder. Ms. Dufour disappeared during a daylight raid on Friday, February 11. An SS Gruppenführer named Reithermann then reported her missing and explained that Ms. Dufour worked for him as a foreign-language correspondence clerk. He exercised his obviously significant influence within the party to arrange for a large-scale search to be carried out. The mortal remains of Julie Dufour were found at the crossroads between Baerwaldstraße and Urbanstraße in Berlin-Kreuzberg on Saturday night. The parallels to the third murder were far clearer this time. The strangled body had also been placed in front of a memorial, the mutilated lower abdomen facing the stone monument. Two long steel nails had been found in Ms. Dufour's ear canals, the tips embedded in her brain. This had been different in Christina Gerdeler's case, but Oppenheimer thought it more than likely that the police had simply overlooked this in the first murder.

The fact that the body had not been found on church premises was not the only difference between the other two murders. The only witnesses in the cases of Inge Friedrichsen and Christina Gerdeler, respectively, were the persons who discovered their bodies. In Ms. Dufour's case, the problem was that there was a flood of potential eyewitnesses, as she had disappeared in broad daylight from the Hotel Adlon, of all places.

Oppenheimer leafed through several hundred pages of interview protocols for hours on end, but try as he might, he could not find a useful lead. She had last been seen at the beginning of the daylight alarm. While the guests from the Adlon went down to the hotel's own air raid bunker, it appeared that Julie Dufour had disappeared in plain sight of everyone. Afterward, no one could say for certain what exactly had happened in the general upheaval, as at the time in question, everyone was busy with themselves. The staff were interviewed, the hotel guests who had a reservation at the time, and also the guests from Berlin who had made a habit of turning up in the Adlon occasionally. But no one could remember where the young lady had last been seen.

Oppenheimer thought about the first two cases. It was understandable that the investigators had initially been unsure whether the Gerdeler case was connected with that of Ms. Dufour. The documentation on the first murder was insufficient. But it seemed that Vogler had gotten it into his head that the first victim, who had been found in Marienfelde, was also part of the murder series, and Oppenheimer tended to agree with him. In conclusion, it could be said that the distinct similarities between the Dufour and the Friedrichsen case at least left no doubt that they were connected and that it was highly likely that the first murder bore the hallmarks of the same killer.

Oppenheimer now knew how he needed to proceed. Top priority was finding additional parallels between the three cases. This was the only way to unravel the perpetrator's motive and possibly discover what type of woman was at risk. But the most salient consistency in the first two cases was not a shared character or physical trait, no; the key to it all was the Hotel Adlon.

■

A lot of things had happened during the week, and Oppenheimer planned to tell Hilde everything on Sunday. Now the time had come to instigate the diversion he had planned. After lunch, he put on his old coat and pulled out an envelope he had received from Eddie a few days ago. Inside was the promised door key as well as the address.

Lisa was doing the dishes when Oppenheimer went into the kitchen. She looked at him in horror. "Richard, you can't go out in that old thing. I have to wash it first."

"It's just a diversion," Oppenheimer replied. Then he slipped into his raincoat, which had also seen better days.

"It's not going to rain today," Lisa said. "You're not going to see a rag-and-bone man, are you? These are the only things we still have!"

"No, I'm not going to give them away. I need to see Hilde and want to try to cover my tracks. Don't worry, I have a plan."

"Did you also plan for the fact that you're going to sweat like a pig?"

The thought made Oppenheimer pause briefly. "Hmm, I don't think there is any alternative. I'll be back by dinner at the latest."

Lisa shook her head.

■

He hadn't been wrong. When Oppenheimer stepped out of the front door, he saw a man leaning against a doorway and reading a paper on the other side of the street. He had probably been assigned to watch him.

The key Eddie had given him was for a room in the Beusselkiez neighborhood. Oppenheimer just had to walk toward the subway station Beusselstraße and then steer west. The area was ideal for disappearing. Originally built to house the Loewe factory workers, it now contained countless flats, all stacked alongside one another like the combs of an enormous beehive. Consequentially, the place was very busy. Thanks to the chaotic building activity, it was impossible to estimate how many people had found somewhere to live here in the last few decades. Numerous backyard flats to the rear of the buildings had turned the area into a labyrinth. Oppenheimer recalled that the Beusselkiez had always kept the police busy. The residents held a traditional sympathy for the Social

Democrats. Many of them were even radical communists. As the leftist Spartacus League had also been very active here, the rise of the National Socialists had led to repeated street fights.

Oppenheimer went straight through the front door upon arriving. On the third floor, he found the small digs to which the key fitted. Once inside, he noticed that there was a window facing out onto the street, though the room was almost empty. A stove whose iron pipe ran straight through the room, a bed, and a sideboard—that was it. So this was the den Eddie had mentioned. However, there was no trace of the things that small-time gangsters tended to keep.

Oppenheimer removed the two coats he wore. Lisa had been right; large damp patches of sweat had appeared under both his arms. He gave himself a couple of minutes to cool down, then took a few tentative steps toward the window until he was able to see the opposite side of the road. Luckily, it was so bright outside that nobody would be able to spot him in the gloomy room. Unsurprisingly, the man who had been waiting for him outside the Jewish House now stood in the doorway of the house directly opposite.

After Oppenheimer made sure that his tail was alone, he put his coat back on. He hung the raincoat across the back of a chair. He wouldn't need it until he headed back home. Luckily, it was possible to exit the building through a back door. Eddie had thought of everything.

The street where the man tailing Oppenheimer stood lay in the sun, but barely a ray of light found its way into the narrow backyard of the block. Still, Oppenheimer put on the sunglasses he had with him. Despite this meager disguise, he hoped he wouldn't be too easy to recognize from a distance with a different coat and the dark glasses.

Apart from a few children playing noisily among the washing that had been hung out to dry, there didn't seem to be anyone around. Without hesitating, Oppenheimer ran across the backyard and disappeared around the next corner.

■

Vogler heard his own steps echo down the corridor. The summons to the Reich Security Main Office had given him an uneasy feeling. He would have been less worried if it had been his direct superior who had asked for him, but the fact that he was supposed to appear before a certain Ober-führer Schröder was anything but a good sign. One could accuse Vogler of a number of things, but not of being naïve. Even before he met this man, he knew the appointment had been arranged for him to justify his collaboration with Oppenheimer.

In the highly bureaucratic SS organization, everyone was busy exploit-ing their comrades' weaknesses. One could not count on solidarity from inside the ranks. When Vogler had come to Berlin, he hadn't been under any illusion in this regard. For someone in his position, the most im-portant thing was keeping the possible target area for attack as small as possible if one didn't want to be degraded or passed over for a promotion.

Vogler knocked and entered the anteroom. "Heil Hitler! Hauptsturm-führer Vogler for Oberführer Schröder."

The male secretary behind the desk looked up from his papers. "Heil Hitler. Please wait here."

The man stood and went into the adjoining room. Vogler heard low voices through the heavy oak door. The secretary reappeared after a few seconds. Before he could ask Vogler to step inside, an authoritative voice called out, "Come in!"

"Hauptsturmführer Vogler, as per your order!"

"Sit down," Schröder ordered. He turned back to his papers, presenting Vogler his profile, which was dominated by his bald head and the black eye patch. For the next few seconds, Schröder continued to make notes. Vogler realized that he was being kept on tenterhooks.

Surreptitiously, he looked around the room. Wood paneling every-where. Two photographs hung on the wall. Both were innocuous images—a portrait of Hitler and one of Himmler. There were no other personal items in the room. Either the Oberführer had not been billeted here for long, or he rarely used the office. Vogler wondered what sort of picture he would present if he were sitting behind that desk.

Finally, Schröder put the pen aside and turned to his subordinate. "You have been charged with the Dufour case?"

"Yes, Oberführer."

"Tell me, what is this I've heard? Although you're looking for the per-petrator among the Jews, you've selected a Yid of all people to help solve the case?"

"Yes, Oberführer." As Vogler answered, he wondered who had betrayed him. Probably Hauptsturmführer Graeter. Right from the beginning, Graeter had demonstrated that he had his own ideas about how the investigation should be conducted and that this did not coincide with Vogler's approach. But Graeter had not gone to his superior to start an intrigue; instead, he'd turned to high brass, to Oberführer Schröder. You had to hand it to Graeter; he had excellent connections within the SS and had no scruples about using them.

"Have you taken leave of your senses, man?" the Oberführer said, crimson-faced. "A Jew joining the investigation? I hope you have a good explanation, Vogler!"

"I made some inquiries, and I was told that Oppenheimer was the best man for the job. He also has a significant amount of prior knowledge."

"And you forgot to notice the tiny details that he is of foreign race? I must remind you that this investigation has the highest priority. Your behavior may compromise us."

"As far as I know, this information was classified, so none of it should become public knowledge."

"If anything does get out, you're going to be in the doghouse, my dear man. I will make sure of it!"

"May I state my reasons for choosing Oppenheimer?"

The Oberführer paused briefly. "Go ahead."

"I consulted him to be able to control the investigation better. It is my intention to work with separate units to whom I give as little information as possible about the results achieved by the other group. I am the only coordinator. The case of the subway murderer showed how careful we need to be."

"What in the world has that son of a bitch Ogorzow got to do with it?" Oberführer Schröder asked in astonishment.

"As an employee of the Reichsbahn, Ogorzow had access to the results of the investigation. He had an impeccable history, and since he was SA sergeant, he was not initially suspected."

"The crazy person we are chasing this time must not be a National Socialist. Does this—this Oppenheimer know that the investigation is top secret?"

"I made it abundantly clear."

"And you think he'll keep mum?"

"Oppenheimer has been under constant surveillance ever since he came on board." This was only half the truth. Vogler had only seen the necessity of putting surveillance on him a day later, but he trusted that Graeter didn't know that.

The Oberführer leaned back in his chair. Vogler sensed that his approach had impressed Schröder in spite of everything.

"I have been watching Oppenheimer," Vogler added. "He is very thorough. Furthermore, we can use his professional experience for our purposes. If we really are chasing a Jew, then it might be an advantage if we also deploy a Jew to catch him."

The Oberführer pursed his lips in thought. "I hope you realize that time is of the essence. Gruppenführer Reithermann is moving heaven and earth, right up to führer headquarters. He is complaining that no one has managed to solve the murder of his foreign-language tart. If we don't get results soon, there will be trouble."

Vogler knew that Reithermann could cause trouble. He had already met the Gruppenführer. He considered Reithermann nothing more than one of these opportunistic creatures that had been flushed to the top with National Socialism. And yet he held a position of power in the party that should not be underestimated.

When Vogler and Graeter were tasked with the investigation of Julie Dufour's murder, it seemed to be a routine case. But by the time Inge Friedrichsen was murdered, even the most senior tiers in the Reich Security Main Office realized that they were dealing with a criminal mind that could become a danger to them. And Vogler also realized that his steps toward solving the case were being closely monitored. He had to provide results. Soon.

■

"Quick, let me in," the man with the sunglasses said and pushed his way into Hilde's treatment room. Taken by surprise, she closed the door before recognizing her guest.

"Richard?"

Oppenheimer removed the glasses. "I've got heaps to tell. Do you have any coffee?"

"I'll make some in a moment. Hmm, I hate to say it, but you smell like a goat. Did you at least manage to shake off your tail?"

Oppenheimer followed her across the living room to the kitchen. "I came up with a small distraction, and it seems to have worked."

Hilde put the coffee on and poured a clear liquid into her shot glass. "I have to admit, I can barely tear myself away from the radio, even if it is dangerous. If the BBC News isn't just propaganda, then the shit really is hitting the fan right now. There were no night raids in the last few days, so there might be some truth to it. It's about time. I can't stand the sight of these Nazis anymore. The bastards have turned the entire country into a comedy dictatorship. As soon as I leave the house, I feel like I'm in a bad production of *The Gypsy Baron*. Just take Göring, that fatso squeezed into his ridiculous uniform like a sausage into its skin. And do you know what a Reich Marshal—or more precisely, Marshal of the German Empire—is, which is what he calls himself? I don't. It didn't exist before; I have no idea what job that is supposed to be. At least I can make sense of Göring's title as Reich Hunting Master. A load of egotistical idiots, these Nazi bigwigs." Before she took a sip of her schnapps, she asked, "Do you want one? It's a special one. Genuine Italian recipe."

"Italian? What's in it?"

Hilde handed him the glass, but the thought of letting this doubtlessly disgusting swill trickle down his throat made Oppenheimer hesitate. "No, I don't fancy it after all. We've found out quite a lot this week. There were earlier victims. The way it looks, we're dealing with a mass murderer."

Surprised, Hilde put the glass down without drinking. "That's shitty news. Tell me more."

While Oppenheimer put on a recording of the Piano Quintet in A Major, op. post. 114 by Franz Schubert, generally known as the *Trout Quintet,* he summarized the most important facts of the first two murders. After he had reported on Inge Friedrichsen's connection to Lebensborn, Hilde frowned.

"The Friedrichsen girl worked for Lebensborn? And the place did not look like an Aryan brothel?"

"No, it didn't. But there were a lot of odd characters running around."

"I would have thought as much. But it would also surprise me if the Nazis managed to raise something other than their right arm."

"Gruppenführer Reithermann doesn't appear to be that type of Nazi. Apparently, everyone is convinced of the fact that Julie Dufour was not only his French foreign-language assistant but also his mistress."

"The case is starting to get interesting. I am not surprised more victims are turning up. The ritual way the murders were carried out is indicative of it. And do you remember whom we compared our perpetrator to? Großmann, Kürten, all mass murderers. The three victims that we know of are just the beginning, that much is certain. At least we can now put together a chronology of the deeds. But I still wonder how to interpret the injuries."

"You're assuming he wants to tell us something?"

"We can probably be sure of that. I don't know whether it is open at all to psychoanalytical interpretation. As we can only examine his victims, it is probably obvious to apply the behaviorist approach."

"Yes, I know what's coming." Oppenheimer sighed. Hilde was on her hobbyhorse, the works of John B. Watson.

"Oh, really?" Hilde asked. "All right, then. Explain it to me. What does Watson say about actions?"

Forced into a corner, Oppenheimer tried to remember. "Well," he began, "all actions can be dissected into a pattern with a stimulus that brings about a certain response."

"Well done. The stimulus-response pattern. Watson assumes that there are just three types of emotional reaction: fear, anger, and love. All other reactions are learned, or, more specifically, learned through conditioning."

They had already talked about conditioning. Of course, Oppenheimer knew of the experiment with the Pavlovian dog, which was always mentioned in this context. "That's all very well," Oppenheimer protested. "But some people are complexer than dogs."

"I don't know. In some cases, I wouldn't be too sure. Look at arse-face Vogler. Pavlov's dog dribbles at the sound of the bell; Vogler kills people when he hears a bell. What's the difference?"

"Hilde, it's not the same. The behaviorists say that the human spirit is nothing but—what's it called again?"

"You mean the black box?"

"Yes. This theory, which says humans are little more than machines that transform stimuli into responses, is not enough to explain responses.

It might work at a desk or even in a laboratory, but not in reality, and as a policeman investigating murders, I say it doesn't work. And anyway, how is it supposed to help us? What should we do if things are as Watson claims?"

"We have to seek out the stimulus that brings about the reaction, so in this case, the murder."

"Then why don't you just say that we have to find the trigger and the cause for the deed? Why do you have to make everything so complicated?"

Hilde leaned back in amusement. "Well, then, we're agreed."

Sometimes Hilde really drove him up the wall. Exasperated, Oppenheimer mumbled something and looked for a new record. Somehow, he felt like chamber music today. He decided to put on Vivace ma non troppo from the Sonata for Piano and Violin in G Major, op. 78 by Johannes Brahms. Brahms's symphonies had always left him cold. Perhaps the first, which was strongly orientated toward Beethoven, was quite acceptable. But in Oppenheimer's opinion, Brahms's strength was his chamber music. The way the composer managed to make the instruments sing, almost like a human voice—for Oppenheimer, there was something magical about it.

As the music played, he thought out loud. "Let's approach this differently. If our perpetrator kills women who happen to cross his path, we won't be able to stop him. Then we can just pray that he will be caught in the act at some point, like Großmann. There is only one realistic opportunity for us and only if he intentionally selected his victims. To determine this, we need to find out what the three women had in common and how that is connected to the motive."

"Were the women similar in appearance?"

"I wouldn't say so. Different builds and hair color. Ms. Gerdeler was a brunette, but quite light, Ms. Dufour was dark-haired, Inge Friedrichsen ash blond. Ms. Gerdeler dressed flamboyantly to emphasize her attractiveness; Ms. Friedrichsen, on the other hand, didn't, as far as I can tell. The appearance cannot be the deciding factor."

"But they were all of a similar age."

"Yes, they were all in their twenties. And if we consider their life circumstances, then they all had something to do with the NSDAP or party members."

The silence that now descended upon them was inadequately filled by the music. The thought and the conclusion that might be drawn from it was not exactly pleasant.

"Wait a moment, though. In the case of Christina Gerdeler, that's not necessarily true," Hilde interjected. "She rooted out rich men in the Adlon and then let them have their way with her."

"And who hangs out in the Adlon? Who has the money to spend there? Usually, it's the party bigwigs. The probability is high that some of them were among her clients. Inge Friedrichsen worked at Lebensborn and was a member of the party; Ms. Dufour worked for an SS Gruppenführer. In this respect, there is a definite connection between these ladies."

Hilde refused to accept this. She shook her head vigorously.

"I doubt that is a decisive factor. I mean, how many females still live here now that the families have been evacuated? Berlin has become a city of males in the last few years. The women who stayed here are normally employed. As the Nazis have infiltrated everything, it is almost impossible *not* to have any contact with them, professionally or privately. In particular here in Berlin, where all the administration offices are. Look at it realistically. Almost everyone had some sort of connection to the party."

"Hmm, maybe you're right," Oppenheimer conceded. "Let's try a different tack. Where does she come from? Inge Friedrichsen lives in Pankow, Christina Gerdeler in Stadtmitte, and Ms. Dufour in Friedrichshain. These boroughs are close to one another."

Hilde reacted with a skeptical look. "Fine, but then look at the places where the bodies were found. Oberschöneweide, Kreuzberg, and Marienfelde."

Oppenheimer thought for a moment, then he looked at Hilde. "Do you notice anything here?"

"Indeed. Oberschöneweide and Marienfelde are both farther out."

Oppenheimer followed her lead. "Both are almost separate towns; both are in the south."

"Kreuzberg is in the center of town, but also in the southern part," Hilde said excitedly. They were onto something.

Oppenheimer concluded, "So while the victim's homes are close to the city center, their bodies were found in the southeast. Why?"

"Because it's more dangerous to transport a corpse than it is someone who's unconscious?"

"Possibly," Oppenheimer replied. "I wouldn't be surprised if our murderer was also based in the southeast. He must have a base there."

"Then we can take the next step and analyze his approach. He transports his victims quite a long way, so he must have a motorized set of wheels spacious enough to transport a dead body."

"He abducts the women from their usual surroundings, takes them to an unknown place where he first tortures and then kills them. Then he deposits their bodies at some point during the night from Saturday to Sunday."

"So this all takes place at the weekend," Hilde added. "Which suggests that he might have regular work with no spare time on weekdays."

"In other words, we are looking for a murderer with a vehicle and a strong work ethic," Oppenheimer said contentedly.

"That could have been something I would have said," Hilde commented.

■

After Oppenheimer had left, Hilde paced the room. She was concerned. Her cheerfulness toward the end of their conversation had been feigned. She could only hope that Richard hadn't noticed. Things were not looking good, and they could get worse. And Oppenheimer of all people, whom she had always viewed as a close friend, might be to blame. If the investigation developed the way Hilde feared, they would soon run into difficulties.

She had another schnapps and reflected whether she would be able to influence Oppenheimer. But the undertaking seemed hopeless. He was incorruptible when it came to his job. He had already proved his extraordinary talent long before they had met and before Oppenheimer was persecuted as a Jew.

It had been one of those small coincidences that can change an entire life when she had discovered him on the pavement outside her house one evening. It was the day of the Reichskristallnacht, the Night of Broken Glass, and Oppenheimer was little more than a terrified figure avoiding the glare of the streetlights and looking to hide from the paramilitary hoodlums of the SA. Was it really only six years since burning synagogues had lit up the sky over Berlin in tones of red? Such a lot had happened since then.

She still had strong memories of the propaganda that preceded the pogrom. The pretext was provided by Herschel Grynszpan, a Jewish immigrant, who shot Ernst von Rath, a secretary at the German embassy in Paris and member of the NSDAP. WORLD JUDAISM UNMASKED, the newspaper headlines clamored in uproar. But the people of Berlin showed little anti-Semitic hate. They remained calm, but an oppressive unease settled on them, as they could sense what was looming ahead.

The perceived *spontaneous public anger* that was then discharged against the Jews was planned with military precision. The Kurfürstendamm was transformed into an icy, glittering ocean. But it was not sudden frost that had covered the streets with ice on a meteorological whim; it was the shattered glass of Jewish shop windows refracting the first rays of sun.

On that day, people sensed for the first time what it was like to be a prisoner in your own state. Hilde, too, drove past the charred remains of the synagogues. The people in the carriage did not rejoice. "Anti-Semitism—fair enough, but this is going too far," the passengers mumbled among themselves, or something along those lines. But no one stepped forward. They were cowards. And were embarrassed by that fact. This was also true of Hilde.

In the days that followed, Jews were fair game. The law of the jungle ruled the country; brute force brought about results without the need for argument. Hilde had watched the events powerlessly, aware that one woman's resistance would not have any effect. To maintain the last scrap of self-esteem, she swore to herself that she would take in the first persecuted person she came across. And that was Oppenheimer. She hid him in her large house for the next three days, until the wave of arrests came to an end and Oppenheimer was able to return home. She met Richard's wife too. Lisa had traipsed ceaselessly around the prisons in Plötzensee, Moabit, and Alexanderplatz, until Hilde was able to tell her that her husband was safe. During those days, Hilde had held highly interesting conversations with Oppenheimer behind closed shutters, especially after she had discovered that her guest had been an inspector on the Großmann case. In those hours, Oppenheimer had found a place in her heart. She had taken him in to save her soul and had received so much more in return.

And now there was a danger that Oppenheimer, of all people, was going to be used by the SD to silence Hilde's kindred spirits.

Of which there were many. In her youth, Hilde had repeatedly visited her uncle and was introduced to the higher circles of society as a matter of course. She had quickly discovered that the military was a caste in its own right—especially the aristocrats among them. But as a vibrant young woman, Hilde also made a lot of other new friends. Her circles grew when she later studied medicine in Berlin. And so, Hilde found a lot of like-minded people who also opposed the ideology of fascism. Ever since that time, she was occasionally invited to "diplomatic teas" and could gauge from her own experience who in the Foreign Office sympathized with the Nazis and who one could trust. Even Hilde's marriage to Erich Hauser, who later became an SS Hauptscharführer, was not held against her in antiestablishment circles. Her friends knew that she was all the more active in her opposition of the National Socialist idea because of her marriage. When Helmuth Graf von Moltke from the clandestine opposition around Admiral Canaris was arrested because he had planned to warn Consul General Kiep of his imminent arrest, Hilde had become more cautious and only kept loose contact with those who thought like she did. But now things had come to a head. She sensed that she had to intervene to prevent worse from happening, even if this meant compromising her friendship with Richard. The time had come to break her silence.

When Hilde had moved into the outbuilding, she had insisted that a telephone line be laid to her new flat. Now she could talk without being overheard by the strangers in her house. However, it was possible that her phone was being wiretapped. But she had become a true expert in talking in code. Her contacts had to be told about Oppenheimer's investigation. She had waited far too long already. Hilde pushed her scruples aside, took the receiver off the hook, and dialed.

11

On Monday, Oppenheimer asked Hoffmann to not bring him straight to Zehlendorf in the morning. Instead, he stood outside the entrance to Höcker & Sons before they opened, his hands deep in his pockets. Lost in thought, he watched the goings-on in the street and chewed on his cigarette tip. He really hoped that his old war comrade Gerd Höcker would not turn up unexpectedly and involve him in inconsequential conversation before he got the opportunity to speak to Ms. Behringer.

A delivery van with a clattering wood gasifier drove past just as he saw her. She had wrapped a scarf around the lower part of her face, but her upright gait and the chestnut-brown curls beneath the black beret were unmistakable. She, too, had already spotted Oppenheimer. When she got closer, she pulled the scarf down and smiled at him. Her bright red lipstick was the only color in the drab grayness of the Monday morning. "Good morning, Inspector," she greeted in a friendly tone. "Have you made any progress with the investigation?"

"Some questions have been raised, which is why I am here. I'd like to ask you something."

"Of course. Go ahead." She looked at him expectantly, pulling out a box of matches. "D'you need a light?"

Oppenheimer hesitated. Then he remembered that he'd followed Vogler's advice and put a cigarette into his tip. "Thanks, but I'm trying to quit."

"Interesting," Ms. Behringer said, unconvinced, looking at his cigarette.

"Did Ms. Friedrichsen ever go to the Hotel Adlon?"

The idea made Ms. Behringer laugh. "My dear Inspector, I don't know what sort of notion you have of our salary. I mean, the *Adlon*! If I could dine there, I wouldn't need to work in this place. Well, I can't swear that Inge never went there, but—no, she would have told me."

"She never spoke of it? Did she perhaps mention the Adlon in another context?"

"You can ask as often as you want. But she never mentioned the hotel and never made any references to it either."

Oppenheimer nodded. "Thank you for your help," he mumbled discontentedly. "If you happen to remember anything, you can always reach me through Hauptsturmführer Vogler."

On the way to Zehlendorf, Oppenheimer didn't even notice Hoffmann's hazardous driving style, he was that disappointed by Ms. Behringer's statement. There were no leads connecting Inge Friedrichsen to the Hotel Adlon. He didn't doubt that Ms. Behringer's statement was correct. No matter how hard Oppenheimer thought about it, he finally had to admit that he was locked in a stalemate.

■

In the living room of the house in Zehlendorf, Oppenheimer continued to sort the facts that had accumulated over the last few days. The sirens howled repeatedly in the distance, but he didn't really pay attention. It took two whole days and the morning of the next day before he had more or less sorted the information and completed the chart on the living room wall. First, he added two further pieces of paper with the names *Christina Gerdeler* and *Julie Dufour* in the middle, right beneath the card with Inge Friedrichsen's name. The doctor's list had also come in. On it were the names of all Lebensborn employees who had known Inge Friedrichsen and who still worked in Klosterheide. There were about forty names. Oppenheimer wrote them on new pieces of paper and pinned them alongside the other suspects. Two people had been absent at the time of the crime: a midwife called Erika Möller, who could prove that she had attended a funeral, and Irmgard Hupke, a party-adhering nurse from the National Socialist Welfare Service, who had resigned her position in Klosterheide just that weekend. Although Oppenheimer thought it unlikely that the perpetrator might be a woman, he moved the two cards with their names closer to the center. Then came the suspects and witnesses from the Dufour case, whose vast numbers constantly forced Oppenheimer to go back to the files to make sure he hadn't overlooked anyone. The number of suspects in the case of the adventuress Christina Gerdeler remained disappointing. There were no reliable leads as to who she might have taken money from. Her notebooks contained only cryptic nicknames that were impossible to decode. A cup of hot coffee in his hands, Oppenheimer stared at the chaos of cards on the wall. Maybe the victims had something other than the Adlon in common.

"I think I'm going to have to speak to Gruppenführer Reithermann," Oppenheimer said when Vogler came by on Wednesday afternoon. "Could you arrange that for me?"

Vogler thought for a moment. "You want to interview him?"

"Well, I don't really have a choice. In the Dufour case, we have lots of witnesses, but the details regarding her person are very limited. I need more background information. And Reithermann is the only one who can provide them."

Vogler nodded. "We'll do it tomorrow. On one condition: I want to be present during the interview."

Oppenheimer was more than happy with that stipulation.

■

The seats in the Daimler were so comfortable that Oppenheimer fell asleep almost immediately. He had spent the early hours of the morning in the cellar together with the other tenants, as there had been another alarm during the night. Over the last few days, Oppenheimer had only managed to keep going with the help of Pervitin tablets. But when he checked the small vial this morning, he noticed that his supply had dwindled to just three tablets. He decided not to take any today, which might be reckless, as he needed to be on track for his interview with Reithermann.

Oppenheimer was rudely awakened by sirens and identified the rising howls as a pre-alarm. Streets slid past his line of vision, his body rocking gently—so he was still in the car.

"We're almost there," a voice came from the driver's seat. Oppenheimer recognized the back of Vogler's head, as he was driving today.

Oppenheimer sat up and rubbed the sleep from his eyes. When he opened them again, Vogler had already parked at the side of the street. They were in Horst-Wessel-Stadt, a borough known to longtime residents of Berlin as *Friedrichshain*. The ruins of a villa rose up before them. The roof beams had collapsed into the inside of the house behind the destroyed façade. It had probably been a direct hit. Large pieces of debris lay next to the building, but they looked more like abstract sculptures that an art-loving owner had placed on the English lawn, which, in a bizarre twist, still looked immaculately cared for.

Vogler scratched his head. "Goddamn it," he swore helplessly. "It must be here somewhere. Number forty-two." He studied his map of the city center. As the course of the roads no longer complied with what was marked on the maps, it was easy to get lost.

"I'll take a look around," Oppenheimer said and got out of the car. A large signpost with the number forty-two hung from the wrought iron gate. As it wasn't locked, Oppenheimer took a couple of steps onto the property and called out to make himself heard. But there was no one there.

An old man hobbled along the pavement, pushing a handcart with possessions.

"Excuse me," Oppenheimer called. "Does Gruppenführer Reithermann live here?"

The old man stopped and replied in a thick Berlin accent, "Don't think you'll find him here no more. See for yerself, the place's been blown apart." The man's teeth were only in a marginally better state than the ruin. "The Epsteins used to live here. The fancy gentleman had them carted off and then settled in. But that's the way things go nowadays. Last week, the Americans dropped a gift here. I didn't think it would ever hit a Golden Pheasant."

Golden Pheasant was the name given to senior party members. The people begrudged them the fact that they skimmed off the cream and lived in the lap of luxury. However, the same people were utterly convinced that the führer would not put up with such excesses if he knew about them. But no one dared to put it to the test and report the profiteers.

"Did Reithermann get killed?"

"No, just bombed out. No idea where he is."

When Vogler got out of the car, the old man touched his hat. "Take a look, if you want. I need to scamper," he said and disappeared around the next street corner.

"Let's have a look," Vogler said. "Maybe Reithermann left a message as to where we might find him."

Oppenheimer nodded and followed Vogler into the ruin. This sort of communication was common. The so-called wall papers were found everywhere on the façades of bombed houses, slips of paper from previous residents with their new address, or notices looking for missing family members. Maybe Reithermann had had the presence of mind to leave his new address behind.

Vogler examined the doorframe; only a few bits of wood were left hanging off the hinges. When Oppenheimer walked around the house, he heard a low drone. He looked up in surprise. He had completely forgotten the pre-alarm that had jerked him from his sleep. Now he realized what a deadly mistake he had made.

Although the sky was hazy, the airplane wings reflected in the sunlight, gleaming bright flecks that floated through the air directly toward Oppenheimer.

"Up above!" was the only thing he managed to shout. Vogler's head appeared from behind a heap of stones. When he followed the line of Oppenheimer's finger and looked up at the sky, he turned pale. "The idiots! There hasn't been a full alarm yet!" he screamed indignantly. "Come! Into the cellar!" He stuck his hand out and pulled Oppenheimer through a gap in the wall. A staircase was visible a few meters away, leading down to the cellar. Oppenheimer thought he could see a door. They stumbled down the steps, stirring up chalk dust. The droning increased. Vogler pushed the handle down, but the door was locked.

When Oppenheimer threw himself against it with all his might, it just shook a little. Vogler also began throwing himself against the door in vain.

Oppenheimer held Vogler back. "Together!" he shouted. Together they stepped onto the lowest step of the staircase and took a run-up. When the weight of their combined bodies hit the door, the frame shuddered. Sweat was pouring across Oppenheimer's forehead.

"Again!" Vogler's voice cracked. The first step, then the second, and run. They rammed the door with the full force of their shoulders. Oppenheimer was barely able to raise his hands to break his fall when the door yielded. He felt his palms scrape across the rough floor. The impact forced the air from his lungs. He crashed against something with the side of his head and landed on his stomach. At the same moment, the cellar seemed to perform a little dance and pivot around itself. Objects around them took on a life of their own; wine bottles rolled in all directions, the whole universe seemed to tremble, and a fiery tinge brushed Oppenheimer's back. He felt like he were in the center of a thunderstorm, helplessly abandoned to the force of nature, a toy for the elements fire and air, when suddenly all light around him disappeared in a deafening roar. The last thing he became aware of was a harsh whistling in his head, paired with the muffled rumble of countless falling stones.

Then everything went quiet. Oppenheimer tried to control his breathing. The whirling dust stuck in his lungs, and he felt the urge to cough. He quickly covered his mouth with the sleeve of his coat and tried to breathe through the material.

They were buried alive. Cubic meters of stone towered above their heads. Oppenheimer hadn't envisaged dying like this. His mind resisted this realization, but finally he accepted the inevitable and prepared to die.

12

———✦———

Vogler's voice became audible from somewhere, distorted with pain. Then Oppenheimer heard a terrible groaning, but initially, he couldn't say which direction it came from. Finally, he realized that it must be him making the noise. He couldn't say how long he'd been unconscious. He had lost all sense of time. Seconds, hours, days, it all had no meaning in the darkness. Only the fact that the dust had settled in the cellar indicated that a certain period of time had passed.

Oppenheimer tried to move. Despite the pain in his left shoulder, he felt around his immediate vicinity. There was a wooden object next to his head. It was probably a cupboard he had crashed into. The floor was covered in sharp objects. He had to get some light; otherwise, he would hurt himself. Shaking, he put his right hand into the inside pocket of his suit and managed to get the matches out with two fingers. Then he reflected for a moment. It could well be that there was no fresh air coming into the cellar. In that case, they needed to save oxygen, and he could only light the match for a brief moment. But it would be best if he could get himself into a position from where he had a good overview. His sideways position was not ideal. Very slowly, he rolled over onto his back, unable to avoid sharp objects poking into his spine. He carefully raised his hand. There was no resistance, so it was possible to straighten up. With a bit of effort, he sat up and lit one of the matches.

A weak shimmer of light filled the space. They appeared to be in some sort of storage room. Countless broken bottles bore witness to the fact that the owner was a wine connoisseur. Oppenheimer noticed the heavy alcohol smell from the spilled beverages. Vogler was lying next to him. His legs were stuck in a pile of rubble where the doorway had once been.

Oppenheimer was just about to blow out the match when he made an important discovery. The flame flickered. There must be a draft. At least they wouldn't suffocate in here. Just before the flame went out, Oppenheimer thought he spotted a candle in a corner of the room. He counted the matches in the box. Eleven. That wasn't very many, but if he found the candles, a single match would be enough.

Oppenheimer reached for the shelf and managed to pull himself up. When he was on his feet, he struck a second match and held out his arm so that the light reached deeper into the room. He hadn't been mistaken. There were white candles over at the back. Carefully, he tried to make his way through the mess on the floor. When he was about to reach for them, he suddenly flinched. The candles were not in a regular candleholder. In the flickering darkness, he realized that he was looking at a seven-armed menorah, one of the most important symbols of Judaism. Pain shot through his fingers when the match went out. The shadows assumed control once more, and the cellar sank into darkness, but the image of the menorah remained like a ghost in Oppenheimer's head. *Is it a sign from God?*

But a few moments later, his powers of critical reasoning took over again, something he'd always been proud of. The menorah was not a sign from God. It just showed that SS Gruppenführer Reithermann had unscrupulously seized the previous owners' fortune. They had surely long been sent to a concentration camp.

When Oppenheimer finally managed to light the candle, he realized that Reithermann had lived in the lap of luxury. Stocks of food were hoarded here, inconceivable to those who had just about managed to get by on ration cards. But Oppenheimer had no time to inspect the cellar any closer. First, he had to take care of Vogler.

"Can you move either of your legs?" Oppenheimer asked.

Vogler shook his head. "I've tried to get out, but it's no use."

Oppenheimer saw that Vogler's legs were buried almost to the knee. He carefully tried to remove a bit of the rubble, but apart from a few small pieces, there was nothing he could do. The larger stones were hopelessly wedged in. "Maybe I could try to get your feet out of their boots," he said to Vogler. "Tell me if the pain gets too bad."

Oppenheimer put the menorah down. Then he bent down and put his arms around Vogler's upper body. Once he'd managed to get his feet into a secure position, he began to pull. Vogler's breath came in short bursts. Oppenheimer gritted his teeth and mobilized his remaining strength. He pulled Vogler toward him, inch by inch. Finally, something gave way, and Oppenheimer landed on the ground. Vogler fell on top of him. For a few seconds, the two of them lay on the floor, completely exhausted. Vogler rolled off Oppenheimer so that he could get up. Vogler's feet had swollen to misshapen lumps. But there was no blood to be seen.

"There is not much we can do at the moment," Oppenheimer said. "We have no way of cooling them for the swelling to go down. We can only hope that someone digs us out."

"The villa was already a ruin," Vogler said in a firm voice. "Who is going to think that someone was buried alive in here recently?"

"I'll take a look around. Maybe there's an emergency exit." Oppenheimer searched the walls, but in vain. There wasn't even a chimney that one could have gotten up. They were trapped.

"Nothing," Oppenheimer said and sighed. "At least we won't starve." He pointed to the tins that were piled up in the cupboards. "And there's enough to drink. It's almost like inside Höcker & Sons in here." Most of the bottles were broken, but the rest was still enough to get drunk for several weeks.

Suddenly, there was a muffled sound. Oppenheimer had to listen very closely to hear it through the thick cellar wall. "It's—there's an alarm outside. It's starting again."

"These bloody bastards," Vogler swore. "Why doesn't Göring do anything about it?"

Oppenheimer searched for a radio transmitter. As there were so many provisions here, it could be that Reithermann had intended this room as a refuge. Through radio announcements, they would at least have some idea what was going on outside and would not have to rely on guesswork, which usually painted the situation as worse than it really was. But no matter where Oppenheimer looked, there was no radio device to be found. They were completely cut off from the outside world.

Just under fifteen minutes later, the ground began to tremble again. Oppenheimer had extinguished six of the candles to keep them for later. He wondered whether Lisa had made it to a bunker in time. The sounds above their heads were muted, but if Oppenheimer listened closely, he could distinguish antiaircraft fire in between the bombings. It seemed to be a heavy raid. His imagination painted gruesome images, images of a flaming inferno that raged above their heads and would heat up the walls of the cellar until they were burned alive, images of collapsing ceilings that would bury them beneath their massive load, images of a demolition bomb that would smash through the cement ceiling and rip them to shreds. He felt the horror slowly spreading through his body. He was no longer an off-duty crime inspector, no longer a Jew; he was simply a helpless creature that feared for its life. Instinctively, he reached for the small medicine vial in his coat. He had to take a pill; otherwise, he wouldn't get through this situation with his head on straight.

He could feel the edges of the pill with his tongue. In his rising panic, it didn't occur to him to open a bottle of wine to wash it down. Soon after he had swallowed the pill dry, he felt the first signs of relief. His body's craving for another dose was finally satisfied; it knew what would follow and prepared for the soothing effect. Soon the situation would lose its horrors. It would be like back in the old days when he had calmly performed his job with the crime squad. Oppenheimer waited for his former personality to gain the upper hand.

Vogler squinted at him.

"What is that?" he asked. He narrowed his eyes to read the label on the small vial. "Is it—Pervitin?"

Oppenheimer nodded.

"Will you give me one?"

The request hit Oppenheimer like a blow. He was torn, as this was his final reserve. On the other hand, Vogler desperately needed it. He was suffering great pain, even if in the last few minutes he had pulled himself together and not made a sound. Hesitantly, Oppenheimer handed him a pill. Vogler chewed and swallowed it.

He sighed contentedly. "Good." After a while, he asked, "Do you need some?"

"What do you mean?"

"Pervitin. I can get it without a prescription. Military service members get their own ration. Did you not know that the stuff is in our *tank chocolate*?" Vogler had to laugh.

Oppenheimer shook his head. Then he also started to laugh.

"My superior at the front always called Pervitin *Hermann Göring pills*," Vogler said, chuckling.

"That's a good one," Oppenheimer panted. Even though it wasn't particularly funny, there were tears of laughter in his eyes.

"There's another term," Vogler gasped. "*Dive bomber* pills!"

They both snorted with laughter. Soon Oppenheimer's diaphragm was hurting.

"I'll get you some if we manage to get out of here. How many do you need? A thousand?"

Oppenheimer grew serious. A thousand pills—an unfathomable amount to him. "Well, if you would . . . ," he stammered.

"But of course. We have to stick together, after all."

Oppenheimer looked around. "Apart from Pervitin and the radio, we have almost everything we need down here. Canned food, alcohol. We could last awhile. Maybe they won't dig us out until after the war is over." He had to laugh once more.

"Then I'll finally get to see Germania," Vogler said. Oppenheimer initially thought he was joking, but the Hauptsturmführer's shining eyes said he meant it. "Perhaps. If they dig us out only in a hundred years' time . . . I wonder what we'd get to see then."

Oppenheimer saw a new facet to Vogler's character: deep down, he was a dreamer. "Do you know, my cousin works in Speer's design office," Vogler said. "There is a drawing. Speer designed it to show the führer what would remain of Germania. What the ruins would look like in a thousand years. Our legacy to those who follow. I've seen the drawing myself. I've never seen anything more sublime. It almost looks like"—he struggled for words—"like ancient Rome."

"So we're living in a new Rome?" Oppenheimer said skeptically.

"There are definite parallels," Vogler insisted. "The German greeting, which the Romans adopted from our Germanic culture, even the SS. Hitler's personal protection squad has exactly the same role as the praetorian guard back in the day," he said proudly. "So which Roman emperor do you think Hitler resembles?"

Taken by surprise, Oppenheimer answered, "I actually only know Caesar and Nero."

Vogler laughed. "In that case, the parallels are more pronounced to Nero, who unfortunately is misjudged nowadays. In reality, he was a good politician. He trusted in the praetorians, understood that you have to rule by force. That the old has to be eliminated to make room for the new."

"I read somewhere that Nero wanted to have his capital turned into Neropolis to consolidate his fame. That's why he had ancient Rome burned down."

Vogler thought about this for a moment, a smile on his lips. "Of course, there is one important difference between Nero and the führer," he then said. "Nero was mad."

Then he laughed again, almost a little too late. Was Oppenheimer imagining it, or had he shot him a confidential look? He was baffled. Was there another side to this SS man? What did Vogler really believe?

"I need to pee," Oppenheimer finally said.

Vogler pointed to a corner of the room. "I think there's a bucket over there."

Oppenheimer relieved himself into the bucket, and Vogler mustered his circumcised penis with interest.

"How do you know so much about Rome?" Oppenheimer asked.

"My father was a Latin teacher. It's about the only thing he taught me."

"You speak in the past tense. Has he passed away?"

"I don't think so," Vogler answered curtly. When Oppenheimer had sat back down again, he said in a confidential tone, "What I don't understand, in your file, it says that you have a daughter, but according to my information, only you and your wife are registered in the Jewish House."

For a few seconds, Oppenheimer said nothing, then he answered, "It was so—unnecessary. She got the measles, like so many other children. We weren't particularly worried. But her body was weak, and then she caught pneumonia. It was simply too much for her. She died at the age of six. She would have come of age this April."

"What's it like when your own child dies?" Vogler wanted to know. Oppenheimer was unsure whether it was sympathy or curiosity he saw in the Hauptsturmführer's eyes.

"At first, you think it's a bad dream, that you'll wake up the next morning and everything will be back to normal. You wake up, and the next day you wake up again, and again and again, but the bad dream never ends.

There is this mystery. No matter what you do, you'll never get over it. You can only accept it. I think I've managed to, over time. And yet there will always be an emptiness in our lives that reminds us of the dead. Especially when"—Oppenheimer's eyes filled with tears, he had to clear his throat—"when you loved them. I never talked much about it when she was still alive. I can only hope that Emilia knew that she was loved. I won't get the chance to tell her anymore or to prove it through action. I miss her every single day. Maybe I'll get to see her again soon."

Silence filled the room. For a moment, the air raid appeared to have stopped as if by magic. But it was just an illusion. When Oppenheimer slowly took in his surroundings again, the noises returned. Metal and explosives continued to hail relentlessly from the sky.

■

Oppenheimer thought he must have slept. A metallic knocking sound filled the room. He looked over to the candle in the menorah. Only a burning stub remained. Quite a bit of time must have passed, but Oppenheimer couldn't estimate how much, as he had no idea how quickly a candle burned down. Maybe he should have paid more attention in school. With difficulty, he sat up and lit the wick of the next candle. The effect of the Pervitin had worn off. His insides were gripped by a bad feeling once more. But Oppenheimer also felt something else. His stomach was rumbling. When he looked around, he discovered Vogler, who had dragged himself over to the water pipes and was banging against them repeatedly. He was signaling that there were people buried down here, in case someone was searching for them.

When he caught Oppenheimer's gaze, he explained, "My radio controller knows where we are. Maybe he'll send someone when they realize we haven't returned."

Oppenheimer examined the tin cans. It was time to start on their stores. While searching through the rows of tins for a tasty meal, he came across canned salted pork leg. It was quite unlikely that the Jewish owners of the house kept provisions that weren't kosher. This meant it was Reithermann who had bunkered the canned goods in the cellar. Oppenheimer wondered where he had gotten so many tins from; there were at least two cupboards full. He reached for the tin with the pork leg. He still had a score to settle with God anyway. He didn't understand why God had allowed all this to happen, not only what happened to his own people but also the suffering that this war brought. This could only mean that he simply didn't care or that he didn't exist. Oppenheimer felt furious with himself, with his childish superstition that had come over him at the sight of the menorah. He finally decided to defy God by flouting the kashruth and eating nonkosher pork.

Oppenheimer extracted his old pocketknife from his breast pocket and repurposed it into a tin opener by stabbing the metal lid numerous times until he could bend part of it up.

While he cut the pork into pieces and ate, he realized that he hadn't eaten such good food for a long time. It had taken him to be buried alive to do so. What a mad world. "Do you want some?" he asked Vogler, who shook his head.

In a dark corner, Oppenheimer spotted a gramophone. Eating was a good thing in itself, but dining to music was much, much better.

"I'm going to make a bit of noise so they can hear us better," Oppenheimer said and reached for the next best record without paying attention to the cover. He expected to hear military marches or perhaps an operetta. But the sounds that blared from the gramophone horn were something completely different. Kurt Gerron and Willy Trenk-Trebitsch sang "Cannon Song." Oppenheimer had almost forgotten *The Threepenny Opera*. The party considered Kurt Weill's music to be abhorrent, deemed it *degenerate*. And as the lyrics were written by Bert Brecht, who openly sympathized with the communists, the work inevitably landed on the index. It was a pity, as Oppenheimer liked the music. Its hectic rhythm reminded him of Berlin in the 1920s. Back then, the city had been loud, vulgar, dirty, daring, and enticing. Although its glittering appearance was probably just cheap tinsel, it had shone far beyond the state borders. At that time, people lived in the fast lane and hurtled at full throttle toward the chasm of the Great Depression. Now Berlin was just a shadow of its former self. The feeling of having one's finger on the pulse of time, of being at the hub of the world, had disappeared. At best, the city was now the hub of the Third Reich, and there was only one color in this gray monotony: swastika red.

Even Vogler's generation had already lost all knowledge of this young, impetuous Berlin that Oppenheimer remembered. But the music from this era seemed to please him. Smiling, he knocked on the pipes in time with the beat. He called over to Oppenheimer. "What is this? I've never heard that before! Ha ha!"

Oppenheimer almost choked on his mouthful of pork. Come to think of it, he was in an interesting situation, buried under tons of rubble with an SS officer, listening to the music of a Jewish composer and a left-wing songwriter. Could this be construed as subversion of the war effort? Well, at least Oppenheimer could claim that he hadn't found any other records down here. "The troops live under the cannon's thunder," the lyrics echoed in the room. It wasn't long before Vogler joined in the chorus.

Once Oppenheimer had finished the pork, he inspected the other records, but even with the best will in the world, he wasn't able to find anything that would *not* have undermined the so-called proper German sentiment. Oppenheimer began to take an almost perfidious pleasure in exposing Vogler to nonconformist music. He switched from one *Threepenny Opera* song to the next. "Pirate Jenny" was followed by "Ballad of the Pleasant Life," which was then followed by "The Useless Song." Vogler did not seem to pay much attention to the lyrics. He only bellowed along to the chorus of the "Cannon Song." Oppenheimer had the uncomfortable feeling that Vogler intentionally refused to understand the satirical intention of the song.

After a few hours, they took turns. While Oppenheimer knocked on the water pipes, Vogler handled the gramophone. He was just raising the tone arm when the lead pipe beneath Oppenheimer's hands vibrated and a light knocking sound could be heard. Both men started. Someone outside had noticed them.

"Hello!" Oppenheimer shouted and banged against the pipe. Then he listened. Once more, someone knocked at the other end.

Oppenheimer knocked twice.

Two knocks sounded from up above.

"They've found us," Oppenheimer whispered. Vogler pushed himself over toward the water pipe and also listened closely.

"We're down here!" Oppenheimer called out. He hoped that the pipe would conduct the sound waves.

He heard something very quiet that sounded like "Hello?"

"In the cellar!" he shouted. "The entrance is closed off! Near the stairs!"

This was followed by a sound he couldn't identify. Then there was nothing.

"Hello?" Vogler shouted.

Nothing.

"Hell and damnation, they can't just bugger off again!" Oppenheimer said angrily. He struck the pipe again. Nothing.

"Wait," Vogler said. He took a large piece of stone in his hand and hit the pipe with the pointed end. After a few strokes, a hole appeared in the pipe.

"Hello!" Vogler shouted into the pipe.

No answer.

"It can't be . . . ," he started to say but didn't finish the sentence.

A scraping noise could be heard from the blocked doorway. They both stared toward it, mesmerized. Slowly the sand began to move, the debris loosened.

Vogler flinched. "Someone is digging!" Then he shouted loudly, "This is Hauptsturmführer Vogler! We're down here!"

An indistinct voice replied from the other side.

"Quick, let's shift things," Oppenheimer said and started to move the stones away from the entrance. Most of them were wedged in, and he needed a lot of strength to pull them out. He didn't pay any attention where he threw them but worked all the more doggedly. Vogler had also started to pull away at the boulders.

Finally, they heard the voice again. It was so close that they could understand it properly now.

"Hello! You got enough air down there?"

"Yes, more or less!" Oppenheimer called out. "But get us out of here!"

"It'll take a while!" came the muffled reply in a thick Berlin accent. "Backup is on the way!"

They spent the next two hours removing the stones. Oppenheimer's shoulder joint began to ache, and his muscles protested, but he didn't stop, kept digging in the rubble, scraping the stones aside until his fingernails were torn and his palms grazed. The air was soon full of dust, but Oppenheimer and Vogler were not bothered by the urge to cough, just continued to dig into the pile of rubble.

Suddenly, stones tumbled toward them. A beam of light cut the shadows, and a gust of wind entered the room, clearing the dust. Oppen-heimer saw someone. Through half-narrowed eyes, he recognized the old man they had met outside the villa, who was now grinning broadly.

"Thought you'd be down here," he called. "Otherwise, you wouldn't have left the car outside!"

They cleared a few more stones, and then they could be pulled through the gap. Strong hands grabbed hold of Oppenheimer's wrists. It was two men in firemen uniforms. Freed from the cellar, Oppenheimer realized that those two didn't even have any facial hair yet. He guessed them to be between twelve and fifteen years old. Their fathers were probably fighting, and so they had to take their places.

"Thank you so much," Oppenheimer said, exhausted, and brushed the dust from his coat.

"What day is it today?" Vogler asked as they sat on a pile of rubble in the corner of the destroyed staircase.

"Saturday," the old man said. "Tomorrow is Whitsun. You made it out in time for the public holiday. You've been buried for fifty hours."

Fifty hours, Oppenheimer thought in dismay. More than two days lost. Maybe the crazy murderer had struck again and they hadn't been able to stop him because they were fighting for their lives under this pile of stones.

"You need to get to a doctor," Oppenheimer said to Vogler. "I will get on with the investigation. Can you stand?"

Vogler tried. Supported by the two young firemen, he managed to get over to the car. After they had maneuvered him into the passenger seat, Oppenheimer got behind the wheel and put the key into the ignition.

"Do you think you can drive?" one of the boys asked.

"Do either of you have a license?" Oppenheimer asked.

They both lowered their heads in embarrassment.

"I can only ride a bike," the old man said.

"Then I don't really have a choice," Oppenheimer said. But before he started the engine, he had a thought. "Well, actually, I don't know if I'm allowed to," he mumbled.

"What?" Vogler wanted to know. "What are you not allowed to do?"

"Drive a car. The thing is, my license was taken away because I'm a Jew. Officially, I'm not allowed to drive this vehicle."

Vogler groaned, annoyed, and said, "Just get on with it and drive!"

While they drove to the nearest hospital, Vogler whistled the "Cannon Song." Oppenheimer grinned to himself, thinking that you had to hand it to the enemies of what was considered *proper German sentiment:* they could certainly write a good tune.

13

When he had taken Vogler to the municipal hospital on Landsberger Allee, Oppenheimer felt an element of restlessness. He didn't want to be idle, so he'd cajoled the Hauptsturmführer into letting him have the car over the bank holiday. This meant he would be mobile without needing Hoffmann. If a traffic policeman or a party loyalist stopped him, which was unlikely given the SS registration number, he should give Vogler as reference. Oppenheimer knew that he couldn't fill the car up anywhere. Petrol was scarce; private individuals had no chance. But the tank was still half-full, which would have to suffice for the next few days.

Oppenheimer had become painfully aware of the fact that he lacked driving experience. So he drove a little more slowly and hoped he wouldn't cause an accident. He was already on his way to Zehlendorf when he changed his plans and drove to the Jewish House. Lisa hadn't seen him for two days and would be worried. But when he got home, she wasn't there. He stood in the kitchen, unsure what to do. Then he tore a piece of paper from his notebook and left a short message that he was fine and would be back in three hours. That was enough time to at least inspect the site where the second victim had been found in Kreuzberg.

■

The stone giant's right hand was clenched to a fist and rested on his thigh, while his left hand was pressed to his chest. He stared down at the ground from his pedestal, his gaze fixed on the exact spot where the mortal remains of Julie Dufour had been found nearly fifteen weeks ago. It almost seemed to Oppenheimer that the grim expression the shadows bestowed upon the statue's face was a comment on this barbaric act, but the inscription on the pedestal clarified that the giant was in mourning for those who had fallen in the First World War. In former times, grass had probably grown at his feet; now carrots sprouted there. The food supplies for the city's inhabitants were so low that every little space of green had been appropriated to grow vegetables, and here, too, green carrot leaves sprouted from the ground. One could no longer imagine a dead woman had been lying here just a few months ago.

A drunken orchestra musician had lurched across the square in the early hours of the morning and had stumbled across Ms. Dufour's body. He had hurriedly tottered over to the nearest house and woken the residents from their sleep. It took a while for the drunken man to make himself understood. However, after two others had ascertained that he was telling the truth and there was actually a horribly mutilated woman lying there, they called the police.

Oppenheimer had read the protocol carefully. The intoxicated man had not seen any perpetrator. The officers investigating at the time had specifically asked him whether he had noticed a suspicious vehicle in the vicinity. But the alcohol had blurred the man's mind to such an extent that he was worthless as a witness.

As Oppenheimer stood in front of the monument and looked at the surrounding rows of houses, he noticed some similarities to the crime site in Oberschöneweide. Once more, the view of the body was obstructed by a dense growth of trees. It had doubtlessly been easy to park the car nearby and carry the dead woman the few meters to the site without being observed. The stone monument concealed the murderer's activities to the north, while the south gave a view of the wide Baerwaldstraße. Although the murderer had deposited the body right in the middle of Berlin, the danger of being caught at this precise spot was relatively low. It was the perfect place to get rid of a body. Oppenheimer wondered if it was a coincidence that there was a war memorial here, too, but when he thought back to the other two sites, he discarded this hypothesis. The murderer had presented the bodies beneath a monument in Oberschöneweide and in Marienfelde. There were many of them in the city and the surrounding area. The perpetrator could have easily chosen those that corresponded to his intentions. This also meant that he planned ahead to a certain degree. He did not carry out his acts on impulse, like Großmann had done. So it was just as likely he had also purposefully selected his victims. But where were the similarities between the three women? Oppenheimer was once again faced by the question that had bothered him all week.

It was already getting dark. Oppenheimer felt himself growing tired, and he had used up all his Pervitin tablets. He could really have done with an energy boost right now. Finally, he shook his head. No, it was time to go home. He had to look after Lisa.

■

When Oppenheimer returned to the Jewish House, Lisa still wasn't there. He just about managed to stumble into his room and take off his coat before he fell onto the bed, instantly asleep.

He was woken by sobs. Oppenheimer felt arms encircle him. He saw Lisa's face through a kind of fog and explained drowsily that he'd been buried alive. But before he could explain it any further, he fell back into a deep, dreamless sleep. When hunger finally drove him out of bed, the sun was shining through the window. Lisa was asleep next to him. He kissed her on the cheek. A careful kiss, so as not to wake her. Then he got up and trotted into the kitchen. He found some cooked carrots in a pot. Involuntarily, he thought of Julie Dufour's body lying on a bed of carrot leaves. But his appetite was in no way impaired by such thoughts. He felt movement behind him, then Lisa hugged him.

All Oppenheimer could do was swallow and place his hands on hers. "Nothing happened," he said. "Did I miss anything?"

Lisa pulled herself together and answered with a halting voice, "Not much. Old Schlesinger replaced the windowpane. You told me yesterday that you were buried alive. Where were you?"

At first, Oppenheimer just wanted to explain in a few words what had happened. But the explanation turned out longer than planned, as he felt that after all these days of worrying, Lisa had the right to know what the investigation was about. So far, he'd avoided giving her any details because the matter was so delicate and also top secret. In the early years of their marriage, it had been a big problem that he wanted to protect Lisa from all the things he experienced on a daily basis. But Oppenheimer had soon noticed that their relationship was burdened by this secrecy. And so over time, they had started speaking about the unpleasant events he had on his mind.

Lisa reacted well to the news that Oppenheimer was chasing a madman. He guessed that over the years of living with him, she had come to accept that whether she liked it or not, she would have to share her husband with criminals and hoodlums. But now she shook her head. "You should stop this. You're taking unnecessary risks."

"I have no choice," he answered. "The SS has me over a barrel. As long as I fulfill their expectations, we're safe. Maybe we can use it to our advantage."

"Don't they have anyone else for the job?"

"Most of my colleagues are at the front or have died."

"Those aren't your colleagues anymore. You are no longer in service."

"You know what I mean. I have to go to see Hilde in a moment to talk about the investigation. Then I'll be right back. Do you want to come to Marienfelde with me tomorrow?" Maybe it was unromantic to take your beloved to visit a place where a body had been found, but after the mortal fear he'd experienced in the cellar of the villa, he wanted Lisa near him.

■

"The sacrificial lamb has sympathy for its slaughterer. Did you ever hear such a thing?" That was typical of Hilde. Oppenheimer had mentioned his suspicion that Vogler might differ from other National Socialists. In the hours they had been buried together, he believed he had encountered a different Vogler, someone who might even carry the potential for good in him. In a certain way that Oppenheimer couldn't quite define, he sensed that since the hours they'd spent together in the cellar, there was a new connection between them.

Of course, Hilde didn't want to hear of it. Oppenheimer almost regretted having mentioned it.

"No, arse-face stays arse-face," she said and downed another schnapps. "Be careful that he doesn't influence you. That's the typical pattern. First gain trust, then manipulate."

"What is there to manipulate?" Oppenheimer made a dismissive gesture. "The facts speak for themselves in an investigation."

"And what if he wants to get you to investigate in a certain direction?"

"What good will that do him? He is just as interested in catching the murderer as I am."

"Vogler is an opportunist, like everyone in the party. He will only do what is most advantageous for him. In a secret investigation, everything is also a matter of politics."

"You're seeing ghosts. The case has only been classified as secret because this Reithermann guy has connections. There is nothing else to it."

"I hope you're right. Unfortunately, recently my fears have had the tendency of turning into reality."

"Tell me instead what you think of my conclusion that the deeds were planned a long way in advance."

"It all sounds logical so far. You haven't been to Marienfelde yet?"

"Unfortunately not. I am going there first thing tomorrow."

"I would be surprised if anything were different. The fact that no one saw the murderer suggests that he probably knew what he was doing. Did you notice anything else?"

"Hmm . . . the women's bodies were all found beneath monuments. They must have something in common."

"The First World War," Hilde finalized his train of thought. "It keeps popping up. Our killer arranges the women beneath the monuments like before a sacrificial altar. Maybe revenge is a motive. But what for? His victims weren't born yet when the First World War broke out. And yet I wouldn't be surprised if the perpetrator had something to do with that era."

"That could only mean that he himself was in the army. If that is correct, he'd have to be older than forty."

"Yes," said Hilde, staring into space.

Oppenheimer changed the record. In hindsight, he regretted not having taken the records from the cellar. He had no idea when he'd next get the chance to listen to pieces from *The Threepenny Opera*. Instead, he pulled the next-best record from his collection and put it on.

"Well, that's something, at least," Hilde said. "We finally know a bit more about our killer. Of course, the question is why he started killing women *now*. He's not that young anymore. I'm guessing that it was a lengthy process until our murderer became the beast who carried out these deeds."

"We definitely need to check whether there were similar cases in the past," Oppenheimer said. "But I fear we won't find much."

"There must have been previous indications of the murderer's sadistic urges. Often these things are simply not put in the right context."

"I know. I would really like to know what's going on in his head."

Hilde snorted derisively. "We'll never find out. If Vogler manages to get his hands on him, then the doctors will be content with measuring his head. I ask myself why everyone is so obsessed with deducing the character of a person from his appearance."

"And I would like to know what the results would look like if one measured the heads of our Nazi elite."

Hilde grinned at the thought. "It will turn out that Rudolf Hess hurried to England because he has a skull like Frankenstein's monster."

Oppenheimer laughed out loud. The fact that Hess, Hitler's deputy, had flown to Scotland in a Messerschmitt during a cloak-and-dagger operation three years ago had caught Goebbels's propaganda machinery unprepared. They couldn't understand why a senior Nazi official would want to pay a visit to the enemy. The population had speculated zealously what might lie behind the operation. There were even presumptions that he wanted to initiate a separate peace with England. Press and radio, caught completely off guard by Hitler's crown prince, published hasty reactions. To limit the damage, they finally announced that Hess was suffering from delusions. But fewer people than the party leaders expected had actually believed this absurd excuse.

Oppenheimer happily quoted a joke that had done the rounds on the quiet. "A song's been passing through the land: We're fighting against Eng-e-land. But when someone actually boards a plane, he is then declared insane."

For a moment, Hilde's laughter drowned out Handel's *Water Music*, which spilled from the loudspeakers. Oppenheimer finally saw a favorable moment to address the tricky subject. He tried to make it sound as casual as possible when he asked, "By the way, would it be possible to get another prescription for Pervitin?"

Hilde grew serious. "Again? You had one about three months ago. Have you used it up already?"

"Just as a precaution." Oppenheimer played it down. He didn't want Hilde to know that he had also gotten some pills from Dr. Klein.

"You know what I told you," Hilde reminded him. "Make sure you don't take too many. Amphetamines are highly addictive, don't forget that. But why do you think you need a prescription for the stuff now? I personally find it completely irresponsible that it was ever sold over the counter."

"I thought it might be a good idea to stock up." Oppenheimer was beating around the bush. "Who knows what lies ahead? Lisa is not coping well with the situation, and . . ." He stopped speaking when he heard a strange noise. "Wait a minute. What was that? Something in your treatment room."

They both listened. Oppenheimer lifted the tone arm from the record. Hilde got up and opened the door to her small surgery. In the silence, they could hear that there was someone outside the entrance. A pained groan. Then timid knocking.

Hilde hesitantly went toward the gate. Oppenheimer prepared for the worst and considered running through the small flat to make his getaway through the front door. There was no other means of escape, as the windowsills were piled up with books. But if Vogler's people had followed him here, then there was no point in fleeing anyway. He had specifically not taken the car Vogler had lent him; it would have been too conspicuous. Had he been careless in spite of everything because he had relied on his ruse with the clothes swap in the Beusselkiez?

Hilde held the door handle but didn't dare move. "Who's there?" she asked.

The reply was a pain-filled howl that sounded like a wounded animal. Oppenheimer and Hilde looked at each other in surprise. They realized that this was definitely not someone from the SD or the Gestapo. Outside, a body fell to the floor with a muffled thump. Hilde tore open the door.

A huddled figure lay on the doorstep. At first, Oppenheimer could only see long black hair. When she bent over to pick the person up from the floor, he realized that it was a young woman. She pressed her hands onto her abdomen. Her dress was soaked with blood.

14

———

Quick, get her up on the examination table," Hilde ordered. Together they took the woman to the far corner of the room. While Oppenheimer propped her up, Hilde put a cloth on the table. Then they placed the girl on it as gently as possible.

"If you want to make yourself useful, wipe the blood off the floor," Hilde said. "Especially outside the front door. And put some water on. I need boiling water as quickly as possible!"

Oppenheimer was not much help. After he had awkwardly cleaned the floor and brought the water, he waited in the living room while Hilde treated the young woman. It took a good hour until she finally reappeared and asked him to carry the patient upstairs and put her to bed. Oppenheimer was so surprised that he didn't ask what the relationship was between the girl and Hilde.

"You silly little goose," Hilde whispered and stroked the sleeping girl's forehead. "First you go and get yourself pregnant, and then this."

"I think you owe me an explanation," Oppenheimer said.

"Hmm, I guess so. Her name is Thea. She came to see me a few days ago. She wanted an abortion. It seems she went to see a quack instead of letting me take care of it. I don't understand why. Now she has internal injuries as a result of the procedure. I warned her. That wouldn't have happened if I'd done it." She turned back to the young woman. "Why didn't you listen to me?"

An incredible suspicion arose in Oppenheimer's mind. "You're a . . . a . . ."

"Backstreet abortionist, terminator . . . call it what you like. I'm not proud of it, but someone has to help these poor women. You've just seen what happens when they go to these butchers who use clothes hangers or the like. Just the thought of it!" Hilde had grown loud in her anger. When the girl groaned quietly, she lowered her voice again. "She'll survive. Luckily, she had the sense to come to me. She almost bled to death; they would definitely have asked questions in hospital. I'm probably the only person who can treat her and won't report her."

Hilde's confession was a punch in the gut for Oppenheimer. Suddenly, everything appeared in a different light. He couldn't deny that Hilde was intelligent, generous, and warmhearted. But he also couldn't deny that she was difficult to read at times. She sometimes judged people's character too quickly, she was cynical, and now it turned out that she terminated human life, for whatever reasons. Oppenheimer shuddered.

"Do you actually know what you're doing?" he asked. "If you're found out, they'll hang you."

Hilde gave a drawn-out sigh. "I know it's dangerous. But I have to do it. Or shall I send someone like Thea to these lunatics at Lebensborn? I couldn't live with myself. Yes, they would help her to have the child, and then what? They'll raise it to become a staunch National Socialist. Have you ever asked yourself what would happen if the child was classified as 'unworthy' to live? Ms. Friedrichsen kept the in-house records. How many fictitious death certificates do you think she signed?"

"That's no excuse."

"Don't you understand? The Nazi bigwigs want to turn women into mere baby-producing machines. Our uteruses can't belong to Hitler! I fight against these bastards with whatever means I have at my disposal."

Oppenheimer shook his head. "I can't see it like that."

"Well, perhaps I shouldn't expect that. After all, you're a man."

"That's not why. I am also an inspector. I chose this career because I want to stop people from killing each other."

"Hmm, I see. And do you think we're in opposing camps?"

"I don't know what to believe. An hour ago, you were the Hilde that I know, and now—now I have to seriously ask myself whether I may have gotten you wrong."

Hilde rubbed her tired eyes. "I don't think we'll solve that today."

"Yes, perhaps I should sleep on it," Oppenheimer said morosely and took his leave.

∎

As planned, Oppenheimer drove to Marienfelde with Lisa on Whit Monday to take a look at the place where the first victim, Christina Gerdeler, had been found. Lisa was about to get into the car Vogler had lent him, ready to leave Moabit, but then she stopped, transfixed. Standing before the open door, she inspected the interior in amazement and allowed her hands to caress the seats. "Oh my goodness," she said, "this is real leather."

Oppenheimer had to smile. "Unfortunately, I don't always travel in such comfort."

In the past, they'd occasionally gone to the summer resorts in the suburbs of Berlin or to the Havelland region when Oppenheimer had a day off. Everything had been so easy back then, when he had his job with the crime squad and there was no need for Lisa to work to make ends meet. Although it was only a few years ago, it seemed like the memories from a past century.

There was not much to be seen in Marienfelde, but at least Oppenheimer was able to draw some important conclusions. The place by the church pond where the body had been found was anything but ideal for getting rid of a body without being seen. The spot was openly visible from the surrounding houses. The murderer had been forced to operate in the open, fully exposed. But as Christina Gerdeler had been the first victim to be found, everything seemed to indicate that this was a typical beginner's mistake. Unfortunately, it couldn't be established whether someone had disturbed the murderer that night, as the police had omitted questioning the neighbors. In any case, after this, the perpetrator had planned his deeds more carefully and made sure that he wasn't seen when he placed the dead women beneath the monuments. He learned and gained more confidence with each murder. Maybe he would become too confident at some point and end up making mistakes. But Oppenheimer could hardly rejoice in this newfound insight, as this also meant that more women had to die.

∎

Vogler reappeared in the Kameradschaftssiedlung right after the bank holidays. He had been very lucky; neither his feet nor his shinbones were broken. He limped toward Oppenheimer, leaning on a cane, as the swelling had not gone down yet. There hadn't been any problem finding Gruppenführer Reithermann, who had been residing in a room in the Adlon since he'd been bombed out. They were supposed to meet him there that afternoon.

"It seems that Reithermann doesn't care too much about details," Vogler added grumpily. "He didn't bother to inform anyone of his new address because he assumes that everyone knows he was bombed out anyway. Of course, it is generally known, but no one bothered to tell *me*."

Oppenheimer barely managed to suppress a grin. He had secretly wondered for quite a while whether the Nazi surveillance state really worked as perfectly as everyone assumed.

Vogler seemed to have similar thoughts and shook his head. "Very well. Here, this is for you. I think it should see you through for a while." With these words, he shoved a Wehrmacht bulk pack of pills into Oppenheimer's hand, who checked the labeling to make sure he hadn't been mistaken. It was Pervitin. Oppenheimer's eyes widened with greed.

"If you need more, just let me know," Vogler said and disappeared into the cellar. As soon as Oppenheimer was sure he was alone, he swallowed three pills at once. Finally. It was high time.

After the effect had set in, he considered where he should hide this immense treasure. Depositing the pills in the Jewish House was too dangerous. The only option was to hide them here in the house.

After he had hidden his stash in the kitchen, Oppenheimer got to work. He wanted to review the chart on the living room wall; he believed that the new insights he'd gained about the perpetrator would help him bring some order to the chaos of notes pinned to the wallpaper. He discarded everyone under forty and moved their bits of paper farther away on the wall. Then he did the same with the female suspects. Finally, only about twenty slips of paper surrounded the names of the dead. The remaining pieces of paper were gathered around the framed picture of Hitler that hung nearby. It almost seemed as if the Reich Chancellor was also among the murder suspects in this investigation. When Vogler entered the room, he acknowledged this with a disapproving look, but refrained from making any comment.

∎

The vaulted ceiling above Oppenheimer was richly adorned with stucco; in its midst, an ornate fresco in a plaster frame. Several more vaulted sections joined to form the hotel lobby's ceiling.

The Adlon was much more than just a hotel. The name alone was enough to spread a hint of exclusivity. It was situated in Dorotheenstadt on the street Unter den Linden, just a stone's throw from the Brandenburg Gate. There was no location more representative than this. The Adlon had already hosted a number of illustrious guests. The tsar of Russia had been a frequent guest, John D. Rockefeller, Charlie Chaplin, and various aristocratic families had resided here, as had Emperor Wilhelm II. In comparison to the National Socialist rulers' pompous new buildings, the Adlon's façade was subtle in its design. The building did not try to show off or even dominate the Pariser Platz but instead integrated itself harmoniously into the surroundings with its clear lines. The interior, however, was dominated by great luxury and comfort. In addition to rooms and suites, it also offered a conservatory, a music room, a library, a ballroom, several conference rooms, a smoking lounge, and even a separate parlor for the ladies. Carpets lay on the gleaming marble floors, exotic palm trees stood in the alcoves, coffered ceilings spanned the numerous arched passageways.

In his function as inspector, Oppenheimer had occasionally visited the Adlon in the past. But he had never really felt at ease in these surroundings. The exclusivity of the hotel had instilled such respect in him that he constantly feared he would slip up. So he had always observed his own behavior, painfully aware that this must make him look like a country bumpkin who had stumbled into the big city for the first time, only able to take in all those new impressions in amazement.

But today, everything was different. Self-assured, Oppenheimer strode across the large entrance hall as if the place belonged to him. He was aware that his confidence was due only to the Pervitin. Despite his scruffy clothing, he had no qualms mixing with the noble guests. He climbed up three of the wide marble steps and leaned casually against the banister to observe the busy goings-on from up above. He saw party loyalists in dress uniform with creaking leather boots and tinsel on their chests, the only purpose of which seemed to be to jingle with every movement; men with briefcases, thick cigars, and fat necks; women in makeup, some of whom wore daring trouser suits, while others presented themselves in elegant evening wear already now, in the afternoon; diplomats and soldiers on leave from the front line. The pages in their dark blue uniforms flitted around in between; occasionally, Oppenheimer also spotted a face he thought he had previously seen on a film poster. It was probably a coincidence that the man hurrying over toward the steps now paid him any attention. His worried glance rested on Oppenheimer for a brief moment, as if he had recognized him. Without slowing his stride, he turned and ascended the stairs.

Oppenheimer's expression turned grim. He had recognized the face all too well, the short, gray hair, the bushy eyebrows, and the distinctive nose. It was his old rival Arthur Nebe who had rushed past him. They had started at the police academy more or less at the same time and had climbed the career ladder. In their time as candidates for detective superintendent, Oppenheimer had still had the edge over Nebe; he had been among the best candidates, whereas Nebe only managed to pass the exam on his second attempt. Despite all his resentment, Oppenheimer had to admit that Nebe was talented and very committed. When he was just over thirty, Nebe was made head of the drug squad. Old Gennat had promoted both Oppenheimer and Nebe to the newly created Crime Investigation Office A shortly afterward. There they became direct competitors and tried to impress their teacher Gennat with their actions, each always eager to outdo the other. Yet it wasn't only Nebe's skills as a detective that smoothed his way to the top but more the fact that in contrast to Oppenheimer, he used politics as a stepping-stone. He had founded the so-called German National Youth Unit Prenzlauer Berg on his own initiative back in the early twenties. Shortly afterward, he joined forces with a like-minded police officer to form a national group that campaigned against Jews and Freemasons in their own ranks. While Oppenheimer was content to become an expert within the Berlin murder squad, Nebe demonstrated that he was much more ambitious. In 1931, he joined the SS as a supporting member. Shortly afterward, he became a party member of Hitler's NSDAP and then went on to join the SA Brownshirts, just to make doubly sure. Although the leadership of the police force in Berlin at the time did not really approve of an inspector propagating his views this aggressively, it soon became clear that Nebe had had the right idea. He was hired to join Göring's secret police, the Gestapo, and so eventually ended up as head of the National Crime Police.

The unexpected encounter with Arthur Nebe brought back Oppenheimer's long-forgotten feelings of jealousy toward his competitor. He had never really known what to think of him. Oppenheimer couldn't tell whether Nebe really was a supporter of the National Socialist ideology or whether he was just using it as a vehicle for his own advancement. At the end of the day, it was irrelevant. As a Jew, Oppenheimer had to fight to survive every day, while Nebe had advanced to Golden Pheasant status.

Vogler limped over to Oppenheimer from the reception. "We've been announced. He resides on the first floor." He looked at Oppenheimer. "What's up with you?"

"I saw an old acquaintance," he replied curtly.

Vogler seemed genuinely surprised. "Here? In the Adlon?"

Oppenheimer shrugged. "Unfortunately, you can't choose who you run into."

■

"Now that the Hotel Kaiserhof no longer exists, this is the best place in all of Berlin," Reithermann said. He beamed with smugness. "The staff, the catering, all top-notch. And you should see the deep bunker in the cellar. No less than nine meters of reinforced concrete. Bombproof. The Tommies can throw at us whatever they like."

Reithermann was sitting on a sofa; he wouldn't have been able to squeeze into one of the delicate chairs. He wore his uniform, which, given his considerable girth, was unlikely to be off the rack. Oppenheimer wondered whether he had the same tailor as Göring. And yet Reithermann's uniform still seemed too tight. He had opened the bottom button of the jacket, from which his shirt spilled out.

Reithermann was one of the so-called old fighters. Hitler had even given him the Blood Order medal, the highest accolade awarded by the NSDAP. This honor was occasioned by a two-year prison sentence he'd been given. That was during the times of the riots at the beginning of the 1920s, when the National Socialists and the communists ganged up to bash each other's heads in. Reithermann had been an accessory to murder. The victim was a party member who turned out to be a communist who betrayed plans of the local SA faction.

After his imprisonment, Reithermann had changed from the paramilitary SA to the SS, where he now worked in the administration. It was a good position, a reward for his efforts in the past. Meanwhile, he ran a brisk sideline trade with loot from the occupied territories; works of art were considered his particular speciality. The party turned a blind eye on these activities.

Oppenheimer had gotten all this information from Vogler, in strictest confidence, of course. Looking at Reithermann now, he thought he knew why the man had hoarded so many tins in his cellar. By all appearances, the Gruppenführer was set on fattening himself to death, as he ate incessantly. Oppenheimer was stunned by this gluttony. The latent aggression that he had felt upon seeing Arthur Nebe was now amplified by Reithermann treating him like a supplicant.

"So you're the chap who's supposed to solve this case?" Reithermann asked. "Why has the perpetrator not been caught yet? What are you actually doing for your money?"

Oppenheimer fought to restrain himself and hoped that his anger was not too obvious as he provided a short summary of the investigation results.

"There is something else that I'd like to talk to you about," Oppenheimer concluded. Vogler shot him a concerned look. Although the sentence seemed entirely harmless, an unfriendly tone must have crept into Oppenheimer's voice. Vogler's gaze reminded him that he needed to keep his wits about him.

"What is it?" Reithermann demanded.

"Do you know this woman?" Oppenheimer handed him a photograph of Ms. Gerdeler.

Reithermann took it, patently bored. However, seeing the young woman in her top hat and tails seemed to arouse his interest.

"Hmm, might I have seen her in a film?"

"Hardly," Oppenheimer said. "She spent a lot of time here in the hotel. One could say she worked here, in a way."

Reithermann looked at him with irritation. "A chambermaid?"

"No. Her name was Christina Gerdeler. She was probably what one would call an *adventuress*. She came here looking for men."

"Hmm, she's a bit too Teutonic for my taste. I prefer the pre-Raphaelite type. Although . . ." Reithermann did not finish his thought, as his gaze had fallen upon the nude photograph. He was breathing heavily and licked his lips, lost in thought. "Unfortunately, I never came across her. I would have fancied having a bit of her."

Oppenheimer did not want to imagine what this would look like. His dislike of this plump bigwig grew with every minute. He took the photograph from Reithermann's pudgy fingers. "So you have never seen this lady before?"

"At least I never noticed her."

"Just to make sure, you've never heard her name? Did anyone ever mention Christina Gerdeler to you?"

"Are you deaf?" Reithermann shouted. "I don't know the little slut. Enough!"

"When Ms. Dufour disappeared, did you see anyone suspicious?"

"There was so much going on—I didn't notice anything. We were here in the building, in the restaurant by the Goethe Garden, when the bloody alarm went off. Ms. Dufour had forgotten the suitcase with her things in Friedrichshain. She just quickly wanted to get some stuff. No idea what. She didn't tell me. I wasn't interested anyway. She was going to meet me in the bunker. I organized a couple of bottles of wine, and then I went down."

"You didn't see which direction she took?"

Reithermann lost control. "Are you all thick or what? I've said it a thousand times. No idea! Go and chase the murderer instead of bothering me!"

"What was Ms. Dufour's position?"

"Secretary. Read your bloody notes before you come here! Is this any way to run an investigation?"

"How long had she been in your services?"

"About two years."

"Did she have any special duties?"

"You want to know if I fucked her? Of course I fucked her! And she liked me giving her a good seeing to! Like all the other women!"

Oppenheimer tried to keep calm. He wondered whether he should leave it at that. But he wanted to clarify one more thing. After all, he'd only wanted to see Reithermann in person to ask him this one question. Oppenheimer looked in his notebook. "One more thing. Could you tell me where you were at the beginning of August last year?" he asked as casually as possible.

"No idea. Why?"

When Vogler realized that Oppenheimer wanted to check Reithermann's alibi with this question, he ended the conversation. "Thank you very much. I think that's all we need." But Reithermann was not stupid. He had seen through Oppenheimer's strategy. Peeved, he heaved himself up from the sofa and planted himself in front of them, a towering threat. "Have you gone completely mad?" he shouted at Oppenheimer. His eyes glinted angrily. "Do you think that I killed them all? I, of all people? I, who arranged for the murders to be investigated in the first place?"

"Wait outside!" Vogler ordered.

When Oppenheimer left the room, he heard Reithermann shouting behind him, "I promise you, Oppenheimer, I'm going to knock you down. Just you believe it!"

■

The light in Vogler's Daimler was pulsating. The constant change in light provided a strange rhythm as they drove through shadowy areas created by the camouflage nets that had been extended across Charlottenburger Chaussee from long wooden poles. These constructions were mushrooming everywhere along the east-west axis. Their strategic usage was simple. Without these nets, enemy planes could easily orientate themselves along the wide streets that led straight to the city center.

The fact that Vogler hadn't said a word since he had emerged from Reithermann's suite worried Oppenheimer. He didn't know how to interpret this silence. Was Vogler disappointed in him? Was he going to take him off the investigation? Oppenheimer considered whether he had behaved too impulsively under the influence of Pervitin. Eventually, he offered a cautious justification. "I genuinely would have asked anyone about their alibi."

"You're really trying to push us deeper into the shit, aren't you?" Vogler hissed. "Reithermann is not just anyone. You shouldn't make him an enemy, regardless what you think of him. He can be truly dangerous."

"There were no details in the investigation files, so I asked."

Vogler laughed briefly. "Yes, that's true. Quite simple, really. Lucky that I was there. I was afraid you'd treat Reithermann like any other suspect."

He leaned forward to the driver. "You can stop at Großer Stern. Mr. Oppenheimer will get out."

Vogler fell back into his seat and looked out of the window. "I shouldn't really complain. This is exactly why I hired you."

"So that I vet people like Reithermann?"

"You can do it. You're unbiased. You can ask questions that no National Socialist would dare even address. That is the only way to lead an investigation."

Hoffmann stopped at the Bellevue Palace gardens, but Vogler wasn't done yet. "I was able to placate Reithermann. He is much more open to arguments once he's let off some steam. I told him that you just wanted to clarify Ms. Dufour's whereabouts in order to find a connection to the other victims. He bought it. You're still on the investigation, Oppenheimer. I'll see you tomorrow morning, as usual."

∎

The next day, a pin board had found its way into Oppenheimer's improvised office. "For your notes," Vogler commented on the new acquisition. "This should be more practical. It also looks tidier should anyone come by." Oppenheimer had to agree. What had once been a dignified living room was turning into a chaotic mess. There were papers and open files on the table, on the sofa, and even on the floor. In addition, the wall, originally reserved for the portrait of Hitler, was now covered in slips of white paper. Each time Oppenheimer walked past them, they rustled quietly.

Of course, Vogler had no idea that Oppenheimer had always worked like this and that spreading out across the room helped him, but he decided to show goodwill and to shift the chart to the pin board.

He was about to put Reithermann's name on the board but then hesitated. Reithermann couldn't really be added as a possible perpetrator, as he had a watertight alibi for the time his escort disappeared. The head waiter remembered him ordering two bottles of wine just after the alarm sounded and Reithermann waiting at his table until they were brought to him. Then there were several witnesses who said they had seen him in the bunker under Pariser Platz, which could be accessed directly from the hotel. And yet Oppenheimer had a vague feeling that Reithermann was involved in the murders.

Oppenheimer acknowledged that his suspicion might simply be caused by his dislike of Golden Pheasants like Reithermann. But certain details did make him wonder. Reithermann's life seemed to consist of consuming things. If he interpreted Vogler's comment correctly, Reithermann employed dubious means to obtain possession of artwork from the countries occupied by the National Socialists. His comments about Ms. Dufour and women in general had put Oppenheimer on alert. Was it possible that Reithermann considered women mere objects, of which he wanted to get as many specimens as possible into his bed? In other words, did he consume people? If he only saw them as objects, might he not see it as a trivial offense if he killed a woman? Or had things gone so far that he secretly hated women?

After some reflection, Oppenheimer realized that this train of thought was far-fetched. Without a doubt, most men had a similar attitude toward the female sex. The fact that Reithermann didn't have a romantic streak did not mean that he was the murderer. And he had been the one to get the murder investigation under way in the first place. If he was responsible for the murders, then this behavior would be hard to understand. Or was it just a perfidious game? Had he commissioned the SS to find a scapegoat for his own deeds, knowing that nobody would suspect him?

Oppenheimer had grouped all the men over forty who had anything to do with the case around the names of the dead women. He was just about to add Reithermann's name in this circle but then reconsidered and placed it a little closer to the middle.

Oppenheimer was still lost in thought when there were steps pounding up the cellar stairs. From somewhere, Vogler called out excitedly, "Oppenheimer! We have to go!"

He looked around, a question in his eyes. Vogler hectically limped over to the coatrack and threw his coat over his shoulders. "We have to go to Zimmerstraße. Now! It's inconceivable, but the bastard has given us a message!"

At first, Oppenheimer didn't understand what he meant. But then he realized that Vogler was speaking of the murderer, and his heart started racing.

Vogler's voice cracked. "The bastard actually wrote a letter!"

15

---

*D*er Angriff, the daily newspaper with a name meaning *attack,* was no ordinary publication. Even when the press was forced into line by Propaganda Minister Goebbels, it was still possible to obtain pamphlets of diverse provenance. All the large party organizations had their own newspaper, from the SS to the German Labor Front.

These papers certainly differed from the bourgeois-conservative press. The most important one was the *Völkischer Beobachter.* It wasn't possible to walk past a kiosk and not notice this official NSDAP newspaper, whose name implied it was "observing on behalf of the German Volk." The front pages were set in large print with shrill headlines in red and black. In addition, the advantage of the *Völkischer Beobachter* was that people didn't need to do much actual reading, as a large part of the paper was made up of photos and illustrations.

Another popular newspaper was *Der Stürmer.* It dealt with only one topic: the Jewish conspiracy. The main focus was to campaign against these so-called subhumans and parasites on the backs of the German people. Accordingly, anti-Semitic demands for the eradication of all Jews were the norm for this publication, which had far more regular readers than its circulation indicated; all big cities had "Stürmer Boxes," special display cases on every other street corner, where good German nationals could get free copies. Particularly popular at the time was its "pillory" column, where people who associated with Jews or those who were rumored to defile the German race could be denounced by their full name.

A large part was taken up by the description of such immoral acts. *Der Stürmer* relished in disclosing smutty details of decadent and perverted sexual practices to its readership so that the article hardly differed from the crudest pornography.

Der Angriff barely distinguished itself from the other publications, neither in its political orientation nor in its tone. What made this paper special was the fact that Joseph Goebbels himself had founded it and still acted as editor. Officially, *Der Angriff* was the NSDAP's Berlin paper and therefore stood in direct competition with the *Völkischer Beobachter.* Goebbels had used it in the run-up to the Nazi rise to power to increase his influence and to hound political opponents. Other party officials had had the same idea and founded their own personal paper to strengthen their influence in the wrangling for party sinecures. While Hitler soon put a stop to this proliferation, *Der Angriff,* Goebbels's own rag, continued to appear and had over the past few years even managed to become one of the most important daily newspapers.

Initially, the editorial office had conveniently been in the NSDAP Berlin main office in Hedemannstraße 10. But since then, the reporting had expanded significantly, so that the editors of *Der Angriff* needed more comfortable offices and had now moved into Zimmerstraße 88–91. Ironically, *Der Angriff* shared the four-story building with the editorial offices of the competition, the *Völkischer Beobachter,* whose name was also flaunted in huge letters, together with a stylized imperial eagle, on the façade with its red flags.

Oppenheimer followed Vogler through the newspaper's offices. They had initially gotten lost, but once it became clear they were looking for the editors of *Der Angriff,* a secretary told them where to go. They passed countless desks before they got to the editor in charge of letters from readers. He didn't waste any time, directly handing Vogler the piece of paper. "This was in the mailbox this morning."

Oppenheimer stepped next to Vogler to read the letter and saw that it had been written on a typewriter. While Vogler gave his full attention to what was written, Oppenheimer turned to the editor. "Has anyone else seen the letter yet?"

"No. I opened it myself and immediately informed the Gestapo. That's standard procedure here. We are in constant contact with the security services and know how sensitive confidential information can be. If you need some privacy, there is an empty office over there with a telephone line."

As soon as they had closed the door behind themselves, Vogler handed the letter to Oppenheimer. The Hauptsturmführer had gone red in the face, his lips pressed tight. "The bastard is toying with us," he growled.

Oppenheimer sat down and read.

> Finished off 'nother whore. I sent letters to the police but they never read them. So Im writing to you insted. They should know why I do what I do now. Those sluts are a danger. More than the Jews and the Bolshevicks combined. Someone has to tell the peopl. The hussy I left lying in Schöneweide aint the last one neither. Why doesnt the party do anything against these parasites? Get ready I will tackl the next one soon.
>
> Haeil Hitler!

Oppenheimer leaned back in his chair and squeezed his eyes shut. The last sentence did not bode well. This lunatic had announced another killing.

Vogler, too, stared grimly into empty space. As Oppenheimer inserted a cigarette in the holder, he said, "Okay, well, it's no use sitting here and moping. It's not going to bring those three women back to life. But with this letter, our killer has given us a few leads. If we can decode them, we can prevent another murder."

Vogler perked up. He ensured that they could use the office for the next few hours, and the two of them got to work.

"All right. Let's take a look at the letter—what can we say about the person who wrote it?" Oppenheimer asked.

"We know his motive now," Vogler said. "He wants to kill whores."

"All the women *he considers* whores," Oppenheimer specified. "That might be an important difference. Were the three victims whores?"

"Not in the classical sense. Ms. Gerdeler probably was, because she slept with wealthy men she picked up in the Adlon."

"And she was getting paid for it. She certainly wasn't an ordinary prostitute. The last victim, Inge Friedrichsen, had to die because she worked at Lebensborn. Our perpetrator probably didn't know that she worked there as a secretary. What's more, he seems to trust the rumors that the

Lebensborn homes are brothels for SS members. This narrows down the list of suspects."

Vogler looked at him questioningly. "How so?"

"The murderer has no idea what really goes on there. He has the same clichéd ideas as I had before my visit there. So we can assume that he is most likely not an employee at Lebensborn."

"Seems logical. But why did he kill Ms. Dufour? She was a foreign-language correspondent, not a prostitute."

"Reithermann didn't care. He still had sex with her. And he probably only employed her for that purpose. Our murderer might think exactly the same." Cautiously, Oppenheimer added, "Then there's one more topic he mentions to justify his deeds. He calls these women *parasites,* says they're more harmful than the Bolsheviks and Jews together. He seems to think that they are going to infect the SS with some sort of illness. He carries out the dirty work that he believes the party should be taking care of—namely, destroying the source of the disease. This indicates that he is a staunch National Socialist."

Vogler grimaced. "It might be a ruse. Maybe that's exactly what he wants us to think."

Of course Vogler had to put forward this argument, but it wasn't plucked from thin air. "Yes, maybe. We have to keep that in mind. The letter might be a red herring, but at the moment, it's all we have."

"He also doesn't seem to be used to a typewriter. He has made a ton of mistakes."

"Hmm. And he creates simple sentences. The punctuation is terrible. When he adds the salutatory address like *Dear Sir,* it sounds like it's alien to him. On the other hand, he is capable of writing 'enemy of the people' without any mistakes. As I said, it could be a ruse, but I'm guessing that the person who wrote this letter does not have a desk job."

Vogler nodded. "Is there anything else you can deduce?"

"No, that's all for now. But you should contact the police immediately."

Vogler looked at him questioningly.

"He mentions several letters he's written to the police," Oppenheimer explained. "We have to find them. Maybe they can enlighten us."

∎

When Oppenheimer returned to the Jewish House, he bumped into Dr. Klein, who didn't seem all that well. His face looked gray. To cheer him up a little, Oppenheimer told him that he had spent the end of last week in Reithermann's cellar and had discovered a hoard of tinned food there.

"Many thanks for the information," Klein said. "But I fear if I turn up there to collect the foodstuff, they will consider it looting."

This hadn't occurred to Oppenheimer. He of all people should have thought of that, given that he was a former inspector. If they caught Klein looting, he would probably be sentenced to death. As he considered this, Oppenheimer realized how his circumstances had changed over the last few weeks. He now had a certain authority from the murder investigation. His advice was heeded; he gave orders that were carried out by the SD. He now lacked any awareness that Jews like him were still being discriminated against, persecuted, and taken away outside the protective space that Vogler provided for him. He lowered his head in embarrassment. "Yes, of course that could be the case," he acknowledged. "You don't mind if I make someone else aware of the situation?"

"Not at all," Klein mumbled. "Have a good day." He went down the stairs, his head bowed. Oppenheimer hardly noticed, as he'd had a new idea. He would pass the information on to Eddie. He had people at his disposal who would take care of emptying the cellar. And that would clear his debts with him. And anyway, it was important to maintain a good connection to Eddie. You never knew when you might need him again.

■

Despite the new information, they barely made any progress at all with the investigation during the rest of the week. The days passed at an agonizingly slow pace. Vogler was out trying to put pressure on the police authorities, as so far no one seemed to have paid any attention to the murderer's letters. Either they had never surfaced or they were buried under a pile of unopened mail.

While Oppenheimer was going through the documents in the living room of the Zehlendorf house once more, summer broke out in Berlin. Temperatures rose daily until Wednesday. The sun was no longer obscured by clouds and heated up the city without obstruction. Oppenheimer was so busy with the investigation that at first he didn't noticed the change in weather. When he drove to Zehlendorf in the mornings, it was only just getting light, and when he went home again, the sun was usually already going down.

On Friday, Oppenheimer decided to make the most of the good weather and take a short walk around the Kameradschaftssiedlung, but the facts of the case were occupying his headspace, so he explored the area only half-heartedly, not really taking in his surroundings. Still, he soon realized how much good the outdoor exercise was doing him. The children playing in the forest, the women who were busy in the gardens or cooking—all this gave the impression of a happy, well-ordered life. But Oppenheimer knew that the houses in this area had been bought at a high price.

He had to keep thinking of Reithermann. He just couldn't get the question out of his mind whether there was a connection to the first victim, Christina Gerdeler. But the big problem was that there was no documentation from Ms. Gerdeler identifying her clients by their full names. Looking through her notes, Oppenheimer had at least found some nicknames and believed that he could prove that over the past two years, she had been kept by a total of eighteen men. Some of them appeared in her notes only once, while four men had met with her on a regular basis. Oppenheimer decided to find out who these gentlemen were, in particular whether Reithermann was among them. Ms. Gerdeler had occupied a small flat near the train station at Friedrichstraße. Her former flatmate, Lizzi Ebner, still lived there.

Oppenheimer had not seen Vogler since Thursday. It was better that way. Let sleeping dogs lie. Maybe he was being overly cautious; after all, Vogler had promised to support him in every respect. But he did not know how the Hauptsturmführer would react when Oppenheimer started investigating Reithermann. Luckily, it wasn't a problem getting hold of a photograph of the SS Gruppenführer. The only picture in the Dufour file that showed the victim while she was still alive had been taken during a party. Ms. Dufour was pictured smiling next to Reithermann, who was guzzling champagne.

Oppenheimer had Hoffmann drop him outside the train station at Friedrichstraße. High up in lofty heights, the train tracks ran along viaducts toward the station, a tall vaulted building stretching across the platforms. However, Oppenheimer did not go up to the platforms but followed the stairs down to the subway. Over the years, the train station had been expanded into a labyrinthine system of underground tunnels. It was ideal for shaking off Hoffmann in case he was shadowing Oppenheimer. But after just a few minutes, he had assured himself that his driver didn't see the need to follow him.

While he walked down the yellow-tiled passageways, he realized how much the station had changed in the last few years. People from all over the world seemed to be meeting down here. Oppenheimer had heard that now there were large numbers of foreign laborers in Germany, who were marked with a blue square with an *F* sewn on it, several million who were occasionally called the *Trojan horse of today's war*. Quite a few good Germans felt unsettled and rambled on about too much foreign influence on society. But too many men were at the front. Without this additional workforce, the Great German Reich would no longer function.

The assembly of foreign nationalities in the station's catacombs overwhelmed Oppenheimer. He hadn't thought something like this possible in a state that was so nationalistic. It was a pleasant surprise, a refreshing contrast to the stupid Germanomania prevalent in the party. He soon slowed down to study the people around him. A lady cast him a salacious glance while she talked to her companion in French. He saw a group of Italians in the next corner, dressed in ragged coats, who seemed to be wheeling and dealing, aided by wild gesticulating. An Eastern worker turned away from Oppenheimer, only to continue watching him warily over his shoulder. With a grin, Oppenheimer thought that they had probably chosen the best possible place for their meeting. After all, the basement of the train station was considered bombproof.

When Oppenheimer found the flat that Ms. Gerdeler had occupied together with Lizzi Ebner, he was disappointed. A new flatmate opened the door and told him that Ms. Ebner was currently doing her duty in an arms factory. She wouldn't be home until the early evening, as she was on shift duty. She had her day off next Tuesday; he should come back then.

Deflated, Oppenheimer walked back to the train station. He was much bothered by the fact that he just would have to wait until the perpetrator struck once more. The thought that so far this had always happened at the weekend made him uneasy. After all, today was Friday, the day when Ms. Dufour and Inge Friedrichsen had disappeared. He could only hope that the next two days would pass without bad news.

16

B illhardt seemed genuinely stunned. "Where on earth have you come from?" he asked and put aside the rake that he'd been using. Although there were clouds in the sky, the skin on his head gleamed underneath his sparse hair. Billhardt had always taken the view that he had a thinker's high forehead, and it seemed as if this had grown a few centimeters since their last meeting. But his colleague had changed in other ways too. He was missing an arm. Oppenheimer tried not to show his dismay too openly.

"Weeds grow tall," Oppenheimer replied. It was a corny line, but as they were in an allotment garden, this somehow seemed suitable. "I was looking for you. Luckily, I remembered where your garden is."

"What's up?"

"It's about an investigation that I'm advising on. Not officially, of course."

Billhardt's jaw dropped. Then he came closer and looked around warily. "I thought you were . . . you know." He nodded toward a sign that had been placed at the entrance to the allotments a few meters away. *German gardens and Jewish smell do not go together well.*

Oppenheimer had always shared everything with him while they were in the force together, but instead of giving a long-winded explanation of his situation, he now resorted to his old white lie. "I converted."

Billhardt seemed satisfied and opened the gate to his plot. "Well, that was just in time. Come on in. Goodness, we haven't seen each other in ages."

At least in the early hours of the morning, it had been a glorious summer's day and warmer than Oppenheimer had initially expected.

But when he took his jacket off in Eddie's place, he realized that he had no idea where he should go instead. Finally, he decided to find Inspector Billhardt. He didn't know whether he was still in the police service, and to be honest, he wasn't even sure if he was still alive. Oppenheimer made his way to the allotments in Neukölln, where Billhardt used to spend his weekends.

"I feared I might not find you here," Oppenheimer said after he'd sat down next to him on a bench.

"I've only been back a few months. You got lucky, Oppenheimer. Now tell me, what's this all about?"

Oppenheimer briefly explained the case he was working on, giving the most important facts without disclosing who was involved in the investigation.

"Well, well, a secret investigation?" Billhardt frowned. "Very interesting, but I don't envy you. It sounds a lot like a madman similar to Großmann. And what's your problem? Are you stuck?"

"The murderer must have gotten himself noticed before. That's why I wanted to ask if you've ever come across a similar case. Not necessarily in connection with a murder."

Billhardt nodded. "I know what you mean. It's about the method he used to attack women, am I right?"

Oppenheimer nodded. "The fact that he strangulated them is not re-markable. I am chiefly concerned with the injuries he inflicted on his victims. On the one hand, the mutilation of the genitals and then the objects in the ears. Have you ever come across anything similar?"

Billhardt went over to his small shed. "Do you want some wine?"

"White wine?" Oppenheimer asked.

Grinning, Billhardt pulled out a bottle. "I also have white wine. I always keep an emergency stash here."

While Oppenheimer tasted the wine, Billhardt seemed to remember something.

"There was something," he said hesitantly. "A colleague told me about it. You were still in the force at the time. It must have been just before the National Socialists took over, 1932 or '33. But I can't say for sure."

"What do you remember?"

"It was an injury. A woman. She was attacked with a knife and had several stab wounds to her genital area. No idea if that's any use."

Oppenheimer held his breath. This seemed to be a valuable bit of evidence. "What happened in that case? Can you remember anything else?"

Billhardt sighed in frustration. "All gone. Completely. I would have to look in the archives. It hit me quite hard when I heard about it."

"So you're still on the force?"

"Yes, if you want to call it that. If you come by next weekend, I can tell you more about the case, provided I find the file. Ever since the police headquarters on Alexanderplatz took a couple of bomb hits, it's complete bedlam. The individual departments, the files, everything is spread over the entire city."

"That would be really helpful. It is terrible having to sit idle and wait for the next murder to take place."

"I understand." Billhardt took a sip of wine. Oppenheimer couldn't help looking at the stump that had once been his colleague's arm.

"What happened with your arm?" Oppenheimer finally asked.

"Left it at the eastern front."

Oppenheimer nodded thoughtfully. "I understand. You don't have to talk about it if you don't want to."

They sat next to each other in silence for a few seconds. But Billhardt seemed to feel the urge to share his story with someone. "You're the only one I would tell. I think you will understand. The other colleagues—I don't even know who I can trust anymore. And I don't want to burden Dorothee with it."

Oppenheimer remembered Billhardt's wife. "How is she?"

"She's lost a lot of weight. There is nothing proper to eat anymore. She's living with her sister, who has a farm. It's better that way, definitely safer than here in Berlin. I see her once a month. I haven't even been able to tell her everything that happened in Poland." Billhardt fell silent. His face turned pale, and an invisible burden suddenly seemed to weigh on his shoulders. He twisted his mouth scornfully. "I killed. For the Fatherland, they said. Will the threat to the Fatherland really be diminished if you kill a child?"

Oppenheimer got goose bumps at the thought of it. He stared at his old colleague, but the man didn't notice.

Oppenheimer asked incredulously, "They made you kill children?"

"It happened. Children, old people, men, women, no difference.

Immaterial, they were all subhumans. Mostly . . . we mostly shot them in forest clearings. Outside the city. They dug huge pits. Usually, we had a dozen men carry out the digging. Once we'd taken the shovels off them, they were shot and thrown in. Then the other Jews arrived from the city. We could hear them singing their songs from afar. But people always fell silent quite quickly when they saw the pit with the corpses. Then they realized what was happening. We were told that they were supporting the partisans. But there weren't only Jews from Poland among them. I once even spotted someone from Berlin. He used to live not far from me. What's he got to do with Polish partisans, I thought. I tried not to look at him. But at the same time, I saw him staring at me. He recognized me. When the order to shoot came, I shot him first. I just couldn't stand the way he looked at me." Billhardt seemed distressed. "Can you understand that? I shot a person because I could not bear his gaze. I didn't think of it when I was at the front, but since I'm here . . ."

Oppenheimer tried to wash down his inner turmoil with a gulp of wine, but it didn't help. Billhardt had gone silent, probably waiting for Oppenheimer to say something.

"If it was an order, then you probably couldn't oppose it, right?"

"A few comrades didn't want to do it. They got a serious dressing-down, but nothing more. Somehow . . . well, yes, I didn't want to back out. After all, we were all there together, in enemy territory. You have to rely on each other; otherwise, you're done. I couldn't just let the others do the dirty work. I can't tell you if what I did was wrong. You know, the strange thing is that once you've done it a few times, the decision is really easy. You just have to be careful when you shoot someone in the head. The skull might explode, and you end up with all the stuff on your uniform or face. There were a few genuine sadists among the men, they really enjoyed it. I wasn't one of those. I didn't take any pleasure in it. After the executions, we always got shit-faced. I don't know where the stuff came from. I drank gallons of it, but I never managed to get properly drunk. At least not as drunk as I'd like to have been."

"How did you get out of there?" Oppenheimer asked.

"My arm was the price I paid." Billhardt moved his stump to prove his point. "We were attacked by partisan fighters. An ambush as we were marching through a forest. They came with grenades. One of them hit me. The commander didn't want to believe it at first. He thought I had the Eastern Meltdown and had held a hand grenade too tightly in order to get home. Well, I was lucky; I didn't get court-martialed."

Oppenheimer took a deep breath, weighed down by what he'd heard. Billhardt was finished with his story. He looked at Oppenheimer nervously, raised his glass, and emptied it in one gulp.

In the ensuing silence, an unpleasant thought occurred to Oppenheimer. Billhardt was without a doubt deeply unsettled by the events, but was he really mourning his victims, or was it the self-pity that bothered him? Billhardt himself probably couldn't answer this.

■

The next day, Vogler appeared with the letters he had managed to get hold of over the last few days. He was still seething with anger when he told Oppenheimer about it. Officially, the police stations were instructed to process all complaints and pass them on to the Gestapo. Usually, the police received anonymous letters from brave citizens who toed the party line, who denounced their friends for offenses against the Treachery Act. But the flood of these letters was so great that the officers couldn't keep up with the processing.

Vogler had had to exert massive pressure to get the police moving. After numerous officers had been commandeered to go through the mountains of paper, on Saturday, they had finally found two letters from the perpetrator. Judging by the postmarks, he'd sent those letters right after the murders of Christina Gerdeler and Julie Dufour. Initially, Vogler had seriously considered asking Reithermann to have those responsible for the sloppy work sent to the eastern front, but there were so many people involved in the processing that he would have had to redeploy entire departments.

They could have spared themselves the hassle, as there were no significant differences in the letter to the editors at *Der Angriff*. The murderer raged about prostitutes and blustered about illnesses they spread, according to his opinion. Oppenheimer's suspicions that the perpetrator had delusions of omnipotence were reinforced. The letters contained invitations to follow suit. After the murder of Julie Dufour, he even called upon Hitler himself to chase all foreigners out of the Reich. This letter was especially insightful to Oppenheimer, as in it he described Ms. Dufour as a "French whore." This confirmed the theory that he had considered the foreign-language correspondent a prostitute.

On Friday, after Oppenheimer had unsuccessfully tried to speak to Ms. Gerdeler's flatmate, he had moved on to Horst-Wessel-Stadt to question Reithermann's neighbor. He had found out that half the district was secretly gossiping about Reithermann and the French girl. Almost everyone who was questioned knew about it and had juicy details to share. So it was conceivable that the perpetrator lived in the same neighborhood. But then, the other two victims lived in different neighborhoods. Oppenheimer went over these facts several times in the living room of the Zehlendorf house, which always ended with him scratching his head in frustration, making more strong coffee. The murderer knew his victims and had clearly followed them for a while. But apart from the assumption that he had submitted them to gruesome torture and then killed them somewhere in the southeastern part of the city, it was impossible to determine a geographic focus. The perpetrator seemed to be everywhere and nowhere.

■

"No, I don't recognize the picture." Lizzi Ebner looked at the photograph of Reithermann with a blank expression. "But I can't tell you that she didn't know him either. She never introduced me to her gentlemen."

The blaring radio in the background irritated Oppenheimer. "Did she ever mention his name? Reithermann, Günther Reithermann, SS Gruppenführer."

"Well, I know she knew a couple of SS guys, but I've no idea of their names."

Her answer made Oppenheimer give up all hope of connecting Ms. Gerdeler to Reithermann. Her flatmate had never seen the men she met with and only knew the nicknames that Christina Gerdeler gave them.

It was ten in the morning when Ms. Ebner had received him, wearing a tattered kimono and torn black tights. But her immaculately coiffured hair belied any presumption that he'd woken her. She was roughly the same age as Ms. Gerdeler but weighed about twenty kilos less. Oppenheimer wondered what sort of job she could possibly pursue in an armament factory.

"Just a moment," she said and turned the radio louder. It was the news. Ms. Ebner had not been able to fully concentrate on Oppenheimer's questions the entire time. She seemed strangely distracted, constantly listening in to the radio program. In all his time with the police, he had never had such an interview. Lizzi Ebner gave the impression of being otherwise occupied.

"May I know what's so important about the radio program?" Oppenheimer finally asked, annoyed.

Ms. Ebner looked at him as if she'd completely forgotten he was there. "I just wanted to hear what they say about the invasion," she replied and turned back to the device.

Even if the party members tended to dismiss the invasion like a bad joke, they had not been able to prevent the entire population being infected by *invasionitis* now. Oppenheimer, on the other hand, had begun to lose faith. He was surprised that even a young woman like Ms. Ebner was gripped by this hysteria.

"Is there any news?" Oppenheimer asked without real interest. "Have our troops completed yet another new building on the Atlantic Wall?"

Ms. Ebner's eyes widened in surprise. "But haven't you heard? They landed last night."

Oppenheimer jumped up from his chair. "What? How do you know?"

"I have an authentic source. My neighbor, Mr. Blank, he told me. He knocked on my door a couple of hours ago. I remember thinking, what could he want at this hour?"

Oppenheimer paid more attention to the radio broadcast now. But by the time the music came back on, the speaker hadn't mentioned anything about an invasion.

"Are you sure that's right?" he asked.

"Yes, I'm sure it is. Mr. Blank works for the papers. He's the first to find out when such things happen."

Oppenheimer was suddenly agitated. "If that were true," he began, but didn't finish the sentence. After all, he didn't know which side Ms. Ebner was on.

"Bad day for the Gröfaz," Ms. Ebner mumbled, meaning Adolf Hitler. Then she realized that she had just let slip the unofficial nickname for the

Greatest Field Commander of All Time, as the führer liked to call himself, and winced. "Of course, I mean . . . umm . . . ," she stammered guiltily.

Oppenheimer had to smile. "I think we can speak openly." Ms. Ebner, too, smiled in relief.

"I have nothing to do with the Nazis," he explained, leaning forward confidentially. "I just want to find out what happened to your friend. If you suspect anyone from the party, you don't need to worry. I won't report it. No one will find out. I just need a lead."

Ms. Ebner looked at him almost beseechingly. "Well, I also want you to catch the bastard who did this. I would really like to help you, Inspector. But I know nothing."

■

There were still many questions Oppenheimer wanted to ask Ms. Ebner, but eventually, he had to accept that there was no point. She was a dead-end lead.

He left half an hour later. Initially, he hadn't admitted it to himself, but ever since he'd heard the news of the invasion, he'd had trouble concentrating on the interview. Instead, he kept wondering whether the Americans and British had finally attacked. He first headed for the train station at Friedrichstraße. He'd seen unusually large numbers of people at the newsstand asking for a paper when he'd made his way to Ms. Ebner's. Now he understood why.

When he got to the station, people were still crowding the newsstand. "What's going on? Aren't there any papers?" Oppenheimer asked.

A man waiting in line turned and shrugged. "No, they haven't arrived yet. Been waiting for ages."

"There they are," someone murmured. Oppenheimer couldn't see anything at first, but then he heard the clatter of the delivery van. The vehicle stopped, and a boy threw a bundle of newspapers onto the pavement from the back of the van. People became restless. The owner of the kiosk heaved the first stack onto his counter so as to cut the string bindings. He was just about the use his pocketknife when two policemen appeared at his side.

"These are confiscated," one of them explained and reached for two of the bundles. His colleague took the other two. Then they walked away.

The people grumbled. Oppenheimer was angry too. He'd almost gotten hold of a paper, almost seen what it said on the front page. It was like Christmas without presents.

"What a load of rubbish!" someone close to Oppenheimer shouted. "Why didn't they confiscate them at the printers?" The man being so addressed just shrugged helplessly.

"I don't give a damn what's on the front page," the man said loudly. "They could have left the back section. I just want to know how the story ends! It's called *Adventures on the Lofoten Islands*. You have to read it; it's brilliant."

■

When Oppenheimer questioned his driver, Hoffmann confirmed that the invasion had begun that morning in Normandy. The man's habitually melancholic gaze became even sadder. Oppenheimer, on the other hand, was electrified by the news. The uncertainty was over. If the attack was successful, then there would once again be a front line in the west, and Germany would be surrounded. The Russians were approaching from the east, and the Americans had made their way to Italy. He had to agree with Ms. Ebner. It really wasn't a good day for the Gröfaz.

Oppenheimer couldn't just go back to Zehlendorf and sit in his quiet little room. He made his excuses to Hoffmann, saying that he had decided to have lunch at home, and instructed him to pick him up in two hours. Hoffmann seemed happy with that. Without waiting, he started the engine and raced down Friedrichstraße at breakneck speed. Oppenheimer presumed he had someone to tell about the invasion.

The city center was pulsating with life. It wasn't just because it was lunchtime. There was something in the air. You couldn't put your finger on it, and yet it seemed almost tangible. People had caught a whiff of something. Oppenheimer went toward Unter den Linden and felt like a twelve-year-old boy at the beginning of the summer holidays. He felt on top of the world and wanted to kick his heels and run through the Brandenburg Gate to his flat. The world suddenly seemed too small for his energy, which had built up over the years of waiting. *Whoopee, here I come*, Oppenheimer thought, just like Hans Albers had sung in the film with the Comedian Harmonists many years ago.

But Oppenheimer didn't act like he was on top of the world. He didn't cheer. And he definitely didn't run through the Brandenburg Gate. For a political demonstration like that, the Gestapo would surely have locked him up in Oranienburg straightaway, Vogler or no Vogler. Walking home, he really had to pull himself together not to show his glee. He met numerous people on the street who seemed to be in a similar situation. Overt grins had spread among the passersby. Only the die-hard party members with the NSDAP party emblem pinned to their lapels looked distraught as they hurried through the streets.

Oppenheimer turned right onto the east-west axis. He went past the Adlon and, for the first time in ages, took the time to look up at the bronze goddess of victory, whose chariot high up above the Brandenburg Gate was being pulled by four horses in the direction of the city center. He went past the gatehouse, where Mars, the god of war, stood sheathing his sword. Oppenheimer hoped that it would all be over soon and Mars out of a job. But he knew the dying was not yet over. It had only just started at the western front. It was too early to start celebrating.

And yet Oppenheimer walked toward Großer Stern with a spring in his step. His mind urged him to caution, but his legs seemed to have a will of their own. As he walked along the wide street, passing the camouflage net, he looked up to the flagpoles. They lined the seven-kilometer-long route up to the former Reichskanzlerplatz in Charlottenburg, which, since Hitler's rise to power, was called *Adolf-Hitler-Platz*. How often had Hitler had this route flagged to celebrate his triumphs? Thousands upon thousands of flags used to line the streets, each red piece of cloth a gaping wound in the blue sky, and in between a martial carnival: soldiers, party officials, flower girls, all united in a slow-moving tide of people that threatened to block the streets.

Today, the flagpoles remained empty. Smiling, Oppenheimer was reminded of their nickname, which was only uttered on the quiet: *bigwig gallows-to-be*. He hoped they would soon be put to use.

■

The sky was overcast once more, but now and again, the full moon broke through the clouds and plunged the square to his left in a pale light. The Giesebrechtstraße was so narrow that the few trees that had been planted alongside the pavement provided sufficient shade to keep watch outside the Guesthouse Schmidt without being seen.

He now knew that they weren't taking him seriously. His letter to the editors of *Der Angriff* had still not been printed. It was inconceivable to him that Goebbels and the führer should not know the depravity that lurked between the spread legs of the painted ladies and that in this ignorance, they even risked causing great damage to the Aryan race. He thought that the reasons driving him spoke for themselves. He had mentioned them in his letters and tried to state clearly what had so far been hidden from the rest of the population.

After killing the last whore, he had lain in wait. He had watched the discovery of the body in the early hours of the morning and seen, shortly afterward, men in uniform appear. This could only mean that the SS had become aware of him by now. This was exactly what he wanted. But it seemed that someone was making sure his deeds were kept secret from the führer and his faithful. That left only one thing to do: he had to show the way, make them understand that he was not working against them. Over the last few days, he had come up with a plan that he was proud of. It would become his masterpiece. This move could not be overlooked. Everyone would understand what he wanted to convey. Although the risk was high, he felt he had to go through with it. But first, he needed a suitable victim.

He was able to find his bearings easily in the dark, didn't require much light to observe his surroundings. In all the hours that he'd already stood here in the Giesebrechtstraße, none of the passersby had noticed him. He knew he would find his victim here, as he considered the Guesthouse Schmidt to be the most disgraceful place in all of Berlin. The painted whores peddled their wares directly opposite him, spreading their disease. The highest social circles frequented the brothel. He had spotted many of them. Soldiers and SS men of all ranks, famous actors, not forgetting the filthy-rich fat cats who got out of their heavy limousines. The whores in Kitty Schmidt's parlor were poisoning the leaders of the nation. He feared that they'd already gotten too far.

He heard steps coming from the direction of the Kurfürstendamm. Figures approached. A man and a woman. They were absorbed in each other, strolling down the street, and had no idea that he was here under the tree, keeping an eye on them.

As they walked toward him, he forced himself to keep still. But his body didn't always do as it was told. Sometimes it seemed to have a will of its own. The whores were surely to blame. They had infected him. Their bad blood had gone deep inside him. They wanted to gain control of his body, but he wouldn't give up without a fight. He had to muster all his powers of concentration to remain still. He held on to the tree and focused on the rough bark beneath his hands. With all his might, he imagined being part of the tree.

But when he opened his eyes again, he flinched.

The couple had not gone away. They were standing right next to him. He could almost feel their breath. Just a few centimeters away, the man had leaned his companion against the tree. They embraced. He barely dared take a breath at the sight of it. He sensed them kissing, heard the quiet rustling of clothes and envisaged the man's knee pushing its way between the woman's legs. The woman sighed. At that moment, the feeling came over him again. Slowly, very slowly, he reached into his jacket.

It felt good to have the knife in his hand. He imagined the woman's thighs spread open and his knife in between, just before the moment where the steel would pierce the skin. Suddenly, he thought of the blood that he had to be careful of, the bad whore blood, as in his mind, there was no doubt that this shameless slut was one of them. He was wearing a raincoat. A pair of gloves in the pocket. If he put them on, he would be protected. So he toyed with the idea of killing the woman next to him, silencing her heavy breathing forevermore, right now. A few stabs in her side, just to keep in practice.

But he hesitated. This whore had someone with her. That would be a problem. Her companion would certainly misinterpret the attack, maybe even think that he was the intended victim.

A car turned into the street. For a few seconds, he was blinded by very bright lights. Then all he could perceive was a red veil covering the black of night. He needed a moment to be able to see his surroundings clearly again. The lovers had gone. He heard rapid steps nearby. A movement in the darkness. The woman had turned briefly to look at him. Doubtlessly, she had spotted him in the headlights.

The car stopped on the other side of the road, its engine running. Because of the blackout obligation, the headlights were little more than two narrow slits in the darkness. That was strange. Earlier, he could have sworn that they were on full beam.

Someone got out, probably a soldier. He wore a uniform, but he couldn't recognize which one. He leaned against the passenger door, swaying. It seemed the uniform-wearer had downed quite a few drinks. With difficulty, he handed the driver a banknote through the window.

"Keep the change," he said.

The taxi driver replied, "Sorry, but are you sure this is right? It's really too much."

The uniformed man waved it aside. "Keep the rest," he ordered, slurring his words. "Now the Americans have landed, it doesn't matter. Spend it quickly." Then he looked around. "Where's the fuck shop, then?"

"Over there. Bell at the bottom." The taxi driver pointed to the door, tipped his cap in a gesture of thanks, and drove off. The soldier watched the car disappear, lurched into the middle of the street, and shouted at the top of his lungs, "Enjoy the war, comrade! Peace is going to be terrible!"

17

The rain just wouldn't stop. For Oppenheimer, last week's summer days were just a distant memory. He hated to admit that his mood was so dependent on something as trivial as the weather. Rain quickly made him feel melancholy, in particular when it was pouring for several days on end. His mood wasn't really helped by the Mosquito air strike last night. At least this was an indication that the German Luftwaffe no longer had much left to beat back the attackers. Air raids during full moons used to be very rare because the chance of being seen was much higher. By now, the Royal Air Force didn't seem to care about such strategies.

Oppenheimer still had quite a way to go. If, after leaving the subway station Schlesisches Tor, he walked along the Spree River, he'd eventually reach Billhardt's flat near Treptower Park. When it had become apparent that the bad weather would be around for a while, Oppenheimer had decided to seek out his old colleague this Saturday already. He didn't feel much like squeezing into the damp allotment shed the next day to have a confidential conversation.

Stupidly, he hadn't thought of getting a second umbrella to confuse his pursuer. He only realized this when he'd already gotten changed in the small flat in the Beusselkiez. He couldn't take his umbrella to Billhardt; otherwise, his cover would be blown immediately. So he had no other choice than to brave the elements, protected solely by his hat. After just a few minutes, the water had poured from the brim of his hat into the back of his collar. As he stepped around the huge puddles, he kept thinking about how much he hated all this water.

Since the news of the landings of the Allied forces in Normandy on June 6, there had been only very few public announcements. On the day of the invasion, there had actually been new editions of the daily newspapers. INVASION BEGINS: IMMEDIATE RETALIATION was the headline in the *Berliner Börsen-Zeitung,* adding: WE FIGHT FOR EUROPE. The reports on the battles were essentially made up of the obligatory triumphant propaganda, which, given the seriousness of the situation, had simply been worded a little more subtly.

Just a few weeks ago, Hitler had boasted of his capacity to retaliate against an enemy attack within nine hours, but since the day of the invasion, there had not been much mention of this promise. Oppenheimer had even flicked through the *Völkischer Beobachter* to get some new information, but the in-house NSDAP broadsheet simply blustered about an insidious *attack on Europe* and spread the rumor that Stalin had forced Moscow's vassals to attack against their better knowledge. The next day, there were reports of heavy enemy losses.

After the initial shock, it became relatively quiet in the city. However, Oppenheimer didn't see many party emblems on the lapels of passersby anymore. Occasionally, he heard someone muttering about a retaliation attack the führer had surely arranged. Vogler and the radio operator looked quite anxious over the next few days, which Oppenheimer saw as a good omen for the Allied forces. But the weather was bad in Normandy as well, which was good news for the Wehrmacht, as the conditions meant that the enemy air force's deployment was restricted. As far as Oppenheimer could assess, the British and the Americans were currently not moving forward.

Like the Allied forces, Oppenheimer had not managed to advance much in the investigation in the past few days. But at least he'd managed to convince Hauptsturmführer Vogler to take the initiative and warn all members of the SS that their female companions and employees might be at risk from a murderer. Oppenheimer wanted to warn all the brothels in the city, but Vogler was adamant in his refusal, as the investigation was supposed to be confidential.

Normally, one would get countless leads from such warnings, but SS members had a far lower urge to communicate than the rest of the population. Maybe they simply felt too safe to take the warning seriously. They'd only had one measly tip-off so far, which had turned out to be entirely made up, as the missing woman had spent the night drunk with some man. Once Vogler's men had clarified the situation, it resulted in the usual jealous drama. Oppenheimer found this episode anything but amusing, as he was painfully aware that they were not getting anywhere.

He rang the doorbell, and Billhardt opened. "I just got back from my shift," he said.

"What are you doing these days?" Oppenheimer asked.

"You'll never guess. I've just come from the train station—on official business. I had to seek out illegal fruit salesmen and confiscate their goods."

Oppenheimer looked at the bulging food basket that was standing in the hallway. Surely Billhardt had been bribed by the traders. "Hmm, I understand," he mumbled. "What do you think about the invasion? Do you think the Atlantic Wall will hold?"

Billhardt didn't react. He led Oppenheimer into the living room.

Even before they sat down, Billhardt announced that he had indeed found the police file. Savoring the suspense with glee, he poured Oppenheimer a glass of wine.

"Turns out, I was right. The whole thing happened in September 1932. There were a lot of cases like that back then. Ideological reasons and so on. A unionist, who was also a Communist Party member, was attacked by a few SA men in his flat. They put him in the hospital, but he escaped with a few broken bones because neighbors hurried to assist him." Billhardt paused for effect. "His wife wasn't so lucky."

"Let me guess," Oppenheimer said. "She was attacked with a knife?"

Billhardt nodded. "Exactly. One of the SA men attacked the unionist's wife with a knife. At least that is what her husband later said. The perpetrator fell upon her in a blind rage and didn't stop even when the neighbors arrived to put an end to the matter. It seems he created a bloodbath. The witnesses reported that the man seemed to have worked himself into a frenzy. He wasn't aware of what was going on around him. It took three strong men to bring him back to his senses. He was sentenced to death."

"And what was so special about this event that you still remember it?"

"The SA man"—Billhardt hesitated—"he stabbed the woman in her pelvic area. The doctors couldn't save her."

Oppenheimer listened attentively. "Interesting. That could actually fit with our perpetrator. But you said he was sentenced to death?"

Billhardt grimaced. "Depends on how you look at it. He was let go."

Oppenheimer almost choked on his wine. "What?" he asked incredulously.

"He only spent six months inside. He got really lucky. While he was waiting for his execution, there was an amnesty. That was in March 1933, just after the seizure of power. The amnesty applied to *all* offenses that had taken place in connection with the national elevation. You hear? All offenses. Immediately, as soon as Hitler came to power, he ensured that his old co-combatants were officially given a clean slate. No matter what was on their record. He made sure their sentences were not carried out. They all got out of prison. Even our murderer went scot-free."

Oppenheimer was speechless for a moment. "Bloody hell," he finally said. "They had him, and then they let him go."

"Careful. Don't fixate on it. I know what you're thinking, but you haven't gotten any evidence that he's the perpetrator you're after now. There are no other indications in his file. He never popped up again. No further offenses. Apparently, he's been living the life of a respectable citizen since then."

"I need to access the file."

Billhardt flinched. "You know that's impossible. You're no longer a police officer."

"Then give me a copy, something. At least give me his name."

Billhardt shook his head. "No, I can't. I've already told you more than I should have. If this gets out, I'm done for. You know I'm no backstabber, but I have to consider my own safety. I told you when all of this took place. That will suffice. The Hauptsturmführer you work for will get you the necessary information."

Oppenheimer thought for a moment. "I don't want to speak to him about it until I have some specific suspicions. I already put my foot in it when I suspected an SS bigwig. And this Brownshirt would be one of his own men once again."

"I really can't help you anymore," Billhardt insisted, but Oppenheimer could see from his expression that he was struggling with the decision.

■

The all clear had finally come at three in the morning. Half-asleep, Oppenheimer had shuffled upstairs from the cellar to his bed, dropped onto the mattress, and gone straight back to sleep. When he woke up, it was already midday. He heard Lisa in the kitchen. Still sleepy, he rolled over onto his back and looked out the window into the gray sky. It was Sunday, but his mind did not allow him to rest. While he got dressed, he thought of the SA man Billhardt had talked about. Maybe he really should turn to Vogler to get hold of the files. A small white lie would suffice. He could claim to have heard about the case while he was still with the force.

When Oppenheimer went into the kitchen, Lisa was at the stove. The kettle was boiling. There was food on the table. To his surprise, he saw valuable items, such as chocolate, coffee, and tinned meat. His reflex was to immediately open one of the bars of chocolate. As the sweet taste spread inside his mouth, he couldn't resist a contented smile.

He put a second piece of this unexpected gift in his mouth and only then asked, "Where did you get this?"

"From Dr. Klein," Lisa answered. Her voice sounded oddly muted. "He handed everything out in the house this morning."

"I thought he must have a secret stash. What are we celebrating? Did the invasion advance?"

Lisa banged the kettle down hard on the stove and looked at her husband reproachfully. "You really don't have a clue what's going on around you, do you?"

Oppenheimer noticed a moist gleam in her eyes but didn't understand her reaction. "What did I do wrong?"

"You're so involved with your investigation that you've forgotten about everyone else."

Oppenheimer felt misunderstood. "Please tell me what's going on!"

"Dr. Klein got his evacuation papers the day before yesterday. Now that his wife passed away, he is no longer classified as privileged. He hoped he would be sent to Theresienstadt, but they want to take him to Poland because he's not sixty yet. They're fetching him tomorrow. So he gave away all his things today. I have a feeling he's going to take Veronal. I don't think the Gestapo will find him alive when they come for him."

The taste of the chocolate seemed to change in Oppenheimer's mouth. Shocked, he swallowed the rest. Then he raised his eyes to the ceiling. Somewhere up there, Dr. Klein was just swallowing a lethal dose of sleeping pills. Oppenheimer felt the urge to do something. He wanted to put an end to this madness. But what could he do? As much as it went against his instincts, he had to accept that it might be better not to intervene. Dr. Klein would spare himself further abuse, wouldn't have to dig his own grave before he was shot or gassed or whatever other atrocities the National Socialists might come up with. The only option he had to demonstrate his freedom, to not capitulate in the face of this extermination machinery, to not resign himself to his fate that the wretch whom the people called führer intended for him, was suicide.

The air in the room had suddenly gone thick and stale. Oppenheimer opened one of the windows and looked out onto the rain-drenched street. He no longer felt like eating chocolate.

■

The cemetery caretaker swore. He hadn't switched on his flashlight, although it was pitch-black all around him. He could find his way around the cemetery in the dark. If he was unlucky, then one of these hoodlums would still be lurking around here somewhere, and in that case, he didn't fancy attracting their attention. He considered himself quite fit for sixty-seven. Should anyone cross his path, he would try to sneak up and overpower him. At the thought of this, the caretaker gripped his hoe even tighter. It was good to have it with him, just in case.

After the all clear came through, he had just gotten comfortable in bed when he had been called out again. He would have noticed early in the morning, when he opened up, that the gate to the cemetery was ajar and that the chain had been cut. But now he'd been obliged to go out into the pouring rain to fulfill his duties. He'd seen Ms. Becker in the neighborhood several times before. He thought she was a silly goose, although she had a nice bum, you had to hand it to her. Out of sheer spite, he'd sent her to the nearest police station to report the break-in right away. Her expression when he said that he had to secure the grounds until the police arrived was simply priceless. Well, yes, one had to have one's revenge. He would have preferred to be in bed now. Maybe even with Ms. Becker.

It was nearly impossible to search the entire cemetery in the dark-ness. The grounds were almost half a square kilometer. And the damp air was unpleasantly clammy, which was why the caretaker decided to go down only the wide path to the water tower. He told himself that then he would've done his duty well enough. He secretly hoped Ms. Becker hadn't gone to the police after all, so he could get some more sleep for a couple of hours. The intruder couldn't really do much here anyway. Maybe steal some flowers. Was there even a black market for that? Otherwise, the most you could do here was desecrate a grave. Not worth mentioning. And this was what they chased him out of bed for. The caretaker shook his head moodily as he walked along the crunching gravel. He could just about make out the huge tower ahead of him at the end of the path. When the sun shone, the cylindrical building's red bricks outshone the entire cem-etery. But during these early hours, the colors were hidden in the black night sky.

The caretaker reached the end of the path and the bottom of the tower and was about to turn back, but suddenly, he froze. There was something there. Had he really heard a rustle? Or was his mind playing tricks on him? He listened carefully, but he couldn't hear anything apart from the large flags flapping above his head. It had probably just been a startled bird. Or could someone be hiding out here after all?

The caretaker raised his hoe, his muscles tensed, and he prepared him-self for an attack. He would show this villain that an old man like him was not a defenseless victim. He slowly began to circle around the tower, moving forward with extreme caution. He tried to be as quiet as possible, but the damned gravel crunched with his every step.

He didn't have to go far to discover the body. The caretaker was just passing the memorial hall at the base of the tower when his foot encoun-tered an obstacle right outside the main entrance. He stopped in alarm. Something he couldn't quite make out was lying in front of him in the darkness. That thing hadn't been lying here yesterday.

The caretaker knew how easy it would be to ambush him here. He was fully exposed. He suppressed his first instinct to examine whatever lay by his feet. First, he had to check that the coast was clear.

Nothing moved. No telltale light in the bushes. Nor was there any-thing coming from the portico of the memorial hall. No shadows waiting behind a pillar, no unusual sounds penetrating his ear. It was just him and the dark something or other on the ground in front of him.

Once he'd made sure there was no one in the vicinity, he focused his attention back on the dark object. If he wanted to be able to see anything, he had no choice but to switch on the flashlight. He adjusted the beam of light down toward the ground and saw what was lying in front of him. He'd seen similar things at the front, but all his war experience could not have prepared him for this human body that had been grotesquely mutilated by crude violence. The caretaker quickly switched the flashlight back off and just about managed to suppress his urge to vomit. Despite his hoe, he felt defenseless.

■

Oppenheimer had not been able to sleep all night. This time, it wasn't the air raid that got him out of bed. Lisa had gone straight back to sleep when they returned to their flat, but Oppenheimer tossed and turned. The thought of Dr. Klein preyed on his mind. He felt a bitterness inside that he couldn't shake off. He lay in bed and couldn't do much more than stare into the darkness.

Suddenly, a muffled sound. Steps. Someone was in the stairwell, coming up to their floor. A few seconds later, the kitchen door opened. Steps approached their room. Was it the Gestapo? Another search? Oppenheimer held his breath. Then someone knocked on the door.

"Oppenheimer?" a voice asked.

Hesitantly, Oppenheimer pulled on his trousers and opened the door. Hoffmann was standing in the brightly lit kitchen. "Mission," he said curtly. Oppenheimer knew what that meant.

"Hell and damnation!" he mumbled. The perpetrator had struck again. He'd killed another victim. In moments like these, Oppenheimer hated his job.

■

The rain had ceased when Vogler arrived outside the entrance to the Bergstraße cemetery at daybreak. His face took on an extremely unhealthy color in this light, but Oppenheimer was certain that he probably didn't look much better either. "We have a witness!" Vogler said with a broad grin.

Oppenheimer's eyes widened in excitement. "What did he see?"

"She. I've sent two of my officers to the police station. The witness will be held there so we can interview her straightaway. As far as I understood from the cemetery caretaker, she saw someone fiddling around at the gate just before the body was found."

Vogler then explained that the cemetery's northern portal consisted of a large iron gate, flanked by two smaller gates. The caretaker usually locked the main gate with a chain. The intruder had cut through one of the chain links, probably with a bolt cutter.

Vogler led Oppenheimer along the wide path straight across the cemetery grounds. Splendid gravestones that had been built shortly after the turn of the century were positioned alongside more recent plain stones, but their contours were still blurred in the shadowless twilight of dawn. The flat-roofed structure they were walking toward seemed rather bulky compared to the brick water tower construction that rose up above it. Oppenheimer vaguely remembered that this tower had never fulfilled its original purpose as a water reservoir. The NSDAP had found better usage for this representative and simultaneously pointless building—namely, a memorial for the fallen of the First World War and the National Socialist movement.

A sudden flashbulb explosion from the direction of the memorial hall. Doubtlessly the police photographer was in the process of securing the evidence.

"Up there?" Oppenheimer asked, quickening his steps. Vogler seemed surprised by Oppenheimer's sudden agility.

"Right outside the main portal," he said and hurried after Oppenheimer. Oppenheimer rushed past an SS man guarding the site, a gun on his shoulder. When he turned around the corner of the portico, he saw the tarpaulin. The photographer was just placing it back over the body. Only a few red curls could be seen poking out of the tarpaulin. The body was near the main stairs that led to the entrance of the building.

The same pattern, Oppenheimer thought. Once again, the body was lying in front of a sort of sacrificial altar, only this one rose up about forty meters above the ground. Before he lifted the tarpaulin, his heart began to pound.

He was presented with a gruesome sight. The woman's pelvic area had been positioned to face the monument, her legs spread. The injuries seemed to be identical with the first three victims. Similar to the other sites, there was little blood. There was no doubt that this was the same perpetrator. And yet Oppenheimer's first impression had deceived him. The pattern was not identical. Something was missing this time.

"What does this mean?" Oppenheimer asked in bewilderment.

"He cut her arms off," Vogler explained. "We're already searching the area to see if they are lying here somewhere."

"No arms?" Oppenheimer thought out loud. Only now did he take in anything besides the injuries. The woman lying on the ground in front of him was dressed entirely in black. The rain had almost washed away her makeup. As if by magic, the woman's face did not show the unimaginable torments that she must have gone through.

Oppenheimer stayed crouched next to her. Anger rose inside him. Anger and despair. She could still be alive if he hadn't failed so dismally. He had wasted the last weeks. The murderer had made him a culprit. He remained an enigma to Oppenheimer. Each time he believed that he could make some sense of the facts, something happened and threw everything overboard.

"Has anyone been reported missing?" Oppenheimer asked.

Vogler, leaning against one of the pillars, shook his head. "Not yet."

Oppenheimer got up, went to the top of the stairs, and looked at the grassy area that stretched out below him. "Right, well, the lady doesn't seem to have anything with her that might identify her. So we'll have to find out ourselves. She looks well cared for; I don't think she works the streets. She is wearing expensive jewelry, and as far as I can tell, she uses perfume. This is too classy. I think you should send someone to the brothels with her picture. If there was some sort of SS connection, we'll soon find out. I doubt no one will miss her. Right, now where is the witness?"

"I believe she's at the police station."

"Then I'll go and question her myself. She's probably the best thing we have right now."

■

Elfriede Becker looked at Oppenheimer with red-rimmed eyes. She'd been in the police station for four hours now, sitting on a wooden bench, exhausted, with her jacket rolled up as a neck support. "I don't want to complain, but your colleagues have already questioned me. I spent half the night in the bunker, and I have to go to work soon."

"It won't take long," Oppenheimer reassured her and sat down next to her. "So you were on your way home and saw the suspect? In Bergstraße, right by the entrance?"

Ms. Becker adjusted her glasses, pulled the jacket from behind her head, and folded it carefully. Her movements were mechanical. "I don't know if it was the perpetrator. Before I got to the gate, I saw a figure there."

"How far away were you?" Oppenheimer automatically moved closer, observing her. Ms. Becker was too tired to notice his behavior.

Her head lowered, she answered, "Maybe fifteen meters. I thought it was odd that the man ran away."

"What did he look like?"

Ms. Becker let out an annoyed groan and leaned back. "I'm afraid I can't say. I couldn't make out much because of the blackout. It was light only for a brief moment because the moon came out from behind a cloud. The light quickly disappeared again, and then I just heard steps. He probably crossed the road or disappeared behind the trees, I don't know. Anyway, by the time I got to the gate, he was gone."

"But you did see him during this brief moment, correct?"

"Well, *seeing* is going too far, but yes, I was able to get a brief glimpse of him."

"What can you say about his appearance?"

"Normal height, maybe five foot seven. Long coat. No hat."

"If he wasn't wearing a hat, what color was his hair?"

Ms. Becker looked at him uncertainly. "I would say light. I can't really remember."

"Light? Do you mean his hair was white?"

"No, it was shiny. Like Jean Harlow in the American films."

Oppenheimer tried to square the image of the peroxide blonde with the suspected perpetrator but couldn't quite picture it. Ms. Becker must have caught Oppenheimer's incredulous gaze. Apologetically, she added, "I think I might be rather tired. I just couldn't see any more than that."

Oppenheimer had learned through experience that every witness can be influenced. Many of them started doubting their own powers of observation after being repeatedly questioned and simply just confirmed what they had been told. He realized that they had almost reached that critical moment.

"We're done," he said. "Many thanks for your efforts."

Without saying good-bye, Ms. Becker grumpily pulled on her jacket and left the police station.

18

Oppenheimer didn't allow himself much sleep that morning. He merely lay down on the sofa in the flat in Zehlendorf and rested for a brief two hours amid the scraps of paper scattered all over the place. Although Vogler's people had searched the entire cemetery and the surrounding area, the victim's arms had not been found.

Vogler had made sure that the autopsy took place right away. They drove to the morgue early that afternoon to attend the examination. Dr. Gebert insisted on carrying out the autopsy himself. It was apparent that he was not very pleased to see Oppenheimer again so soon. His expression, already glum, darkened even more when he saw the body.

Oppenheimer was particularly interested in the surfaces of the cuts at the shoulders.

"Interesting," Gebert said when he inspected the area.

"How did he manage to cut the arms off?" Oppenheimer asked.

"He probably used a knife. It's quite straightforward. I'll try to put it in layman's terms. This is where the caput humeri, the upper arm bone joint, would normally sit in the socket of the shoulder blade." Gebert pointed to the light piece of bone that was visible in the flesh. "There's a hollow there. The perpetrator cut into the tissue here, and then he simply had to cut around the joint."

"So he had some knowledge of anatomy?" Oppenheimer asked.

"You mean that he might be a doctor? Not necessarily. Animal and human joints are quite similar in their construction. The method he deployed here is also used to dismember cattle."

Based on the body temperature, Dr. Gebert estimated that the murderer had killed the woman about eighteen hours ago. Her remaining injuries, including the steel nail in her ears, proved to be identical to the findings made with Inge Friedrichsen.

Oppenheimer had heard what he wanted to know and left the morgue even before Dr. Gebert had properly begun the autopsy. He wondered what the murderer had done with the woman's arms. Back in Zehlendorf, he contemplated the photographs taken at the other localities. He tried to find a pattern in the injuries that would fit with the severed arms. But hard as he tried, he couldn't discover a reasonable connection.

At least the SD, which had been called in, had hit a bull's-eye. Late afternoon, Vogler entered the room, grinning from ear to ear. "We've identified the body and know where she went about her business," he reported triumphantly.

"So she was a professional prostitute?" Oppenheimer asked.

"You were right. The woman had too much class to be an ordinary streetwalker. I got Güttler to look into it. He took the photographs to the best-known upmarket brothels. He got lucky right in the first one—Salon Kitty in Giesebrechtstraße."

∎

The next day, Oppenheimer sat in the back of Vogler's Daimler on the way to Salon Kitty. The SD man Güttler, who had discovered the dead woman's connection to the brothel, was with him. He was a nimble, friendly man and almost bald, even though he was probably only in his midthirties. Oppenheimer himself couldn't really say what had made him take Güttler along. Maybe it was the urge to have a chaperone in the shady establishment. Vogler had described him as a competent and reliable man, and Oppenheimer thought this to be an advantage in any situation. He had wanted to visit Salon Kitty already yesterday, but the owner, Kitty Schmidt, had asked him to come at a later time when the place wasn't quite so busy. It was early afternoon now, apparently the ideal time.

The Giesebrechtstraße was on the southern edge of Charlottenburg. Officially, the salon operated under the name *Guesthouse Schmidt,* but because of the raucous parties in the dead of night and the big limousines that parked outside the house almost every night, all the neighbors knew that clients were being offered more than board and lodgings. It was quite a prestigious neighborhood; SS Gruppenführer Dr. Ernst Kaltenbrunner lived right next door in number twelve. In his function as head of the Reich Security Main Office, he was also head of the Security Police and the SD. This also made him Güttler's direct supervisor. Eduard Künnecke was also said to live on the street. Oppenheimer liked his operetta *The Cousin from Nowhere,* which was really funny and masterfully orchestrated with popular tunes. It was a nice change to the operatic tragedy that Franz Lehár had become addicted to and that had drained the swing he used to have in his earlier works.

All things considered, Kitty Schmidt could not have found a more exclusive address for her house of ill repute, just a short walk away from the Kurfürstendamm. The hustle and bustle on the exclusive boulevard fitted admirably into the concept of an upmarket brothel set on attracting well-known visitors from the higher society. According to Güttler, there had been endless comings and goings of illustrious personalities, among them high-ranking militaries, diplomats, and party officials. Currently, however, the clientele was made up mainly of soldiers on leave from the front. Given just how familiar Güttler seemed to be with Salon Kitty, Oppenheimer wondered if he wasn't perhaps a client himself.

During his time with the crime squad, Oppenheimer had occasionally heard about this particular pleasure dome. Salon Kitty had an excellent reputation in the city, not only because of the ladies who plied their trade there but also because the owner, Kitty Schmidt, and her staff took discretion very seriously. Oppenheimer vaguely remembered having once heard an anecdote that a party had taken place in Kitty's spacious flat on the day of Hitler's seizure of power, which had been attended by both SA leaders and Jews. Of course, Güttler withheld this particular detail from his stories.

Hoffmann stopped outside house number eleven, while Güttler explained, "It's just here on the ground floor." It took a bit longer to get out of the vehicle because of Güttler's wooden leg.

Oppenheimer looked up at the façade. He thought he could see the edge of a provisional roof. Clearly, the building had been hit by a bomb a while ago.

When they were in the hallway outside the door to the flat, a maid in a white apron and bonnet opened the door.

"We have an appointment with Mrs. Schmidt," Oppenheimer's companion explained.

"Please come in," the maid said.

They entered a foyer with several doors leading off. The furnishings were exactly as Oppenheimer had imagined: plush, heavy curtains everywhere, a palm tree in the corner, thick carpets on the floor, stucco on the ceiling. The girl was just about to announce the visitors when one of the doors opened.

"The men from the SD," the maid said to the woman who swept into the room.

"Many thanks, Elvira. I'll take it from here," she replied.

Mrs. Schmidt played her part with courteous ease. Although Oppenheimer was in no doubt that her accommodating manner was rehearsed, it still had the desired effect. Kitty made her guests feel immediately welcome. "I'm so pleased you could arrange to come today. You have no idea how things are right now. One client after the other." It was only now that Oppenheimer got to take a closer look at Kitty Schmidt. She was a handsome woman with a pleasant face, one of those women whose precise age is hard to determine. Oppenheimer presumed she was in her late thirties.

A young woman entered the foyer. She was clearly tired, but when she saw the two men, she pulled herself together. "Good-bye, Kitty," she said as she opened the door to the stairwell. Oppenheimer wasn't sure, but it almost seemed as if she'd given Güttler a familiar wink as she passed by.

"Good-bye, my child," Kitty dismissed her employee before turning back to Oppenheimer. "As I said, lots of traffic. I don't know why, but things have been really busy in the last few weeks. It's probably best if we go to my boudoir. We won't be disturbed there."

In the so-called boudoir, Oppenheimer spotted a large oil painting. It portrayed Mrs. Schmidt with her arms folded, in half profile.

"Ah, you're admiring the painting," Mrs. Schmidt said when she noticed Oppenheimer's interest. "Yes, unfortunately no Tintoretto, but that was *way* before my time." She accompanied her comment with an indulgent smile.

"You are Mr. . . ."

Oppenheimer flinched when he realized that he hadn't introduced himself. He shook her hand. "Inspector Oppenheimer. I presume Mr. Güttler has already informed you about the matter, Mrs. Schmidt?"

Kitty hesitated briefly when she heard Oppenheimer's name. "Oh, please, do call me Kitty. Everyone does." Her smile disappeared when she remembered the murder. "Yes, Mr. Güttler already mentioned the matter of Friederike. It really is terrible. Can I offer you something to drink? Champagne, cognac, coffee?"

Kitty pressed a bell push. The maid appeared a few seconds later. "Do we have any Number 1 left?" Kitty asked.

"I'm afraid we're all out of champagne. We haven't received the new delivery from the wholesaler's yet. We'll have to order elsewhere."

"Oh, I'm so sorry." Kitty looked at Oppenheimer. "I'm afraid my guests are very thirsty. Unfortunately, it is sometimes not that easy to get your hands on champagne."

"Oh, please, don't trouble yourself," Oppenheimer said. "I'm on duty anyway. But you mentioned coffee?"

"Of course. Real coffee. Two cups, please, Elvira."

The maid curtsied and disappeared.

"You just mentioned a Friederike?" Oppenheimer said. He consulted his notebook. "According to my information, she's called Edith Zöllner."

"Of course. I forgot. Our girls all have aliases." She opened an album and passed it to Oppenheimer. "Here, our photo of her."

It was not by chance that Oppenheimer was forced to think of Christina Gerdeler when he saw the photograph. Like her, Ms. Zöllner was stretching languidly, naked, in front of the camera. The remaining photographs in the album showed other women in similar poses.

"I suppose I can remove this picture now." Kitty sighed dejectedly and fetched a bottle of gin from behind her desk. "Would you like one too, Inspector? Oh, I forgot, you're on duty." She poured herself a glass of the liqueur and took a sip.

"Your girls don't live here, do they?" Oppenheimer asked.

"No, that's not possible. I have thirty-five women working for me. That would be too much for this flat. I have their telephone numbers. My guests get presented with the albums, and they can choose which lady they want to spend time with. Then I call them at home or send someone for them, and we wait here until they appear."

"When did you last see Ms. Zöllner?"

"On Saturday evening. We were very busy. She went home around three thirty in the morning. She wanted to discuss something with my housekeeper before she left, but the woman had already gone to bed. And then on Sunday, I couldn't reach Friederike—I mean Ms. Zöllner—anymore."

"Who else works here?"

"Just two servant girls and the housekeeper."

"So you only employ women?"

"That's right."

Nobody who worked in the salon fit the description of the perpetrator. The amount of useful information that Oppenheimer got from Kitty was limited. She had no idea who the killer might be, and she couldn't remember the names of Ms. Zöllner's regulars.

Next, Oppenheimer questioned the housekeeper, who wore a simple dark dress, her hair in a bun, whose reserved demeanor didn't fit in with the setting at all.

"Rosalie, this is Inspector Oppenheimer," Kitty introduced her guest. Rosalie looked at him in surprise for a brief moment, then she mustered him as if she were looking for something.

"Hello," she said and then looked at Kitty again, who nodded almost imperceptibly and led Rosalie to a chair. Oppenheimer had a bad feeling. The women's behavior was unmistakable. They had seen through him. They had put one and one together—his name, the holes in his coat where the yellow star had been. They both knew he was a Jew. But neither said anything.

Rosalie had no idea why Ms. Zöllner had wanted to speak to her. The two women hadn't even seen each other the day she disappeared. Disappointed, Oppenheimer took his leave. He was already in the stairwell with Güttler when he heard Kitty's voice speaking quietly behind him.

"Inspector Oppenheimer?" Kitty briefly pulled him aside so that Güttler couldn't see them.

"Times must be very tough for you right now," she whispered. Then she pressed a few banknotes into his hand and said in a normal voice, "Come and see us again soon. New faces are always welcome here. Good-bye."

Then she closed the door in front of Oppenheimer's nose. He froze in surprise for a moment before hurriedly putting away the money.

Güttler was already out on the street when Oppenheimer stepped out of the building. He could not have witnessed any of the transaction. And yet Oppenheimer felt the need to explain why he had taken so long.

"She seems very keen on attracting new clientele." He did his best to smile sheepishly.

Güttler didn't comment. Instead, he nodded over toward a lorry, from which a delivery boy was unloading champagne. "There are the supplies for Kitty. Pity, we were too early today."

■

Ms. Zöllner's flat was easy to find. She lived just a few hundred meters away from Salon Kitty. The owner of the house seemed to have no idea of Ms. Zöllner's occupation and described her as a pleasant tenant who didn't make any noise, paid her rent on time, and didn't entertain any men. She'd last seen the young lady on Saturday afternoon as she left the house. This suggested that Ms. Zöllner had probably been kidnapped by the perpetrator on her way home on Saturday night. For inexplicable reasons, the murderer had not struck on Friday night as usual; this time, the body wasn't discovered until Monday morning.

Rarely had Oppenheimer had such scant evidence. Even the description of the perpetrator was so vague that they couldn't put it to good use. When he again went through the report Vogler's men had put together based on Ms. Becker's interview, he stopped short. He compared their notes to his own and realized that Ms. Becker's statements differed. In the first interview, she had said that the man she'd seen was dark-haired. But to him, she'd described him as being blond. Oppenheimer could clearly recall her saying that the hair color was like Jean Harlow's. Witnesses were often uncertain, but it was more than unusual for them to give such completely opposing details. Oppenheimer grabbed his jacket and called, "Where is Hoffmann?"

■

MEN *aged between 16–70 should be at the front, not in the BUNKER,* the graffiti on the house wall urged. *Our walls are breaking, but our hearts aren't—the führer commands, we follow,* a placard clarified the situation.

These were the usual paroles that could be found all over the city and also adorned the house that Ms. Becker had given as her place of residence. But as Oppenheimer stood outside the building, he found himself at a loss. It was highly unlikely that Ms. Becker was going to ask him into her flat—her house no longer existed. The external walls remained as if to add insult to injury. The house would have looked untouched if the façade had not been covered in soot and if through the window frames one had not been able to see the gray sky instead of curtains.

Still bewildered by this discovery, Oppenheimer shifted from one foot to the other. He went through the chronology of events in his mind. The bombing had taken place the night from Sunday to Monday. When he'd interviewed Ms. Becker, she'd just returned from a nearby bunker. Could it be that she hadn't known about the destruction of her flat?

There was a butcher's directly opposite. When Oppenheimer walked in, the place was empty, which wasn't unusual in these times of rationing. The butcher was sitting behind his display on a stool, having a nap.

"Excuse me?" Oppenheimer said loudly to wake the man in the white apron.

But the man just mumbled, "Come back tomorrow. Nothing here today."

"Maybe you can help me. I'm looking for Ms. Becker. She lives opposite, in number thirty-four."

The butcher pushed his cap back and sat up. "Number thirty-four? You're out of luck. Didn't you know? Berlin is a city of used-to-be houses. There used to be one here. There used to be one there." He chuckled contentedly.

"Was Ms. Becker bombed out Sunday night?"

"On Sunday? No, that happened about two weeks ago."

Oppenheimer thought he must have misheard. But when he asked again, the butcher confirmed that Ms. Becker had been bombed out before the invasion began. He had no idea where she was living now, but she occasionally passed by to buy some meat.

Oppenheimer trudged back out, crossed the street, and examined the pieces of paper stuck on the front door. There was no new address for Ms. Becker among them. So the only remaining option was to question the neighbors.

Like everywhere in the city, the neighbors tended to gather at the public water pumps. As many pipes had been destroyed and the water supply was interrupted frequently, the street fountains had become the new focal point of daily life. Oppenheimer had to search for a while, as the access to the water supply was hidden behind the gutted remains of a car. A woman was filling her two water buckets. Another was sitting on the pavement, soaping her washing, chattering to her neighbor. Although the two women turned out to be very willing to help, they couldn't tell Oppenheimer where Ms. Becker had moved to.

Disgruntled, he had the driver take him back to Zehlendorf. While Hoffmann indulged in his speed rush, Oppenheimer, crammed into the sidecar, thought hard. Their witness had given two differing statements regarding the perpetrator and then had gone on to give a false address. "Has everyone gone bonkers?" Oppenheimer swore loudly.

∎

That same afternoon, he called for Güttler to come and see him. "I have a job for you," Oppenheimer explained. "Find Ms. Elfriede Becker for me. It's urgent. Here is her old address. She was bombed out about two weeks ago. I have no idea where she lives now. But it must be somewhere in Steglitz. She still shops at her old butcher's."

Güttler took the piece of paper with the address. "I understand. I suggest I first go to missing persons and then to the registration office. It's pretty chaotic there nowadays, but maybe I'll get lucky. As it's urgent, I would also suggest that we position a colleague outside the butcher's. If Ms. Becker should shop there again, the butcher can point her out to us."

Oppenheimer was happy. Vogler hadn't promised too much; Güttler was a quick thinker. "That sounds good; let's do it. If you manage to get hold of the new address, please inform me immediately."

Güttler hesitated. "Just one more question. I am currently assigned to another investigation."

"Talk to Vogler. I'll take responsibility. And tell him that I specifically asked for your support. I give you free rein, Güttler. I don't care how you go about it, just find the woman."

"Right away," Güttler said and put his hat back on. His eyes shone with the zeal of a hunter.

∎

Despite quite some hustle and bustle, the next day passed uneventfully. As Kitty couldn't or wouldn't name her clients, Oppenheimer put together a list of all suspects. When he asked her if one of her clients was among them, she couldn't identify anyone but promised to ask her girls later.

Meanwhile, Vogler had the editor's mailbox of *Der Angriff* observed. The killer had posted the last letter himself, but since the latest murder, no new letter had arrived at the newspaper.

Güttler also hadn't had any luck. Ms. Becker remained untraceable. She was not registered anywhere and had not reappeared at the butcher's either. Güttler's next step was to check the registration offices in the nearby vicinity. His determination to find the woman seemed to have been spurred on even further by the setback.

Vogler was in high spirits on Friday, which surprised Oppenheimer a little, as there were still no new leads. He concluded that it must have something to do with the military situation on the western front. Frustrated, he sat among mountains of papers, drank coffee until his stomach rebelled, and finally headed off home.

When Oppenheimer returned to the Jewish House, Lisa was still at work. He found an old piece of bread and ate it, together with some of the late Dr. Klein's sausage. It required quite some effort to eat the donated food, as Oppenheimer kept thinking of the old doctor. He was hoping fervently that the Allied forces would soon reach the city and put an end to the nightmare. But the eastern front line was still far away, in Karelia, things were progressing slowly in Italy, and the invasion at the western front seemed not to have advanced much in the last days either. The fact that there was so little news from Normandy suggested that both sides were probably still gathering their troops, not yet prepared to strike. The weather in Normandy also remained bad, and the enemy air force only saw limited action. In this situation, the hopes of the National Socialists lay with General Field Marshal Rommel, who had taken over the defense of the Atlantic Wall. Oppenheimer considered Rommel to be undoubtedly capable, but unfortunately, he was on the wrong side. The Americans and British had so far been unable to capture a single harbor in order to organize their reinforcements from there. As long as that didn't take place, everything was left hanging.

When Lisa came home, Oppenheimer found out the reason for Vogler's euphoria.

"The bastards shot flying bombs at England," she said before she'd even taken off her coat. "Can you imagine? Simply fired them across the channel. The whole time, my colleagues were talking about the V-1. Apparently, the whole of London has been destroyed."

Oppenheimer's mouthful got stuck in his throat. "What are you saying? I thought that was just propaganda."

"Apparently not. People are already placing bets that the war will be over in a week. Maybe you should organize gas masks for us."

"You mean the British might risk a gas war?"

"A lot of people are talking about it."

Just the thought of it was horrifying to Oppenheimer. He had been exposed to numerous gas attacks in the last war, always anxiously hoping that his gas mask would work. He had been incredibly lucky back then to have gotten off scot-free, in contrast to some of his comrades, who had died in insufferable agony. One thing was clear: with the V-1, the führer had heralded a new phase of war. It wouldn't take long for the British to reciprocate. But Oppenheimer didn't want to give up hope that they would not resort to this final, dirty method. "Maybe it won't be as bad as all that. You shouldn't measure the English by German benchmarks. Churchill is no Hitler."

"Nonetheless, will you promise to get masks?"

Oppenheimer thought for a moment. "As soon as I get back to Zehlendorf, I'll see what I can do."

As the situation was very worrying, Oppenheimer decided to invest some of the money Kitty had given him in a visit to the cinema. He hoped to discover more in the weekly newsreel. They could make the evening performance at seven thirty. "What do you think?" he asked Lisa. "Do you fancy watching a film?"

Oppenheimer needed a while to convince Lisa to come along. She thought it too risky, as Jews were not allowed to go to the cinema. Finally, he promised her that they would only sneak into the auditorium once the lights had gone off and the preview was running. Just as they were going down the stairs, Old Mr. Schlesinger emerged from the cellar. When he saw them, he said, "Mr. Oppenheimer, I have a letter for you!"

Oppenheimer and Lisa exchanged glances. They had occasionally talked about why Schlesinger should be entitled to accept the entire postal delivery from the postman, to then distribute it to the tenants. Lisa suspected that the old man opened all the envelopes over steam to read them. But Oppenheimer didn't want to get involved in lengthy discussions and decided to grin and bear it.

"Most kind of you to have collected my post for me," he replied amiably.

Schlesinger went back into his room and returned with an envelope. Oppenheimer looked at it briefly. There was no sender on the envelope.

"For you," Schlesinger said, a challenge in his voice.

"Many thanks, Mr. Schlesinger," Oppenheimer said and tucked the letter into the inside pocket of his coat.

"What could that be?" Lisa asked as they walked down the pavement.

"No idea," Oppenheimer replied. "But I didn't want to open it in front of Schlesinger."

Oppenheimer had decided against changing his outfit in the Beusselkiez. He didn't care if a pursuer saw him sneaking into a screening. It was a risk he could take as long as he was working for Vogler. They got on the subway at Tiergarten and stayed on for two stops until Savignyplatz. There were several cinemas on Kurfürstendamm, but Oppenheimer didn't know exactly which one had been bombed. Luckily, the first one they came across was the UFA Palast Kurfürstendamm, which still seemed to be operating. Today, they were showing a film with Gustav Fröhlich and Otto Wernicke. But Oppenheimer didn't really care what film they bought tickets for.

While they waited in the foyer to be admitted, Oppenheimer checked that the envelope was still in his inside pocket. He didn't dare to open the letter while the audience was pouring into the auditorium. It was safer to wait until the weekly newsreel started.

The gong sounded, and the room went dark. Oppenheimer and Lisa sneaked into the auditorium and sat in the first free seats they came across. The curtain opened, displaying the imperial eagle that marked the beginning of the weekly newsreel. A stylized calendar sheet appeared showing the date of June 6, 1944. "A date of global significance," the speaker said. "Under pressure from Moscow, the British and Americans have finally begun the long-announced invasion we had been expecting. It finds Germany at the ready."

This was followed by images of soldiers running through the corridors of the Atlantic Wall. A nighttime artillery skirmish was shown, during which Oppenheimer was unable to recognize much more than the glowing traces of the projectiles. There was the sound of artillery and the flare of an explosion. So far, the footage was not unusual, but the next scene caused the audience to freeze. It had been shot with a remote camera just before the invasion began. Only two camera angles were shown, but these few seconds took Oppenheimer's breath away.

He saw the Atlantic. Dancing on the waves were not white foam caps but millions of tons of iron. The horizon seemed to be filled entirely with ships. Then there was nothing but artillery fire, flames from flamethrowers, smoke everywhere. The action on the beach was not shown, just empty landing boats, and the commentator claimed that their crew had been killed or captured. Then came images of smashed military gliders, parachutes hanging in trees, the destroyed city of Caen, captured assailants, and time and again images of German soldiers who seemed to be in complete control. After a while, Oppenheimer barely listened to the shrill voice coming from the loudspeakers. He had never seen anything like it in his life. It didn't matter what the commentary to the newsreel was; these forceful images rendered moot all attempts to play things down.

The National Socialists' opponents seemed to have inexhaustible reserves at their disposal; they had enough weapons and were clearly not suffering from a lack of petrol. The rest of the world was sending their sons to sacrifice themselves on these shores for freedom's sake, and there were enough of them. Oppenheimer physically felt the cinema audience being gripped by a frozen discomfort. Lisa, too, had reached for his hand in agitation. The people stared at the screen in horror.

It took a few minutes after the coverage finished for the first people to stir. Several members of the audience left their seats, no longer interested in the main film that was about to start. Quiet whispers started in the row in front of Oppenheimer.

"Well, our flats will be nice and toasty soon."

"Why is that?"

"When they take down all the portraits of the führer, we'll have plenty of firewood!"

The usual reaction to a joke like that failed to materialize. No giggling, just an acknowledging murmur could be heard.

Oppenheimer furtively pulled the envelope from the inside pocket of his jacket. The light reflected from the screen was just enough to be able to read the words.

Hilde had sent him a message. But what could be so important to make her send him a letter? He held the piece of paper up close to his eyes.

I must talk to you. It's very important. Come and see me at 1:00 p.m. on Saturday. That was all it said. Signed with an *H*.

∎

The sirens howled. Swaying unsteadily on her high heels, Traudel Herrmann stepped into the dark street.

"Are you sure you don't want to come into our bunker?" Marga, the wife of Gruppenleiter Kriegler, asked. They'd had a merry evening. The other guests had already left, but Traudel stayed on as usual. "We can also go into the cellar," Marga said. "It's safe. Reinforced concrete. We can get comfy down there."

Traudel shook her head. "It's best I'm home when Rainer gets in. He had to go to a meeting and didn't know how long he'd be." Of course, Traudel knew he'd lied. Rainer was having an affair with another woman. She had seen the telltale signs—strange lipstick on his collar, scratch marks on his back one time. He couldn't hide it from her even if he tried. But she didn't care which slut her husband was humping at the moment. Life with him offered enough comforts for her to ignore this small detail. And anyway, Rainer was similarly tolerant in these matters.

Something in Marga's gaze said that she wasn't prepared to let her friend leave like this. "It's dangerous. Please stay here. You don't know what might happen. Didn't you hear about the warnings?"

Traudel vaguely recalled a warning of potential kidnappings directed at family members of SS officers. "Nothing's going to happen to me. Gustav is driving me. He can take care of me. We'll manage the few kilometers to Köpenick before the attack."

"Wait, I'll come with you," said Marga and tied her head scarf. Traudel thought it a good idea that Marga accompany her, as she was feeling quite tipsy from all the wine.

"You know, our new girl," Traudel began as Marga supported her, "I think it was a mistake to hire her. I have to keep checking up on her to make sure she's doing her job. When Rainer gets home and nothing's been prepared for him, he'll get very angry."

Marga stopped and looked around. "Where is the car, actually?"

Traudel joined her in staring into the darkness. The limousine was not waiting in the street. She was just about to take up Marga's offer and return to the house when she suddenly remembered. "Ah yes, he's waiting in the side street. Over there." She changed direction and headed toward a dark alley. In the pitch-black night, one could barely make out the chassis. Traudel had no idea why, but Gustav didn't like to park on the main road. Maybe he feared that an envious passerby might damage the car. Not everyone could afford such a luxury vehicle, let alone the petrol that the engine guzzled.

Marga accompanied Traudel to the corner. The car door opened, and the familiar figure of Gustav in his chauffeur's uniform became discernible.

Traudel stopped. "It's all right. Go back to your bunker." She gave her friend a good-bye hug and disappeared into the darkness. Marga could just make her out approaching the vehicle. Gustav held open the rear door and helped her get in.

The engine started.

When the car drove past Marga, she waved. Traudel waved back from behind the window. For a moment, it occurred to Marga that the heavy vehicles with their large windows sometimes looked like aquariums. The passengers seemed like trapped fish. But then she put the thought aside and laughed at her own eccentricity. The sound of the engine disappeared into the distance.

Marga was about to turn around and return to the bunker when she noticed something. A movement. She had had the experience before that she could distinguish things better in complete darkness if she looked past them. Something was lying on the ground in the alleyway. It was nothing more than a light shimmer.

Marga hesitated, wondering what to do. She remembered the warning that had come through a few days ago. Wasn't she putting herself in unnecessary danger if she walked down a dark alleyway in the middle of the night? She looked around once more. There were also other people on their way to the bunker, walking along the main road. The sight of them made Marga feel safe. She could always call for help if necessary.

She took a hesitant step into the alleyway, then the next. It was only five strides until her right foot touched something. She hadn't been mistaken. It was a body.

When she knelt, she realized what the light shimmer had been. A man wearing a white shirt was lying in front of her. She felt the stranger's face. She felt his stubble, stroked his cheek to wake him up.

"Hello. Are you unwell? The alarm has sounded. You have to get to the bunker."

The response was a groan. Marga realized that her left hand was damp. She held her fingers in front of her face and perceived the metallic smell of blood.

"Oh my God, what happened to you?"

The man was coming around. He tried to sit up. Marga helped as well as she could, but it took a while for him to sit up against the wall of the building. Marga took his hand. "Come along. We have to get to the bunker."

She began to pull him behind her, past her front door that was still partially open. The light from the hallway spilled out into the street. Annoyed, Marga thought how careless she'd been. She'd completely forgotten the blackout order.

"Wait here." She leaned the man against the doorway. And hesitated. In the weak light, his face somehow seemed familiar. She went to the front door and opened it, disobeying all blackout orders.

When the lamplight lit up the man's face, Marga froze. Her eyes widened in disbelief. Of course she knew him. It was Gustav, Traudel's chauffeur. "Gustav, what are you doing here?" She quickly went back down the steps to the front door to look at him more closely. There was blood on the back of his head. Someone had struck him down.

Confused, Marga looked in the direction her friend had just disappeared. If Gustav was here, who was at the wheel of the car? She felt her insides clench. Now she was seriously worried about Traudel.

■

When Oppenheimer arrived outside Hilde's house, it was a quarter to one. He was early, but he didn't want to wait any longer. He knocked on the door of the side building where Hilde had her flat. She opened after a few seconds. Her face revealed that she had not been expecting him yet.

"Oh, you're here already," Hilde said and glanced out into the street.

"Nobody followed me," Oppenheimer reassured her.

"Well, come in, then."

After he took off his coat, they faced each other, both of them embarrassed. Then Hilde said, "Shitty weather, right?"

"I hope the summer doesn't stay this rainy."

"I presume you don't want a small schnapps?" Hilde went through the treatment room into the living room.

"I'd prefer coffee. If you happen to have any left over, that is."

"Of course. Coming right up." She seemed happy to have an excuse to disappear into the kitchen and left Oppenheimer standing there, all dressed up with nowhere to go. Then he saw his gramophone and the record collection. He felt like listening to Johann Sebastian Bach today. He picked out a recording from the so-called *Coffee Cantata*. This seemed a suitable choice in the given situation. The actual title, *Be Still, Stop Chattering*, was an irony that Hilde would surely not appreciate. As soon as the first sounds emanated from the horn, Oppenheimer went over to the kitchen door and asked, "So, why did you ask me to come? What's so important?"

Hilde poured steaming water into the coffee filter, then she replied, "There are a few things that you should know about the prostitute that you found in Steglitz."

Oppenheimer looked at her in surprise. "Hilde, how do you know about that?"

"You have no idea of all the information I've managed to obtain." While the coffee passed through, she leaned against the kitchen table and crossed her arms. "Richard, I have a confession to make. I let a few people in on the matter. Please understand, it wasn't about having you followed, but when I found out the murders were all somehow linked to the party or party officials, I had no other choice. You have to trust me. This case is politically charged and could become dangerous to you. I wanted to know what was going on, which is why I consulted some experts in the matter."

Oppenheimer wanted to ask what she meant by that when there was a knock on the door.

"I presume that's them," Hilde said and left the kitchen to open the door.

Voices could be heard from the treatment room. Hilde spoke to the newcomers, then they appeared in the living room. Two men in suits. While the clothing could be described as inconspicuous, the same could not really be said of its wearers. Hilde introduced her guests to one another. "This is Inspector Oppenheimer."

"Lüttke," said the taller man with round spectacles, shaking Oppenheimer's hand. His movements were precise. Oppenheimer suspected a military background. Then the second man shook his hand. "Bauer," he said and nodded affirmatively. The man named Bauer was of a compacter build. His elegant movements were in stark contrast to his partner's. His left cheek was embellished with a so-called Schmiss, an old fencing scar that had left a deep gash. It was the usual mark of members of a dueling fraternity at university.

When they had made themselves comfortable in the living room, Hilde served coffee. Despite the warm beverage, the atmosphere remained cold. Oppenheimer studied the two men in an attempt to suss them out. Lüttke and Bauer were doing the same with him. They watched one another like poker players; neither of them wanted to be the first to show his hand. This could have gone on for minutes, had Hilde not taken the initiative.

"Well, you're all a right bunch of mystery-mongers," she said after she'd looked back and forth between the men. "I'll make a start, then." Hilde looked at Oppenheimer. "So this is top secret. Not even arse-face Vogler has the guts to tell you this. The dead girl you found in Steglitz was a member of the SS paramilitaries."

19

Over the next few hours, Oppenheimer could hardly believe his ears. The woman whom he had found dead in front of the water tower was a person with many identities. In Kitty's Salon, she was known under her alias Friederike, she rented her flat under the name Edith Zöllner, but in her former life, she'd been known as Verena Opitz.

She'd been a highly intelligent woman, spoken fluent French and Italian. Before she'd started working for Kitty, she'd been ordered by the SS to take a course in home economics and catering at an NSDAP Order Castle in the Bavarian town of Sonthofen and had also received training in pistol shooting and judo. However, Friederike, alias Edith Zöllner, alias Verena Opitz, was not the only prostitute working in Kitty's Salon with a background like this. She belonged to a group of around twenty women who were trained by the SS to spy upon clients. They were all extremely attractive, came from various parts of the German Reich, from Austria, from the protectorates Bohemia and Moravia, even from Poland. Each of them had been known to the police for sexual offenses in the past.

"They spy for the SS," Lüttke explained. "Initially, they were answerable to the security service of the Reich Leader SS, which has since been absorbed by the Reich Security Main Office, the RSHA. We believe that SS Oberführer Walter Schellenberg is behind the matter. He heads up Department IV, the foreign intelligence service."

Oppenheimer looked doubtfully at the man explaining all this. "Who comes up with something like that?" He shook his head. "I've never heard anything so stupid. I mean, prostitutes with judo training who act as spies? It sounds just like a child's image of Mata Hari."

"The idea is said to have come from Heydrich himself when he was still head of the RSHA."

Upon mention of that name, Bauer gave a derogative snort. "Heydrich definitely read too many cheap novels and confused them with reality."

Oppenheimer recapitulated in his mind what he remembered about Heydrich to properly classify the information. Basically, he only knew that Heydrich used to be the head of the RSHA. At some point, he was made deputy Reich Protector of Bohemia and Moravia, which was why he had to move to Prague to take care of the official business. He was assassinated in 1942, and the party organized a huge funeral ceremony when Heydrich was buried in the Invalids' Cemetery in Berlin. He was elevated to be a martyr, while others wearing the party uniform filled his post. Whoever these two visitors might be, they seemed to have little sympathy for the RSHA in general and for Heydrich in particular.

"Schellenberg and the people in his intelligence service are amateurs," Bauer concluded. "But that's exactly what makes them dangerous. Their reactions can't be gauged. The plan was to systematically introduce the female agents to military personnel, foreign diplomats, and high-ranking party functionaries in the brothel so that they could spy on them. During the act of love, so to speak. They had bugged the entire place and listened in on everything. We only found out in January 1941 when Obersturmführer Schwarz arranged for a direct line to be laid to the RSHA offices in Prinz-Albrecht-Straße."

Oppenheimer looked somewhat confused, and Bauer felt the need to explain in more detail. "Schwarz was entrusted with carrying out this project. But the idiot actually thought we wouldn't notice that he had ordered miles of copper cable. It was obvious that something was going on. There were dozens of shorthand typists at the RSHA transcribing the conversations transmitted directly from the brothel. They also made wax disc recordings."

"Originally, the brothel was on the third floor," Lüttke said. "After the house was hit by an aircraft bomb, they had to move down to the ground floor. We're assuming they didn't put in any new listening devices.

Officially, the project seems to have been shelved for the time being. The yield seems to have been too limited."

"Naturally, they didn't inform their whores," Bauer said with a slimy grin. "They still think they are being shagged for the German Fatherland."

"That means that all of Kitty's whores are from the SS?" Oppenheimer wanted to know.

"No, only about half of her good-time girls are SS," Lüttke clarified. "The rest more or less take care of walk-in customers."

Bauer disagreed. "That used to be the case, but now they go on the game in the usual way, write the odd report, and that's it. Nobody at the RSHA gives a damn about them anymore. The project is dead." He cast Lüttke an amused glance. "I bet Schellenberg was irritated by the fact that none of our boys spilled when they were at Kitty's."

"Lucky we picked up on it in time," Lüttke agreed.

Oppenheimer interrupted them. "I'm sorry, but what organization are you from?"

"They're on our side," Hilde said categorically.

"What's that supposed to mean, *on our side*? Who am I dealing with here? Why am I here?"

Lüttke and Bauer looked at each other in silence. Hilde finally said, "They're on our side. They're from the Bureau Canaris."

"Or what's left of it," Lüttke said in resignation.

Oppenheimer shook his head. "Doesn't mean anything to me."

"I'll try to summarize," Hilde said with a sigh. "Correct me if I get anything wrong. There are two organizations here in Germany that deal with foreign espionage. There is Department IV in the Reich Security Main Office run by Heydrich. Since his death, Schellenberg is the big boss. The second organization is the Wehrmacht Intelligence, headed up by Admiral Canaris."

"So there are two organizations doing the same job?" Oppenheimer asked incredulously.

"Are you surprised? There must be a reason for the huge growth of the party machine."

"And if two organizations do the same thing, how is that meant to work?"

"That, precisely, is the problem," Lüttke said. "It doesn't work. It never did. Officially, our services' competences were divided up. We call it our ten commandments. Each was supposed to be active in a different field. We were meant to cover the military section."

"But no one sticks to it," Bauer added. "The SS bastards kept interfering. Even when Heydrich was still alive, he was always at loggerheads with Canaris."

Hilde cast Oppenheimer a smug glance. "You can imagine what this means. One spy service poaches in the other's territory. And on top of that, they spy on each other too. The situation is as follows: Canaris also employed people who openly worked against the regime. He knew about it and so far has been able to cover for them."

"That was the case until February, to be precise," Lüttke said.

Oppenheimer had never heard of anyone opposing Hitler from within his own organization. He suddenly realized what the connection to Hilde was. Among her acquaintances, there were many who worked against Hitler, and she was also the niece of an officer. The Wehrmacht had been around a lot longer than the NSDAP. The SS men could parade their martial behavior as much as they wanted; officially, they were just party loyalists and didn't have much in common with the long-established military men. Oppenheimer could imagine military personnel acting against the upstart Hitler. Seen from that perspective, it was understandable that both organizations tried to outstrip each other. And espionage seemed to be one of the main sites for battling it out.

"Why can Canaris not provide more cover for his men? What happened in February?" Oppenheimer wanted to know.

Lüttke explained, "One of our female agents defected to the British while she was in Turkey. It was a welcome opportunity for Schellenberg to remove Canaris from office. He had to step down at the end of the month. They packed Canaris off to Lauenstein Castle in Frankenwald, where he's passing his time until he's forced out of office. We don't know what's happening to our service after that. It will probably be dissolved, and our employees will have to report to the RSHA."

Oppenheimer shrugged. "That's all very well, but I don't understand what I've got to do with it."

"This is where the murder cases you're working on come into play,"

Hilde replied. "When I got the impression that the murders were politically motivated, I told Mr. Lüttke about it."

"We want to ask you whether you would consider working with us," Lüttke said.

"And what would that require me to do?"

"We need information, nothing more. Details about the ongoing investigation. In particular if a connection to the intelligence services or one of our employees should emerge."

Oppenheimer grew curious. "Do you really think that someone from your ranks is the murderer?"

"Of course not, no," Bauer interjected. He had been shifting on his chair restlessly for a while now, watching Oppenheimer with a hostile expression. "Of course it wasn't one of us. But these bastards are going to try to link our department to the murders. The murder of that prostitute from Schellenberg's shop gave them that opportunity. Then they'd have free rein and could throw each and every one of us to the wolves. Just as they see fit. And Hauptsturmführer Vogler is a flunky. He probably works for them. It's all part of one and the same shop anyhow."

"We don't care who carried out the murders," Lüttke clarified. "We just want to protect our own people."

"Hmm . . . of course, I'll have to think about the offer," Oppenheimer said.

"I've already spoken to Richard about the matter," Hilde suddenly said. Oppenheimer looked at her in surprise. This was an outright lie, but she seemed to be up to something. "He would be prepared to pass on information about the investigation if you arrange for him to get out of the country. Him and his wife."

"Completely out of the question!" Bauer blustered.

Lüttke leaned back with a sharp breath. Then he said slowly, "It wouldn't be impossible. Just very, very difficult."

"We would never get authorization," Bauer replied.

Hilde had done a good job. Oppenheimer realized that she hadn't abused his trust without reason. With a bit of luck, this was his ticket out of the murderous madness that Hitler and his helpers carried out day after day. Oppenheimer decided to join the gamble. "As Hilde said, that's my offer."

"Ask for something else," Bauer demanded.

"Don't give me that," Hilde said. "You have the means. If anyone can manage to smuggle people out of Germany, it's you. We're just talking about two false passports. The intelligence service has years of experience of transporting people over long distances. Two more people is not going to be noticed."

Bauer shook his head vehemently. "You women and your ideas!"

"I am still an officer's niece," Hilde retaliated, her chin thrust out. "I know how things get done. Richard is a person entrusted with confidential information. Do you have any idea what will happen if it becomes public knowledge that he spied for you? If he gets involved with you, he's vulnerable. So at least make sure that he gets out of it all in one piece."

Lüttke considered the matter for a moment. "Obviously, I can't decide immediately. We'll be in touch." He picked up his hat, shook hands, and left.

"Well, I'm against it," Bauer grumbled.

■

When the two had left, Oppenheimer gave Hilde the latest news. The discovery of the letter of confession, in particular, got Hilde very interested. "Thinking about it, I'm almost inclined to believe that Dot and Anton are on the wrong track," she finally said.

Oppenheimer shot Hilde a questioning look, but then he remembered that she liked to give everyone nicknames and concluded that she meant Bauer and Lüttke. However, it seemed that Hilde had confused Erich Kästner's children's book *Dot and Anton* with *Emil and the Detectives*.

Hilde shook her head, lost in thought. "I believe that our murderer's political agenda is just a pretext."

This conclusion came as a surprise to Oppenheimer. "How do you mean?"

"If your information is correct, then he's targeting prostitutes. He has a pathological aversion to them that goes so deep that he kills them. Sometimes mass murderers justify their own deeds. Why they have this urge has not yet been fully explained. I'm guessing that each perpetrator has a different reason. Many will surely have the need to justify their deeds to themselves. Don't forget that with the first murder, the perpetrator doesn't have a routine yet; he might well even be shocked by his own deed. And yet he feels the urge to kill again. So a sex murderer needs a reason to justify further deeds to himself."

Oppenheimer wanted to make sure he'd understood everything properly. "You mean it's like with schizophrenics who say their deeds were guided externally?"

"Yes, sort of, only in this case it's not an external power that seems to influence the murderer but he himself who is searching for reasons for his behavior to be able to accept it. Mentally stable people have a hard time understanding this logic. From a distance, I can't say for sure where our murderer's delusions originate, but looking at his letters, he seems to want to justify his deeds to himself."

"And you think that the reason he gave, National Socialism being infected by prostitutes, is not the decisive one?"

"You can forget the whole political rubbish he spouts. He states quite clearly that he hates prostitutes because they transmit diseases. It wouldn't surprise me if something similar happened to him. He's projecting his personal experience onto the state, which obviously shows clear signs of delusions of grandeur."

"If that's true, then why of all people did he choose a prostitute who worked as a spy for the SS?"

"That might just as well have been pure coincidence. Salon Kitty is almost tailor-made for our murderer. A renowned house of ill repute that is frequented by prominent party cadres and the military. These circumstances alone suffice to make the place interesting to our murderer. Sooner or later, he simply had to show up there. If I'd known about his letters earlier, we might have realized this sooner and could have prevented the most recent murder."

"Around half the women are supposed to have been spies," Oppenheimer pondered, the cigarette tip in his mouth. "The likelihood that he was going to get one of them was relatively high. So the murderer doesn't necessarily have to have known about the espionage activities. It's a pity, actually; otherwise, the pool of suspects would have grown smaller."

"At least Dot and Anton will be happy to hear about the murderer's letter." Hilde added, in a confidential tone, "I wouldn't tell them about it too soon, though. Let them squirm for a while and try to get as much out of the situation for yourself as you can."

"I wonder what they want with the information," Oppenheimer mumbled, lost in thought.

"It doesn't matter. That's the way the intelligence services work. Everyone tries to gather as much information as possible. Whether it's actually useful is another matter. They both say they want to protect their colleagues who are working against the party. That may be. But maybe they just want to use their insights to obtain a better position when their shop gets subordinated to the RSHA. Don't worry about it. You now have the chance of getting out of Germany. Use it."

■

By the time Oppenheimer headed home from the Beusselkiez, it had started to bucket down from the gray, overcast sky. Like Oppenheimer, Hilde had been surprised to hear that the murderer had abandoned his usual pattern. The fact that he hadn't sent a letter particularly irritated her. In contrast, Oppenheimer, for his part, was unsettled by Hilde's assumption that the perpetrator might have stopped communicating by letter to soon do so by other means. He wondered what that might be. Oppenheimer had a sense of foreboding.

As he climbed over several piles of rubble that littered the pavement, he was annoyed by the torn soles of his shoes. His socks soaked up the water in the puddles and ensured that his toes felt uncomfortably cold. Hilde had given him a new pair of shoes from her stash. But Oppenheimer carried them under his arm to protect them. At least his other decision, to take along a second umbrella today, had been a good one. This way, he could lead his pursuers in the Beusselkiez on a wild-goose chase and still stay dry.

Oppenheimer only had a few more meters to go when he heard a siren in the distance and then another noise nearby. Initially, he couldn't place it, until he spotted an air raid warden's steel helmet. The man was banging a gong to warn the residents of the air raid. It appeared that the nearest siren had been destroyed.

Because of the gong, Oppenheimer couldn't hear his pursuer's footsteps. As usual, the man had followed him to the Beusselkiez today and was now approaching. When Oppenheimer heard someone wading through a puddle behind him, it was already too late. Suddenly, a hand reached out and descended on his shoulder.

An unfamiliar voice asked, "Richard Oppenheimer?"

Oppenheimer spun round. Facing the man, he realized that he was armed only with two umbrellas. A car glided by a few meters behind the stranger and stopped at the side of the road. At the man's next words, Oppenheimer knew resistance was futile. "Sicherheitsdienst. Get in."

20

Goddamn it, where have you been?" Vogler was completely beside himself. "We've taken apart the entire building you disappeared into—nothing! No Inspector Oppenheimer!"

This meant his cover was blown. Oppenheimer stood in the hallway of the Zehlendorf house, still in his coat. So he would have to come up with another way of visiting Hilde in the future. "I went for a walk to clear my head," was Oppenheimer's lame reply, which sounded even absurder given the fact that he was holding two umbrellas and a pair of shoes in his hand.

"I don't care what you do as long as you tell me where you are! He's struck again."

Oppenheimer felt the blood freeze in his veins. As usual, Hoffmann had said nothing in the car when he had brought him here. "Already?" he asked in anguish.

"Yes, already! Traudel Herrmann, the wife of a Gruppenleiter. She was reported missing a few hours ago. Leave your coat on. You're going straight to Köpenick."

■

He hasn't killed her yet. We can still stop it, Oppenheimer thought when he stood in the Herrmanns' living room. It seemed that the Gruppenleiter was a vain man. There were photographs of him in his full SS uniform everywhere—*in full dress,* as the saying went. There he stood, his chest proudly pushed out above the beginnings of a paunch, a well-built man in his prime with steel helmet and combat pack. Almost no one would have recognized this man in the huddled bundle in the armchair. His body seemed to have shrunk over the last few hours, his face was red with anxiety, his gaze already a little glassy as if he'd already tried unsuccessfully to comfort himself with hard liquor.

"Please try to remember," Oppenheimer addressed him once more. "Every tiny detail can be important. When exactly did you come home last night?"

"I didn't look at my watch," Herrmann said hoarsely. "It must have been around three in the morning. At first, I noticed that the car was parked at the side of the road. I wondered why Gustav—he's our chauffeur—hadn't put the car into the garage. That's negligent. You never know what's going to happen if you just leave it outside. Gustav is usually very conscientious. I decided to speak to him about it in the morning. Then I went straight to bed and fell asleep."

"You and your wife have separate bedrooms?"

"Exactly. Silke hadn't put out my pajamas, but I was so tired that I didn't really think about it much. I just flaked out."

"Silke is . . ."

"Our maid. We haven't had her long."

"What happened this morning?"

Herrmann got up and went over to his cocktail cabinet. He poured himself a cognac. "It was just a couple of hours later. Marga Kriegler, my wife's friend, finally managed to rouse Silke. She said she'd tried to reach us several times during the night after the alarm, but no one had answered. She told us that Gustav had been beaten up, that a stranger had taken our car and kidnapped my wife. Initially, I didn't want to believe her, but Traudel wasn't in her room, and Silke hadn't seen either of them yet either. So I called the police. I've been sitting here ever since waiting for something to happen."

"Have you moved the car?"

"No, it's exactly there where I found it."

The car, at least, was a lead. Oppenheimer stepped outside into the rain, Vogler close behind.

"What did Mrs. Kriegler say?" Oppenheimer asked. "When did the stranger disappear with Mrs. Herrmann?"

"Around midnight."

"So three hours at most. Three hours to move the woman and park the car here again. Why did he take the risk of bringing it back?"

"Maybe a limousine like this would be too conspicuous in his neighborhood," Vogler said.

"Good point," Oppenheimer concurred. Then he turned to the vehicle. "Has anyone secured the evidence in the car yet?"

"I wanted you to look at it first." Vogler opened the rear passenger door. Oppenheimer leaned across the seats.

"Leather, that's good. Maybe he left some fingerprints. Hmm. A fight took place. I presume that this tuft of hair belongs to Mrs. Herrmann." Oppenheimer showed Vogler some hair he'd found on the back seat. "Do you have an envelope?"

Vogler pulled out an envelope, and Oppenheimer placed the hair inside. Then he turned to the back seat. "There is blood here. Doesn't look good. But it's just a few drops. Mrs. Herrmann was overpowered and immediately removed from the car."

When he finally turned to the driver's seat, he paused. "Hello."

"What's the matter?" Vogler wanted to know.

Oppenheimer bent down and pulled out a pocketknife. Then he asked Vogler for a second envelope and scraped something off the brake pedal. He straightened up again and examined the substance in the envelope.

"Clay," he said.

Vogler also looked at the contents of the envelope. "Quite a large piece."

Oppenheimer took a piece of the dried mud and rubbed it between his fingers. He remained standing on the damp pavement for almost a minute, staring at the clay between his fingers. Then he had an inspiration.

"Very good. This is what we'll do," he said to Vogler and pointed to the vehicle. "Secure the evidence immediately. Then we need a search party, tracker dogs, all available personnel. I think I have an idea where to find our perpetrator."

■

There was another alarm in the evening, but Oppenheimer didn't even notice. He was up all night, pacing up and down the living room in the Zehlendorf house while Vogler gave orders by radio from the cellar to round up all available men for the search parties. The rain had stopped a few hours before, and when Oppenheimer finally walked across the fields with one of the search parties in the early hours of the morning, the air was still cold but already carried the scent of a breaking summer day.

The clouds had disappeared. The first delicate gleam of dawn could already be made out in the distance. It was going to be a gorgeous, sunny day today, the kind of day that used to be known as *Kaiserwetter,* weather fit for an emperor. However, Hitler's ascent to power had also had impacts on general linguistic usage, and so people now called a day with blue skies and sunshine *Führerwetter.*

The search party that Oppenheimer had joined was combing the area north of Köpenick. Additional troops were located on the edge of the city in Treptow and Schmöckwitz. Farther north, a group was searching the area around Dahlwitz. Time was of the essence, as the first city residents would soon be setting off toward the suburbs on their weekend trips. Within a few hours, the extensive forest region would be teeming with day-trippers wanting to leave the rubble of the city center behind them and recharge their batteries in the open countryside or heading to the racecourse in Happegarten.

"We're looking for a building on the outskirts of the city," Oppenheimer told the men. "The remoter, the likelier it is to qualify as the murder scene." *The victim's screams couldn't be heard from there,* he thought.

The first train juddered across the rails. Meanwhile, they had managed to cut across the forest to a desolate marshland.

"It's the famous needle in the haystack," Vogler said. He placed his hands on his hips and looked toward the area of garden allotments that stood out from the nearby forest edge in the morning mist. "Are we in the right place?"

Oppenheimer also stopped. Although it wasn't that warm yet, he was already sweating. He wiped his face with his handkerchief. "The perpetrator only had three hours to kidnap Mrs. Herrmann, get her out of the car, lock her in his hideout, and then drive back to Köpenick to drop off the car. He didn't have much time. He *must* be somewhere here in the district. The lump of clay that I found on the brake pedal contained neither stone nor chalk. The city center is full of that. Bombed-out houses and rubble piles everywhere. The perpetrator cannot have spent time in the middle of town."

"The area is bloody big. Gruppenleiter Herrmann wants to recruit a troop from the Hitler Youth in Köpenick to help with the search."

"Excellent idea. They know their way around secret hideouts better than anyone. I'm guessing they are not going to be told that this is a murder case?"

"That's taken care of. I gave Herrmann specific instructions."

"Good. We can hardly search the entire area. We'll just have to hope that we get lucky."

Oppenheimer was just about to take off his coat when they suddenly heard barking noises just a few meters away. Both men started.

"They've found something," Vogler said and ran straight through the reeds toward the dog handlers. They were outside a wooden shed. When Oppenheimer finally arrived, Vogler had already gone into the hut. He came out looking disappointed. "Nothing, completely empty. It wasn't even locked."

"What was going on? The dogs picked up on something!" Oppenheimer said.

The dog handler looked embarrassed. Finally, one of them pointed toward the nearby bushes.

"It can happen with the animals," he said with a sheepish shrug.

Oppenheimer lowered his head in disappointment. A dead rabbit lay in the bushes.

■

Oppenheimer was on his feet almost the entire Sunday. The Pervitin helped him through it. He had taken a pill every four hours to combat the symptoms of fatigue. When their efforts hadn't brought about a result by late afternoon, Vogler almost had to force him to allow Hoffmann to drive him home. Oppenheimer finally agreed when he realized that he hadn't had any sleep for thirty-six hours. They had been unlucky. There had been no quick solution.

As the work would continue the next day, he had to pace himself. He knew that his body would reclaim the missed sleep. He wasn't all that young anymore after all.

When he went into the kitchen looking dejected, Lisa was already waiting for him with a worried expression.

Oppenheimer sat down on the nearest chair. "The case. I was busy. Did Hoffmann tell you what was going on?"

"He just said that you'd be late, nothing more. What happened? Is it over now?"

"No. Not for a long time. The next few days are going to be difficult." He leaned back in his chair, exhausted. Then he placed the new pair of shoes on the table. "Here, these are from Hilde. I need to stuff them with paper so that they fit me."

He gave Lisa a tired look as she sat down next to him with two cups of coffee substitute. She stared into her brew for a few seconds and then said, "I guessed the investigation wasn't over yet. Hilde mentioned something along those lines."

Suddenly wide awake, Oppenheimer pricked his ears. "You spoke to Hilde?"

"Not only spoke. She was here a few hours ago."

"Here at ours?"

"You should have seen Old Schlesinger. He was beside himself with curiosity. Hilde finally told him that she was my sister from Leipzig. She had an important message."

"What was it?"

"She said that Dot and Anton accepted your conditions." Then she lowered her voice. "They want to talk to you. You're to head down toward Hansa Bridge at ten o'clock tomorrow evening. They will make contact. Hilde said that those two are going to get us out of the country. Is that right, Richard? Is there a way to get out?"

He leaned over toward Lisa. "It is possible. The intelligence services are behind it, but it is a bit precarious."

Over the last few years, Oppenheimer and Lisa had often talked about leaving Germany. His sister had fled to Paraguay with her husband. Judging by her letters, she was managing quite well, as he was an engineer and after some initial difficulties had managed to secure a job. However, Oppenheimer doubted that there was much demand for criminal inspectors from Berlin there. And when, with a heavy heart, Oppenheimer finally decided to turn his back on Germany, it had been too late. They had managed to get a British visa, but when Hitler invaded Poland shortly afterward, the borders were closed off. Later, there had been an option to get to America via Shanghai, but the Oppenheimers hadn't been able to find anyone in the USA to put up the $400 and the travel expenses. Now, out of the blue, there was an additional option. However, he didn't know what Lisa thought of the plan. So he asked her, "What do you think? Would you want to leave?"

"I would do anything for us to be able to leave this dreadful place," Lisa said with unfamiliar vehemence. "I no longer want to be a German. All this madness. I hate the people here."

Oppenheimer had to smile. "Now you almost sound like Hilde. The problem is that I have to inform Dot and Anton of the results of the investigation. But the murder cases have been classified as secret."

"Just do it. Otherwise, you'll never get out of here. Although Vogler treats you with respect, they're still using you. I know you'd like to believe it, but these members of the master race will never accept you as an equal. You're not one of them, and you never will be." Then she looked him straight in the eye. "Don't feel too safe in the presence of SS members, Richard. Don't forget who you are and where you come from. It's not a betrayal if you pass information about the investigation on to the intelligence services. This is not the time for loyalty. We should take up the offer and flee."

21

Infinity stretched out above them. The stars had returned to Berlin a few years ago. The blackout regulation had freed the universe from the light of the city, and Cassiopeia shone brighter than ever before. The planets didn't care whether there was a war raging on the sun's satellite named Earth or not. They continued along their trajectory, allowing nothing to stand in their way. From the depths of the universe, Algol, the Demon Star, stared down coldly at the three people who met at the Reich Sports Field at four in the morning. The men appeared small and insignificant on the grounds that had been designed for the Olympic games a decade ago. One of them unlocked the iron gate next to the elongated building that served as a ticket check and allowed the other two to enter. They walked past the gigantic sphere of the Olympic stadium and approached the green area called *Maifeld*. They had to go through an entranceway that consisted of two slender pillars stretching up into the night sky and disappearing into the darkness somewhere above their heads.

"Why did Hoffmann have to let us out at the south entrance?" Oppenheimer complained as they still had around one kilometer to go.

"It's the only entrance that's open at night," Vogler said.

"I thought that the west gate had been broken into anyway. I'm not interested in looking at the entire grounds."

Oppenheimer couldn't understand it. Even the SS people were bureaucrats at heart. His curses were muffled by the scarf that Lisa had forced upon him. Oppenheimer hadn't been able to prevent her from waking up, too, when Hoffmann had appeared to bring the bad tidings. It didn't matter what they did now; it would be of no use to Traudel Herrmann anymore.

Although it was still quite early, it was already growing light. Oppenheimer remembered that it would be solstice in two days' time. The National Socialists had always held large festivities in the Olympic stadium on this date, with thousands of burning torches forming a gigantic swastika. But over the war years, the people had lost all taste for such events. Oppenheimer had not heard of any festivity taking place this week, given that huge flaming swastikas were probably not in keeping with the general blackout regulations. The party liked to use the Reich Sports Field for other events as well. Several years before the war, while the rest of the world was still hoping that the First World War would end all other wars, Germany was already making plans for the next one. Hitler and his helpers weren't even very subtle in preparing the people for it. For example, the nationwide competitions by the SA took place in the Olympic stadium every year. Entirely new categories of sports had been devised for the occasion, such as grenade-throwing or relay racing with gas masks, which was extremely popular with the audience in the prewar years. It would soon turn out that the healthy Germanic body propagated by the party was not an end in itself. Anything that toughened German men—in the stadium or at the front—was praised.

Oppenheimer had ample time to think about these things while he and Vogler followed the night watchman, who led them across the seemingly never-ending field. They were heading toward the bell tower that rose up above the so-called west wall. Oppenheimer glumly thought how the murderer always managed to find a phallic symbol in front of which to place his victims. Despite its name, the building ahead was not really a wall but an elongated grandstand with countless rows of seats, one of those typical stone blocks that had been erected all over the city by the party architects, none of which had a real purpose unless there was a parade or some other pompous festivity.

Finally, they reached the bottom steps on the edge of the grandstand. They climbed a balustrade and then had to walk along the semicircle before they reached the VIP stand that was installed directly beneath the bell tower. Oppenheimer spotted a landing with a stone stump on it. This observation platform was the führer's podium, upon which, visible to all, he could take the salute.

"Halt! Who goes there?" someone called. Oppenheimer was blinded by the light of a flashlight. Then he heard the heavy boot heels clack and could make out the shadow behind the flashlight saluting Vogler.

"Carry on," Vogler commanded, and the SS man disappeared again to guard the crime site. Vogler pointed his light downward. Below them lay the human remains of Traudel Herrmann.

The murderer had arranged the body in the usual fashion. But once again, something was different. Frowning, Oppenheimer looked at the victim's head. The perpetrator had taken the time to shave Traudel Herrmann's hair.

"Hmm," Oppenheimer considered. He had heard of women being shorn in the streets because they had made the mistake of getting involved with a man who, according to Nazi definition, was not of German blood or even belonged to the so-called subhumans. According to the Law for the Protection of German Blood and German Honor, if you chose a partner that the National Socialists considered to be wrong, you needed to be punished. Oppenheimer wondered whether the shorn women were meant to serve as a warning or as entertainment for the audience.

"Is there some sort of secret meaning? I presume that Gruppenleiter Herrmann at least must have an Aryan certificate. I suggest you have it checked. Maybe that will get us somewhere."

Vogler didn't answer but stared at the body, his expression grave.

Oppenheimer sat down and looked across the parade ground, which was still dark; the sun, however, was already rising behind the distant houses. Blue was slowly creeping into the sky so that the Andromeda galaxy that had been visible to the naked eye alongside Pegasus just a few hours ago could no longer be distinguished. Clearly visible, on the other hand, were Capella in the northeast and the razor-thin moon sickle. Even the moon seemed to bow to the architecture of the Reich Sports Field. It was situated directly above the Marathon Gate, a wide swath that sliced through the circular Olympic stadium. Oppenheimer thought hard.

"This is not really our murderer's territory."

"If your assumption is correct, then he took a serious risk," Vogler said. "He had to transport the corpse across the city, which someone could have noticed. And there are several Wehrmacht stations just around the corner here."

"He's becoming careless. That is typical for repeat offenders. He hasn't been caught so far and now feels safe. And he also feels let down by official party representatives, so he places the body directly below the führer's podium. One could interpret it as a personal appeal to Hitler."

"Yes, that would be one explanation," Vogler agreed. "In his delusion, he believes the führer would approve."

"Only this place where the body was found has nothing to do with the First World War. It's a mystery. In all the other cases, there was some sort of memorial to the fallen."

"But we have one of those here too," a voice said out of the dusk. It was the first time the night watchman had spoken. "The Langemarck hall. Just down there."

"That's right," Vogler said. "This place perfectly fits with the other crimes."

Oppenheimer looked at the two men. "What hall are you talking about?"

"Come along," said the night watchman and jangled his keys.

■

In the beam of the flashlight, Oppenheimer recognized the contours of blockish letters. In the darkness, the room seemed like a pharaoh's tomb that had been hidden beneath thick blocks of stone waiting for archaeologists to find it. Oppenheimer felt like Howard Carter and wouldn't have been surprised if they'd come across a mummy in one of the corners.

It had happened on November 10, 1914. In Langemarck, a little town in Flanders, war volunteers, sixth formers, and students had charged against the enemy, the national anthem on their lips, and were brutally massacred. Oppenheimer had never heard of any of his former comrades bursting into song under the enemy's artillery attack, but that's how the night watchman told the tale, his eyes shining and a rapturous smile on his lips. According to his description, two thousand German soldiers had fallen there.

In Oppenheimer's mind, it had been nothing more than one of those questionable battles fought during the First World War.

"I need some fresh air," Oppenheimer said and left the hall. "I presume you found the body?" he asked the night watchman.

"I saw a delivery van parked at the west gate," he replied. "I had just gotten to the broken gate when the engine started and off he went."

Oppenheimer stopped and grabbed the night watchman's arm. He must have surprised the perpetrator. "Can you show me exactly where that was?"

■

They stepped outside. The Maifeld could not be seen from behind the towering grandstand. The night watchman pointed to a free spot. "If you look over there, those are the parking spaces, right by the entrance to the outdoor stage. But the delivery van was right here around the corner."

"Can you show me the exact spot where the vehicle was parked?"

The night watchman started moving. Oppenheimer could feel the blood pulsating in his head with anticipation. He wanted to quickly get to the spot where the vehicle had stood, but the night watchman was shuffling down the steps at an irritatingly slow pace. Oppenheimer decided not to let the time go wasted and continued his questioning.

"Given that it was a delivery van, were you able to recognize an inscription anywhere, or remember the number plate?"

"I just saw a great big shadow. Nothing more. I don't know if there was anything written on the tarpaulin."

Oppenheimer pricked up his ears. "What tarpaulin?"

"Well, I could see the lorry drive away. It went over a large pothole, and the whole thing juddered."

"You mean the tarpaulin was stretched across the truck bed?"

"Yes, up high, just high enough for a man to stand under."

The night watchman went over to the structure in front of the wall, a stone pedestal approximately two meters high. A vehicle parked here during the day could only be seen from the higher tiers of the grandstand. At night, this spot would be almost invisible.

As they approached the area, Oppenheimer saw something glimmering on the ground. He flinched. "Stop!" he called out and held back his companions. Excitedly, he grabbed the flashlight from Vogler's hand and inspected the ground.

In front of them was a puddle. It had rained a lot over the last few days, and the ground was still drenched. Yesterday's sunshine had not been enough to dry the earth completely here in the shadow of the stone pedestal. Oppenheimer bent down and examined the ground. He could see a clear and precise pattern. The truck had gone through a puddle and left a tire print in the damp earth.

"I need someone from forensics here straightaway," Oppenheimer ordered. "We need to make a plaster cast of the tire print immediately."

"Right," Vogler said and turned to leave. When he realized that Oppenheimer wasn't moving, he stopped. "Are you not coming?"

Oppenheimer snorted obstinately. "Hell no. Wild horses won't drag me away until the forensics is done. I'm not taking the risk of some drunken idiot ruining the prints. Get someone, as quickly as possible."

Vogler and the night watchman disappeared. The flashlight beam grew smaller and got lost in the shadows of the west wall. Oppenheimer strained his eyes and searched the ground for additional evidence. He finally found a footprint just a few centimeters away.

For the first time in this investigation, Oppenheimer began to feel a little hopeful.

◼

"Psst." It sounded from the right, then a husky whisper, "Oppenheimer, come over here."

It was ten in the evening. Oppenheimer had been wondering where exactly he was supposed to be meeting Lüttke and Bauer. He was just about to cross the Hansa Bridge when he heard the whisper.

Lüttke stood on the steps leading down to the banks of the Spree and waved to him. Oppenheimer went over to him as discreetly as possible. Bauer stood farther down, gesturing excitedly.

"Come on, hurry up. Take your coat off," he said and handed Oppenheimer his own coat. After they had swapped clothes and hats, Bauer went back up the stairs. "You've got two hours."

Lüttke and Oppenheimer watched Bauer walk across the bridge. In the growing darkness, it was difficult to make him out properly, when suddenly another figure appeared. The man briefly glanced down the steps, but Lüttke and Oppenheimer had already withdrawn to the shadows of the bridge. Then the man crossed the Spree. He followed Bauer from a distance of about a hundred meters. This had to be the man tailing Oppenheimer today.

"Close shave," Lüttke said and exhaled, relieved. "If we'd taken any longer, it would have been tight. My colleague will lead him on a wild-goose chase so that we can talk in peace and quiet. Come along. I have a car nearby."

As Oppenheimer was about to get into the car, he saw that there was a man sitting inside. Dark hair was plastered to his round skull in precisely styled waves.

"Don't worry," Lüttke said. "That's one of our stenographers. Just in case we come to an agreement." Then he started the engine and drove off.

On Lüttke's orders, they pulled down the blinds on the side windows. The stenographer seemed to have been waiting in the car for quite a while, as the interior stank of his oily hair pomade. Unfortunately, it wasn't possible to let in any air with the blinds drawn down. Oppenheimer resigned himself to his fate.

Lüttke confirmed Hilde's message that the intelligence services were prepared to agree to his demands and get him and Lisa out of the country. Once that had been clarified, Oppenheimer gave Lüttke the most important facts he had come across during the murder investigation. He even mentioned the vague references he had received from his colleague Billhardt. The stenographer took notes eagerly.

"That sounds very interesting," Lüttke commented. "It's understandable that your colleague wasn't able to help with the SS suspect. The police system has changed a great deal since you were with the force. Normal officers no longer have any real power. The Gestapo and the SD have their fingers in every pie. They decide which cases they handle, and the rest is then distributed among the others. If you manage to elicit the name of the SS man, we could activate our people to find his file."

"I'll have another go," Oppenheimer said. "But I can't promise that Billhardt will give it up. How can I get the information to you?"

"We've already set up a drop point for this purpose. But first you need to familiarize yourself with the code words you'll be using when you contact us. From now on, your cover name is *Schiller*."

This all seemed like a game to Oppenheimer. But regardless of how stupid it seemed, people like Lüttke and Bauer were deadly serious about this game. This really was like *Emil and the Detectives*, Oppenheimer thought and sighed.

■

Vogler shook his head. "If what my people have found out is really true, then Traudel Herrmann was a real scapegrace."

Although it was only ten in the morning, Vogler had to switch on the desk lamp in his cellar office to have sufficient light. There had been another alarm half an hour ago, which was why Oppenheimer had also made his way down there.

As soon as the body had been found, Vogler had background checks carried out at the special courts in Berlin. These courts handled the so-called incidentals. Any offense that wasn't considered to be politically motivated was dealt with here. The special courts were keen to resolve things quickly; minor offenses could often even be taken care of immediately.

Those unlucky enough to have to appear before such a court had a hard time of it. According to the so-called Volksschädlingsverordnung, an ordinance governing people that were considered "parasites" to the German society, prison or even the death penalty could be imposed for almost anything. It sufficed if the deed exploited the war-induced state of emergency or damaged the "healthy German sentiment," which the legislator had failed to define clearly.

As a result, the special courts had carte blanche to do as they pleased. There were almost daily reports of new death sentences. Once a sentence had been passed, it was not possible to appeal. The only option was a petition to have the sentence annulled, but the chances of success were extremely low. If Mrs. Herrmann really was guilty of racial defilement, then it was more than likely that she would have appeared before this special court. But the sheer number of Mrs. Herrmann's offenses surprised even Vogler.

"Between 1938 and 1942, she appeared before a special court no fewer than six times," he reported. "Each time because of racial defilement. She seemed to have a predilection for having sex with wealthy Jews. It was always the same: someone reported her, she was accused and sentenced. Her lovers were sent to concentration camps; the last two were sentenced to death. But Mrs. Herrmann—or Traudel Tuggenbrecht, as she used to be known—always received a conspicuously low sentence. Normally, she would have also been sent to a concentration camp for each of her offenses, but she was only given a few weeks' imprisonment. And there are no indications that she ever served her sentences. She never actually saw a prison from inside. And as far as the wealthy geezers' money is concerned . . ."

"Let me guess: the Jewish lovers' possessions miraculously ended up in the hands of Gruppenleiter Herrmann, correct?"

"Correct. At least as far as we can ascertain. Then last year, he married her. It seems the foray was over."

Oppenheimer's compassion for Traudel Herrmann had plummeted abruptly.

"This would indicate that Herrmann bribed people. They bagged the assets and did so in a seemingly legal way. A profitable business model." After he had briefly scanned the files, Oppenheimer added, "Looking at the offenders' addresses, it seems like Mrs. Herrmann slept her way through the beds of half of Köpenick. Now at least we know why the murderer chose her. The most important question is who knew about the fact that she seduced Jews in particular."

"I'm sure she didn't boast about it," Vogler replied. "To pick up on this, the perpetrator must have seen her on numerous occasions, maybe an old acquaintance. She lived in Köpenick the entire time, so it might have just been a former neighbor. Other than that—" Vogler cleared his throat. "Other than that, there is the judge who sentenced her. It was always the same one."

Surprised, Oppenheimer took another look at the papers. Vogler was correct; the sentences were all handed down by one and the same judge. The longer he dealt with the matter, the more the whole thing felt like a prearranged affair.

"If my suspicions are correct, then the judge also profited. This doesn't fit with our murderer. The perpetrator strongly condemned Mrs. Herrmann's behavior. If he were a judge, he could just as well have sentenced her to death, and no one would have been able to hold it against him, not even the Gruppenleiter. We might consider another court employee, but due to the large number of proceedings, it's not very likely that any of the bailiffs came across Mrs. Herrmann more than once or even remembered her. I don't think there is a connection to the court."

234 I HARALD GILBERS

Thoughtfully, Oppenheimer chewed on the mouthpiece of his cigarette tip. Then he slammed his hand flat on the table. "No, the murderer must have lived in Köpenick between 1938 and 1942, at least for a while. I am sure of it."

Oppenheimer felt agitated, so much so that it forced him up from his chair. He started pacing the small cellar. "Very well, we are getting more and more information about the murderer, but it's time this should be enough for us to catch him. There's no way around it; you have to send your men to the registration offices."

Vogler looked at him attentively, clearly trying to follow the former inspector's thoughts. "So we should find out which of the suspects lived in Köpenick at the time in question," he mumbled.

"Exactly. It's a bit of a slog, as we don't have a specific suspect right now. Every man we came across throughout the investigation needs to be closely looked at. We must find out which one of them had the opportunity to observe Mrs. Herrmann's activities. I'll put a list together in a moment and mark those who most likely match our preliminary description of the perpetrator. Their whereabouts must be established first."

"I'll get right onto it," Vogler said and sat down at the radio. Then he paused. "We need to interview Gruppenleiter Herrmann again to find out who his wife had contact with recently."

Oppenheimer nodded. "I fear it won't be much help, but we should at least try."

"I'll do it myself," Vogler said. "I suggest you check the files to see if there were connections to Köpenick in the other murder cases too." Then he instructed the radio controller to set up a line. Like Oppenheimer, he seemed happy to finally have something to do again.

■

Oppenheimer left the cellar of the Zehlendorf house while the alarm was still on and in the living room wrote down the names from the pieces of paper on his chart. Then he studied the files, searching doggedly for another connection to Köpenick, until the radio controller came up from the cellar to black out the windows. It was only now that Oppenheimer realized it was already getting dark outside and that it was too late to pay Billhardt a visit.

Later, as Hoffmann chauffeured him home, he realized that he would have to come up with a new way of shaking off his pursuer when he visited his old colleague. He didn't fancy Vogler finding out that he had an informer on the crime squad.

When Oppenheimer opened the door to the kitchen, Lisa was preparing dinner. But she wasn't alone. Old Mrs. Schlesinger was sitting at the kitchen table chattering. Lisa had her back to her so as not to encourage her, but this clearly wasn't proving successful. When Mrs. Schlesinger saw that Oppenheimer had come home, her eyes widened in delight. She had a new victim.

"Ah, Mr. Oppenheimer," she called. "How fortunate that you've arrived. I already informed your wife that the toilet on your floor is broken. My husband is taking care of it, but I don't know how long it's going to take. You know how difficult it is to find a handyman who is willing to work in a Jewish house. So my husband said, 'I'm not even going to try this time,' and took the matter into his own hands."

Oppenheimer thought that Mrs. Schlesinger and her husband would have been the ideal informants for the SD. They always had to stick their noses into other people's business. While her husband went about it in a rather gruff way, she was exactly the opposite. She was always almost manically happy. It didn't matter what was going on, she always had a smile etched on her face.

"Well, that seems to be the most sensible thing to do," Oppenheimer answered. Then he took off his hat and coat and hung them on the hook. When Mrs. Schlesinger looked him over, her cheerful gaze suddenly grew reproachful.

"But, Mr. Oppenheimer!"

Surprised, he turned to her. "What is it?"

"But—your star! Pray tell me, where have you left your star?"

Initially, Oppenheimer didn't know what she meant. When he followed her gaze, he realized that the Star of David was missing from his coat. Recently he hadn't bothered sewing it back on each day.

"Oh, it was a silly misunderstanding," he lied. "I—the coat has just been cleaned. I completely forgot to sew the star back on."

Mrs. Schlesinger looked at the dirty coat and turned up her mouth pointedly. "Well, then you're very lucky that no one caught you. I don't know what the point of the whole thing is, but it's better if we stick to the rules. Otherwise, we'll just get in trouble. Wear the star with pride, Mr. Oppenheimer. With pride."

■

This time, there hadn't been any pre-alarm. At nine o'clock, the sirens suddenly started howling. Oppenheimer was in the sidecar of Hoffmann's motorbike, being driven along Kronprinzallee at breakneck speed.

The signal, which could be heard despite the loud clatter of the engine, was unmistakable. "Full alarm," Oppenheimer whispered. This could only mean that bombers had appeared out of nowhere and were heading straight for Berlin.

He looked at his driver. Hoffmann, too, had understood. They had about a kilometer to go until they would reach the Kameradschaftssiedlung. Hoffmann pressed his lips together and went full throttle.

Oppenheimer had thought Hoffmann had already been driving at full speed the entire time, but he'd been mistaken. The renewed acceleration pressed him back in his seat. Hoffmann swerved elegantly around the piles of rubble that dotted the road here and there. The potholes, on the other hand, were far less easy to spot from a distance, especially from the passenger's perspective. Mostly, Oppenheimer only realized they were approaching a crater when Hoffmann suddenly wrenched the handlebars to one side, veering this way and that without slowing down. Oppenheimer wondered whether it wouldn't be safer to sit at the side of the road, wait for the bombs, and put his trust in God instead of being at the mercy of Hoffmann's driving skills, which was equivalent to being on a launching platform.

The capital of the Reich had been lucky over the last few days. After Hitler's buzz bomb had hit London, the people of Berlin had anticipated a strong British counterstrike. But although there had been constant alarms, the big attack had failed to materialize. By now, Oppenheimer found the alarms more annoying than threatening. And anyway, most of the time he was so absorbed in studying the results of his investigation that he barely noticed the sirens.

With an effort, Oppenheimer managed to look up at the sky. He thought he could hear a hostile droning and wanted to localize the source.

But with each of Hoffmann's handlebar moves, pure survival instinct directed his gaze back to the road. Finally, they came to a stretch of road that was in a tolerable state.

When Oppenheimer was finally able to turn around, he froze. The sky behind him was studded with dark spots that carried white condensation stripes behind them. They were headed straight for the city center. Without a doubt, this was the big retaliation attack.

Suddenly, Oppenheimer shouted at his driver, "Get on with it, man!"

■

Although the Kameradschaftssiedlung remained untouched, Oppenheimer knew that terrible things must have happened in other parts of town.

They had spent hours in the cellar, waiting restlessly. The radio controller listened carefully on his headphones while Vogler sat on the chair with his arms folded. Oppenheimer couldn't think of anything meaningful to do either. He thought of Lisa. What might have happened to her? He had seen her this morning. If he remembered correctly, she was on early shifts this week. That meant that she would already have been at work when the attacks started.

When the sirens blared the all clear at quarter past one, they received a radio message. The radio controller handed Vogler the headphones. "Hauptsturmführer Vogler," he said. Even from the opposite side of the room, Oppenheimer could hear the fuzzy crackle from the headphones. Somebody seemed to be bellowing at the top of his lungs on the other end of the line. Whatever the message was, it seemed to make a big impression on Vogler. While he listened, he turned ashen. Initially, he seemed to have problems speaking, but then he swallowed and uttered a croaky, "Yes, sir."

Vogler numbly took off the headphones. An uncontrollable twitch in his face showed Oppenheimer that something monstrous had happened.

"What is it?" Oppenheimer asked.

Vogler didn't react. He hastily charged upstairs and called out, "Where is Hoffmann with the car?"

22

It was as if they had stepped onto the surface of a foreign planet, a bizarre landscape with an atmosphere utterly hostile to life. But after some hesitation, Oppenheimer decided to trust his eyes. This all *had* to be real. His imagination would barely have sufficed to paint such a scenario.

It had been a very heavy attack. The closer they got to the government district, the more the daylight darkened. They soon encountered vehicles with their headlights switched on to see anything in the fog created by soot and dust. Then they reached the first streets where the electric streetlights were on. Hoffmann also switched on his headlights. He did his best to reach Voßstraße, but this was a difficult undertaking in this chaos.

The rubble from the destroyed buildings cut off entire streets, and emergency services blocked their way, desperately trying to quash the fires; survivors wandered around aimlessly while others tried to rescue their belongings from the houses. The drive through the bombed-out streets resembled an obstacle course. Their driver tried various alternative routes, but eventually, he had to give up and let them get out.

When Oppenheimer opened the door, he was assailed by hot air. Although he hadn't moved yet, he already started to sweat. He pulled off his jacket and hung it over his arm. Then he looked around and registered the unfathomable.

The sun was just a milky disk behind the blue-black fumes that had settled upon the entire city center. Despite the extreme heat and the fact that houses were on fire and sparks rained down from the sky, the ground was thick with snow. But even in the gloom of the polluted air, it was clear that the snow was not white. The olive-green flakes on the ground consisted of dust and limestone debris.

Vogler, too, failed to get his bearings. "Bloody hell," he swore. "Where are we, Hoffmann?"

"We've already crossed the canal. It can't be far now. Leipziger Straße is somewhere over there. A bit off to the left, and you'll get to the building of the Reich Chancellery."

Vogler slammed the car door shut and looked up and down the road. The streetlights were powerless against the smoke. The street disappeared into the gloom just a few meters away.

"Right. Off we go, then," he said to Oppenheimer and strode off ahead.

After just a few minutes, Oppenheimer's eyes began to smart. His lungs hurt from the heavy smoke. It occurred to him that he could have made good use of the gas mask now, which he had organized on Lisa's prompting, but unfortunately, that was at home. While he stomped through the dust and clambered across empty window frames, he searched through his pockets. He finally found the motorbike goggles that Vogler had given him for his reluctant trips in the sidecar. He put them on and briefly blew into the gap between goggles and eyes to dispel the worst of the dirt before pressing them down tightly.

The streets were teeming with firemen, SS men, forced laborers, and prisoners who, with the last of their strength, were trying to battle the effects of the bomb attack.

And then there were the others.

The victims.

The people who had been bombed out moved mechanically through the inferno, rags and burned flesh clinging to their bodies. "Why doesn't anyone protect us?" a woman called. Others sat outside their destroyed homes and were happy to still be alive, while teenage boys from the Hitler Youth gathered up the bodies in zinc tubs just a couple of meters away. A man with shriveled eyeballs lurched toward them. Oppenheimer tried not to look, but there were too many horrors around them to not take it in. Wherever he looked, there were new details, each gruesomer. A mother packing her burned child into her air raid case to take it with her; the corpses in the open shelter; curtains of fire whipping out of empty window openings.

Oppenheimer walked quickly, but there was no way of escaping these impressions. However, he did notice something else. While some housing blocks were blazing fiercely, others didn't have a scratch on them although they were right next door. The streets were too wide for the fire to spread uncontrollably. Berlin did not burn well, although the sheer number of hits during this attack had been more than enough to keep the fire brigade busy.

Toward the Berlin Palace, streaks of flames kept flaring up into the sky. It seemed that this area had suffered the worst hits. Vogler led Oppenheimer in a semicircle around a bomb crater full of bubbling water.

A sudden detonation!

A pressure wave shot through the streets, then stones clattered to the ground from the black cloud above them. Vogler and Oppenheimer jumped aside and sought refuge behind a wall. "These bloody time fuses!" Vogler shouted angrily. Impossible to know how many bombs were still lying around, waiting to detonate in order to send rescue teams, those who'd already been bombed out, and firefighters to their deaths.

A few meters away stood a sooty wire mesh that had once been a stroller. The sight of it made Oppenheimer painfully aware of the fact that even Hitler's opponents were willing to sacrifice their higher ideals for a cynical rationale. Their bombs were not able to differentiate between Nazis and opponents to the regime, not to mention the Germans who couldn't be categorized as either. It might be a controversial question whether all humans were equal before God, but there was no doubt in regard to the bombs: they claimed any life. The question of how bad the good were allowed to become when they fought the bad no longer existed for Oppenheimer. Terror was answered with sheer terror.

It took three-quarters of an hour for them to make their way to the Reich Chancellery. A man in uniform was already waiting for them. It seemed that he was the commander of the Leibstandarte, the SS bodyguards whose task it was to guard the building.

"Are you that Vogler fellow?" he called out to them.

Vogler saluted. "Hauptsturmführer Vogler at your service!"

"It's about time you got here," the commander said. "Where on earth have you been?"

"We had trouble getting through," Vogler replied.

The response was a croaky laugh. "Oh, really? Well, get a move on. We want to get rid of all traces as soon as possible!"

The new Reich Chancellery consisted of several buildings that lined the northern side of Voßstraße. In between the Führer's Chancellery and the actual Reich Chancellery, there was a middle section, slightly set back. This building's courtyard was separated from the path by a waist-high stone balustrade.

The commander led them to a passageway on the western end of the building. A piece of tarpaulin lay right in the middle of the courtyard, guarded by two SS men. The tarpaulin had an unusual format. It was almost square, maybe five by five feet, definitely too small to cover a corpse.

The commander removed the tarpaulin, and Oppenheimer pulled his motorbike goggles off in disbelief. It seemed that the human flesh had not only been burned, it was warped, had melted away, only to clump together in a new, bizarre shape right here in the heart of the government district. This was the only explanation Oppenheimer could come up with at first sight.

The murderer had arranged four arms on the ground. Oppenheimer knew that they must be the arms of Kitty's missing worker. The other two arms would no doubt turn out to belong to Traudel Herrmann.

Oppenheimer found his voice again. "Fingerprints?"

"All done," the commander interjected. "We also have photographs. Do you gentlemen have any other requests?"

Oppenheimer shook his head. "No, all good."

"Many thanks," the commander responded. Oppenheimer stepped back onto the path and leaned against one of the waist-high pillars. Although he had slept well that night, he suddenly felt utterly exhausted. He fished a Pervitin tablet from the small vial, swallowed it, and thought about what he had seen.

The murderer had achieved something that rarely ever happened. He'd succeeded in shocking Oppenheimer. After the investigations in the Großmann case, he'd thought that nothing else would shock him, but today, this had turned out to be an illusion.

At least the mystery of what the murderer had done with the arms of the last two victims had now been solved. He hadn't wanted to draft one of his usual letters to appeal to the NSDAP leadership but instead had come up with this surprise to show everyone he supported the party.

Oppenheimer wondered where all this was supposed to lead. He leaned against the stone pillar for a moment with his eyes closed.

When he opened them again, he flinched. He thought he'd seen something on the other side of the road.

There was an old crime squad rule that a perpetrator always returned to the scene of the crime. Hilde had often made fun of this, but Oppenheimer knew it was true. There were different reasons for this behavior. Some criminals wanted to make sure that they had covered their tracks; others relished in the spectacle the police made and felt vindicated in their superiority. Oppenheimer knew that their murderer was out for recognition; his letters made this all too clear. Now he had possibly taken the biggest risk of all, leaving body parts right under the noses of the SS men who were guarding the entrance to Hitler's Chancellery just a few meters away. And all of this during a heavy bombardment, which had worked to the murderer's advantage in a treacherous way, for while the place was usually crawling with party officials, they had all taken to the bunkers when the attack started. And so the murderer had been able to implement his plan without being seen by anyone. Nonetheless, Oppenheimer had not expected the perpetrator to be as daring as to observe the scene of the crime. But a glance at the opposite side of the street sufficed to convince him. When Oppenheimer had opened his eyes, he had looked straight at the beast.

Several curious passersby watched what was going on in the courtyard from opposite the Reich Chancellery. But the presence of the SS bodyguards scared them away. However, in the direction of Wilhelmstraße, one person stood outside the building of the German Reich Railway Company and looked across toward Oppenheimer. While everyone around him hurried on, this man seemed to have all the time in the world, his hands casually stuck in his leather coat and his hat low on his forehead. But it hadn't been the man's immobility that Oppenheimer had noticed first. It was his mocking grin and his gaze that was fixed on Oppenheimer, allowing only one conclusion: the man knew what was going on there, knew precisely what gruesome find they had just made.

A wave of energy shot through Oppenheimer's body. "Hauptsturm-führer?" But Vogler was gone. When he looked back at the opposite side of the street, the man had also disappeared. Oppenheimer had been too fixated on the grin to memorize the face properly. He couldn't let him get away. He quickly crossed the road. The stranger must have gone in the direction of Wilhelmstraße. And indeed, he saw the man hurrying away from the site, now about two hundred meters ahead. Oppenheimer's coat over his arm hampered his pursuit, so he quickly slipped it on.

The man seemed to have noticed that someone was following him, but he didn't increase his speed. He crossed the road, went past the steps to the subway station at Kaiserhof, and continued straight toward Mauerstraße. Oppenheimer noticed the man's strange gait. Although he was limping, it didn't prevent him from walking fast.

As they walked along Zietenplatz, Oppenheimer tried to reduce the gap between them, but the rubble everywhere made the pursuit difficult. Swearing, Oppenheimer stumbled past the destroyed Hotel Kaiserhof. Strange growths rose up out of the rubble toward the sun. Twisted steel girders.

The clatter of bricks. "Careful!" A brick wall bulged toward Oppen-heimer from the right and caved in.

"Watch where you're walking!" an old woman with a lined face called out through the cloud of dust. Oppenheimer nodded briefly. He didn't have time to reply, as the man he was pursuing had made good use of the distraction. When Oppenheimer looked ahead toward Mauerstraße, he could just about spot the man disappearing around the corner.

Oppenheimer started to run. When he reached the corner, the man had veered off and was now running diagonally opposite behind the re-mains of the Holy Trinity Church. The roof dome had been completely de-stroyed by a bomb; empty window openings jutted upward. Oppenheimer hurried around the nave of the church and at the last moment managed to see the man turning into Kronenstraße.

Oppenheimer no longer paid any attention to what was going on around him. He ignored the shoveling forced laborers and the honking fire engines. He hastened across the street, an obstacle course amidst peo-ple and building materials. He sensed how close he was to solving this case. He could not afford to mess up this opportunity.

Next, his prey had to cross Friedrichstraße. It was one of the main thoroughfares and quite wide, so there was no cover. The man in the leather coat sought to make up for this by running even faster, taking the crossroad to Leipziger Straße. Oppenheimer's mouth was dry. Dust and ash burned in his chest. His eyes began to water, as in his haste he'd completely forgotten to put the goggles back on.

His breath rattling, he managed to cross Leipziger Straße. His legs felt wobbly. He wouldn't be able to keep up this pace for much longer.

The man had run into a closely built-up neighborhood. Oppenheimer had to stop at the next crossroads to get his bearings. Frantically, he glanced left and right into corners and alleyways. Just when he feared he'd lost him, he spotted him again. His target also seemed to be out of breath. He was leaning against a wall, his chest heaving. His lead had dwindled. Oppenheimer was just about to set off again when something held on to him.

He looked down in irritation. Next to him stood a member of the Hitler Youth in uniform. He was barely five feet tall and held a shovel out toward Oppenheimer.

"Hey, Jew!" he shouted. Oppenheimer flinched. *How on earth did he recognize me?* Then he realized that he'd forgotten to take the yellow star off his coat after Mrs. Schlesinger's visit. He had been running right through the center of Berlin with the Star of David.

"Help clear the rubble!" the little rascal commanded and continued to hold on to Oppenheimer. But Oppenheimer had more important things to do than clear the streets.

The man in the leather coat had noticed him and set off at a run, gasping for breath, increasing the distance. Oppenheimer wanted to tear himself away, but the boy continued to cling to his coat.

"Don't you understand, Jew?" he shouted in his boyish soprano. Oppenheimer did what he felt the boy's parents should have done a long time ago. Without a word, he slapped him round the face.

Oppenheimer just caught a glimpse of the boy's astounded expression before he set off to chase the murderer. When he got to the next crossroad where the man had vanished, he heard distant shouts behind him but didn't pay any attention. When he got to the next corner, he stopped. The man had disappeared.

Oppenheimer looked to the left, but the alleyway was empty. Nor was there anyone in the alley to the right. His thoughts were racing. The man couldn't have gotten far. The row of houses was quite short, but it seemed impossible that he'd made it to the next side street. And yet the man seemed to have disappeared from the face of the earth. Oppenheimer was completely baffled. His target must have run through the rubble piling up along the street.

Oppenheimer was about to cut straight across when his gaze fell upon an open doorway. It was possible that his target had run in there, either to hide or to find another way out. One side of the building was already destroyed, but the other part still looked inhabited.

Oppenheimer pulled the door open and entered the building. In the dim light, he could make out the faint outline of a handrail. He tried to control his breath and listened. Initially, he only perceived the throbbing of his own pulse. He was surrounded by silence. Nothing appeared to move. But something was there.

Oppenheimer listened very carefully. There it was again. A noise from the floors above. Someone was up there. Hoping not to be discovered. Or *did he want* to be discovered? Was he trying to trap his pursuer? Get rid of him here, unobserved?

Carefully, Oppenheimer crept up the stairs. He moved quietly, tried to avoid sudden movements, but the wooden steps creaked.

It seemed to take forever to reach the first landing. Oppenheimer broke out in a sweat; his muscles were tense. He stopped and looked around, peering into the twilight.

But there was nothing here. Just a few doors and the staircase to the next floor. He stood by the banister and listened for the noise from above. Where had it come from? Was it the next floor or the one above? Oppenheimer had his eyes half closed, concentrating on the silence, and tried to hear all the way up to the roof. A mistake, as the next noise didn't come from above.

One of the doors burst open with a loud rumble. Daylight poured into the staircase. Oppenheimer spun around—too late. A hand gripped his throat, the other pressed his upper body back over the banister. Helplessly, he grabbed his opponent's wrists and tried to wriggle his way out of the grasp. When he looked into his attacker's face, shock waves ran through Oppenheimer's body.

The face was not human. Two cold insect eyes hovered a few centimeters above him. A tube protruded from the head in place of a mouth. The creature appeared as grotesque as if it had risen from a bad dream. Its breath came in jerky bursts. Then Oppenheimer understood. The man was wearing a gas mask! As soon as he realized this, he changed his approach, let go of the opponent's wrists, and grabbed the lower part of the mask with one hand while trying to get hold of the head strap with the other. Frantically, he tugged at the mask, trying to displace it and block his opponent's view.

All of a sudden, his attacker let go. But Oppenheimer had no time to react. With one swift move, the man had grabbed his legs and lifted them up. Oppenheimer was hanging in the air.

Panicking, he reached backward as the man was trying to heave him over the banister. He felt something solid. Instinctively, he clung to it. When he was thrown over the bannister, his arms gripped the handrail.

He hung helplessly in the air. The man with the gas mask tried to loosen Oppenheimer's grip. Oppenheimer clung on desperately. He didn't know how far down the fall would be, how long it would take until he hit the floor. He grabbed the attacker, clung to his jacket with his right hand, but it was hard to pull him closer through the railing. Perhaps he could get him to lose his balance. If the attacker didn't let go, they'd fall into the depths together. Oppenheimer was determined to make his opponent pay a high price for his victory.

Through all this struggling, Oppenheimer failed to hear the shrill voices calling from below. He felt his opponent let go of him, hasten back into the room, and close the door behind him.

Footsteps could be heard on the stairs, but Oppenheimer did not pay them any attention. He pulled himself up over the banister and finally felt firm ground beneath his feet again. But there was no time for feeling relieved. He flung open the door through which his opponent had disappeared and almost didn't see the precipice he headed toward.

Oppenheimer found himself in a flat, or rather the paltry remains of such. Wind blew into his face. The open façade gave an indiscreet view of the striped wallpaper. Only a narrow ledge remained of the room, in whose corner a left-behind armchair was exposed to the elements. A bomb had destroyed the remainder of the flat.

Oppenheimer carefully peered over the crumbling edge. The man was below him. Oppenheimer spotted the gas mask just a few meters away. The man was laboriously clambering his way down the side of the façade. Oppenheimer knew he would be faster if he used the stairs. He whirled around and was back on the landing when he ran into the group of youths. "That's the Jew!" the boy he'd encountered earlier shouted and pointed at Oppenheimer. Hands grabbed him. He desperately tried to get free, but resistance against these boys was pointless. They were all dressed identically: narrow leather straps across their chests, a buckle rather than a properly tied knot to hold the neckerchief in place below their Adam's apples, shoulder straps sewn onto their shirts—Oppenheimer was surrounded by a horde of Hitler Youths.

"He hit me and then ran off!" the boy said. "We can't take that from a Jew!"

The other boys were also in a flurry of excitement.

"Heini, what's he doing here anyway?" one of them asked.

The Hitler Youth whom Oppenheimer had slapped had a quick response. "He's probably a spy. Passing coordinates to the British or something like that."

Further protest came from the other boys. Oppenheimer was wedged in among them. He could feel the situation getting out of control. In an attempt to calm things down, he said, "Speak to SS Hauptsturmführer Vogler; he can explain everything."

"I bet that's just a trick," a boy of perhaps thirteen said. "The SS would have locked him up a long time ago."

Oppenheimer was desperate. "You don't understand, I work for the Hauptsturmführer. There is a murderer out there. He's going to escape if you don't let me go."

The Hitler Youth named Heini laughed derisively. "People like you don't work for the SS," he declared categorically. The freckled boy looked at him with hostility. He pulled something from his pocket and held it under Oppenheimer's nose. It was a knife like the one every Hitler Youth member carried. "You're not getting away. It doesn't matter how much you beg." First, he shoved Oppenheimer against the wall, then he asked his comrades, "What shall we do with him?"

"We should shoot him in the back of the head," one of the boys said.

"Hang him!" another said.

A slender boy disagreed. "Oh no, Jürgen. We can't just kill him."

"Why not?"

The slender boy didn't seem to have an answer. He shrugged unhappily. "I don't know," he finally sighed.

The point of Heini's knife came dangerously close to Oppenheimer's throat. The glint in the boy's eyes betrayed the fact that he knew what power he possessed all of a sudden. Oppenheimer recognized the sadistic impulse in Heini's gaze. The half-open mouth in front of him was distorted.

"You heard. We have to punish you," Heini hissed. Then he commanded, "Bring him downstairs. There's a streetlight over there."

"You can't do that!" Oppenheimer protested. To no avail. The boys had already taken him in their midst and were stumbling down the stairs. Oppenheimer didn't know what was happening.

They stopped on the pavement. Two boys twisted his arms behind his back and held him tight while Heini pranced around with the drawn knife. "Has anyone got a rope?"

"Where are we meant to get that from?" one of the boys said.

"Detlef's father has a haberdashery!"

Heini considered this alternative. Then he said, "No use. It will take too long. Let's just stab him."

The slender boy cleared his throat once more. "We can't just kill someone."

Annoyed, Heini closed his eyes. Then he pushed the knife into the slender boy's hand. "Right, you do it, Götz. That's an order."

Götz looked at Heini in dismay, then at the knife in his hand. He was breathing heavily, shook his head. "I can't," he said, his voice constricted.

The boys were silent. Heini stepped close to Götz. "You're not going to chicken out, are you?"

"But I can't just . . . a human being—" he began.

Heini interrupted him. "It's not a human being. It's a *Jew*."

Götz slowly raised the knife. His hand was shaking. Doubt was written all over his face, but he didn't dare object. Everyone was looking at him.

"Get on with it, or are you a chicken?" Heini whispered.

Götz stared numbly at Oppenheimer. Then he took a hesitant step forward, then another. He was just a few centimeters away from Oppen-heimer. He bent his arm.

Oppenheimer's initial instinct was to call for help. But he was sure that no one would save him. He tensed his arm muscles, but the two boys behind him were holding on tight.

Now Götz was so close that Oppenheimer could hear his breath. Tears had gathered in the boy's eyes.

"You've seen what our enemies have done here," Heini whispered. "It's his fault."

Suddenly, Götz pressed his lips together in determination. All empathy was gone from his face. He reached back. Oppenheimer realized that the boy was about to deal a death blow.

"Stop!" a shout came from farther back. A deep voice, an adult.

Götz stopped and turned around. Oppenheimer also looked up.

"Well done, boys!" Vogler was approaching. "I've been looking for him. I'll take him into custody."

The boys from the Hitler Youth saluted. Only Götz still stood in front of Oppenheimer with the knife. He lowered his arm. All tension had left his body. He didn't appear relieved, but instead confused. With an embar-rassed shrug, he gave Heini the knife back. Then he, too, saluted Vogler.

"You've been a great help," Vogler praised the boys. "I will put you forward for a reward."

The Hitler Youth boys beamed full of pride.

■

"Did you see his face?" Vogler wanted to know. They were sitting in a conference room in the Reich Chancellery.

"Only very briefly," Oppenheimer replied. "I wouldn't be able to de-scribe him in detail. I just saw his eyes, and then he was gone. When he tried to overpower me, he wore a gas mask."

Vogler hesitated. "A gas mask?"

"Yes, but not one of the current models. He wore one from World War I. They are pretty much obsolete now. You can't even get a filter for the old things."

"What is he doing with that? Why wear a gas mask that no longer works?"

"No idea. Maybe he just wanted to disguise himself. Or maybe it has sentimental value. We've already ascertained that there is a connection to World War I. These damn boys! I almost had him!" Oppenheimer was still furious about the fact that the Hitler Youth members had been praised by Vogler. Although the chances of catching the suspect were practically nil now, Vogler had immediately started a manhunt.

Oppenheimer couldn't forget the image of Heini walking up and down in front of him with the knife. He considered in what sense there was a similarity between Vogler and the Hitler Youth. It was an interesting question, whether the adolescents nowadays imitated the adults or whether the adults behaved like children.

Oppenheimer was exhausted and took the rest of the day off. Vogler didn't object, as he still had to interview the Reich Chancellery employees and monitor the manhunt for the fugitive. He seemed to understand that Oppenheimer wouldn't be much help today. And anyway, it was highly unlikely that someone from the Reich Chancellery had seen the perpetrator place the body parts.

When Oppenheimer got up to go home, Vogler stopped him.

"Wait," Vogler said and tore Oppenheimer's Star of David from his coat. "I think I'll confiscate that."

Oppenheimer nodded. "Yes, I suppose I'll be more useful alive," he said bitterly.

But when Oppenheimer set off toward Levetzowstraße, he changed his plan and decided to seek out Billhardt. He had to find out the name of the SA man, the suspect, regardless of how tired he was. He was determined to pester Billhardt until he disclosed the name. And anyway, now seemed like a good opportunity. Oppenheimer considered it unlikely that he would be tailed, given all the chaos around him.

■

"Tell them it's a message from Schiller. The suspect's name is Johannes Lutzow. The investigation was in September 1932. I need all the files connected to the case. Lüttke knows what to do."

Hilde wrote down everything Oppenheimer had said. "Johannes Lutzow, right," she mumbled. "Did Billhardt give you the name straightaway?"

Oppenheimer grimaced. "It was hard work getting it out of him. Could I maybe have a schnapps or something like that?"

Hilde looked at him in surprise. "Well, I never thought I'd see the day."

"You have no idea what I've been through this week."

"What happened?"

"Schnapps first," Oppenheimer stated.

Three glasses later, he'd described the latest murder and the finding of the four arms outside the Reich Chancellery.

"I really don't like the sound of that," Hilde said, worried. "It's escalating. The time in between the murders is diminishing. He seems to be feeling more pressure. At the same time, he is taking more risks. That was quite a feat today. He must consider himself vastly superior."

"That precisely is our advantage," Oppenheimer replied. "He'll expose himself. He made a big mistake by appearing at the crime site today."

"Of course that's our advantage. But I wonder what price we have to pay until he's captured. I don't mean the stupid cow who was his last victim. I worry about the fact that he now knows who's chasing him. It can become dangerous for you."

"Let him come. I'm just waiting to get my hands on him again. I found the Hitler Youth a lot scarier." Oppenheimer paused to think. "Where does the hate come from? They were *children,* for goodness' sake."

"The hate has always been there. It's not unusual in young men; they like to rebel, participate in all sorts of crap. No idea where it comes from. It's probably the way some of them establish their self-worth. Hitler exploited the hate for his purposes. That's what's so insidious about it."

"I ask myself what will happen to these children when the war is finally over."

"This generation is lost," Hilde said and knocked back a shot of schnapps. "They have been conditioned from a young age. They were taught everything: racial science, anti-Semitism, all the rubbish."

"If they've been conditioned, then you should be able to reverse it all again."

"Possibly. But you're not working in laboratory conditions out there. They're unlikely to be able to shake it off. I fear that the damage that these criminals have caused to those children is beyond repair."

Oppenheimer thought back to the Hitler Youth boy Götz, to the doubt in his eyes. He wasn't so sure that Hilde was right this time.

■

The following afternoon brought devastating news. "Oh, hell and damnation!" Oppenheimer shouted and threw the next-best folder across the room. "What is that supposed to mean—none of the suspects ever lived in Köpenick? They *must* have! I can't be wrong! Otherwise, the latest murder just doesn't make sense!"

Vogler sat on the sofa and watched Oppenheimer's outburst without commenting, but his gaze showed how disappointed he was. He indicated Oppenheimer's slips of paper. "We've been through all the people whose names you put on the board. If your assumptions are correct, then none of them can be our perpetrator."

Oppenheimer took a deep breath and slowly ran his fingers through his hair. "Right. Let's look at it from a different angle. Let's concentrate on what we have. Yesterday, the murderer deposited four parts of a dead body in the city center during a bombardment in broad daylight. How did he get there? Why did no one notice him?"

"The Reich Chancellery employees were still in the bunker," Vogler started his summary. "The SS men were guarding the main portal from the inside during the attack. After the all clear, everyone returned to their posts. A secretary noticed the body parts when he looked out of the window. The four arms don't take up much space; the perpetrator might have carried them in his air raid suitcase. No one would have noticed."

Oppenheimer took up this train of thought. "The only thing that would have been noticeable was the smell of decay. Judging by their state, they weren't kept in a chilled environment. This means that the murderer couldn't have traveled by train or bus. Someone would have noticed the smell."

"So he walked or had some other means of transport."

"Means of transport," Oppenheimer mumbled. His gaze directed down, arms crossed, he paced the carpet. "The perpetrator has a delivery van; we know that now. There are not many of those left in Berlin. Most of them are in use at the front. This has to be useful for us. Do we have a plaster impression of the tire yet?"

"I had an additional copy made, just to be on the safe side. If you need one, we can fetch it from police headquarters. The same goes for the footprint."

Oppenheimer continued to ponder. The night watchman from the Olympic stadium had said that a tarpaulin had been stretched across the loading area. Oppenheimer had seen a similar delivery van during the investigation. Suddenly, the image appeared before his inner eye. Salon Kitty. Drinks. The delivery van. The driver unloading crates of spirits. Of course. There could be a connection. At least between the Adlon and Kitty's place. Alcoholic beverages were delivered to both establishments. Höcker & Sons had several of these delivery trucks standing in their yard.

"Tell Hoffmann. We need to go to police headquarters immediately. I need a copy of the tire print straightaway. It's the only reliable lead we have right now. I'm going to take a close look at the vehicles at Höcker & Sons." Oppenheimer glanced briefly at his pocket watch. It was five o'clock now. Höcker & Sons would be closing in an hour. But he didn't have the slightest doubt that Hoffmann would get him there in time, driving at his usual breakneck speed. Just to be safe, he rang the office to tell them he was coming. Miss Behringer was on the other end of the line.

"Inspector Oppenheimer here. I'll be coming by shortly to clear up a few details. It won't take long. I'll be there by seven at the latest, probably before six. Would that be all right?" A noise came from the receiver that Oppenheimer interpreted as a quiet sigh. Miss Behringer didn't seem pleased with the announcement. But she remained friendly. "I presume it's urgent?"

"I think we have a lead. The quicker I can determine whether it's a solid one, the better."

A brief hesitation. "I'll be in the office until seven, Inspector."

Oppenheimer went to the coatrack and slipped into his coat. He had no time to lose. "Where is Hoffmann?" he shouted down the cellar. Without waiting for Vogler's reply, he opened the front door.

Suddenly, he heard a metallic click. But he reacted too late; the door was already wide open. The barrels of two guns were pointing directly at him.

Oppenheimer instinctively took a step back, but the two SS men followed him in and kept him in their sight with routine precision. A man in civilian clothes entered his line of vision. He seemed to be in command. Something flickered briefly in his hand when he showed Oppenheimer a metal badge. Even without reading it, Oppenheimer knew that the words

SECRET STATE POLICE and a number were engraved on it. A man from the Gestapo. Was he going to take him into protective custody? Send him to a concentration camp?

"Mr. Oppenheimer, I presume?"

Oppenheimer swallowed before he was able to nod. Vogler also seemed to have heard something. "What's going on?" he called, coming up the stairs. When Vogler saw the men, he snapped his heels and saluted. "Hauptsturmführer Vogler!"

The Gestapo men looked from one to the other. Oppenheimer wondered whether he had actually briefly seen a trace of amusement in the face of the man in charge. "Follow me. Both of you," he ordered.

There was no point in refusing.

23

———+———

Oppenheimer stared at the bare stone wall. They'd been waiting for over two hours now. Vogler, too, sat forlornly on his chair, staring ahead morosely. If the waiting was supposed to intimidate them, the strategy was fulfilling its purpose.

At least Oppenheimer knew where they were. But this information didn't do much to reassure him. He hadn't been able to recognize much in the black limousine because of the lowered screens on the windows, but when they'd gotten out, he'd recognized his surroundings. The day before, they had inspected the body parts just a short distance away. They were in the government district again. The old bombed-out Reich Chancellery was on the other side of the road, so they were in Wilhelmstraße. The building they'd been taken to had a bulky gray façade. A pillar had been embedded into the façade of the building to the right of the big doors; a stone eagle perched high above, clutching a swastika in his claws. This had confirmed Oppenheimer's suspicions. They'd been taken to the Propaganda Ministry.

This was the building where Joseph Goebbels, Reich Minister of Propaganda, personally pulled the strings, told the newspapers what to print, approved the weekly newsreel before it flickered across the screens in the remotest villages. From here, he controlled a huge think tank. Everything that was supposed to enter the heads of the German people was conceived, censured, and prepared here. But Oppenheimer had absolutely no idea what all this had to do with their investigation.

He wriggled around restlessly on his chair. Muted steps could be heard outside the door, the handle was pushed down, and a young man with a neat side parting looked into the room. "Ah, there you are!" he said, pulled out a document folder, and riffled through it. He made a note of something, closed the folder again, and put the pencil behind his ear. "If you'd like to follow me," he requested politely and held the door open for them. Oppenheimer and Vogler exchanged a brief glance.

The young man strode ahead and led them down a wide stairwell. Each of their steps was answered by a dozen phantom steps. The sober environment demonstrated that cool logic reigned here. Oppenheimer was not unimpressed by the architecture, but at the same time, he felt his soul freeze. They reached another floor. The young man opened a heavy door that was covered in thick leather from the inside. A second similarly upholstered door came right behind it. It was like an air lock. Oppenheimer recognized the architectural principle. These double doors served to insulate the sound. But what sort of sound wasn't allowed to escape from the room on the other side? The screams of mistreated prisoners? Were enemy agents interrogated here?

The young man opened the second door and pointed into the room. "Please take a seat. If you'd just like to wait for a short moment."

Oppenheimer stepped hesitantly into the artificial light. He stopped in amazement. Vogler also hesitated for a moment and quickly assessed the new surroundings. He was quite good at hiding his surprise. The door closed behind them with a satisfying smack. Now they were completely cut off from the outside world.

Although no daylight could penetrate this room, it was in no way dark, as they were standing in front of a snow-white screen. Oppenheimer looked around curiously. Two small windows were embedded in the wall opposite. Behind these, the glass eyes of the film projectors stared out. They were in a viewing room. Oppenheimer had never seen a private cinema like this before. The raked rows of seats would accommodate maybe a dozen viewers. The room appeared almost gloomy when not in use. The light in the projection room was on, and a film projectionist was busy at the machines.

"Right, well, we've had the tour," Oppenheimer growled. "Now what?"

They didn't have to wait long until the door opened again. Oppenheimer knew the face of the new arrival only too well; everyone did. Before them stood the person who ruled over this building and all its staff. Now Oppenheimer understood why he was commonly—and disparagingly— known as the *Shrunken Teuton*. Joseph Goebbels was at least half a head smaller than Oppenheimer.

Vogler quickly stepped aside for the minister and saluted. Then he stood in front of the wall as if turned to a salt pillar. Oppenheimer initially didn't know how to greet the man. He didn't consider the Hitler salute appropriate; after all, he was a Jew. Simply shaking Goebbels's hand was also out of the question. Instead, Oppenheimer removed his hat and bowed politely.

But Goebbels ignored him. He appeared a little distracted, seemed to have had a tiring day. In place of a greeting, he pressed an envelope into Vogler's hand. "Could you please explain this to me?"

Vogler came back to life. He opened the envelope and pulled out a few pieces of carton. The edges were wavy, and Oppenheimer knew it had to be photographs. Vogler stared at the pictures, bewildered. Oppenheimer went to stand next to him and have a look too. In stark black-and-white contrasts, the image depicted a swastika on a stone floor, comprised of four arms. It was possible to make out the Reich Chancellery in some of the photos. Without a doubt, these were pictures of yesterday's body parts.

Goebbels watched their reactions, his arms folded. "Well, cat got your tongue?" he finally barked. His body was tense, the day's exertions forgotten. "I'd like an answer to my question."

The SS men who had shielded the site from the public were missing from the images. "Who took the photographs?" Oppenheimer asked.

"That's neither here nor there," Goebbels said. "I want to know what the hell is going on there. Now tell me, Hauptsturmführer, what or whom are we dealing with here?"

"We are hunting a mass murderer," Vogler explained. "Gruppenführer Reithermann initiated this investigation after his foreign-language secretary was found dead." He roughly outlined the five murders and summarized the results of the investigation so far. Goebbels was not particularly amused. "This case was declared top secret. It is irresponsible that these images were leaked."

Oppenheimer intervened. "I can say that these are not the images that we had taken of the site. These were taken earlier. I am guessing it was shortly before the all clear was given and before anyone in the Reich Chancellery discovered the body parts."

Goebbels looked at Oppenheimer intently. He considered briefly and then replied, "To your first question: the images were taken by a photographer who occasionally works for various newspapers. The gentleman has already been given his marching orders. We shall see if he is similarly conscientious at the front."

Oppenheimer was disappointed, as he would have liked to have questioned the man. He must have been at the site before they arrived. Had he seen anything else? Thanks to Goebbels, there was now no way of finding out.

"Are these all the pictures there are?" Oppenheimer asked.

"I bloody well hope so!" Goebbels bellowed. "He tried to sell them to the highest-bidding newspaper. Luckily, one of the chief editors called me immediately. Are you aware of what would have happened if someone had published these pictures?"

Vogler deliberated this. He wanted to make sure he didn't give the wrong answer. Finally, Oppenheimer said, "It would probably have caused a mass panic."

"A mass panic? Yes, *at best*." The propaganda minister was one of those people who liked to hear themselves speak. Steeped in his own importance, he puffed out his chest, raised his index finger, and began his lecture. "Our situation probably isn't clear to you. We are in a strategically important moment. We have regained the people's trust in us by deploying the V-1. But we cannot carelessly gamble away this political credit. Especially as we are nowhere near total and complete activation of our war efforts. A great deal is going to happen, gentlemen. We must put an end to the luxury enjoyed by people in the homeland. The nation must be combed even more radically to seek out men fit for military service. Depending on the situation, it may even be necessary for the führer to appeal directly to the people and organize a national uprising against the enemy. But if we start letting such horror stories become public knowledge, it's only a small step for defeatism to spread. We simply cannot afford that."

Oppenheimer stood next to Vogler, but he didn't feel part of the conversation. While the Hauptsturmführer listened to his superior, evidently contrite, Oppenheimer allowed his thoughts to wander. In these surroundings, Goebbels seemed like a bad actor who had jumped off the screen. Oppenheimer had to think about the situation he was in. He was here alone with the minister and an SS man whose weapon was in immediate reach. He weighed up his options. Would he be able to overpower Vogler and get control of his weapon? Should he shoot Goebbels? He probably wouldn't get far. Oppenheimer calmly considered whether he had what it took to be a martyr. But was there any point? Wouldn't another Nazi soon succeed him as propaganda minister? Even after Heydrich's death, the gap had quickly been filled, everything had continued in the Reich Security Main Office as if nothing had happened. Countless party lackeys were frothing at the mouth, waiting to take over from Goebbels. To Oppenheimer, the NSDAP seemed like a hydra with countless heads that couldn't be chopped off quickly enough before they grew back. Or did he only think that because he was such a coward?

Goebbels was talking at them, but it was as if someone had turned down the volume. Oppenheimer noticed the minister moving up and down nimbly but with a certain amount of effort, as he had a clubfoot. This reminded him of an additional nickname the people of Berlin had given Goebbels: *Hobblestiltskin*. It was interesting that someone like him, of all people, propagated a worldview that indulged the idol of a blond superman made of Krupp steel. How would Hilde interpret that? Had Goebbels learned to be tough on himself to compensate for his disability? Had the National Socialists' racial fanaticism been so enticing to him because he could use it to detract from his own deficits, to be on the same level as the pure-blooded Aryans, to subsequently humiliate anyone who had ever derided him in his life? He decided to discuss this with Hilde when the opportunity next arose.

He observed Goebbels carefully. The minister's hair was dark, his nose prominent. Vogler's facial features were far less distinctive. Oppenheimer had to smile. In this particular group, he was the only one who looked a bit like an Aryan, he of all people, a Jew. After what seemed like forever, Goebbels finally got to the point. "To put it in a nutshell, I'm giving you a week to clear the whole matter."

"Yes, Minister," Vogler said in a loud voice.

"There will be no further deferment. Hand me the perpetrator and all the files next Thursday, or else I will hold you personally responsible."

Vogler swallowed hard. "Yes, sir!"

But Goebbels still hadn't finished. He sat down and shifted his gaze to Oppenheimer, mustering him critically from top to toe. "So you are Jewish, Oppenheimer?"

"Yes."

"Well, these things happen. Hauptsturmführer Vogler seems to have a lot of faith in your capabilities. However, no one should find out that you are of non-Aryan origin. If it weren't for your name, one could easily be deceived. I presume that you've been given new quarters for the duration of the investigation?"

Oppenheimer looked at the minister in surprise. "I live in a Jewish House."

"And in the mornings? What do you do? Do you drive to work from there every day?"

Oppenheimer wasn't sure what Goebbels was getting at. Vogler answered, "One of my drivers picks him up in the mornings. We have set up an office in the Kameradschaftssiedlung in Zehlendorf for him."

Goebbels jumped up all of a sudden. "Are you out of your mind, Vogler? No, this driving around Berlin has to come to an end. Give Oppenheimer a flat nearby. Most definitely *not* in a Jewish House!" He then turned directly to Oppenheimer and commanded, "For my part, you are suspended from the affiliation to the Jewish people until the end of the investigation. Until then, you are to be treated as an Aryan. Vogler will take care of everything. That will be all, gentlemen."

Oppenheimer looked at Goebbels, completely taken by surprise. He hadn't known that the propaganda minister's authority stretched as far as religious affiliation. What would happen now? Would he miraculously grow a new foreskin?

The minister waved his guests off distractedly. He seemed to want to expel them like an annoying thought. His gaze already focused on the screen, he reminded them once more, "Don't forget, you have one week. Dismissed."

The two men obeyed and left as the light around them slowly dimmed. In the doorway, Oppenheimer looked round once more. Goebbels had already instructed the projectionist to start the film. A close-up of a pretty actress flitted across the screen.

∎

"Pack your things," Vogler ordered. They were sitting in the back of the limousine again. The hands of the Hauptsturmführer were still shaking. The encounter with Goebbels seemed to have made a deep impression on him. "Get everything ready before Hoffmann comes to pick you up. My staff will come tomorrow lunchtime and shift everything."

"It's not much," Oppenheimer replied. "Maybe two or three suitcases in all."

When Oppenheimer stepped into his room fifteen minutes later, Lisa was already asleep in bed. It was past midnight. He gently woke her up; after all, the matter was important.

"We're moving tomorrow."

Lisa looked at him drowsily. She needed a bit of time for the news to hit home. Then she sat up abruptly. "Who says so?"

"I fear you won't believe me." And Oppenheimer began to tell his story.

∎

Oppenheimer carefully clasped the two tins left over from Dr. Klein's legacy between his knees. That was probably the safest place for the valuable treasure, while he himself was being flung from side to side and had to endure several bursts of acceleration in the sidecar of Hoffmann's motorbike.

He had gotten up earlier that morning to help Lisa pack their belongings. To be honest, neither of them had really been able to sleep with excitement. The packing took no time at all, as they'd been sitting on half-packed suitcases for years and barely had any belongings to call their own. As he was unable to tell Lisa where Vogler would accommodate them, Oppenheimer suggested to Lisa that he'd pick her up outside the rubber factory at the end of her shift.

Despite the uncertainty, he left the Jewish House without much regret. Nor was there much of a farewell from the Schlesingers. He simply deposited the suitcases with them, saying that someone would be coming to pick them up, then he got into Hoffmann's devilish vehicle, picked up the plaster cast of the tire print from police headquarters, and went directly to Höcker & Sons.

Ms. Behringer received them in the office with an ominous frown. "Ah, Inspector. I'm guessing you weren't able to make it last night?"

"I'm terribly sorry that I kept you waiting," Oppenheimer said apologetically and handed her the two tins. "Here, to make up for it." When Ms. Behringer read the label of the tins, her discontent evaporated. She was speechless and cleared her throat several times. "Oh gosh. I'm not sure. I can't really accept this."

"Of course you can, I owe you. After all, you spent the evening in the office last night because of me."

In passing, he noticed how well proportioned her face was. When she began to smile, her eyes took on a lively gleam. Would he have given her the tins if she hadn't been as attractive? Oppenheimer didn't want to consider this any further. He excused his behavior with the fact that he needed information and that this justified almost any means. "I need some information," he said quickly before Ms. Behringer had similar thoughts. "Are the Guesthouse Schmidt and the Hotel Adlon on your client list?"

"One moment, please. Do take a seat." Ms. Behringer went over to the huge filing cabinet and took out a box of files. "I can tell you that we occasionally supply the Hotel Adlon, I know that for a fact, but a Guesthouse Schmidt . . ." She looked through the files until she found an entry. "Giesebrechtstraße 11?"

Oppenheimer felt the blood shoot to his head when he heard the question. "That's correct."

"Well, the Guesthouse Schmidt is not a regular customer, but we have delivered to this address. Yes, we've supplied them several times over the last few years."

It all made sense. Everything came together at Höcker & Sons. Oppenheimer was sure he was on the right track. Christina Gerdeler frequented the Adlon to acquire wealthy clients. Together with Gruppenführer Reithermann, Julie Dufour often frequented the hotel that was supplied by Höcker & Sons, the company where Inge Friedrichsen had worked as a secretary. And the same company also supplied the Salon Kitty, whose employee with the pseudonym Friederike had found a violent death. This could not be a coincidence. Although it didn't yet explain how Traudel

Herrmann, the latest victim, fitted into the scheme of things, Oppenheimer was optimistic that there was a connection.

"Right, I will need to inspect all the companies' lorries."

Ms. Behringer, who was putting the tins of meat in her desk drawer, paused for a moment. "You mean you have a lead? Do you know who killed Inge?"

Oppenheimer shrugged. "At the moment, it's just a hunch," he reassured the young woman. It was still too early for a triumph.

■

When war had broken out, the party had drafted motorized vehicles to the front, and so the sight of them was rare in Berlin. The few automobiles that still drove around the city were largely official cars. It seemed that Höcker had successfully used his connections to the SS to organize a small vehicle fleet for his business.

But Oppenheimer didn't care about these details. He hurried down the steps. He was in luck. Ms. Behringer had told him that the entire fleet of Höcker's lorries was in the courtyard. She had just been preparing the delivery slips for the first load when he surprised her with his gift. He approached the open warehouse door with big strides.

A man in a long smock turned around. It was Häffgen, looking just as cranky as during Oppenheimer's last visit. He did not seem pleased at the sight of this unauthorized person in his warehouse, crime officer or not. "Ah, you again. What do you want?"

"I need to inspect the tire profiles of your delivery vans."

"Are you also with the traffic department?"

Oppenheimer ignored the comment. It was better to present Häffgen with a fait accompli. "How many vehicles does the company own?"

"There are four delivery vans in total."

"The other three are still in the shed?"

"I suppose so."

Oppenheimer took out the plaster cast that he had wrapped in a piece of cloth, bent down, and compared the profile with the tire of the vehicle that was currently being loaded. They didn't match.

Next, he went to the shed where the other vehicles were parked. One driver was already in his vehicle, dozing. The front tire of the lorry was easy to compare to the plaster cast, but it was more difficult with the back tire, as the sky was overcast and there wasn't much light in the back of the shed. Oppenheimer had difficulty recognizing the profile. He crawled from tire to tire on his knees, bending toward the rubber profile. He also checked the grooves with his fingertips just to make sure.

Oppenheimer spent almost half an hour there to be completely sure. He even checked the spare wheels. He inspected them several times over, until he came to the devastating conclusion that none of them matched the print that the murderer had left at the site where the body had been found.

Of course, Oppenheimer knew that so-called hot leads were all too often deceptive. Which was why he'd become relatively careful about drawing conclusions during his time with the murder squad. But he'd been so sure this time. Maybe it was because he had missed the important clues. Oppenheimer walked unhappily across the yard, racking his brain, his hands deep in his coat pockets, the cigarette tip between his lips. It would all have fitted so well together.

When he reentered the office, Ms. Behringer looked at him expectantly. "And? Did you find anything?"

"Unfortunately, I was out of luck," Oppenheimer replied, his head bowed. "Just one more question: Were any of the vehicles in the garage this week? Have any tires been replaced?"

"Not that I know of. I didn't get an invoice. And if one of the vehicles had broken down, I would have had to inform Mr. Ziegler." Ms. Behringer thought for a moment. Then she said slowly, "Of course, Ziegler. There is one more vehicle." Her eyes wandered around the room absentmindedly, then she nodded.

"What were you saying?" Oppenheimer pressed her.

"Ziegler. Karl Ziegler. We call him when one of the lorries breaks down or we have more to deliver than our four vehicles can manage. He has his own lorry. Well, actually, it's little more than an old boneshaker, but at least it has a loading area. If we need Mr. Ziegler, I call him at short notice."

"I've never heard of a Karl Ziegler. He wasn't on the list of employees Mr. Höcker gave me."

"He's not on the payroll because he doesn't receive a regular salary. Wait a moment."

Ms. Behringer went over to the filing cabinet and after a brief search pulled out a file. "Here, his address and telephone number."

Oppenheimer took the card. When he saw the address, his hands began to shake. "Ziegler lives in Köpenick?"

"As you can see."

"What sort of person is this Ziegler guy? How would you describe him?"

As usual, Ms. Behringer spoke frankly. "He's not very bright. Barely speaks. That's why everyone here calls him *Gormless Kalle*. And, well, he's a creep."

Oppenheimer pricked his ears. "Did something happen?"

"It's not really worth mentioning. I caught him looking under my skirt. He stood right under the stairs and stared up at me through the steps. I've switched to wearing trouser suits since then. Better safe than sorry."

The building blocks fitted together. This also explained how the murderer had probably come across Traudel Herrmann. He knew his first victim through his work with Höcker. He knew Mrs. Herrmann because he lived near her, just as Oppenheimer had presumed. They had a suspect. Now they just had to find him.

24

Although Billhardt was in his own sweet home, he felt anything but comfortable in the presence of his unexpected guest. Reluctantly, he thought of how, in a sudden moment of obedience, he'd written that bloody letter. When he'd passed it round at police headquarters, he'd never expected someone would come by and see him about it the next day. And even less so that the someone would be an SS Hauptsturmführer. Billhardt swore quietly to himself. That's what you got for doing your civic duty.

Despite the awkward situation, he tried to keep calm. And in actual fact, his thoughts were clear as rarely before. He was in a bit of a dilemma. He had to find a way to play down his role. It must not become known that it had been he who had made Oppenheimer aware of Lutzow.

The SS man who'd introduced himself as Vogler seemed to be in a hurry. He'd refused to sit down, simply stood in front of the window and fixed Billhardt with a challenging look.

Billhardt said vaguely, "The day before yesterday, he came to see me in the afternoon. Inspector Oppenheimer. I mean the former inspector, of course. It was just as I described it."

"I want to hear it from you," Vogler demanded.

"He'd already paid me a visit the week before. Initially, I didn't know there was a purpose to his visit. I thought he just wanted to get back in touch with an old colleague. Then he came out with it the day before yesterday. He wanted to get his hands on an old file. I was meant to procure it for him, but of course, I sent him away and told him that I couldn't do something like that."

"Which investigation was this?"

"It involved a member of the SA. His name is Johannes Lutzow. He was arrested in September 1932 because he attacked a Bolshevist in the man's flat. It seems Lutzow created a right bloodbath. The victim's wife sustained bad knife injuries."

"Were there injuries to her genital area?"

Billhardt couldn't hide his surprise. Angry with himself, he immediately lowered his gaze again. He mustn't show any emotion. That could be dangerous. It was better not to admit the details that Oppenheimer had given him on the current investigation. "Maybe. I believe I heard there were injuries of that sort. It was an unusual case that quickly spread around police headquarters. Lutzow was sentenced to death, but he was let off the following year. The führer's amnesty, you remember. It seems that Oppenheimer had also heard of the case at the time. He was still in service then. And now that he's involved in this new investigation, he remembered the old case and wanted me to get hold of the old file. Just like that. Of course, I refused."

"Did Oppenheimer give you further details of what he is currently working on?"

Billhardt shook his head vigorously. "He didn't want to tell me anything. He just mentioned something about female corpses. But I didn't press him. Then out of the blue, Oppenheimer asked about the Lutzow investigation. At first, I didn't know what to think of it, but then it seemed suspicious, and I considered it my duty to report it."

"But he must have at least given you my name; otherwise, you wouldn't have been able to write me this letter."

"I must have picked it up." Billhardt looked guiltily at Vogler. "But I know nothing more about the case that he is working on right now. I swear an oath to the führer on that, Hauptsturmführer Vogler."

Vogler frowned and paced up and down with his head lowered. "Does anyone else know about it?"

"I went directly to my superior."

Vogler stopped and looked at Billhardt. Doubt was reflected in his gaze. Billhardt tried with all his might to control his eyes. He knew that he mustn't look away if he wanted to convince Vogler of his story. Finally, the Hauptsturmführer said, "Very good. You acted perfectly correctly,

Billhardt." To reinforce this, he approached Billhardt and patted him on the shoulder. "If only everyone were as vigilant as you are. You see, I have a very particular task. The case is still classified as top secret. Whether the results of the search are made public or not has not yet been decided. It is also not for me to decide. My instructions are to ensure that all possible connections between the murder case and our party are not made public. Do you understand what I'm saying?"

Billhardt nodded. He had understood only too well.

"There is more to this case than meets the eye. Enemies of the state may be at work. They have an interest in damaging the party. They're probably fabricating evidence so it appears that the perpetrator comes from our own ranks. Even a hint or a rumor could severely damage national uprising, especially in times like this. You do understand that you must keep this matter in the strictest confidence?"

"Of course," Billhardt replied automatically. "My lips are sealed." He breathed a sigh of relief. Fortunately, the Hauptsturmführer had confirmed that he had done the right thing. Therefore, nothing would happen to him. And yet he felt a certain restlessness that had come over him several times in the last few hours. Could his behavior be considered a betrayal of Oppenheimer? He placated his conscience by telling himself that it hadn't been anything personal. He had only done what a good German had to do. It was that simple. Billhardt told himself that there was no point in thinking about it any further.

■

Although Oppenheimer was lucky and the telephone line was working, he was unable to reach Vogler in Zehlendorf. The radio operator who was manning the desk in the cellar of the small house had assured him that he would inform the Hauptsturmführer immediately and that backup was on its way.

Restlessly, Oppenheimer paced up and down in the dark entrance, his gaze fixed on the building opposite. He had set off for Köpenick immediately. Although he couldn't do much without Vogler, he wanted to play it safe and observe Ziegler's house so that the man couldn't get away. Not now, not after all the effort it had cost him to finally find a connection between the murder victims. Hoffmann was somewhere around the back of the building, guarding the back exits. Now all they could do was wait until Vogler arrived with his men.

In situations like this, time stretched out unbearably. An eternity passed until he finally spotted Vogler's Daimler. The vehicle stopped a dozen meters away. Three men in civilian clothes got out of the car with Vogler. Oppenheimer stepped out of the building's entrance and approached the group.

"His name is Karl Ziegler," Oppenheimer whispered. "He's a tenant with the owner of the garage, Mr. Braun. It is possible that Ziegler knew the victims."

Vogler inhaled loudly. "Well, let's get to it, then."

They crossed the street. The entrance to the garage was open. Before they reached it, a gentleman came toward them. He was in his early sixties. "Can I help you?" he asked as he cleaned his oily fingers on a cloth and took in Vogler's uniform.

"Mr. Braun, I presume?" Vogler inquired.

"Yes."

"We're here to speak to your tenant, Mr. Ziegler."

"You want to speak to Karl? No idea where he is. Haven't seen him since yesterday."

Oppenheimer stepped in. "Could you show us his flat?"

■

There wasn't much to see. Ziegler's accommodations were little more than a wooden hut behind the garage, just a few meters away from an old privy, consisting of two rooms, an anteroom where some shabby clothing hung, and the actual living room, which was just large enough to house a bed, an old cast-iron stove, and a table. Oppenheimer was glad that Vogler's men had waited outside. It would have been a squeeze if they'd all made their way into the room together.

"It looks like a pigsty in here," Oppenheimer said and pushed his hat back on his head. Ziegler had few possessions; the showpiece was the gramophone that was enthroned on its own stool. Several records in their paper sleeves were arranged next to it in an orderly manner. But Ziegler didn't seem to pay much attention to the rest of his belongings. Clothes strewn everywhere, old newspapers, in between cheap tat that looked like it had been won at a funfair. Ziegler did not take care of his things.

Oppenheimer picked up a pair of shoes from the corner of the room. After a brief inspection, he showed Vogler the soles. "Just like the print found at the Olympic stadium."

"Has Karl been up to something?" Mr. Braun asked curiously from the door. They turned around.

Vogler cleared his throat. "No, it's just a routine matter. We think Mr. Ziegler might have been a witness to a traffic accident, and we have a few questions for him."

The look on Mr. Braun's face showed that he didn't believe a word of Vogler's white lie. But he didn't ask any more questions. Instead, it was Oppenheimer's turn to pose a few questions. "How long has Mr. Ziegler worked for you?"

"Let me think now. It'll be four years in August. Karl is not the brightest spark. He can just about read, but only when he really concentrates. But he can repair machines, yes, he can. He's not too stupid for that. I wouldn't have believed it until I saw it."

"So he works in the garage and delivers for Höcker as a sideline?"

"Insofar as anything comes from them. I used to do it myself, but lifting all those crates has become too much for me. But Karl can do it."

"Is he gone a lot?"

"He's usually gone at the weekends. He gets restless by Friday afternoon and leaves as soon as he can. Sometimes heads off on Thursdays already. No idea where he goes. He's always back on Mondays. You can set your watch by him."

Oppenheimer looked around once more and thought for a moment.

"Where is the delivery van that Mr. Ziegler uses to deliver to Höcker & Sons?"

"He took it with him, just like every weekend."

Oppenheimer hesitated. It seemed that Braun gave his employees a lot of leeway. "You mean he drives around with your delivery van?"

"No, you don't get it. The van's his. Karl claims he put the whole thing together himself. Using individual parts from the scrapyard. Think he used to live in it, too, before he came to me."

Braun led Oppenheimer to the shed where Ziegler usually parked his van. Oppenheimer crouched down and examined the ground. It had been damp yesterday. The soil had had enough time to soak up the rainwater, a good prerequisite for getting a tire print. And Oppenheimer did indeed discover a clear print not far from the shed in between clumps of grass.

"This profile is a bit smudged," he said to Vogler. "At the Olympic stadium, the van had driven directly across the damp clay, which then dried. This print here is much harder to read. It probably couldn't be used in court, but the similarities are enough for me." Oppenheimer stood up and turned to Vogler. "I would say it's the same tire. Send out a search party for Ziegler. We need to catch him as quickly as possible. He's a prime suspect."

Vogler's men were already searching Ziegler's accommodations. "If you find an address, on a piece of paper or wherever, or maybe a street map, a sketch, or anything like that, please tell me," Oppenheimer instructed. "We are looking to establish the gentleman's whereabouts. Any little thing might help."

The men stopped rummaging. One of them glanced in Vogler's direction. When he nodded almost imperceptibly, they continued with their work. The men's hesitation once again reminded Oppenheimer that he had no official authority here. He was barely able to stop himself from joining the men in their search, but the hostile attitude of those around him made him reconsider. After just a few minutes of poking around, they had actually managed to worsen the disarray in Ziegler's room. The men worked almost soundlessly as they cut open the mattress with precise, rehearsed movements, raised the planks on the floor, and sounded out the walls for cavities that might contain something. Their faces reflected no hunting fever; they emotionlessly carried out their tasks. There was no doubt that these men were experts.

Oppenheimer stood in the backyard, indecisive, looking around. Church bells rang in the distance. His pocket watch showed a quarter to five. Soon it would be time to pick Lisa up from work. He realized that he still had no idea of where they would be housed after Goebbels had forbidden them to continue living in the Jewish House.

He turned around and knocked on the doorframe of Ziegler's hut. "Position someone in Ziegler's place just in case he comes back," he said to Vogler. "I need to head off to pick up my wife. Do you know where we are supposed to stay?"

Vogler looked at him blankly. Then he remembered the problem with

Oppenheimer's housing. "Yes, of course. We've found a solution. But we had to improvise a little bit."

■

As it was inconceivable for a second person to be transported in the side-car of Hoffmann's motorbike, they took a detour via Zehlendorf to exchange their vehicle for a car. When Hoffmann turned into the street, Lisa was already waiting outside the black iron fence of the factory building, looking expectantly down the street. Hoffmann came to a halt right next to her with screeching brakes. Lisa stopped short at first, until she spotted her husband in the back of the car. Oppenheimer got out with a smile and held the car door open for her. "In you get. We have our own chauffeur."

Lisa's colleagues, who were leaving the factory behind her, hesitated at the unfamiliar sight. When Lisa became aware of their quiet whispers, she quickly got in the car.

"We celebrated for hours in the factory today because we had no raw material," Lisa said. "And? What's happening? Where are they putting us up?"

"Nothing dramatic," Oppenheimer replied. "It's actually quite comfortable there."

He saw that Lisa had more questions, but she made do with the reply. Oppenheimer wouldn't have said anything anyway, as he wanted to surprise her.

The sky had been cloudy and gray all day, and now the treetops were enveloped in fog. Hoffmann, an old-school gentleman, opened the car door for Lisa. She got out in a daze, wide-eyed. She wasn't looking where she was going but stared incredulously at her surroundings. The almost autumnal weather reinforced the impression of stepping into a magical world. Lisa breathed in the smell of the forest and felt far away. "It's beautiful here."

Oppenheimer could understand Lisa's surprise. He thought of his own reaction when he'd first come to the colony. By now, these surroundings were increasingly becoming part of his daily routine and progressively losing their magic. Lisa turned to him, a question in her eyes. "But . . ."

He simply said, "Zehlendorf."

She immediately understood. "You mean we are being housed in the Kameradschaftssiedlung?"

"Out of the frying pan and into the fire. It seems that's all they have available right now. But you'll like it, despite the neighborhood." He winked at her. "It's over there," he said and pointed toward the little house.

Although he didn't really have the heart to destroy Lisa's illusions, he thought it best to warn her gently. "Remember, it's probably just for a week. I doubt they'll let us live here after that. Even if we do manage to catch the perpetrator by then."

"Then I'll consider it a holiday," Lisa said, looking at him.

"Yes, let's have a holiday," Oppenheimer said. With a sigh, the entire weight of the last weeks was lifted from his shoulders. He took Lisa's hand and led her toward the front door.

Oppenheimer almost stumbled across their three suitcases in the hallway, which someone had placed there, when footsteps could be heard stumbling up from the cellar. The radio operator's neatly drawn parting came into view. "I'm sorry, I didn't get a chance to take the suitcases upstairs yet," he said, clamping one of the pieces of luggage under his arm and picking up the other two by the handle. "There are two bedrooms upstairs." Then he carried everything up.

Lisa smiled, surprised that they even had their own porter here. "It's been a while since someone carried our suitcases for us."

Oppenheimer smiled. "And the best thing about it is we don't even need to tip."

There was a bathroom and two bedrooms on the upper floor. The radio operator zealously offered to unpack their suitcases, but that was too much attentiveness for Lisa. She had always wanted to have a house of her own, but Oppenheimer had never been able to put aside enough money to afford one. When he saw his wife in the new surroundings, he realized that this house came pretty close to Lisa's ideal home.

She surveyed the bedrooms. The second room was larger and had a double bed. Even the beds were made up. "Let's see what the mattress is like," Oppenheimer said, slipped out of his shoes, and lay down on the bed. His back had bitterly missed such comforts over the last few years. The beds in the Jewish Houses were not nearly as soft, and recently, they'd spent most of their nights on the hard cellar floor because of the air raids. He was just about to stretch out when he saw Lisa's expression shift.

"That ruins everything," she said and placed her hands on her hips. But she wasn't looking at Oppenheimer; rather, she focused on a spot somewhere above him. He followed her gaze and discovered a framed picture hanging directly above the headboard. Curious, he inspected the glass frame, but from his position he could see little more than the bright reflection of the window. He sat up, expecting to see an image of a saint, only to see Reich Leader SS Heinrich Himmler staring at him through his spectacles.

Oppenheimer was deeply shocked. "Enough is enough," he snorted. Was Himmler's picture hanging there to encourage his subordinates to procreate for the Fatherland? Oppenheimer doubted whether this strategy was very promising. "We really have gone from the frying pan into the fire," he said and turned the image of the so-called Reich Heini to face the wall.

"Better tell me now," Lisa said. "Are there any other pictures of party barons in the house?"

"That's nothing. We've got the full chamber of horrors here," Oppenheimer fibbed. "A picture of our special friend Goebbels is hanging above the radio. And then there is one more of Göring stuffed in his uniform like a sausage. Where do you think that one's hanging?"

"Let me guess, in the larder?"

Oppenheimer became aware of an unusual sound coming from Lisa's throat. She was laughing.

■

Vogler wasn't going to be stopped by the secretary this time. He briskly strode down the corridors, the police file on Lutzow clamped under his arm. He was finally confident enough. He'd gathered everything together to extract himself from the entire affair and to satisfy the party leaders. Actually solving the case was purely a matter of form now. The time had come to make sure that everything else went according to his plans. His competitor Graeter must not be given the opportunity to pass the solution off as his own success. To give his career the urgently needed push, Vogler had to impress Oberführer Schröder, that much was clear.

Vogler saw an opportunity to be given a new, more important task after having solved this murder case. And the chances were actually good, as the war had entered a decisive phase these past few days. Everyone knew that a struggle for victory or defeat was taking place in the west. Sepp Dietrich, Oberstgruppenführer of the Armed SS and head of Hitler's Leibstandarte, had made a complete fool of himself two weeks ago when he'd tried to score a propaganda coup by reinterpreting the failed attempt to drive enemy soldiers into the sea as the result of brilliant warfare. The British and American forces were initially meant to be *sucked in*—his own terminology—so that they could then be wiped out in a blitz move by the German forces. Like most people, Vogler considered the Oberstgruppen-führer to be an idiot. However, he was a dangerous idiot you didn't want to get on the wrong side of. If Dietrich considered it a particular success to have as many enemy troops as possible on the continent, then he might soon be right. Cherbourg was about to fall. Vogler knew that this would be a severe setback for the Wehrmacht High Command, as Cherbourg was a harbor town, and the enemy would then get the opportunity to support their invasion with deep-sea vessels. Heavy materials, tanks, the entire supplies for the military alliance would no longer be a problem. Vogler strode through Schröder's anteroom, paying no attention to the flustered, gasping secretary. He briefly knocked on the heavy oak door as a matter of form. When he entered without waiting for a reply, he saw that Schröder was not alone. Another man was sitting in the room, in conversation with him. With a sour expression, Oberführer Schröder took note that someone had the audacity to disturb him. Graeter flinched when he looked around in surprise and recognized Vogler. The Haupt-sturmführer stopped in the doorway, his chin thrust forward proudly. His theatrical heel-clicking echoed from the wooden paneling. "Hauptsturm-führer Vogler!" he called into the room and saluted. He'd realized years ago that simulating overly officious submissiveness was the best method to legitimize disrespectful behavior toward superiors. He did not respect Schröder as a person, only his power as an SS Oberführer. That was an important distinction to him.

At first, Schröder was perplexed. But he rallied quickly. "Bloody hell, Vogler, what do you think you're doing? Have you taken leave of your senses?" His bald head almost glowed with agitation. "If there isn't a damn good reason for you bursting in, then there will be repercussions!"

Vogler observed the two men. It was just as he'd thought. Graeter had ambitions to take over the investigation from the start. Everyone knew he had connections. Of course it had been he who had informed Schröder of the fact that there was a Jew on Vogler's team. Graeter had done all he could to put obstacles in his way. Maybe he'd even ensured his summons to Goebbels. Was it just a coincidence that he was in the same room, or was it fate? In any case, it would be all the more satisfying for Vogler to see the noose draw more tightly around his adversary's neck.

"There has been an important development in the Dufour case," Vogler said. "I considered it my duty to inform you immediately. We have a strong suspect. The case should be solved within a few hours." The news caused all color to drain from Graeter's face. Schröder, too, stared at him from his cyclops eye and slowly got up. "I hope that is true."

"The manhunt for the suspect is already in full swing. I demand that all teams involved in this matter be put under my command so that this criminal can be apprehended as quickly as possible."

Schröder paced the room, thinking. He had lost all interest in Graeter. However, Vogler knew that his sense of authority prevented him from simply fulfilling a Hauptsturmführer's every wish. "I will consider the matter. As soon as I've come to a decision, I will let you know. Anything else?"

From the corner of his eye, Vogler saw how Graeter had sunk down in his chair. Served him right. The time had come to savor his triumph. He knew that his next move would deeply humiliate Graeter.

"I have one other, extremely important task that needs to be dealt with."

Surprised, Schröder looked up. "Speak."

"There is a second suspect in the murder series. I set great value on solving this internally. This is the only way we can ensure absolute secrecy."

Schröder grew serious. "Why the caution? Are we dealing with a second Ogorzow?"

"It is not likely, but we can't rule it out. The man's name is Lutzow, a member of the SA, who got in trouble with the law a while back. Here is his police file." He handed Schröder the file. "I need all information we can get hold of. It would be best if we arrested him immediately. Better safe than sorry. But we have to proceed with extreme caution. There must be no leaks. This task can only be given to an extremely reliable man. I would like to nominate Hauptsturmführer Graeter."

With contentment, he noted the shocked expression on his adversary's face, who had immediately realized that Vogler's praise was poisoned. The seemingly important task that he was to be given was highly unreward-ing. Graeter had to investigate a party member, which was an extremely delicate task. If he didn't find anything, the matter would come to noth-ing, and if it turned out that there was some dirt on Lutzow, then only a handful of people would find out. In any case, Vogler would get all the recognition because he had found the murderer.

Schröder shifted his weight from the front to the back of his feet and considered Vogler's suggestion. Finally, he nodded. "I share your assess-ment of the situation. Graeter, as of now, you will report to Hauptsturm-führer Vogler. You must inform him immediately of any findings." Then he looked at Vogler. "And you, dear Hauptsturmführer, now carry the ultimate responsibility for the investigation being successfully completed. I don't care how you do it! I hope you've understood."

Schröder's conditions certainly met with Vogler's gambler's mentality. It was all or nothing now. He saluted. "At your command, Oberführer!"

■

Hilde needed a moment to digest the news. Then she burst out laughing. Her laughter caused the telephone receiver to shake. "In the Kamerad-schaftssiedlung? Holy shit!" was all Oppenheimer could make out be-tween her gasps. After an early dinner in their new accommodations, he had taken Lisa to the nearest pub to call Hilde with the latest news.

Slowly, she calmed down again. "That really is a smart move by arse-face. How long has Joseph given you?"

"Till the end of the week. But as I said, we already have a potential candidate."

"I still don't like the sound of it. It's too dangerous. I'll inform Dot and Anton and get them to start the operation. You know what I mean. Best you don't even unpack."

"Hilde, the matter hasn't been solved by a long shot," Oppenheimer protested weakly.

"That's rubbish. Save your bacon!"

Despite the foggy weather, it was still light enough to show Lisa the Kameradschaftssiedlung. The seasons seemed to have gotten confused, for although it was mid-June, the air was as crisp as in autumn. The forest was visible only as outlines that got lost in the fog. Wrapped tightly in their coats, they dived into the soft twilight.

With Lisa's arm tucked under his, Oppenheimer wandered past a street named Dienstweg. *Path of duty,* succinctly Prussian. "Nice," was Lisa's comment on the street sign.

"A bit farther down there is a street called *Im Kinderland,*" Oppenheimer explained. An ironic smile played around his lips. "I don't know whether there is any significance to the fact that it's a dead end. I haven't seen any children around here."

Lisa shook her head. "These people are mad." She reflected for a moment. "Still, it's very beautiful here. If only we could stay. I'm finally getting some peace." She stopped and took a deep breath with her eyes closed. Then she looked back at her husband. "But it can't be forever, right?"

"They won't let us stay here. Only privileged SS people are allowed to. I am sure the party bigwigs are queuing up to accommodate their families here. But at least we've earned ourselves a few days in this idyll."

"And then . . ."

"Hilde is already working on it," Oppenheimer whispered. "We can count on her. If anyone can get us out of here in one piece, then it's she."

"I know we can count on her. But it's still better not to think what will happen later."

"There is no point in grieving about things in advance. Now we're here, and that's wonderful."

They embraced and stood there as if time no longer existed. Oppenheimer felt taken back to the phase in his life when he'd met Lisa and everything about her had been new and exciting. He thought of the nape of her neck, of her long hair that seemed to flow down like water when she bent over him, of her feeling of shame when they'd first made love naked. He felt an unexpected knot in his stomach. He felt like a silly schoolboy, and yet he couldn't withstand the urge to kiss Lisa. When he leaned forward, she initially looked at him in surprise, but then she understood and with a generous smile allowed him to proceed.

Oppenheimer tried to memorize every little detail of this moment, to capture it for the difficult times that without a doubt lay before them.

25

———✦———

Oppenheimer was sure he'd been woken by a noise. The sun was shining directly into his face. Squinting, he sat up in bed and looked around the room. He was irritated by the flowered wallpaper; these were not his usual surroundings. Then he remembered that they were in Zehlendorf.

Lisa was asleep next to him. It was ten o'clock. By his standards, he'd slept a long time. His curiosity was stirred by the fact that the bedroom door was slightly ajar, although Oppenheimer specifically remembered having closed it last night. *Lisa had probably gone to the bathroom,* he thought. Then he perceived a cautious knocking on the door. Someone cleared his throat noisily. "Mr. Oppenheimer, are you awake now?" It was the radio operator.

"What's the matter?" Oppenheimer grumbled.

"Hauptsturmführer Vogler instructed me to wake you. It's urgent."

Oppenheimer immediately realized what this meant. They had found another body. It couldn't be anything else. He lay back morosely and closed his eyes. The bed was pleasantly warm. He hated the thought of there being another world outside the sheets.

"Mr. Oppenheimer? Are you coming?"

"Come on, out with it if it's important! What's happened?"

"We've caught him."

Afterward, Oppenheimer couldn't even remember getting dressed. A moment later, he stood next to the bed, fully dressed. Lisa was waking slowly, stretching beneath the sheets. Her smile disappeared when she saw her husband hasten through the room.

"Richard, what's the matter?"

Oppenheimer leaned over her. "Go to Hilde's," he whispered. "Go as soon as I've left. Tell her that we've caught the suspect. Karl Ziegler. And make sure no one follows you."

■

The big windows on the side of the huge mansard roof were visible from afar. The building used to house the Arts and Crafts School, but meanwhile, the studios and lecture halls had a new purpose. The Department IV of the Reich Security Main Office, responsible for "enemy assessment and combating," had moved in here in 1939. In less bureaucratic terms, this was Gestapo headquarters.

Rumors about the building had been circulating throughout the city for a long time. There was talk of a special prison that held influential opponents of the regime. Reports of brutal torture made the rounds, played down by officials as *intensified interrogation*. And as no one really knew what went on behind those walls, a paralyzing fear had spread, which had been the party leadership's intention. It was noticeable that none of the party leaders had ever seriously attempted to deny these horrors; the worse the rumors within the population were as to what the Gestapo did with their prisoners, the better. Already during the first years of the street fights, the National Socialist rulers had understood that fear played into their hands. The system of spies that Göring had installed by means of the Gestapo after the seizure of power was the most consequent continuation of this concept.

This was why Oppenheimer felt extremely unsettled when Hoffmann dropped him off at the corner of Prinz-Albrecht-Straße. Hesitantly, he approached the massive stone pillars that flanked the portal. In front of those, two guards stood with their weapons shouldered. There was hardly a place on earth that Oppenheimer felt more aversion to. Besides, it wasn't very advisable for a person in his situation to enter this building, but he had no choice if he wanted to solve the case.

The sky had clouded over. The raindrops that had accompanied Oppenheimer's drive into the city center were cold and hard. The passersby who hastily sought cover from the first hailstones looked at him in bewilderment. Oppenheimer's steps had slowed. Eventually, he stood in the middle of the pavement, unprotected, shifting from one foot to the other, not daring to enter. One of the guards looked at him skeptically, and he realized what he must look like. Oppenheimer decided that there was no point waiting outside the entrance and thinking about the possible dangers. He plucked up his courage, climbed the steps, and pulled open the big door.

He entered the lobby. The porter was on the right. "Where you goin' then?" he asked.

The porter's voice was not hostile, rather bored. Nonetheless, Oppenheimer flinched. "I have an appointment," he stammered, feeling guilty.

"He's with me!" came a voice from the building's interior. Vogler joined them. "Hauptsturmführer Vogler. This is Richard Oppenheimer. I need him for the interrogation."

The porter acknowledged this explanation with a shrug and waved Oppenheimer through. Behind the massive entrance door stretched a pompous hall with curved arches, stucco ornaments, and large windows, but Vogler turned left into a long corridor that had a comparatively sober appearance. "Ziegler is downstairs," he said. A few meters on, a staircase came into view. The corridor in the cellar looked almost identical. Only the window at the end of the corridor upstairs was missing down here. There were doors on either side, leading to the interrogation rooms.

As Vogler marched purposefully down the corridor, a muffled scream came from one of the rooms. Oppenheimer paused and stared in the direction of the noise. He had to swallow hard when he imagined what was probably going on behind that door right now.

A second scream could be heard. Oppenheimer's shadow danced on the floor as he started moving again to follow the Hauptsturmführer. Vogler was already waiting outside the door of another room.

"Just for your information, Mr. Ziegler was arrested at five o'clock this morning near his flat. He has not made any statement as to why he returned. He was on foot. No trace of his delivery van."

"Hmm, so he is saying nothing?"

"I want the thing wrapped up as soon as possible. We've got enough evidence, although of course a confession from Ziegler would be ideal."

Oppenheimer wanted to object. Things were proceeding too rapidly for his liking. Important questions remained unanswered. Where had the perpetrator taken his victims to mutilate and kill them? What was the purpose of it? Was there any way to explain his behavior? Oppenheimer's work ethic as a crime inspector called for as few questions as possible to remain open, and he wasn't planning on changing this approach now, even if Goebbels himself was breathing down his neck. But he didn't bother to hope that Vogler would understand. The Hauptsturmführer just wanted results, as quickly as possible. So he replied, "Let's see what can be done."

Oppenheimer was just about to go into the room when the door from which the screams had come opened into the corridor. Everything had gone quiet. A burly, purple-faced man stepped out, carrying his suit jacket folded over his arm. He was sweating, fumbled around for a handkerchief, and wiped his damp brow. Then he noticed a dark red stain on his white shirt. He swore and tried to remove the blood with his handkerchief. When he noticed he was being watched, he paused for a moment. He looked at Oppenheimer and nodded as if to a colleague. Then he continued his unsuccessful attempt to clean his shirt.

Oppenheimer entered the interrogation room. It was strange that he felt safe there of all places.

■

"Would you like a cigarette?" Oppenheimer asked and opened his cigarette case.

Gormless Kalle looked at him with a blank expression, then took a closer look at the white cigarettes. There was not the slightest glimmer of craving in his face, a sentiment that would have overcome any smoker, given the lack of tobacco products. Oppenheimer took a cigarette and offered it to Ziegler. In the last half an hour that Oppenheimer had spent in the room with him, Ziegler had uttered a dozen words at most. This was not a good setup for an interrogation.

Ziegler searched his pockets for a match, without avail. The SS people had already removed all his possessions.

"Do you need a light?"

Ziegler nodded.

Oppenheimer slowly went around the table and lit the man's cigarette.

The stenographer, a young man of about twenty, sat in a corner, waiting, his pencil at the ready. When Oppenheimer looked at Ziegler, he wondered what might be going on in his head. It was not really possible to find out when the suspect wouldn't talk.

"Why don't you tell us where you were last night?" Oppenheimer suggested. "Are you embarrassed?"

Gormless Kalle's reply was a shrug. Oppenheimer had tried an interrogation method that Old Gennat had taught him. He'd often had the opportunity to see how Gennat managed to crack even the hardest cases. Although his mentor had always exuded a certain authority, he very rarely grew loud during an interrogation. The chief superintendent had always appeared like a bastion of calm through his sheer physical presence, a wise and empathic Buddha whom even the most stubborn criminals ultimately entrusted with their secrets. And Gennat had definitely been interested in the people he interrogated. He was not only concerned with solving cases, he also wanted to know how things had come about, wanted to expose deficiencies that could be addressed. At the time, this approach had been very audacious and at the same time groundbreaking, as Gennat had been very successful with it.

As a young assistant detective, Oppenheimer had internalized Gennat's much-cited maxim: *If you touch a suspect, you're out on your ear! Our weapons are our minds and our senses!* The Gestapo didn't seem to think a great deal of this motto. But now it was up to Oppenheimer to stay calm and win Karl Ziegler's trust. However, Gormless Kalle was definitely not making it easy for him.

"Do you know what you're being accused of?"

An empty gaze.

"Five women were found mutilated. They were kidnapped and then brutally tortured. Do you have anything to say about that?"

Ziegler's face showed no reaction, neither surprise nor disgust. He also wasn't denying anything. He was too cool to be innocent, that much was clear to Oppenheimer.

"Do you know what I'm talking about? These women's lower abdomens were one big wound. The perpetrator has to be a veritable animal. No, he is worse than an animal, because he delights in his victims' anguish."

284 | HARALD GILBERS

Ziegler began to show some reaction. He cleared his throat. "I didn't break no one."

"So why won't you tell me where you were last weekend? We can check that. It's very straightforward. If your information is correct, we'll let you go immediately."

Ziegler seemed to consider that. Then he shook his head.

"I didn't break no one," he repeated stubbornly.

"How is it working for old Braun? Do you enjoy working in the garage?"

"It's all right."

"He told me you own a delivery van. Did you never think to set up by yourself? Open a business? Transport, removal, and things like that? Surely that would be of interest for a man of your capabilities. You did some jobs for Höcker & Sons if I remember correctly?"

Ziegler puffed on his cigarette. Blue smoke enveloped his face.

When Oppenheimer noticed, two hours later, that he was doing all the talking, he realized that he wasn't going to get anywhere with this approach. Ziegler didn't even want to talk about cars, a subject that Oppenheimer had hoped would get him talking. But Gormless Kalle remained a mystery. Oppenheimer was forced to admit that he had no idea how to position himself with him. One thing was clear: there was still more homework to be done.

■

Oppenheimer looked around searchingly in the chaos that Vogler's security people had left behind in Ziegler's hut. He had to find something that would give him access to Karl Ziegler. Did he have any wishes? What were his dreams? What did he hate? What did he do in his spare time? Old Mr. Braun was unable to help Oppenheimer with this matter. Mrs. Braun also seemed to know nothing about her husband's assistant. Although he had been working for them for almost four years, he appeared to have remained a stranger the entire time. When you considered how uncommunicative Ziegler was, this wasn't surprising.

Gormless Kalle was in the habit of retiring to his hut in the evenings. The Brauns didn't know what he did there. They were not interested in him as long as he kept quiet. Once, Mrs. Braun had attempted to bring him a pot of soup, but Ziegler had thrown her out. She had not made any further attempts to enter his domain.

Oppenheimer scratched his head in frustration. When Ziegler went out, he always locked his hut. It was quite likely that he stored something here that meant a great deal to him. But what could it be? Maybe there was an item that had some meaning to Ziegler while others just considered it jumble. Oppenheimer had been given a list of the items in the hut. There was nothing of value. Ziegler had no photographs or similar souvenirs that would allow any conclusion about his background. He seemed to have appeared out of nowhere.

With a dissatisfied sigh, Oppenheimer started to search the hut once more. Ziegler's entire record collection was scattered over his dirty laundry. The men from the SD had pulled the records out of their paper sleeves and then thrown them carelessly on the ground. This was a sacrilege to Oppenheimer. If someone had treated his records like this, he would have confronted them, even if it had been Vogler. He almost followed his instinct and sorted the records, but then he reminded himself that this was not the purpose of his visit. So he searched through the chaos for reference points.

There was a bed, a chest of drawers, and two tables. He carefully stepped around the records. The bed was just a simple wooden frame to accommodate a mattress; nothing could be stored here, let alone hidden. Oppenheimer pulled the chest of drawers forward and inspected the back. Of course, the SD people had done that, too, but that didn't stop him from pulling out the small drawers, inspecting the bottoms from underneath, and reaching into the empty spaces to feel for items that might be hidden there. The two tables had no drawers; they were nothing more than crude wooden planks on four legs. Nothing could be hidden here either. Oppenheimer swore under his breath.

When he took a step back and onto the laundry, he felt something hard beneath his foot. He believed he'd heard a muffled crack. Surprised, he turned around and carefully picked up a pair of underpants. He'd been right. Underneath the laundry lay a broken record. At the sight of it, Oppenheimer decided to gather up all the records so that he could move freely without running the risk of breaking any more.

As he looked around for the paper sleeves, he remembered that Ziegler had arranged his records just as diligently as Oppenheimer did with his own treasures. Hope surged through him; he might be able to break Gormless Kalle's reserve using their joint love of records. Ziegler's taste in music might be a way to get to know him. The more he thought about it, the more this approach appeared promising. He searched the floor, found around thirty records, and arranged them one by one in an orderly manner in the empty metal stand. Some of the paper sleeves were torn, but most of them were in good shape so that he was able to slip the records back inside.

Ziegler did not have eclectic taste. There were a few marches and popular tunes entitled "Home, Your Sweet Stars" and the like. Some of the records, however, had no label. Curious by now, Oppenheimer examined them more closely. They couldn't be normal records like those found in shops. And indeed, they were acetate discs. Ziegler appeared to have made his own recordings. Four of the matrices were blank, but the rest had soundtracks on them. Oppenheimer wondered what sort of things Ziegler had recorded. Possibly radio broadcasts?

He placed one of the acetate discs on the record player and carefully placed the needle on the ridge.

The gramophone began to scream. A woman's voice. A low whimpering ensued that grew to another panic-filled scream. Oppenheimer had always considered himself a seasoned police officer, and although he had seen a lot and was generally considered case-hardened, the blood froze in his veins. He was listening to the recording of a torture session and became a witness to unfathomable horror. Although it had all taken place in the past, the recording took Oppenheimer right into the middle of the action. He heard the metallic banging of a hammer hitting steel, a nail that with each thrust was driven further into the victim's auditory canal. Now he got an idea of what the women in the clutches of this madman had had to suffer.

The recording lasted about four minutes on this side. Oppenheimer almost regretted having played the record, but at the same time felt a grim sort of relief that this nightmare would now finally be over. When he lifted the needle from the acetate disc, he was sure that he would never in his lifetime forget this particular recording.

26

———•———

D o you want to die?" the voice hissed.

"Yes," the woman sobbed.

"You need to ask me for it first."

"Yes, please kill me! Please kill me!"

Oppenheimer couldn't bear it any longer. He switched the gramophone off and looked at Ziegler. The man's eyes were open wide, his face was red, but he said nothing, stared wordlessly at the device's horn.

"What kind of recordings are these?" Oppenheimer barked at him. His voice was a little louder than planned. He tried to swallow his anger. It cost him a lot to speak calmly to Ziegler.

"If you don't tell me what these recording are, I'll have to assume that you made them. That you are the sadist who kidnapped these women and tortured them."

Ziegler grew restless.

"There are no more excuses. These records were in your possession. They are recordings of an abominable deed. There is no point denying it, Kalle."

"I didn't break no one!"

Oppenheimer had to take a deep breath to be able to ask the next question in a matter-of-fact manner.

"Where did you make these recordings?"

"Wasn't me!"

"Kalle, don't you understand that you're making everything worse?"

"I ain't crazy! I'm not gonna tell you . . ." Ziegler broke off.

"What don't you want to tell me?"

Ziegler screamed from the top of his lungs, "It wasn't me, Inspector!" Then he collapsed. "You all just want me to hang! Right from the start! You ain't gonna get nothin' out of me. I'm not snitching on no one!"

"What are you talking about, snitching? Are you trying to tell me that it was someone else?"

No reaction.

"Kalle! I'm talking to you!"

Was Ziegler trying to weasel his way out? Such a reaction wasn't unusual. People accused of crimes often tried to put the blame on an imaginary acquaintance or even a stranger, a phantom that no one would ever catch because it didn't exist. But Oppenheimer had proof that Ziegler was in trouble and wanted to find out what was behind it. Was the man crazy? Or was he just imagining an accomplice to not have to admit his own guilt? Oppenheimer tried to recall what Hilde had said about schizophrenia.

"Kalle, do you hear voices sometimes?"

"When someone speaks to me, sure. I'm not loony, you know, Inspector."

Oppenheimer tried again, trying to be lenient. "Did someone order you to kill these women?"

Ziegler went berserk. "Goddamn it, I didn't break no one!"

Oppenheimer considered whether Ziegler was actually intelligent enough to put such a hideous plan into action and play cat and mouse with the SS for weeks on end. Then he thought of Karl Großmann and how he'd realized that the less clever murderers in particular were harder to catch because you couldn't really predict their actions. Oppenheimer recalled the undignified exhibition of the mutilated bodies, five women whose lives had been obliterated just because this stubborn idiot wanted it so. And bit by bit, something happened that had never happened to Oppenheimer during an interrogation. Hatred rose up in him, a hatred he could barely control.

Morosely, he watched the pathetic wretch babbling away to himself so that Oppenheimer had trouble picking up any useful information. It was obvious that Ziegler was involved in the murders and was trying to play for time. He was uncooperative on principle. Any trace of pity that Oppenheimer had ever had for Kalle was eradicated at this moment. He just wanted answers. He didn't care anymore what means he used to get them.

Before Oppenheimer knew what was happening, he took a mighty leap forward and grabbed the suspect by the neck with both hands.

The chair shattered beneath their weight. They landed on the floor, but he didn't let go. He wanted the little shit to pay for the suffering he'd caused. The face in front of him turned purple, the eyes started to bulge, the mouth opened into a silent scream. Oppenheimer registered that Ziegler was hitting him on the back, but he could barely feel the blows. He was too possessed with making Kalle accountable, an eye for an eye, one life for the lives of many.

Oppenheimer caught a movement on the edge of his vision. It had to be the stenographer. Two strong hands gripped him and dragged him off Kalle, who was gasping for breath.

Oppenheimer didn't want to let go, reached out his arms, but he was jerked back and manhandled out into the corridor. He heard the door to the interrogation room close.

"What's going on?" he asked. "I almost had him there!"

Oppenheimer was let go, and he realized that it was Vogler who had dragged him out of the room.

"From now on, that's our job," Vogler said. "Many thanks for your help. Now that we have the murderer, the SS will take over."

Oppenheimer was too agitated to understand. "Give me an hour. Just one. I'll get the information out of him!"

"Thank you for the offer, but we have our own methods. Wait for further instructions. I'll be in touch if there is anything else you can do for us." With that, Vogler returned to the room.

Oppenheimer's breathing returned to normal. The throbbing in his head stopped. He slowly realized that he no longer played a role in the investigation. It was over, and he had delivered an unworthy spectacle in the final stages. Gradually, he realized what he'd done. He had almost killed a suspect. Within just a few seconds, he'd thrown everything he'd ever believed in overboard. He'd flouted his mentor's maxim. He'd attacked a suspect to force a confession. Oppenheimer didn't know whether he'd ever be able to forgive himself. What would have happened if Vogler hadn't stopped him in time? He didn't dare think of it. Through the door, Oppenheimer heard Vogler begin to shout at the suspect. "We have witnesses who saw you, Ziegler!" Vogler was clearly gambling. He was probably planning on putting Kalle under pressure with false evidence until he confessed to everything. Oppenheimer had heard that this was the Gestapo's standard method. But he was not interested in the SS man now; he was preoccupied with himself.

He had caught the murderer and suffered a huge defeat at the same time. Oppenheimer stood in the corridor, dazed, deeply ashamed by his own behavior.

■

He held on to the smooth enamel of the sink. It was dark. A thin ray of sunshine fell into the room through the window that was as narrow as an arrow slit. Despondency had gripped him and had become so strong that he almost believed he would never be able to escape it. He had to concentrate, recover his control so that he could think straight once more. He didn't know what to do. Only the belief in his mission prevented him from giving up.

He had already found pleasure in killing during the war. But at the time, that was nothing special. After all, his comrades at the front had endured the same fate. Back home, it had taken him a few years to realize that he was different.

When, in an attack of rage, he had throttled a prostitute who'd laughed at the sight of his member, he'd still been naïve. He'd actually felt panic back then when he realized that the wench with the brightly made-up face was dead. He'd fled from her digs, hoping that nobody had seen him. In the days that followed, he avoided his room, lying low in town, always ready to move on at the sight of a policeman. But no one looked for him, no one wanted to bring him to justice. When he dared to go back to his lodgings, his life returned to its usual rhythm. And yet to him, the world had changed irrevocably.

He turned around and looked at the alarm clock. After having checked that the color had had enough time to work, he leaned forward and started to rinse it from his hair.

When he thought about how awkwardly he'd gone about killing the first wench, he almost had to laugh. What an amateur he'd been back then. Insecure. Fearful. Driven by an urge he initially couldn't understand.

But after he'd spent a lot of time thinking about it, the time had come when everything made sense. He'd suddenly appreciated how everything hung together and understood the role he himself played in it. Since then, he'd been aware that something had embedded itself deep inside him a long time ago, something that grew incessantly, became stronger, and then freed itself with a forceful outburst.

He dried his bleached hair. When he put the towel aside, he couldn't help but stare at himself in the mirror. Now he once again resembled the person he wanted to be. Full of pride, he looked at the deadly monster, the führer's prophecy come true.

After he'd made sure that his original hair color was no longer showing at the roots, he was content. But he knew that the creature in the mirror was not yet complete. It was a constant learning process. In the last few years, he'd already taken many steps in the right direction. And he was particularly proud of one of his skills: the keen sense he'd developed in finding his victims. He was able to discover prostitutes in places where in his naïvety he initially hadn't assumed them to be. Even the doctors who had treated him for a while were unable to imagine the danger that emanated from the prostitutes. He was almost grateful to the stupid wench for laughing at him and awakening his distrust.

He had placed the four cut-off arms in front of the Reich Chancellery to provoke a reaction. But that had turned out differently from what he'd expected. Now the roles had been reversed. He had become the prey. The SS lackeys followed him like a criminal. They wanted to eliminate him. No question, the situation was serious.

He went toward the door but stopped after a few steps. Heeding an inner impulse, he approached the preserving jars that were arranged on a shelf in an orderly row. He hoped to feel some sort of reassurance at the sight, but doubt had already gripped his heart again. He didn't know whether he was still capable of continuing his mission, despite his many capabilities. The next step would be to manage without Kalle.

He reproached himself for being naïve enough to trust an idiot like Kalle. But the man had been useful, taking on the tasks from which he himself shied away. Without Kalle, it would have been difficult to protect himself from the prostitutes' contaminated blood. Kalle wasn't afraid of carving the genitals out of the women's bodies and putting them into saline solution. He knew that his helper didn't believe in the same things, and he hadn't considered it appropriate to enlighten him. Kalle didn't care about anything, as long as he could play his games with the women. And now he'd gone. Disappeared, just like that.

He leaned against the cold wall and asked himself the unavoidable question. Had all his work been in vain? He looked across toward the preserving jars once more to gather courage. But the malignant genitals trapped in there just looked like dead pieces of meat. He realized that the memories of his deeds were fading. But he needed these memories, needed them as confirmation that he was not idle, but continuing to follow the right path.

He thought he could hear the shrill laughter of the whore in the distance, but he knew it was just his mind playing tricks on him. He pulled on the gas mask he always carried with him. Underneath his second face, he felt secure. Once he'd affixed the mask, he felt his former assurance slowly return. When he took a deep breath, the distant laughter had disappeared. The only sound that remained was the sharp hiss of the filter, and there was no more room for doubt.

Calmly, he weighed the options. The fact that Kalle had disappeared probably meant that the SS people had picked him up. They would interrogate him, and he didn't doubt that Kalle would crack at some point. His storage hut was well hidden in the woods, but he wasn't safe here anymore. His pursuers could turn up any second.

He now knew what he was looking at. He realized he had a head start. He could calmly make all the arrangements before snatching the next prostitute.

And he had no doubt that he needed to continue with his task. Even if they were chasing him, he would not stop. Catching. Killing. There were still so many who needed to be punished. He couldn't stop now.

At least Kalle had left the delivery van behind. That was very valuable. Now he just had to find a way of protecting himself in case someone found his hideout.

He stood in the middle of his storehouse, looked around, and thought about how the attackers would proceed. They would have to take the deserted forest path to get onto the property. There were two doors to the building, but he'd already closed the back entrance off with bricks several years ago so that the prostitutes couldn't flee. Then there was the iron hatch down to the coal cellar, but that was hard to find because it was overgrown with shrubs and could be opened from the outside only with a blowtorch. So it was obvious which way the intruder would have to come in to overpower him: through the front entrance, straight through the storage area to the workroom. Where he killed the women.

He tried to put himself in the pursuer's shoes. Crouching down low, he crept along the wall and jumped through the doorway.

Now he was in his workroom. When the wooden floor creaked beneath his feet, he looked down. Seen from the outside, the storage hut seemed to consist of strong brick walls, but the inside was a ramshackle construction. Only a few rotten beams ensured that he didn't break through the floor and fall into the cellar.

Suddenly, he had the idea he'd been waiting for. No, they couldn't touch him. Now he knew how he could get away. Now that he'd resolved this, he felt ready. For the next deed.

■

"The race is almost over. There's a hot favorite now, but the horse was replaced shortly before the finishing line. I think we can fetch our old nag from Happegarten now."

Hilde understood Oppenheimer's description of the situation. "The knacker has been informed. However, we'll need at least three hours to get to Happegarten. It's quite a long way to the trotting track."

There was a note of disappointment in Oppenheimer's voice. "As I said, there is nothing more we can do. See you later."

He replaced the handset on the cradle and contemplated the telephone a while longer. He had to think of other things now. Very well, Vogler had taken the case off him, and the ending had been disappointing, but there was nothing to be done about it. Now that Oppenheimer was no longer needed, he was in an extremely dangerous situation. He could not afford to look back. The next goal had to be to get out of Germany and seek refuge somewhere. He still had three hours. All of a sudden, that seemed an extremely long time to Oppenheimer. So much could go wrong.

He exited from the post office and at first didn't know where to go. Potsdamer Platz lay before him; countless people were walking to the train station, which was not really surprising, as the first people were leaving work for the day. A horse-drawn cart turned from Leipziger Straße into

Hermann-Göring-Straße and almost forced a cyclist off the road, who rang his bicycle bell wildly. Life in the city was running its usual course, but Oppenheimer felt cut off from it all. He stood in the midst of the hustle and bustle, suddenly a stranger in the pulsating metropolis.

Hoffmann was nowhere to be seen; he probably had to drive more important people through Berlin now. Oppenheimer decided to take the subway line A-II to the Krumme Lanke station. He estimated that this would get him closer to the Kameradschaftssiedlung than the commuter train to West Zehlendorf. However, the roof of the subway station at Potsdamer Platz had been bombed during the big attack on Wednesday. Oppenheimer could see it was cordoned off. It seemed they were still working on it. He hoped that some sort of replacement transport had been arranged.

He was just about to cross Saarlandstraße when someone called out his name. "Mr. Oppenheimer! Wait!"

He turned but couldn't spot anyone familiar. A figure limped through the crowd, waving his hat, his head almost bald. Güttler. Oppenheimer remembered. He'd given the man a task after they'd found the body of the whore called Friederike, who had been Verena Opitz before the SS gave her the alias Edith Zöllner. Ms. Becker had seen the murderer creep away from the graveyard in Steglitz, but her two descriptions of the perpetrator had contradicted each other.

"There you are!" Güttler said happily. "I was just about to go to Hauptsturmführer Vogler because I didn't find you in Zehlendorf."

"How are you, Güttler?"

"That's quite a job you gave me. A veritable Sisyphean task, finding Ms. Becker." With a proud smile, he then announced, "I've been successful, though."

"You know where she lives?"

"Ms. Becker is staying in Dahlem. Her name was misspelled at the registration. Elfriede Bäcker, spelled *ä* instead of *e*. It took a while for me to figure that out. She claimed that all her papers were destroyed during the bomb attack."

Oppenheimer stopped. This didn't make sense. When he'd questioned Ms. Becker, she'd had no problem identifying herself. And there had been no further bomb attacks until she'd disappeared without a trace. This was not the behavior of an innocent person. This lady was hiding something. Oppenheimer made a note of the new address.

"Has anyone been informed about this yet?"

"Of course not. You set me on the task, and I wanted to report only to you."

"Thank you, Güttler. Good job. I hope we see each other again. Maybe on the next case."

With this empty promise and a handshake, Oppenheimer took his leave of the SD man. Before he knew it, his thoughts were revolving around the case again. Once he'd checked that the subway was working properly, he decided to get out a few stops earlier. Dahlem-Dorf was four stops before the final stop, Krumme Lanke. So paying Ms. Becker a visit was not a detour, and after all, Oppenheimer still had just under three hours.

■

CLOSED UNTIL THE ULTIMATE VICTORY, the large letters on the yellowing sign said. The tailor had placed the note behind the glass entrance door. Whether this was his cynical comment on the current war situation or whether he possibly still believed the German army would win was not clear.

Oppenheimer looked at the house. This was number seven, the address Güttler had given him. If his information was correct, this was where Ms. Becker was living.

So far, the building had remained untouched by bomb hits. In fact, the entire street was still intact. There were two floors above the tailor shop. Curtains hung in the windows. So someone was living here.

The entrance to the flats was at the side of the building. Oppenheimer looked for Ms. Becker's name on the four mailboxes, and there was one with the name *Becker* on it.

When he reached the top floor and rang the bell, he heard agitated clattering inside the flat. A moment later, the door opened, and Elfriede Becker squinted at him from behind her glasses.

"Yes?" she asked. Oppenheimer felt that her voice sounded shaky.

"Elfriede Becker?" he asked.

The woman instinctively pulled her cardigan closer around herself. "What can I do for you?"

"Inspector Oppenheimer. We've met. Back at the cemetery in Steglitz. I have a few more questions. Could I come in?"

"I . . . That's not convenient. I have to leave in a moment. I have an appointment."

"It will really only take a few seconds," Oppenheimer assured her, and before she could react, he had pushed his way into the flat. She appeared just marginally younger than that night at the police station. Oppenheimer guessed she was in her early to midthirties. Hesitantly, she led the way into the living room.

"You really are hard to find," he said as he sat down in the armchair.

"How do you mean?"

"The address that you gave us doesn't exist anymore. The house. And you gave a false name at the registration office."

"What? That can't be right. One of the clerks must have written it down wrong. It's not my fault. It's always so busy there."

A framed photograph stood beneath the table lamp. A young Elfriede Becker was beaming at Oppenheimer from a wedding photograph. So, in actual fact she was Mrs. Becker, not a Miss.

"Do you live alone?"

"My husband fell at the eastern front last year, if that's what you mean. It's probably best if you ask your questions frankly."

"You said that you saw the person leaving the cemetery on the night in question. Unfortunately, you gave two contradicting descriptions."

"That was a mistake. It was only later when I thought about the event that I remembered everything in detail."

Oppenheimer pricked up his ears. Someone had coughed in the next-door room, muffled, but quite clearly perceivable.

"The neighbors," Mrs. Becker hurried to explain.

Oppenheimer looked her in the face. Then he got up and went straight into the room that the noise had come from. A bedroom. The back wall was taken up by a large wardrobe.

"I told you, it's the neighbors," Mrs. Becker protested.

"Is that your wardrobe, or was the room already furnished?"

"It was already here. Just like all the other items."

Oppenheimer walked up and down in front of the wardrobe and

examined the large doors. In a loud voice, he then addressed the large item of furniture. "You can come out now! The game is up! Do you hear me?"

Silence.

Very slowly, one of the wardrobe's doors began to open. Two eyes stared at Oppenheimer, full of fear.

"I'm waiting."

A rustling noise. Caught out, a man made his way out from between the clothes. He was in his early twenties, definitely of an age fit for military service. Now Oppenheimer understood Mrs. Becker's strange behavior.

"Which battalion?"

"Eighth," the young man answered, intimidated.

Of course, a deserter. Like so many others who didn't report back to the front after their leave, preferring to take the risk of being shot by a firing squad should they be caught. When he saw how Mrs. Becker put her arms protectively around the shaking young man, he understood what had happened. If what she'd told Oppenheimer was true, then her husband had been killed, and she had fallen in love again. Unfortunately, her lover was a deserter. No one must know of his existence. Doubtlessly, she was crazy about the boy; otherwise, she wouldn't have taken the risk of hiding him in her flat. His life depended on her behaving correctly. Hence the deception once the police had become aware of her. But now the house of cards these two had built had collapsed.

"I told you there was no point, Friede," he said resignedly to Mrs. Becker. She began to sob quietly.

"I'm not interested in you," Oppenheimer said as calmly as possible. "I just care about the witness statement. When I leave, you'll never see me again. No one will find out about this from me. I give you my word of honor. But I ask you to now give me a genuine report of what you saw at the cemetery that night."

Mrs. Becker turned toward Oppenheimer in surprise. The young man's eyes also held renewed hope.

"What shall I call you? Just your first name so that I can address you."

"Ernst," the young man said.

"So, Ernst, were you there when Mrs. Becker made the observation at the cemetery in Steglitz?"

"We'd only met a few days before," it suddenly burst out of Mrs. Becker. "We saw each other for the first time during an air raid. We were in the same bunker, and, well, we liked each other straightaway."

"I accompanied her home that night," Ernst added.

"Right. I don't need any further details. So you were walking along the wall of the cemetery. Now to the important question: Which one of you actually made the observation? Let's start with you, Ernst."

The man named Ernst swallowed and thought hard. "It was like this: I saw someone tampering with the gate."

"A man?"

"I would say so, yes. He moved like a man. I could not really make out what he was wearing."

"Hair color?"

"I would say brown or black. Definitely not light. But he could have been wearing a hat."

"What did you do after you'd seen the man?"

"It seemed quite strange. The man was pushing a handcart. But who has any business in a cemetery at night? I told Friede—I mean, Mrs. Becker—what I'd seen."

"You didn't see anything else after that? Did the man vanish? He can't have disappeared into thin air."

Ernst looked down in embarrassment. "Well, I quickly looked around for a spot where I might hide. I didn't know who it was. You understand, in my situation, I have to be careful."

By and large, his description corresponded with the first witness statement given by Mrs. Becker. "Now to you, Mrs. Becker. Ernst pointed the man in the cemetery out to you. What did you see?"

"The moon was just coming out from behind a cloud when I looked. Usually, you can't see anything because of the blackout. Everything was light, very briefly, and the first thing I saw was a head of platinum-blond hair."

"Platinum blond, just as you described him."

"Yes, I know it sounds crazy because it was a man. I don't know any men who dye their hair. But anyway, he ran across the street really quickly, and then he disappeared into the darkness."

"And the handcart?"

"I heard something but couldn't see what it was."

"Which one of you noticed that the gate had been broken open?"

"That was me," Mrs. Becker said. "Someone had broken in. I wanted to report it to the police immediately, but it was too dangerous. I had to tell someone; I couldn't just slink off. With hindsight, that wasn't very clever of me." She smiled grimly. "Ernst says it's my Prussian blood. Anyway, I told the cemetery caretaker. That seemed the best compromise."

"But he sent you straight to the police."

In response, Mrs. Becker shrugged.

"And at the police station, you were worried about getting more involved because of Ernst and therefore gave a false address?" Oppenheimer asked.

"It wasn't wrong. Just not up to date. It was a snap decision. It might have been easier to give a different name, but then I would have had to lie. The situation with Ernst and everything else—I couldn't think straight anymore."

"Why didn't you just stick to the first version of your witness statement?"

"Initially, I only repeated what Ernst had told me. He was completely convinced that the man had looked like that."

"But then you began to doubt, and when I questioned you, you described the scene as you yourself had seen it," Oppenheimer finished.

Mrs. Becker sat before him on the edge of the bed, clearly contrite.

"I'm a silly idiot. But I couldn't lie. I'd seen the man with my own eyes. But he looked different to me."

Oppenheimer thought about it. Her description seemed credible. There was a very simple solution for the discrepancy between their two statements. "Is it possible that you saw two different men?"

"I asked myself that too," said Ernst. "We can't rule it out entirely."

"Thank you very much," Oppenheimer finally said. "I think you've answered all my questions."

He went to the front door and turned once more. Mrs. Becker and Ernst looked at him uncertainly.

"That's it from my side," Oppenheimer said, his hand on the door handle. "Take care of yourselves, you two." When he closed the door behind himself, the two lovers were already embracing. Mrs. Becker held on tightly to Ernst, who was doing his best to calm her.

"Friede, it's all right," he said and gently stroked her hair.

Friede. *Peace.* Ernst had given his lover a beautiful nickname. And somehow it fitted his situation as a deserter.

As Oppenheimer headed for the subway, he went through the information that Mrs. Becker and her lover had given him.

Inevitably, his thoughts wandered back to his unsuccessful interrogation of Karl Ziegler. He had assumed that Gormless Kalle had wanted to extract himself from the situation and had therefore invented an imaginary partner, giving him the blame. Oppenheimer had to admit that he might have formed a hasty judgment. Ziegler having recordings of the torture only implied that he was involved in the crime. No more and no less.

An important aspect was the fact that in the Gestapo office he'd only seen Ziegler seated. The suspect whom he'd followed across the city center of Berlin had had a limp. But Oppenheimer hadn't taken the time to check whether Ziegler had a limp.

He swallowed hard when he considered the consequences. If the ominous partner did exist, and the most recent witness statements corroborated this, then the murderer was still on the loose. As he'd lost his assistant, he would change his modus operandi, but he wouldn't stop kidnapping and killing women until someone stopped him. Although it wasn't cold, Oppenheimer shivered. He turned up the collar of his coat and stomped grumpily down the street. After these new witness statements, the end of this nightmare seemed ever further away.

■

"That was damned close. The next time, you'll have to give us more time." Bauer looked at Oppenheimer reproachfully from the side.

"Where is Hilde?" Oppenheimer wanted to know from the back of the car, trying to catch his breath.

"We're meeting her later," Lüttke explained, put the car into second gear, and shot off.

"Amateurs," Bauer swore under his breath and crossed his arms, a sign he wasn't happy with the entire situation.

Dot and Anton had discovered Oppenheimer near the "Onkel Tom" housing project; he'd been on his way to the Kameradschaftssiedlung. Bauer had appeared out of nowhere and bundled him into the car. It had all happened so quickly that Oppenheimer was still surprised to be sitting next to the man from the resistance. Even the pedestrian who'd been walking his dog just a few meters behind him was completely taken by surprise by the move. The man had barely turned around, curious about what was going on, when Oppenheimer had already disappeared into the car. It seemed the two men from the resistance had adapted classic Gestapo methods for their own purposes. And they seemed to be quite talented in this regard.

Exasperated, Lüttke sounded his horn. Another vehicle had cut across them. "These bloody rubble heaps! Everyone just drives as they see fit!"

"Has my wife been informed?" Oppenheimer demanded.

"We haven't been to your flat yet," Bauer grumbled. "Just tell me what's new."

With as much detail as necessary, Oppenheimer recounted the day's events, but he decided to keep Mrs. Becker's new statement to himself for the time being.

"Ah, right, so Vogler has found his scapegoat," Lüttke summarized the situation. "He's sure to make it to the top."

"The question remains whether he contents himself with this solution to the case," Bauer said with a gloomy look. But Oppenheimer was only half listening. At the moment, he didn't care about Vogler. More important things were occupying his thoughts. He was relieved that he would be getting out of Germany in a few hours, but he was unable to really look forward to it. The devastating fact that there were two perpetrators could not be ignored. So he asked, as matter-of-factly as possible, "Did you get hold of the Lutzow file, by any chance?"

"That file has disappeared off the face of the earth," Bauer was forced to admit. "Our contact went through the entire archive. There are no notes, no file memorandum, nothing."

"Interesting," Oppenheimer mumbled. "Either the files were lost when the police headquarters on Alexanderplatz were bombed, or someone had them removed."

"That's exactly why we wanted to speak to you," Bauer interrupted. "There is something you have to do for us."

Oppenheimer cast Bauer a questioning look—and froze. At that moment, he noticed for the first time the rows of houses they were passing. He quickly looked over his shoulder. Despite the twilight, he was able to discern the square called *Führerplatz* disappear into the distance. They had driven past the entrance to the Kameradschaftssiedlung. What was Lüttke doing? Didn't he know where they were going? "We've gone past the entrance!" Oppenheimer protested and grabbed Lüttke's shoulder.

"As I said, we've got things to talk about before we can get you to safety," Bauer repeated.

"What's going on? Hilde didn't say anything about this."

"Not so fast, my friend." Now it was Lüttke speaking to Oppenheimer. "We have no idea what Karl Ziegler testified today or what might be pinned on him. We know that the SD works with false confessions. It is possible that they will subsequently try to denounce one of us. These murders would be a welcome excuse for Schellenberg and consorts to silence their adversaries once and for all."

"You've already explained that to me at great length, but what am I supposed to do about it?"

"If we're to help you get away tonight," Bauer explained impassively, "then you have to go through the interrogation transcript one more time. Tonight. Because the government district is constantly being bombed, the SD is moving all its departments to the Wannsee. They have requisitioned several villas there. Vogler has also been given an office there for the duration of the investigation. He keeps all the files on the case there."

The only noise that could be heard was the sound of the tires splashing through the puddles. Bauer waited for a reaction, but Oppenheimer sat huddled in his seat and thought morosely of how many more delays there would be. Finally, he tried to squirm his way out. "Do you really think that's necessary?"

"We need to know what Vogler might have added to or changed in the confession. It's too dangerous for our contact to find that out, and it would take too long. But you are familiar with the case; you know what to look for. It probably won't take you more than twenty minutes."

"And you think it's that simple? I'm supposed to break into an SD building? The place will be guarded like a high-security prison."

Bauer didn't take no for an answer. "It's not as complicated as it looks. There is so much going on there, what with all the departments moving right now. Our contact will be able to help us. It's all arranged. We just need to be there at ten o'clock. We'll smuggle you in, and you then pick out the information we need. Quite simple."

So everything had been arranged. Oppenheimer needed more time to decide. "I am sure you'll understand that I cannot make this decision alone. I need to speak to my wife first."

Bauer snorted, dissatisfied. "Mr. Oppenheimer, there is no alternative."

"Mr. Bauer," Lüttke intervened, "give him a bit of time to think things over. You've already been a great help, Mr. Oppenheimer. We have our reasons for asking you for this last favor. It's a matter of life or death for some of our colleagues. I can assure you that we haven't taken this decision lightly. If you agree, you can save our men from worse fates."

After these words, he drove back to the Kameradschaftssiedlung, and they didn't speak for the remainder of the drive.

Bauer's usually brusque manner had morphed into a huffy sulk. Oppenheimer could guess the differences of opinion between the two of them. Bauer had clearly wanted to present him with a fait accompli, while Lüttke thought it would suffice to appeal to Oppenheimer's decency. Sometimes these two seemed to him like an old married couple who were always at each other's throats but couldn't be one without the other.

When they entered the Kameradschaftssiedlung, Lüttke switched off the headlights. The narrow band of light that had lit up the road ahead of them disappeared. Barely visible to the naked eye, the black vehicle glided the last few meters and slowly approached the turning loop to park there.

Lüttke didn't switch off the engine, ready to roar off again instantly should their plan go wrong. Oppenheimer also felt uneasy. He cleared his throat.

"How are we going to proceed?"

Bauer spoke again. "Is there anyone in the house at this time?"

"Not usually. Possibly the radio operator. He sometimes holds the fort in the cellar."

"Then be on your guard. Come out with your wife and the luggage and get in the car immediately. The quicker we get out of here, the better. We can discuss the rest during the drive."

Oppenheimer slowly got out of the car. He hesitated, crouched beside the car door to check the surroundings, but then realized how suspicious he must look. So he put his hands in his coat pockets and tried to walk toward the front door as casually as possible.

He could already discern from the outside that no lights were on in the house. Oppenheimer was a little surprised. Had Lisa already gone to bed? She normally managed to get by without much sleep and had slept in late this morning.

He stepped into the hallway. Fearful that the hinges on the door would squeak, he moved the door very slowly. The door fell shut behind him with a muffled click. He stepped toward the door that led down to the cellar and carefully pushed down the door handle. Locked.

He was hugely relieved. This could only mean that the radio operator had already gone home. To make sure, he let his eyes wander through the living room that contained his office. Nobody to be seen here.

He felt reassured by this discovery. Everything was going according to plan. Secretly, Oppenheimer had suspected that Lüttke's escape plan was too good to be true. He had constantly feared it wouldn't work out. And yet he'd played along simply to not give up hope. Oppenheimer told himself that he couldn't always be dogged by bad luck. He had to get lucky at some point.

Holding on to this thought, he went up to the second floor. But what he saw there made his half-hearted optimism fade again.

The bed was still unmade. Their packed suitcases stood in the corner of the room. But something was missing: Lisa.

27

———✦———

O ver here! I saw him over here!" More excited shouts followed. He'd jumped onto the loading area at the last second and immediately pulled the tarpaulin over himself. His heart beating madly, he tried to lie still and cover the unconscious prostitute at the same time.

His pursuers had taken up the trail, were close on his heels. He knew that the feeling of being protected by the tarpaulin was deceptive. The cover that shielded him from the SS men consisted solely of a thin sheet of plastic. He racked his brains, but he couldn't see what mistake he had made. One thing was clear—something had gone terribly wrong this time.

The tarpaulin was torn, just a few centimeters from his face. He could see the men's arms and legs through the opening. He couldn't make out how many there were. His view was additionally obscured by the fact that he was staring through his gas mask.

More men arrived and formed a group. Right next to his vehicle.

"The alleyways are clear!" someone called. "He can't have disappeared!"

"He has to be here," a cutting voice said. "Somewhere very close."

Then silence. The men turned in circles, searching the surroundings.

When he heard heavy steps, he pressed himself as close as possible to the prostitute's limp body. Again, he heard the voice of the man who'd spoken last. Although he was whispering, it was clear that he was used to giving orders. "I tell you he's here somewhere!"

More and more uniformed men arrived, until the commander rebuked them harshly. "Stand still. And be quiet, for heaven's sake!"

The men's murmuring stopped. His breath came in bursts. They were listening attentively. He knew that the slightest movement would blow his cover. A low harrumph sounded outside.

"I said quiet!"

"But, Obersturmbannführer, we can't—"

"Didn't you hear that? There was a noise! It sounded like a hissing."

He flinched in shock. At first, he didn't understand what the Obersturmbannführer meant, but then he understood. The filter! They could hear the filter of his mask! Of course. With each breath, he made a noise.

His mind raced. He must not draw attention to himself. And yet he had to breathe somehow. Doggedly, he tried to come up with a solution for escaping this trap.

Slowly, very slowly, he let the air out of his lungs. The filter rustled just a little. But even this barely perceptible noise was still too loud.

"There it was again!" he heard someone say. "Can you hear it?"

He had to make a decision now that was essential to his survival. Did he want to protect himself from the prostitute, or was his mission more important? He didn't need long to make up his mind.

His lungs rebelled, demanding more oxygen, but he didn't yield. His free hand inched closer to the filter, which was hanging somewhere from his belt. His fingertips finally found the tube. Now he had a point of reference. When he finally realized that he couldn't manage any longer without air, he slowly breathed in, a barely noticeable sigh, without the filter making a sound. When his lungs were half-filled, he held his breath once more and moved his hand down the tube until he finally encountered the filter.

His next task consisted of twisting the tube out of the filter mechanism without making a sound. With just one hand.

An oppressive silence filled the air. The men outside were still immobile. Their hunting instinct had kicked in. They didn't want to return home without their prey.

Now he needed all the self-control he possessed. While his thumb pressed against the filter, he slowly started to unscrew the tube. The mechanism squeaked quietly.

Instinctively, he paused mid-movement, realizing that he'd turned the tube too quickly. Cold sweat broke out on his brow.

When he risked a cautious peek through the gap, the men were still standing in position. But no one seemed to have noticed anything. Finally, he dared to continue turning the tube. This time it worked.

"I'm afraid there's nobody here," a voice said.

At that same moment, the filter came free from the tube with a jerk. It made a metallic sound as the end of the tube encountered his belt buckle.

The sound seemed deafening to him. The men outside also flinched. They turned warily toward the vehicle. Through the gap in the tarpaulin, he could see a figure bend down as if in slow motion. He flinched when a face entered his line of vision.

Damply glimmering eyes stared straight at him. The man's hair was streaked with gray, his features hard. It had to be the Obersturmbann-führer. Like the others, he was basically helpless in the darkness. He remained poised for several seconds, eye to eye with his enemy.

A voice came from somewhere. "We have to report this, Obersturm-bannführer; otherwise, valuable time is lost!"

The commander straightened up. His face disappeared. "Whatever. You go, Plate! And the others, search every last corner!"

The men moved away, complying with this order. It took several minutes until the strides of their heavy boots faded away. It was only then that he dared breathe again. At first, he felt only relieved, but then the burning feeling of resentment also returned. Disdainfully, he twisted his lips as he thought of the SS men and their arrogance. They considered themselves to be something better, and yet they were so blind that they hadn't discovered him.

Despite these thoughts, he remained cautious and decided to wait awhile. If the men were too close, they'd certainly hear the motor starting. And he couldn't reveal himself. Not now, after having shaken them off successfully.

He lay on the wooden floor of the loading area without moving. His breathing slowed. The air was crisp; he could feel the pleasant warmth of the wood gasifier behind his back. He was quite calm now.

As he lay there, he realized that he was completely alone with the wench. He held her in his arms. It was precisely these moments that he liked so much, the moment when he felt the intoxicating certainty of having complete power over his victim's life. But this feeling of elation ended abruptly when he realized that other things were going on with his body.

The woman's perfume had made its way under his mask. Through her clothes, he could feel the softness of her flesh. Despite his gloves, he could easily feel the hollow of her belly button with his index finger. As her backside was pressing against his loins, he had gotten an erection. His breathing had become heavy, but not out of fear of being discovered.

Disgusted, he rolled on his side. His eyes filled with tears when he realized how weak he was. This sort of thing must not happen. Even when they lay there unconscious, there was still a lot of danger emanating from the prostitutes. He mustn't allow himself to be beguiled. They had already brought him a lot of bad luck. Any thought of their bodies was bad.

He remained lying on his side until his erection had subsided. When he'd regained his composure, he peeked out from under the tarpaulin to make sure his pursuers had disappeared. He'd been right. The men in uniform were no longer to be seen.

After provisionally gagging and tying up his victim, he slipped off the loading area and pulled the tarpaulin tight. In the shadow of the trees, he sneaked over to the driver's cabin and slipped silently onto his seat.

The noise of the engine was unavoidable, but luckily, the vehicle started immediately. To avoid attracting any more attention, he drove off with the headlights off. It was only when he turned off at the next housing block that he felt safe enough to switch on the lights and increase his speed.

Suddenly, everything seemed so simple that he almost felt as if he were floating across the asphalt. He didn't need to think about what would happen if someone got onto him anymore. He had long made the necessary preparations. He would take the prostitute into the workroom through the cellar to kill her there. Just to be on the safe side, he was going to block the access behind him with heavy coal sacks. Then there was only one way left to get into his hideout—the door that led directly into the workroom. He'd sawed one of the supporting pillars in the cellar halfway through so that the floor would collapse under any intruder as soon as they entered the room. He could then take advantage of their surprise and escape through the iron hatch in the coal cellar and disappear into the undergrowth. This carried a certain risk, but he was prepared to take it. The diversion he'd thought up was further confirmation that he was vastly superior to his pursuers. Secretly, he almost hoped that someone would get onto him so that he could put it to the test. The thought made him chuckle.

He was gripped by unbridled pride. He'd managed everything even without Kalle's help. Now he was driving through the city with an unconscious prostitute on the loading area, and all without external help. He'd managed to overpower the wench all by himself and then drag her to the vehicle.

But when he thought of the woman's body, bitterness seeped into his feeling of triumph. Luckily, he'd managed to overcome his urge and maintain control. And control was the most important thing if he wanted to get through this in one piece.

The real test was still to come.

He carefully removed the mask from his head as he drove, then off came the gloves, with which he'd touched the prostitute. His gaze darkened when he realized that he had a long night ahead of him. A night ruled by the poison that was still pulsing in the prostitute's veins but that he would soon release. He couldn't be so careless as to allow himself to be infected by it.

■

The three men had sat in the car in silence for several minutes. Despite the engine's low, soporific humming, they were all wide awake.

"And she didn't leave a message?" Lüttke asked once again.

"I've been through everything," Oppenheimer responded, his voice throaty. "Nothing."

"Where could she have gone?"

"I sent her to Hilde's this morning, but she should have been back hours ago."

Bauer could barely sit still. "We should head off."

"I won't do anything until I know where my wife is," Oppenheimer said.

"And where are we supposed to conjure her up from?"

"I don't care. I want the situation clarified before I go anywhere."

Bauer was about to start berating Oppenheimer when Lüttke cut him off. "Look. What's that, out there?"

Oppenheimer peered out of the window. And indeed, someone had approached the house. He was able to recognize the dark outline of a bicycle that leaned against the wooden lattice fence. The person who had just gotten off now headed straight for the front door. Her gait was stiff, as if she could sense the men watching her. Oppenheimer got out of the car. He thought he recognized the figure. When he grabbed her shoulder, the woman whirled around in surprise. It was as Oppenheimer had thought. Hilde.

"Goodness! I almost wet myself!" Hilde's voice was a flustered whisper.

"Where is Lisa?" Oppenheimer hissed.

"Everything is fine. She's with me."

Oppenheimer breathed a sigh of relief. "This way." He led Hilde to the car.

Once she was seated, Lüttke headed off. Oppenheimer could tell that he had to force himself not to make a racing start. "It's less conspicuous if we keep moving," he said, taking the next corner.

"She was still with me when you called," Hilde explained. "We lost track of time. Anyway, I considered it safer not to send her back. I was just about to fetch the suitcases and leave this." She handed Oppenheimer a piece of paper.

"What is it?"

"A farewell letter." When Hilde saw Oppenheimer hadn't understood, she explained. "Lisa wrote it. I dictated it. A red herring for arse-face Vogler. If they think you've committed suicide, it might give you a head start."

Oppenheimer nodded. Hilde really had thought of everything.

"A good plan," he agreed.

"Does that mean we need to go back there?" Bauer interjected.

It was only now that Hilde paid the two men from the resistance any attention. "Do you have any objections?"

"We have to get to Vogler's office," Bauer protested, irritated, as if he couldn't believe his bad luck in having to work with such people.

Hilde suddenly grew serious. "Hang on a minute. What's that all about? That wasn't part of our agreement."

Once Lüttke had explained their plan, she was seething with anger. "Goddamn it, have you gone completely mad? You've been reading too many spy novels! Break into an SD house, really? Sending him to Wannsee now has got to be the dumbest thing ever. Why should he take the risk?

Richard has given you all the information. He presented the facts on a silver platter. What more do you need? Do your own bloody jobs and get us out of here!"

"There are some important questions that haven't been answered," Bauer countered, shaking his head vehemently.

"That may be, but things are getting too hot for Richard now. You can't just rope him into a stunt like that just so you can write a nice report. Your inside man can steal the interrogation protocol, whatever, but Richard has more than fulfilled his duty."

Bauer wiped his brow and cursed loudly. Oppenheimer intervened. "One moment. I suggest the following: we head back as quickly as possible, leave the farewell letter, and then I'll look for the protocol."

Hilde stared at him, her mouth agape. "Richard, are you completely mad?"

"However, I have one condition," he continued and looked at the men from the resistance challengingly. "There is a second perpetrator. If I find out who it is, will you help me take him down?"

Oppenheimer's news was a bombshell. All color seemed to fade from Bauer's crimson face.

"Are you quite sure?" Lüttke asked.

"There is a new witness statement. Two perpetrators."

Hilde shook her head. "It's no longer your case, Richard. Accept it. Vogler has homed in on Ziegler."

Oppenheimer turned to Hilde. "I can't just disappear. If I don't do anything, more women are going to get killed, and I will be to blame for that. Don't you understand? It's the weekend again. He's almost certainly kidnapped another victim and is in the process of torturing her right now. It won't end if I don't intervene."

He could tell from Hilde's face that she didn't agree with his view of things, but she finally gave in. "Well, I guess there's nothing more to discuss."

Oppenheimer leaned forward to address Lüttke. "What do you think? I'll get you the information, and you help me arrest the perpetrator. A straightforward deal."

"I'm in," Lüttke said without hesitating.

"All right," Bauer growled.

312 | HARALD GILBERS

They returned to the Kameradschaftssiedlung once more, and Oppen-heimer entered the house for the last time. While deliberating where to leave the farewell letter, his gaze fell upon the wall chart with the suspects.

Spontaneously, he took a drawing pin and pinned the piece of paper right into the middle. Content, he examined the board, but then a feeling of restlessness rose up inside him. There was one more thing he had to do here in the house, and that was the real reason why he'd urged Lüttke to turn around.

First, he made sure that no one had followed him into the house. Then he quietly crept into the kitchen. He was not proud of what he was doing now, but it couldn't be avoided. He had to be on his toes tonight, and he realized that he'd only be able to do this with the help of Pervitin. With a practiced grasp, he pulled the packet from its hiding place and immediately swallowed one pill, then washed it down with water.

It didn't take long for it to take effect. For a few seconds, he considered taking the entire packet with him, but he knew that Hilde would never allow it. He was angry that he hadn't thought to put them in his suitcase. He gave his treasure one last, yearning look. There was nothing he could do about it.

He filled his small vial with the pills. Then he stuffed his pockets with them as well. Oppenheimer hoped that Hilde wouldn't notice. He could do without a sermon this evening. After all, he was an adult and respon-sible for his own behavior. Suddenly, he thought how pathetic he was. *Of course I'm not an addict,* he reassured himself and stared in disgust at the white pills in his shaking hands. A brief hesitation, then he continued to put the pills in his pockets. Although he didn't like to admit it, he knew that he would need them.

■

"Here is a copy of Karl Ziegler's interrogation protocol. The case is solved." Vogler passed Schröder the documents. He thought he could sense the Oberführer's harsh gaze even through the eye patch.

Schröder took the papers without comment, leaving Vogler to remain at attention while he himself sat down and, his lips pursed, thumbed through the pages. Although the protocol wasn't very long, he needed quite a while to get through it.

They were in the entrance hall of Oberführer Schröder's town house. Vogler had delivered what had been asked of him. Yes, he had personally interrogated Ziegler after Oppenheimer had been taken off the case, albeit just pro forma. Vogler knew every single word in the interrogation protocol; after all, he had written it himself. Even before they'd picked Ziegler up, the results of the investigation had long been put into words. The document that Schröder now held in his hand had preempted what Ziegler needed to say so that the matter could be concluded and all loose ends tied up. This also included the accused not surviving the interrogation.

After he'd executed Ziegler, Vogler had driven straight to his office to prepare the documents. As it was now Saturday evening, and Vogler wanted to get the entire matter over and done with, he had driven to Schröder's town house, even if this meant disturbing him at home. Truth be told, Vogler was actually keen to find out what was behind Schröder's façade, what he looked like in private. But the meeting with his superior was not very enlightening. Vogler had to wait in the entrance hall of the large villa, and when Schröder appeared shortly afterward, he was already in full regalia. There was no sign of anything that could have compromised the image of the authoritative superior. There was neither the telltale smell of alcohol nor an entirely unheroic cardigan that would have testified to Schröder having any private life at all. Only his so-called town house was conspicuous, given its country-style interior. Nothing reminded one of the fact that they were in the middle of the capital of the German Reich. The place was decorated with rustic wooden furniture, roughly carved and heavy. Instead of paintings, several hunting guns hung on the walls, which were covered with a veritable forest of antlers. Vogler wondered where one could shoot that many deer in Berlin.

But the longer he waited, the harder he found it to concentrate on his surroundings. Although he had carried out the order, a certain restlessness gnawed away at him. He tried to ignore it and told himself that he'd done exactly what Schröder had commanded. Vogler had supplied a perpetrator who did not compromise the party. He might have tampered with a few facts here and there, maybe the leads were a little incomplete, but this did not shake his conviction that he'd arrested the right person.

Finally, Schröder placed the document aside, looking satisfied. Then he pulled an envelope from his inside jacket pocket and handed it to Vogler.

"Our plans regarding your further deployment have changed. We desperately need men on the western front. Here are your marching orders. You leave for Caen in the morning. There you'll report to the Ninth Panzer Division Hohenstaufen."

Vogler clicked his heels in a salute. So it had all been prearranged. Schröder had had the marching orders ready the entire time. Vogler was not bothered by this, as the result was better than he'd hoped. He no longer needed to bide his time with gloomy civilians. The quicker he got to the front, the better.

Vogler considered the meeting over and waited for Schröder to dismiss him. But his superior seemed to have something else on his mind. In an unusually familiar tone, he whispered to Vogler, "Tell me, what did the Yid do to Reithermann?"

The mentioning of this fat cat's name made Vogler listen up.

"How do you mean?" he asked.

Schröder's face grew serious. "I received a direct order to get rid of Oppenheimer as soon as the case was solved. So what happened?"

"Oppenheimer insisted on interviewing the Gruppenführer himself."

"And? Stop beating about the bush, Vogler!"

"He asked him whether he had an alibi."

This reply seemed to make Schröder freeze with shock. Then he started to laugh loudly. "This Oppenheimer fellow, priceless." He wiped tears of laughter from his eyes. "No one has ever dared do that. We should almost let him go just for that. I would have liked to have been there." Once his exhilaration had abated, Schröder put on his unreadable face again. "He seems to take his job very seriously?"

"Oppenheimer is very conscientious."

"Well, nonetheless, make sure the order is carried out. It's probably best if you take care of it yourself."

"Yes, sir!" Vogler replied without hesitation.

As he strode through the garden to return to his car, accompanied by the rhythmic crunching of the pebbles beneath his shoes, Vogler understood the order he'd just been given. He was supposed to kill Oppenheimer.

The entire time, he hadn't wasted a thought of what was going to happen to Oppenheimer once the investigation was over. He had fooled himself into believing that he could simply return him to where he'd found him. But things were far complexer than they had seemed initially, and Gruppenführer Reithermann had made the decision for him.

He glumly kicked a pebble onto the manicured lawn. He had to admit that he didn't like this order. For a while now, he'd had this feeling toward Oppenheimer that he couldn't really place.

Vogler contemplated the essence of their relationship. Over the past few weeks, he'd always known that he could rely on Oppenheimer. After all, the man came from a completely different world and was a homicide inspector. Almost everyone else Vogler knew was SS and therefore potential competitors. Oppenheimer's skills were equal to his, but there was never any danger of him challenging Vogler's rank.

Vogler got behind the wheel and caught himself trying to find an alternative. In actual fact, Reithermann was going against Goebbels's personal orders. But no, the propaganda minister had only taken Oppenheimer under his wing for the duration of the investigation. He didn't care what happened to him after that. Vogler pondered the matter for several minutes, but he could not find a way out of this dilemma and reluctantly concluded that it was pointless to think about it any further. After all, he was a member of the SS. Although it hit a sour note, by the time he started the engine, Vogler knew that he would carry out this order. Just like every other order.

■

No, it had been a false alarm. He listened carefully into the night, paying attention to every tiny detail. Oppenheimer pressed himself flat against the villa's stone wall. But as hard as he tried, he couldn't hear anyone. He was completely alone.

This meant that everything had gone according to plan. Bauer had given him a leg up over the fence. Under the cover of darkness, Oppenheimer had run across the garden and around the building until he reached the back. Now all he could do was wait.

The drive from Zehlendorf to the small villa that housed Vogler's office had only taken a few minutes. They had gone a few kilometers westward and crossed the Wannsee Bridge. The lakeside was a very popular residential area. Many rich aristocrats had built palatial villas here around the turn of the century, with Mediterranean-style gardens. Berlin celebrities had always been drawn to the Wannsee. A wide variety of personalities, such as the world-famous surgeon Ferdinand Sauerbruch and the actor Heinz Rühmann, resided just a few hundred meters away from Vogler's office. During the time of runaway inflation, scandal-ridden speculators had moved into the exclusive neighborhood, and eventually, so had the NSDAP bigwigs. In addition, various convalescent homes and schools had been requisitioned by such party organizations as the National Socialist Women's League or the National Socialist Insurance Company.

Wannsee was considered a quiet part of town and had largely been left untouched by bomb attacks. The neighborhood was therefore down-right predestined to be used for carrying out discreet tasks. According to Lüttke, the SD and the Gestapo, too, had requisitioned several properties here or forcibly transferred them into Aryan ownership. To his astonishment, Oppenheimer had found out that besides several institutes, the SD even maintained a palatial guesthouse right on the banks of the lake. The villa that Oppenheimer was due to visit was not that big, but still large enough to house several SD offices. Bauer had insisted that only the front entrance was guarded. This was the reason why their inside contact was planning to smuggle Oppenheimer in through a window at ten o'clock sharp.

Oppenheimer stretched. Morosely, he wondered whether he could trust the resistance people. The window directly above his head was supposed to be opened now. But their contact had not yet appeared. Oppenheimer looked at his pocket watch, but it was too dark to recognize anything. He'd left the car at five to ten and had climbed over the fence. Could five minutes really last that long? Or was his watch broken? He listened; it was ticking.

Oppenheimer surveyed his surroundings and double-checked that he'd gotten the right window. It had to be the assigned place. It was exactly as Bauer had described it. This was the only place where Oppenheimer could climb in through the window without leaving tracks in the flower bed. But still nothing moved.

Oppenheimer filled his lungs with cold night air and cursed quietly. Anything seemed possible in this dangerous situation. Maybe their contact had been discovered. Or they had gotten the wrong time. Or the SD had eliminated everyone a long time ago and had forgotten him.

Suddenly, he heard a noise. The window above his head opened. Oppenheimer flinched when a rope landed on him. Someone was leaning out of the window. A whisper in the night. "Hello? Is that you, Schiller?"

For a moment, Oppenheimer had almost forgotten that this was his cover name.

"Here," Oppenheimer whispered just in time before the rope was pulled back up. Unfortunately, he wasn't practiced in climbing up house walls on a rope. Groaning, he progressed hand over hand. He only made slow progress. A hand grabbed him and pulled him up the last few inches into the inside of the building.

He was in a corridor with many doors. A single ceiling light in the nearest hallway cast long shadows across the floor. A figure stared at him in the twilight. He stopped short when he recognized a middle-aged woman. "Are you the inside man?" he asked in surprise.

"The resistance only has male terms for someone in my job," she muttered while she rolled up the rope, released it from the radiator, and closed the window. "No idea why. There are no guards in here. If you encounter anyone, just behave normally. Don't draw attention to yourself. There are some people who work nights, but come along; we don't have time for lengthy explanations."

She pressed the rope into his hands and headed off down the corridor, Oppenheimer right behind her. As hard as he tried to be quiet, the sound of his steps seemed to be amplified a hundredfold. Luckily, it wasn't far to Vogler's office. The woman pulled out a metallic gleaming object and put it in the keyhole. The lock clicked, and his accomplice opened the door. Oppenheimer was about to enter the room when he froze.

"What is it?" the woman whispered when she noticed him hesitate.

Finally, she impatiently pushed him into the room. He barely noticed the door closing behind him. He stared intently at the pin board directly in front of him.

During the investigation, he had always believed that no one was particularly interested in what he did, as long as he provided results. He had been followed, sure, but he had always presumed that this was the only surveillance activity. Now he realized that this assumption had been an illusion.

Clearly, Vogler had tried to reconstruct every one of Oppenheimer's moves here in his office. Oppenheimer was easily able to recognize the pieces of paper on the board that made sense only to him. Vogler or one of his staff had gone to the trouble of arranging them in exactly the same order as in the Zehlendorf house. The results from the last few weeks, the results from his work before they had caught Karl Ziegler, hung there before him.

"What's the matter?" his companion asked impatiently.

Oppenheimer's mouth felt strangely dry.

"Nothing," he finally muttered.

"Over there." The woman pointed to the desk in the corner. "The files on the table are new."

Oppenheimer had to force himself to concentrate on his original mission after this surprise discovery. He tore his gaze from the board and turned toward the files lying on the desk.

Hastily, he thumbed through the documents, but it was too dark to recognize anything. He dared to switch on only the desk lamp to examine the documents. An interrogation protocol was at the front of the file. Oppenheimer quickly flicked through it, searching for a name or an address, for hints as to who the second perpetrator might be and where the kidnapped women had been taken. He soon concluded that the confession was false. Ziegler admitted to having kidnapped and tortured the women alone. His motive was that he wanted to see how the human body worked. He had simply been curious. And in his, quote *congenital ignorance,* with regard to good and evil, he did what was most obvious to him—he cut the bodies up, in the same way as he tinkered about with an engine, to inspect the individual parts. But it wasn't in his powers to rebuild the women afterward, which was why he simply got rid of the bodies at night.

Oppenheimer's gaze flew anxiously across the pages, word for word, line by line. The confession made no mention of the places the bodies had been found. The monuments for the fallen of the last world war were not mentioned. Of course, there was no way to make a connection between Ziegler and the First World War. It simply didn't fit with the concept of a single perpetrator.

Oppenheimer read on as quickly as possible. Ziegler's work for Höcker & Sons was given as the connecting link between the murders. So far, so good. The fact that the murdered women were connected to the party was not mentioned at all. Nor was the hiding place where the mutilations had taken place. Disappointed, Oppenheimer flicked through to the final page. He saw that the confession was not signed. The dotted line for Ziegler's signature was empty. Then his gaze fell upon the last sentence.

The suspect died during the interrogation, it said matter-of-factly. So they'd made short shrift of Ziegler and had killed him.

Oppenheimer shook his head. "They really went all out on this," he mumbled to himself. He knew that they would have sent Ziegler to the gallows anyway. What made the situation all the more difficult was the fact that he couldn't be questioned anymore. Ziegler could no longer reveal where the hiding place was.

Disappointed, Oppenheimer put the protocol aside. For several seconds, he sat immobile and stared into space. He knew what that meant. The murderer would continue his gruesome game, hurting women, torturing and killing, when he'd had enough of them.

"Are you finished?" Oppenheimer flinched. The woman shifted restlessly from one foot to the other.

"Just a moment," he mumbled absentmindedly and concentrated on the remaining documents. There were two files. The first one had Karl Ziegler's name on it. He quickly scanned the pages. There was nothing much. His past addresses, his medical examination for military service, a certified copy of his birth certificate. When Oppenheimer looked at the second file, he froze. It was labeled *Johannes Lutzow.* Oppenheimer remembered: the storm trooper, the file that Lüttke and Bauer had not been able to find—it was right in front of him.

This couldn't be a coincidence.

A spark of hope flickered up inside him. Had Billhardt's information been right after all? Was Lutzow the actual brains behind the crimes?

Hectically, he searched through the file. Police protocols, photographs of the union man's wife he had attacked, doctors' reports. As thin as Ziegler's file had been, this one was voluminous. Oppenheimer turned page after page, searching through each document until he suddenly paused. Someone had included a section of a city map in the file. He recognized the outline of the Müggelsee and, right next to it, a cross drawn in ink.

The mark was just under the spot marking the Bismarckwarte, a famous watchtower. There were blotches next to it. They were brown, probably dried blood. And at the edge of the section was a signature, Karl Ziegler's signature, missing from the interrogation protocol. The blood rushed to Oppenheimer's head. Before his death, Kalle had disclosed the hiding place to the investigators after all.

"We have to go," Oppenheimer said and took both the files.

His escort looked at him in confusion and pointed to the files. "You can't take those."

"Special orders," Oppenheimer lied. "Let's go."

Before he stepped out into the corridor, he hid the files beneath his coat. This way, he wouldn't attract attention. Oppenheimer had walked just a couple of paces down the corridor when suddenly everything lit up.

Someone had switched on the overhead lights.

He quickly turned to slip back into the office, but the door was already locked. There was no sign of his companion.

Steps echoed down the corridor, approaching. Finally, Oppenheimer resigned himself to the inevitable and looked at the approaching figure. He recognized the man immediately. It was the burly man that he'd seen in the Reich Security Main Office that afternoon, the man with the pristine white shirt. Recognition flickered in his eyes. He stopped in surprise and then headed straight toward Oppenheimer, approaching ominously. Escape was out of the question. It was over. He'd messed up.

28

———————

S till here, this late?" the man asked. Then he added guilelessly, "Probably had a briefing meeting, right?" Oppenheimer stood lost in the
corridor and watched the huge man absentmindedly rub his knuckles.

Oppenheimer was surprised. The man spoke as if he thought he was
a colleague. Could it really be that he didn't smell a rat? Oppenheimer
pulled himself together. He had to reply. "Yes, all this bloody paperwork,"
he answered vaguely. He hoped the man wouldn't notice that his voice was
shaking. "All has to be done by the morning. No idea where the secretary
is. I had to type it all up myself."

"Do you mean Iris? *Fräulein* Haferkamp? Right little corker, that one.
Marvelously equipped too." The man began to grin at the thought. "But
careful. Married, unfortunately. And to make matters worse, happily.
Someone should do us the favor of sending her old man to the front,
right? Well, as you said, she's not there. I think she's gone to a funeral.
Unavoidable these days. What a waste of human material."

Oppenheimer decided to make use of the situation. He frowned and
glared at the man. "What are you trying to say? Are you criticizing the
führer's methods?" It seemed that in this case, attack was the best form of
defense. The man's eyes widened with fear for a second. It was extremely
dangerous if someone questioned your adherence to party principles.
Almost any good German national could be cornered this way. Pleased,
Oppenheimer noticed that members of the SD were no exception. The
man opposite him clumsily fumbled around for a handkerchief and wiped
his brow.

"What? No, no, my dear colleague, I—of course not," he stammered. "Of course, I completely support our führer, 100 percent!" As if he couldn't think of any other arguments, he suddenly shouted, "Heil Hitler!" and raised his arm in the German greeting.

Oppenheimer imitated Vogler, clicked his heels together, ramrod straight, and reciprocated the greeting. To his horror, he realized that the files he'd hidden beneath his coat were slipping. The other man must not see this. If he guessed that Oppenheimer was smuggling files out of the building, the game would be up. He desperately pressed the files against his body. To distract from this, he slapped the man jovially on the shoulder.

"Don't get the wrong idea, my dear colleague. I didn't mean to criticize. I understand some of your thinking. However, you have to be careful with such statements nowadays, they can easily be interpreted as undermining military morale. With all due respect, you do need to be a little more careful who you share these thoughts with."

The man breathed a sigh of relief. "Yes, I quite understand. Quite so. Quite so. My name is Holm, by the way, Peter Holm."

"Richard," Oppenheimer replied. And after a brief pause, he added, "Richard . . . Opel."

When the man called Holm stopped short, Oppenheimer realized what a stupid choice he'd made.

"Opel? Oh, like the car manufacturer? Related?"

"Unfortunately, not."

While they shook hands, Oppenheimer had to be careful that the files didn't slip. Holm put on his coat and headed off. Oppenheimer decided it would be less conspicuous if he accompanied him.

"Ah, right. Are you also heading home?"

Oppenheimer's mind raced. He was standing here in his coat, so he couldn't really say no.

"Yes, I must make a move so that I can get at least a couple of hours' sleep," he lied.

Holm stretched and reached for his shoulder. "I think I'm getting old. I had a difficult client today. I'm out of practice. It didn't used to bother me. Could interrogate people for hours on end."

Oppenheimer's companion was still nowhere to be seen. He joined Holm to turn right. They headed straight toward the large entranceway and approached the door. Oppenheimer could see a uniformed officer, a weapon over his shoulder, guarding the exit. He was painfully aware that he couldn't simply leave Holm without some excuse. He had said he was going home, so his companion would assume that they were leaving together. Even a brief hesitation would immediately be conspicuous. But it was too risky to simply stride through the main entrance; no, it was absolute madness when one had furtively climbed into the building shortly beforehand. On the other hand, Oppenheimer had company now. He was with someone who seemed to be in the building a lot, who would not be suspected of smuggling an intruder out right in front of a guard.

Mechanically, Oppenheimer carried on walking. He had no choice; he had to stake everything on one card. Either he would manage to escape in this way or not at all.

He heard a voice. Someone at his side said something. It must have been Holm. Oppenheimer hadn't heard what he'd said because he was concentrating on the guard. "Sorry?"

"Your wife—is she also in the country?"

"No, she's here. Close by."

"Ah, I understand. I sometimes quite like having Margarete off my back. But it's not a long-term solution. And the children. I do worry about them when they're gone."

"I understand. That's the way it is with children."

The guard looked at them briefly. Then he looked past them again.

"Good-bye," Holm said on his way out to the guard.

When the heavy door closed behind them, Oppenheimer breathed a sigh of relief. He crossed the garden by Holm's side and eventually exited from the front gate into the street. He'd made it. He had escaped. Oppenheimer had not considered it possible that it could be that easy. He could see Lüttke's car at the next corner.

"Do you want to come for a drink?" Holm asked.

"Another time. My wife is waiting."

"See you soon, then."

"Indeed," Oppenheimer said, relieved. He turned away hastily. Too hastily, as suddenly the two files slipped out from under his coat and landed directly in front of Holm's feet on the pavement.

Oppenheimer felt his heart stop. He'd betrayed himself. Bauer and

Lüttke were too far away to be able to help. They also weren't counting on him coming out of the front gate.

"Whoops!" Holm said and bent down with a groan. He picked up the files and looked at them curiously. "What have we got here, then?" He was unable to read the labels on the file in the darkness. Holm looked at Oppenheimer attentively. "Are they yours?"

"I—I took them with me," Oppenheimer stuttered.

Holm looked doubtfully at the files. He seemed to be considering what to think of this. Then a grin spread across his face as he thought he understood. "Homework, what? Good for you."

He handed the file to Oppenheimer, who tried not to appear too frantic as he took them back. "Many thanks. Yes, work, work."

Holm chuckled. "Carry on, my diligent chap. Heil Hitler!" With these words, he turned around and a few seconds later had disappeared into the darkness.

■

The glow of his lighter would have to do. Although they were outside the city now, Oppenheimer didn't dare to switch on the flashlight because of the blackout order.

Bauer and Lüttke had not been particularly happy about him having taken the two files, but Oppenheimer had talked his way out of it by saying that after having run into the man named Holm, he wouldn't have been able to get rid of them unobtrusively. Now, he and Hilde at least had the opportunity to scan the files during the drive and find out who their perpetrator was. They put their heads together over the papers. They had quickly decided how to divide their tasks. While Hilde went through Lutzow's medical report, Oppenheimer browsed through the two men's files, looking for consistencies. After only a couple of minutes, he came across something.

"Here it is." Oppenheimer could barely contain his excitement. "The connection between Ziegler and Lutzow. Here are copies of the registration entries. They lived in the same block of flats in Köpenick for several months, three and a half years ago."

"That means they know each other."

"It's likely, but we can't prove it. We'd have to ask former residents. If I were still with the crime squad, I'd also go through the files there to see if there were any unsolved murder cases in the Köpenick area at the time. Maybe other women fell victim to them."

"Bullshit. You're always too cautious, Richard. Common sense tells us that they met there."

Oppenheimer couldn't prevent himself from smiling. "Common sense? Wow! From you of all people? Normally, you base everything on facts!"

"Look, Lutzow definitely fits the age profile that we have. If we assume that the two of them worked together, this also explains the differing injuries the victims had. It's been bothering me the entire time. I couldn't explain it properly, but now it makes sense."

Oppenheimer interrupted her before Hilde could continue. "Wait a moment. You're already three steps ahead."

Hilde took a deep breath. With all the forbearance she could muster, she began to explain her train of thought. "It's quite simple. Let's assume that Ziegler was just an assistant. Let's say he just wanted to satisfy his sadistic impulses. In that case, the recordings are probably a sort of souvenir—a trophy, if you will. The recordings show the victims begging for mercy while nails are being hammered into their ears. That is connected to Ziegler."

Oppenheimer nodded. "Right, that could be the case. What about the mutilated genitals?"

"I was just getting to that. It has to be connected to the second perpetrator, to Lutzow. Judging by the letters, he hates women. His motivation is to put the so-called prostitutes out of action. Which is exactly what he does. He doesn't only kill them but also steals their genitals so that they can no longer be a danger. In any case, it has to be Lutzow who wrote the letters; Ziegler is simply too stupid. Lutzow dressed up his deeds ideologically, he wants public recognition, and he goes as far as displaying the corpses in public. He is definitely the driving force behind these murders."

"Well, here is a document that shows Lutzow was at the front during the last war. So there is a connection to that time, that much is true. It seems he didn't get any sort of award, but there aren't any indications that he was dishonorably discharged either."

Hilde cast a brief glance at the piece of paper and then pointed to it. "Lutzow's abnormal behavior must somehow be connected to this period of time. Otherwise, it makes no sense that he presented the women in front of the First World War monuments."

"So you mean that he had some sort of experience with women during this time that shaped his thinking?"

A cynical smile played around Hilde's lips as she waved the medical report in front of his face. "Do you know when this was dated? In 1920. Lutzow was treated for syphilis during this time. Did you read it?"

Oppenheimer shook his head in surprise. "What does Lutzow's former illness have to do with it?"

"He experienced exactly what he describes in his letters. He contracted syphilis from a woman, and years later, he blusters on about how the German man's body is damaged by prostitutes. This speaks for itself. He probably saw some sort of connection to his own wartime experiences. Maybe he visited a brothel for the first time at the front, possibly even had his first sexual experience altogether. This wouldn't be unusual. He is young, lives among soldiers, feels grown-up and paints the town red."

Oppenheimer frowned. "That's quite a few *ifs* and *buts*."

"It doesn't matter as long as it's the truth. All that matters is whether Lutzow believes it. He must have construed some connection, and this experience later shapes all his actions. And the crazy thing is that we might have been spared all of this."

"You mean Hitler's amnesty? Billhardt mentioned it. It must be mentioned farther on." Oppenheimer started to thumb through the file, but Hilde interrupted him.

"Not Hitler. I mean the doctors Lutzow consulted back then. They definitely didn't treat him correctly. Do you know the symptoms of syphilis when it is not completely cured?" Hilde didn't wait for Oppenheimer's answer. "Sometimes the nerve tissue in the spinal cord or brain slowly degrades. Personality changes, hallucinations, delusions of grandeur, the full range. These are exactly the symptoms that can be deduced from our murderer's letters. Lutzow was not insane when he sought treatment. This only happened because the doctors mistreated him, these stupid idiots."

After this observation, Hilde sighed deeply and looked outside where the moonlight was shining onto the flat fields. Lüttke had decided to take the southern route around the city. It was the shortest way to the murderer's hiding place. But Oppenheimer barely knew where they were right now.

"Lutzow might have become a bastard," Hilde mumbled, "but he is also a pretty interesting case. If only I'd gotten my hands on this file earlier. What happened to him after the war?"

Oppenheimer briefly looked at the papers. "Well, for the first few years, there is no trace of him. The medical report that you have is the only document from this time. The rest sounds like the usual party career. The court files paint a pretty good picture of what he was getting up to. He was a war veteran, but he's not able to get established. I'm guessing that he didn't feel accepted by society, like so many returning German soldiers. In any case, he kept the wolf from the door by working as an unskilled laborer, took every job he could find. He even worked at a butcher's once, which would fit in with the precise cuts found on the victims. But he didn't stay for long anywhere. Then, in the mid-1920s, he signed up with the SA storm troops."

Hilde snorted derisively. "Of course. The perfect refuge for the chronically disadvantaged. So Lutzow haunted the streets with his Nazi activists. Doesn't surprise me."

"Well, here it's paraphrased as *political activities*. But now things are getting interesting. At the time, Lutzow lived in Charlottenburg. The SA people have a meeting place there, the restaurant Zur Altstadt in Hebbelstraße. Once they'd set up camp there, they turned the place into their 'Storm Joint.' The owners apparently tolerated it, although their regulars seem to have been more communist than socialist. There was also some sort of dungeon for locking up political prisoners."

Hilde's features had hardened during Oppenheimer's description. "You don't need to explain that to me."

When she sensed Oppenheimer's questioning gaze, she added, "I had a patient at the time. He was unlucky enough to get taken to such a place. They beat him with burning torches, and when he got thirsty, they gave him wood preservative to drink. It's almost unimaginable. When they finally let him out, all I could do was send him to hospital. He lay in a bath of boracic acid for a week, suffering terribly, before he died. Considering that there are probably dozens of such hideouts here, it makes you wonder how many more Lutzows are running around Berlin."

Oppenheimer stared ahead glumly. After clearing his throat, he said, "Well, nobody is likely to be able to answer that question. In any case, the authorities didn't become aware of Lutzow until he attacked the unionist's wife in Moabit. That was in September 1932. These files were originally put together for the murder case. The judge considered Lutzow's behavior to be a malicious attack and sentenced him to death."

"And then Hitler came to power just a few months later."

"Exactly. Lutzow got lucky. His murder was seen as a politically motivated attack, and the sentence was never carried out. They let him go without further ado. But a short while later, Lutzow's career within the party falters. When the power struggle within the various camps of the NSDAP flared up, he seems to have remained loyal to the SA."

Hilde considered this. "In that case, he was pretty stupid. If he really only wanted to climb the career ladder, then he would have joined the SS no later than the Night of the Long Knives, when Röhm and the entire SA leadership were massacred."

"Well, I can understand it," Oppenheimer replied. "He was probably of the opinion that he and his SA comrades had been doing all the donkey-work. The street fights had laid the foundation for Hitler's rise to power. But the führer's gratitude failed to materialize, and the competitors from the SS gained ever more influence."

Hilde shook her head. "Hang on; don't forget that it was the SS who were primarily responsible for the SA being scrapped. Röhm was stupid enough to pick a fight with the Reichswehr. That egotistical idiot dreamed of having the entire military dancing to his tune."

"Of course I know that," Oppenheimer protested. "Maybe Lutzow hoped for the same. In any case, the SA had no chance of asserting themselves. Hitler deemed the brown-shirted rabble that had brought him to power too unrefined. He was Reich Chancellor now and trying to appear respectable. It was just inconvenient that Röhm of all people was heading up the SA in this situation. Röhm saw his own people as the spearhead of the new ideology and played the part of the revolutionary, while Hitler primarily wanted to secure his power. When Röhm refused to be fobbed off and became too recalcitrant, he basically signed his own death warrant. Now imagine what Lutzow thought in this situation. The way was cleared for the SS; the SA officially continued to exist but no longer held any power. Now all Lutzow and his comrades were good for was making up the numbers during parades."

Hilde's eyes narrowed as she spun this idea on. "Initially, Lutzow would certainly have felt alienated. He saw that National Socialism was going in a direction that didn't suit him. This could have been the trigger for him to begin distancing himself from the party line."

"But there is one important point to all of this." Oppenheimer raised his index finger. "He does not question the foundation of this ideology. He just wants his own form of National Socialism."

"But his attitude is getting ever more bizarre." Hilde was clearly agitated. She seemed to have come across something. "Not even the politics of a madman like Hitler can keep up with this. Of course, Lutzow's latent hatred of women plays an important role once again. When he discovered he had syphilis, he started to demonize the women he considered to be whores. Regardless of how exactly his definition runs, he classifies them as unclean and is afraid of renewed infection. It all comes to a head with the murder of the unionist's wife. At the latest since that deed, his hatred of women becomes intertwined with the National Socialist ideology."

Oppenheimer considered Hilde's comments. "After that, Lutzow cobbled together his own ideology from these elements. And we are now dealing with the result. You're right, Hilde, it would fit."

"Bother!" Lüttke swore. Oppenheimer and Hilde were flung to the side. From the corner of his eye, Oppenheimer was just able to see that they had avoided a pile of rubble in the middle of the road at the very last moment. A sure sign that they were approaching the outskirts of the city again.

Hilde also focused on their surroundings again. Her gaze fixed on the city map, and she scratched her chin thoughtfully. "Lutzow chose a strange hiding place."

Oppenheimer looked at the map too. He'd been to the Müggelsee countless times. The Bismarckwarte lay on the southern side between Köpenick and Müggelheim. It was a popular destination, as the building also had a viewing platform that provided a fabulous view of Berlin. The view was so impressive that there was a second platform on the same hill, as well as a tavern in the forest and, a little farther on, the idyllic Teufelsee. Almost everyone who lived in Berlin had taken a weekend trip there once. And while the day-trippers happily splashed around in the water or wandered across the hills, they had no idea that an indescribable horror was taking place just a few hundred meters away from them.

"You mean it's strange that Lutzow chose a place that is heaving with people at the weekends?" Oppenheimer asked. "Yes, it does increase the danger of being discovered."

"No, I don't mean that. The hiding place is very close to the Bismarck-warte. Doesn't that tower make you think of the place the bodies were found?"

At first, Oppenheimer was puzzled as to what Hilde meant. But when he recalled the image of the Bismarckwarte, he understood her reference. The huge tower structure with the large entrance gate was similar to the water tower in Steglitz. With its blunt top crowned by a mighty fire bowl, the Bismarckwarte could almost pass as a vastly enlarged version of the monuments in front of which the murderer had placed his victims.

"Fair enough," Oppenheimer finally said. "There may be certain similarities, but in contrast to the other sites, I don't see a direct connection to the First World War. The Bismarckwarte was built around the turn of the century. It might just be a coincidence."

"That may be right," Hilde admitted, "but Lutzow had an affinity for phallic symbols. And what does he do? He finds a safe house in the direct vicinity of the biggest stone willy to be found far and wide."

Oppenheimer continued to be skeptical, but he saw no point in digging his heels in.

"It doesn't matter anyway," he conceded. "The main thing is that we've figured it out."

The car stopped, and Lüttke said, "Right. We're here."

Covertly, Oppenheimer watched Hilde assessing the surroundings. To her surprise, she realized they were outside a subway station.

"Hey, what's going on?" Hilde protested. "We're not in Adlerhof yet. This is wrong."

"We're in the right place," Oppenheimer replied calmly. To enforce his instructions, he looked Hilde straight in the eye. "You're getting out here."

Hilde was speechless for a moment. Then she said in a shrill voice, "I damn well won't! You've taken me this far, so it doesn't make any difference now. I want to see the matter through!"

"Hilde, it might get dangerous. The trains are still running. Take the next one to the city center. We'll meet at your place later."

"Men!" she said in bewilderment. "Will you stop with the whole gallantry thing!"

"You don't understand; I'm worried about Lisa!"

Hilde paused when she heard Lisa's name.

Oppenheimer continued, tried to explain. "If something happens to me, someone has to take care of her. Hilde, it's the last thing I'm going to ask of you. Promise me you'll take care of Lisa?"

When Oppenheimer saw that Hilde's features relaxed, he knew that she understood. But he also knew that she wouldn't simply agree with him. Finally, she shrugged and said with a feigned sigh, "It would be better if I came along, but if you insist."

Oppenheimer had to smile. "Come on, then. Out with you."

Hilde seemed reluctant as she opened the door. Once she was on the pavement, she looked back and nodded toward the files lying on the seat next to Oppenheimer. "What about those? Do you need them?"

"What do you want with them?"

"Well, they're of huge value to research. This case could be useful for solving future sex crimes."

Oppenheimer considered for a moment. Then he handed her the files. "It's probably better this way. Just in case someone surprises us, then at least there is no proof that we broke into the SD building."

Oppenheimer felt there was nothing more to be said. The moment had come to say good-bye. Hilde had also realized it. She gave him a long look and whispered in his ear, "Take care of yourself." Then she added a little more loudly, "And give Lutzow a hefty kick in the balls from me."

"You can count on that," Oppenheimer added grimly and closed the door.

He stared out of the back window until Hilde disappeared into the night. Shortly afterward, they were already driving through the dark streets of Köpenick. Just a few more kilometers, and they arrived at the Müggelsee. Suddenly, it occurred to Oppenheimer that they would soon be approaching the place where he'd searched for Traudel Herrmann a week ago. They'd been so damn close; they had missed the murderer's hiding place by just a few kilometers. Oppenheimer couldn't suppress a quiet curse at the realization.

A few minutes later, the water reflected the light of the moon, which was just bright enough to lend the surface a hazy sheen. They were in the forest area around the Müggelsee.

Bauer turned to the back. "Where exactly are we going now?"

Oppenheimer switched on the flashlight and handed it to them, together with the section of the city map. It was the only document from the files that he'd kept. "Simply turn right into the entrance. We have to head up the Müggelberg. It's more or less in between the viewing platform and the Bismarckwarte. Lutzow has had some sort of business out here for the last few years. He grows mushrooms or something like that. Anyhow, there has to be a house or a hut that belongs to him."

Bauer frowned. "He grows mushrooms?"

"It's very practical nowadays," Lüttke said. "I also thought about doing it. Much simpler than vegetables. They're guaranteed to grow, just need moisture. Unfortunately, I don't have enough space at home."

Bauer stared at his colleague as if he seriously doubted his mental faculties. "Mushrooms," he mumbled, shaking his head.

■

Somewhere up there, a huge lion was lying sprawled across the main entrance. It was the only sculpture that had been mounted on the façade of the Bismarckwarte. Feeling tense, Oppenheimer looked up the hill and wondered whether the lion could be seen from here in daylight. But the tip of the Bismarckwarte was lost in the blackness of the night sky.

They'd had to turn around again on the Müggelheim dam and only then had discovered the narrow forest path. The access to Lutzow's building was a little-frequented track for agricultural vehicles that led straight to the Müggelberg. When Lüttke finally stopped the car, they were in front of a wooden fence that shielded the property from uninvited visitors. In the bright light of the headlights, they had made out a small sign with the name of the owner next to the gate. Oppenheimer was now standing in front of it, very nervous. Lüttke had already switched the lights off again, but the few seconds had sufficed to etch the writing on the sign into Oppenheimer's memory.

Lutzow.

He pushed the gate. Of course, it was locked. There was no building to be seen. Oppenheimer wondered whether the hideout still even existed. Maybe it had already been destroyed and Lutzow had found new quarters somewhere else. A deep silence emanated from the dark forest. It seemed inconceivable that this was a place where gruesome torture had taken place, but on closer examination, it was precisely this that made the site suspicious to Oppenheimer. It was too peaceful here. Too normal.

Initially, he didn't dare to take even one step onto the property. His instinct told him that there would be a trap waiting for him. On the other hand, it was also conceivable that they would not find anybody. That Lutzow hadn't kidnapped another victim, because he was worried about Kalle's disappearance. He was probably long gone. Oppenheimer took a deep breath and prepared himself mentally to find this out.

Lüttke joined him. "Take this," he said and pressed a gun into Oppenheimer's hand. "A loan, until this is all over. Do you want the flashlight too?"

"I'd better not. It might give me away. I'll try to creep in under cover of darkness. If he's in his hiding place, I might get lucky and be able to overpower him. Wait five minutes, and then follow me with the light. As backup."

Bauer had also gotten out of the car and nodded briefly.

"Good luck."

Oppenheimer climbed over the fence and tried to follow the trail he'd briefly made out in the beam of the flashlight. Unfortunately, the moon was hidden by the treetops. Oppenheimer peered into the darkness. If Lutzow had been waiting for him and would attack now, he was completely at his mercy. Well, not completely. Oppenheimer released the gun's safety catch.

Suddenly, he sensed a bump on the ground beneath his foot. Luckily, he'd withstood the urge to put on the good pair of shoes that Hilde had given him. The tatty soles of his shoes were coming in useful now, as he was easily able to feel any unevenness in the ground. Oppenheimer stopped and bent down. Yes, there were tracks made by a heavy vehicle. Excellent. Now Oppenheimer had something to help him find his orientation. The tire tracks would lead him to the hideout. He carefully set off again to follow them.

The path curved, and Oppenheimer discovered light between the trees. There it was, a small storage hut—Lutzow's hideout. A few steps on, he discovered that the light was coming from a lamp hung over the entrance. Because of the air raid provisions, the glass was blue.

Just a few meters farther on, and he was able to make out an object. Oppenheimer gasped when he realized what it was, right there next to the entrance. It was a delivery van with a tarpaulin cover. *Ziegler's van,* he thought. This could only mean that Lutzow was here and that he'd kidnapped a further victim.

Instinctively, Oppenheimer stopped and looked around. He waited a few seconds, but no one came. No sudden attack in the darkness, no murderer assaulting him.

Nervously, Oppenheimer put his left hand in his coat pocket, all the while keeping an eye on his surroundings. He pulled out a Pervitin pill, put it in his mouth, chewed, and swallowed.

He considered why Lutzow had left the light on. But then he remembered that the light couldn't be seen from the path anyway, so Lutzow was not running any risk by leaving it on. He appeared to feel safe in his hideout. Too safe? Did he never expect that someone might show up and force their way in?

Normally, Oppenheimer would have circled the building first to find a back entrance. But there was probably a woman begging for help inside the building at this very moment. He had no choice. He had to get inside. Immediately.

Oppenheimer braced himself and approached the door. He gently placed one foot in front of the other, trying all the while not to make any noise. He pushed the door handle down. In contrast to the gate, the door was not locked.

A fusty smell hit him, and he gasped. Carefully, he peered through the narrow crack of the door, but he wasn't able to recognize much in the darkness behind.

He pulled himself together and quickly entered the room, his weapon at the ready. Only the blue light of the outside lamp lit up the inside of the storage hut.

He could just about make out some outlines. He needed a moment to understand. Those were basins for growing mushrooms, about waist-high, huddling together in the constant shade. Oppenheimer realized with apprehension that there were lots of nooks and crannies, perfect hiding places. And yet there didn't seem to be anyone here. There was no trace of Lutzow and his victim. Close by, Oppenheimer spotted a black square in the ground. That opening had to lead down to the cellar. He quickly considered the options. It was highly likely that Lutzow was hiding down there. Oppenheimer had to take the risk and descend. Silently, he approached the opening in the ground. He had just bent down to feel around for stairs when he heard something.

Desperate whimpering.

Oppenheimer was startled. He sensed that the muffled sound had not come from the cellar. This meant that the victim had to be here on the ground floor. Could there be another room? He looked around searchingly, but the light above the entrance didn't reach far enough.

At that moment, Oppenheimer wondered where Lüttke and Bauer had gotten to. Would it not make more sense to wait for them in order to join forces and then attack?

Fear threatened to befuddle Oppenheimer's mind. He suddenly felt uncertain; his thoughts revolved around the single question of what might be awaiting him in the darkness. This could only mean the Pervitin hadn't taken effect. Now, when he needed it most.

A creaking noise. Oppenheimer whirled around with his weapon raised. He stood still. Waiting for the attack. It failed to happen. False alarm. There was no one behind him. No one wanted to attack him.

Oppenheimer took a deep breath and tried to calm down. Until he felt the effects of the Pervitin, he must not allow himself to be misled by the demons that imagination projected into the darkness. His heart thumped. He had to hold on to something. Shakily, he felt around.

His fingertips touched something firm. He gently stroked across the surface. A wall. Eventually, he risked feeling his way along it.

He crept forward centimeter by centimeter. Hasty movements increased the danger of making a noise that would give him away.

To make matters worse, Oppenheimer realized that the ground was quite uneven. He shuffled alongside the mushroom basins, but there was no way of telling what distance he had already covered.

Oppenheimer flinched. His fingertips brushed something. On closer inspection, it turned out to be another wall that stood at a right angle to the first one. Oppenheimer carefully followed the second wall.

He crept on until he saw something on the ground in front of him. At first, it seemed nothing more than a light pattern, but when he looked closer, he saw that it was the relief of the wooden planks. The ends of the roughly timbered planks protruded upward. Taking this in, Oppenheimer made an important discovery. The strange form of the splintered wood chippings cast long shadows. This could only mean that the light source was also at ground level.

When Oppenheimer bent down, he saw a strip of light just a few centimeters away. He was standing directly in front of a closed door. The light was coming from an adjacent room. So he had been right. If Lutzow had a new victim, then she had to be behind this door.

Oppenheimer held his breath and pressed himself against the wall, his weapon at the ready. Now he could clearly hear something moving in the room. Then he heard a rustling and a woman's suffocated cry. Lutzow had indeed kidnapped another victim. Oppenheimer realized this woman was still alive.

From his many years of experience as a police inspector, he knew that in this situation, there was only one thing to do. He had to try to get Lutzow away from his victim by whatever means.

Oppenheimer prepared himself for a frontal attack. He took a deep breath, and when he felt he was ready, he took a run-up.

When the lock burst out of the frame, he jumped into the room, his weapon ready.

The gleam of the naked bulb blinded Oppenheimer. Before he was even able to recognize anything, he thought there was some movement on the right-hand side of the room.

The sound of hasty steps. When Oppenheimer pointed his gun in the direction of the noise, he froze in mid-movement.

A woman was sitting bound and gagged on a chair in the far corner of the room. She offered a pathetic sight. She was still wearing her evening dress, ready for a ball. But her long brown hair was tousled. Tears had left traces of mascara on her pale cheeks. Her body was slumped, and she seemed to have surrendered to her fate.

But as soon as Oppenheimer entered her field of vision, life returned to the woman. Her head jerked up in shock, and she began to scream desperately through her gag. She tugged on her fetters, twisted her body on the chair.

Where the hell was Lutzow?

Oppenheimer turned around, cast a quick glance to the corner behind him. No. The room was still empty. He was alone with the victim.

The situation was clear to Oppenheimer. Lüttke and Bauer would show up any minute. They should take care of Lutzow. He instinctively wanted to help the woman; he couldn't leave her in this hell. But he realized too late that this reaction, precisely, had led him into a trap.

When Oppenheimer ran toward the woman, he initially didn't notice the muffled sound of the collapsing wooden beams. What happened next made no sense. Oppenheimer ran and ran.

This place seemed to be bewitched. Lutzow must have found a way to outwit nature here in his realm. The faster Oppenheimer ran, the greater the distance to the bound woman became.

With a deafening noise, the room changed shape. The image of the panic-stricken, screaming woman grew smaller and smaller until she finally disappeared from Oppenheimer's view. At the same time, he felt the pistol slipping from his grasp. Instead of the wall, the roof beams towered above him. He was thrown onto his back, the air pressed from his lungs, then it was over.

Silence.

Dazed, Oppenheimer rolled onto his side and took a deep breath. He grimaced when he felt a stabbing pain in his back.

He looked around, searching. He had no idea where he was. There were wooden beams everywhere he looked. The dust in the air got caught in his lungs. Oppenheimer had to cough.

The boards slipped twice when he tried to get up, but finally he managed to find direction in the confusion.

As well as he could, Oppenheimer sat up and squinted upward. It was only now that he realized what had happened. It seemed that Lutzow had notched the floor's supporting pillars. Oppenheimer's weight had been enough to bring everything down. Now he was in a cellar room. Water was running down from above, possibly from the mushroom basin. But maybe the collapsing wooden floor had also damaged a water pipe. Oppenheimer bent down to pick up his gun.

A shot fell outside. Oppenheimer froze. A second shot, a third, then everything went quiet. Something must have happened out there. He stretched upward but couldn't see anything.

Oppenheimer tried to find a way out but realized that it was hopeless to try to climb up the slippery wooden planks. Before he could come up with a solution, heavy steps sounded above. Men were moving through the building, entered the room the woman was in.

Oppenheimer breathed a sigh of relief. That had to be Lüttke and Bauer! They'd clearly caught Lutzow.

Oppenheimer called out, "I'm here! Down here!"

But there was no answer. Impatiently, he pushed the loose boards aside to explore the cellar room he'd crashed into. There had to be an exit here somewhere. Then he heard more steps. They seemed to be coming from next door. Oppenheimer followed the noise, and indeed, he came across a door behind which voices could be heard.

Then he was once again enveloped by a leaden silence.

Oppenheimer pulled at the door handle—the door was locked. He aimed his gun at the lock and fired. As his aim was terrible, he needed two more shots before he was able to open the door.

Across the room, there was another door, wide open. Cool air blew toward Oppenheimer. But everything was quiet. He could not detect a single movement.

To his left, stairs led up toward the light. That was where he'd seen the kidnapped woman. Carefully, he approached the stairs and started to go up. He had to find out what had happened to the victim.

When he arrived at the top, he stopped in surprise. There was nobody to be seen. Oppenheimer almost wanted to believe that a bad trick had been played upon his senses. But no, there were telltale details. It was clear that something had happened here in the last few minutes. The chair the woman had been sitting on had toppled over. Severed rope lay all around it. So it was true. Lüttke and Bauer had already freed the victim. Oppenheimer could finally breathe easily.

But then the doubts began.

He wondered why the men from the resistance hadn't shown their faces when he'd called. Could this mean that Lutzow had gotten away after all?

Or had he somehow managed to trick Lüttke and Bauer? Were there other accomplices? The trap Oppenheimer had walked into showed that the man had prepared for all eventualities. His opponent might be mad, but he definitely wasn't stupid. Oppenheimer realized that he needed to get out of here quickly to clarify the situation. Unfortunately, the rear half of the room no longer had a floor. It was not possible to get around the chasm to reach the door that Oppenheimer had come in through. He remembered hearing steps in the cellar. He'd felt a draft down there, so there had to be an exit.

When Oppenheimer was about to turn around to go down the steps, he heard a voice.

"We caught Lutzow. He was trying to run."

Oppenheimer froze. He hadn't expected to hear this voice here of all places. He knew it all too well. And he was right. When Oppenheimer turned around, he was facing Vogler.

29

———•———

Vogler didn't seem in the least surprised to see Oppenheimer. Instead, a contented smile played around his mouth. "This time our early-warning system worked," the Hauptsturmführer said.

After a moment's consideration, Oppenheimer nodded. "So you were informed about the kidnapping?"

"When I was told, I set out immediately with several men. Just in time. We shot Lutzow when he came out of the boiler room."

So Vogler had drawn the same conclusions as Oppenheimer. After Ziegler's torture, Vogler knew the two perpetrators' hiding place. It had been highly likely that Lutzow would come back here as soon as he'd found a new victim.

Oppenheimer realized that he had no explanation for his presence. And he didn't think it was a good idea to tell Vogler that he'd broken into his office. "Right," he said vaguely. "I'm sorry, but I need some fresh air."

Vogler didn't stop him. Oppenheimer followed the draft. Suddenly, he couldn't bear to be in this shed for another second. He just wanted to get out of Lutzow's torture chamber, which contained a whole universe of pain and madness.

Disoriented, he stumbled around the dark cellar until he finally came across a coal chute that led up to a heavy iron door. The evening air that greeted him outside felt good after his exertions. Oppenheimer took a deep breath. It was over. Lutzow was dead. He slowly calmed down again. Vogler appeared shortly afterward. They stood together outside the storage hut, two figures illuminated in blue by the night forest.

Oppenheimer looked around. The reinforcements Vogler had spoken of seemed to have already disappeared. The only company they had was a corpse lying on the ground a few meters away, still with the old gas mask covering his face.

"Lutzow?" Oppenheimer asked.

Vogler crossed his arms and leaned against the outside wall. "Your sleuthing instincts didn't mislead you, Oppenheimer. Lutzow colluded with Ziegler."

"What about the woman?" When Vogler shot him a puzzled look, Oppenheimer clarified. "The victim. Where is she?"

"Don't worry, she's unharmed. My people have brought her to safety. We won't bother her for too long with our questions."

"That's good."

"And then there's one more thing," Vogler added. He hesitated, searching for the right words. "We picked up two, well, strange gentlemen nearby. Unfortunately, they didn't want to tell us what they were doing here so late. You don't happen to know anything about it, do you, Oppenheimer?"

Oppenheimer froze. He knew what that meant. It was over. He was ruined. Secretly, he had hoped that Bauer and Lüttke would be able to disappear in time. But Vogler had caught them, and without those two, it would be impossible for Oppenheimer to leave Germany. He would no longer have a chance to make it up to Lisa for all the difficult years. In just one second, Vogler had managed to destroy the vague hope of being able to forget all that.

Oppenheimer knew he was a bad liar and that the shock was etched in his face. So he tried to avoid Vogler's attentive gaze. As indifferently as possible, he asked, "What am I supposed to have to do with that?"

Vogler laughed out loud when he saw what an appalling actor Oppenheimer was. "I don't really care, Oppenheimer. Those two are probably already being interrogated. Who knows what they'll tell us. I have nothing more to do with it. I am off to the front tomorrow. And about time too. You see things more clearly when you're under fire."

With this comment, Vogler's gaze wandered off into the distance.

Oppenheimer nodded. He thought he understood what the Hauptsturmführer meant. At the front, it was all about survival. There were only two types of reaction there—a right one, which meant you survived, and a wrong one, which meant you died. Although your life was occasionally also in danger at the home front, the decisions you had to make here were a lot complexer.

Both men were having similar thoughts. Although the Pervitin was now pulsing through Oppenheimer's veins, he felt a great emptiness within.

He had to employ quite a bit of willpower to push himself out of this state, to get his stubborn body moving again. But Oppenheimer wanted to have a last look at Lutzow. He bent down and after a moment's hesitation pulled the mask off the face.

Oppenheimer didn't really know what he'd expected.

Maybe a sign of the madness that had eaten into Lutzow's features? A manic expression? A jeering grin? But all his expectations were disappointed. The dead Lutzow looked ordinary. The open eyes were dull. His face, framed by a fringe of platinum-blond hair, radiated a serenity that is specific to the dead. Oppenheimer realized that he wouldn't find any answers here. What remained was an unsettling helplessness.

When he perceived a reflection of light on Lutzow's eyeballs, Oppenheimer turned around.

Vogler stood next to him, lighting a cigarette. "Is it always like this?" he asked after blowing out the match. "Is the solution to a case always different to what one expected?"

Oppenheimer straightened up and thought about this question for a few seconds. "It happens. But I think it's less the result that is a surprise. It's more the things one is confronted with during the investigation. You don't really notice it, but the view you held in the beginning slowly changes."

Vogler made an affirmative noise. "I now understand what you meant at the time. That you have to approach the matter without any preconceptions and so on." He was just about to put the packet of cigarettes in his pocket when he changed his mind and offered Oppenheimer one. "Here. To celebrate the successful closing."

As Oppenheimer struck a match to light the cigarette, he heard another sound right next to him.

A metallic click.

Oppenheimer immediately understood that Vogler had released the safety catch of his gun. He stood stiffly and tried not to make any sudden movements. Oppenheimer felt the weight of his own gun. Stupidly, he'd put it in the inside pocket of his coat when he'd climbed up the coal chute. He would never be able to pull it out fast enough.

For a few seconds, the two men just stood there without anything happening. Finally, Oppenheimer inhaled deeply so that the end of his cigarette began to glow. When he dropped the match, it had almost burned down. He knew he had no chance; he was at the Hauptsturmführer's mercy. Oppenheimer dared to turn toward Vogler only very slowly. But the SS man wasn't looking at him. He was staring at the corpse.

"No one will find out that Johannes Lutzow was involved in these deeds," the Hauptsturmführer said. His voice sounded strangely croaky. "Does that surprise you, Oppenheimer?"

Oppenheimer had to swallow hard before he could answer. "I thought as much."

"Tomorrow morning, there will be no evidence that he ever existed; this building will no longer exist. No one will remember it."

Oppenheimer realized what Vogler was trying to say. He was an accessory who had to be silenced. Sweat appeared on his brow. Silently, he observed Vogler aiming at something in their surroundings. Oppenheimer had forgotten the cigarette between his lips. Panicked, he searched for a way out, a means of escape. It was only now that he noticed how light it was. The bloody lamp over the entrance! There was no chance of disappearing into the darkness. Oppenheimer assessed the distance to the lorry, the distance to the nearest trees, but everything was too far away. If he ran for it now, Vogler could get him with a single shot.

When Oppenheimer looked back at the Hauptsturmführer, the man's mood had changed. He had a rakish grin on his face and looked like someone who was laughing about a joke that only he understood. He briefly closed his eyes, then lowered his gun. "It is better for you if you don't return to the Kameradschaftssiedlung. And don't go back to the Jewish House either. Reithermann, the fat pig, will move heaven and hell to get you. And please don't make the mistake of trying to shoot me. I'm a quicker draw." With that, Vogler threw away his half-smoked cigarette and blew a final cloud of smoke into the night air. "This conversation did not take place. It seems like this is it, Inspector." Oppenheimer looked at the

Hauptsturmführer in surprise. Why was he letting him go? Were Hilde's gloomy intimations unjustified in the end? Had Oppenheimer been right after all? Was Vogler capable of more than blind obedience? Oppenheimer understood Vogler's words as a prompt to go. So he cleared his throat and turned to leave.

He had only taken a few steps, when Vogler said, "Oppenheimer?"

The Hauptsturmführer approached him and handed him a small, longish metal cylinder. Oppenheimer examined it curiously.

"A cyanide capsule," Vogler explained. "I think you might need it more than I do."

■

Berlin spread out before him beneath the crescent of the waxing moon. The clear air worked as a magnifying glass, making distances shrink. Oppenheimer was convinced he could touch the nearby buildings with his hands. Tonight, the pale green light of the burning phosphor lent the city a ghostly aura.

Just a few minutes after Oppenheimer had taken his leave of Vogler, his old suspicions had returned. The realization that he was now free game made him cautious. It had occurred to him that perhaps Vogler had only let him go so that he didn't need to get his own hands dirty. Oppenheimer knew that Vogler's men were probably waiting for him at the bottom of the hill, in case the Hauptsturmführer didn't really want him to get away. But there was an alternative to returning to the Müggelheim dam. This pathway down the hill was a bit more challenging, but it had the advantage of leading in exactly the opposite direction. Oppenheimer knew he was capable of finding his way even during the night. He just had to follow the crest of the hill in a westerly direction until he finally reached the observation tower on the Kleine Müggelberg. From there, he could simply climb down the steps on the southern side of the hill to the Langer See lake and try to make his way along the bank toward Köpenick.

But instead of choosing the 347 steps down, he decided to sneak onto the terrace of the pub next to the observation tower under the cover of darkness. It seemed to make sense to get an overview of the situation before he returned to the hellhole down there. Although the panorama from the edge of the terrace was not as impressive as from the observation tower, which you had to pay to access, it proved to be sufficiently impressive to take Oppenheimer's breath away.

From this perspective, it hardly seemed possible that there was still life in the city. And yet Oppenheimer knew that millions of people had sought shelter somewhere in the depths of the city. In a ring around the city, the light beams of the antiaircraft guns projected up into the air like transparent spider's legs, slowly gliding across the sky. There was something else up there. Airplanes with bellies full of explosives hung over the city like a mobile over a baby's crib. Blaring artillery fire was spewed into the sky, bombs fell toward the ground with a whistling sound. This was no large-scale, minutely planned attack but one of the usual British night attacks in the cover of darkness. And yet it released enough destruction to wipe out hundreds of lives.

Again and again, blue flashes shot upward. A phosphor canister detonated with a buzzing sound, scorching the streets with its burning breath. Mesmerized, Oppenheimer leaned against the railings and watched the goings-on. His box seat offered an almost obscene perspective, but he knew that he could not stay any longer. After all, he had to get to Lisa, had to support her, reassure her that he was still alive. And yet something made him hesitate.

He realized that he'd involuntarily put his hand on his breast pocket. Beneath the material, he felt the hard object Vogler had given him. Curious, he pulled the cylinder from his pocket and unscrewed the lid. The poison capsule was see-through, narrow, and about two to three centimeters long. Ideal for hiding in your mouth and then biting on it, should the circumstances require. Oppenheimer held it up in the moonlight. The pockmarked moon lent the clear liquid a tempting sheen. He could barely tear his eyes away.

And then, a completely different sensation came over him. Oppenheimer was filled with an inexplicable feeling of calm. It took him a while to understand that this wasn't his body's chemical reaction to the Pervitin pills. Instead, he realized that this was his reaction to the poison capsule.

It was strange, but when Oppenheimer looked at the means that offered him the option to commit suicide, he felt more alive than ever before. With this capsule, he had the power to choose his own end. No Gestapo officer or other Nazi loudmouth could intimidate him now. They couldn't

346 | HARALD GILBERS

touch him anymore. He was the master of his own destiny once more, and this thought gave him courage. He wondered what Vogler had intended by giving him the poison. Was it an unspoken order to take his own life? Or was it his bizarre way of showing him his appreciation, a whiff of humanity because Vogler was still counting on Hitler's victory? However long Oppenheimer would think about this, it would remain a mystery. Only one thing was clear. From now on, this poison capsule would be his most valued possession.